ROOM 40

25 Years Before Bletchley Park, Codebreakers Gather

Dominic Hayes

To Fran

'First gain the victory and then
make the best use of it you can.'

ADMIRAL NELSON, 1797

CONTENTS

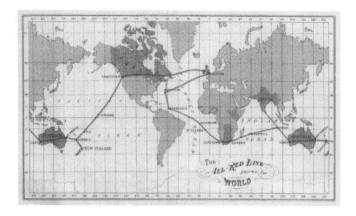

Map Of The All Red Line

PROLOGUE

26th August 1914, thirty minutes past midnight.

A bank of dense, swirling fog enveloped the SMS Magdeburg as she inched towards the entrance of the Gulf of Finland. This close to the island of Odensholm, the only sounds on deck came from the leadsmen, muffled and uneasy, calling out the depth of water around the keel.

In the telegraph room, thick strands of mist seeped under the door, while Radio Officer Bender continued to tap out messages. Only the ship's mascot behind him seemed aware of impending danger.

The dog lifted his head, eyed his master and whined.

'Shh, Schuhmchen, I'm busy.'

The ship lurched and the transmission key fell silent. Officer Bender stared at the deck as his seat thrust him upwards. Schuhmchen gave a muffled yelp, and moments later, the wireless room rose again, accompanied by a metallic groan. Four more jolts were followed by a long silence.

The door to Bender's cubicle was wrenched open by the First Officer. 'Signal the *Augsburg*. Tell her we're grounded at 59 degrees 18 minutes north, 23 degrees 21 minutes east. Order V-26 to come and tow us off.'

Bender reached for the codebook.

'No, we don't have time. Broadcast in clear - then burn the blasted book.' The officer hurried away.

As Bender tapped out the instructions, the dog growled at raised voices beyond, hearing but not understanding the shouted orders to throw coal and munitions overboard. Senior officers yelled orders to lever the steel bulkhead doors from their hinges and jettison them over the rails. Shrieks of tortured metal echoed around the walls as sailors wrenched coaling gear from mounting points and dumped them into the sea. The engines thundered, driving the propellers forward and then into reverse. Despite all their efforts, they were not moving.

Through his headset, Officer Bender heard the leadsmen cry out.

'Sixteen feet to port bow, and nine to starboard.'

'Port stern, thirteen feet. Starboard stern seventeen feet.'

The keel drew twenty feet. He calculated they would not get rid of enough weight to float. Unless the torpedo boat could pull them off, they were stuck fast. He clamped the earphones against his ears, noting V-26's signal of its intention to manoeuvre into position.

'Stay Schuhmchen,' he commanded, grabbing the codebook as he rushed to the door. 'I'll be back, whatever happens.'

Outside, deck lights materialised like starbursts in the dense fog. Officers roared directions from the bridge lookouts. Men struggled to lift heavy iron rails, their grunts deadened by the mist. He caught sight of two ratings carrying codebooks similar to his. They threw them from the starboard rail, and he wondered who had made the order; in such shallow waters, there was a strong probability they could be located later and recovered.

He hoisted his codebook under his arm and found the companionway to the engine room. When he opened the hatchway, heat enveloped him and sweat popped on his exposed skin. He climbed down the ladder and sought out the chief engineer. They had rehearsed this procedure several times, so there was no need to talk above the clatter of the steam engines. The engineer unclipped the furnace hatch, and Bender hurled the tome inside as far as it would go. He saw the leather binder curl, waiting long enough to witness the paper burst into flames.

On deck, lights from V-26 emerged from the darkness. He heard the confirmation a line had been secured. But as the ship backed off, a crack like rifle-fire sounded, and the hull shuddered. The line had snapped.

A massive detonation from the direction of the bow threw him off his feet. He slid across the deck, coming to a sudden stop when his head met a rail stanchion. Seconds later, he regained consciousness to the sounds of thrashing engines and the cries of sailors. Over the uproar was the faint but familiar sound of a barking dog.

'Schuhmchen!' He pulled himself upright and used the railings to shuffle to the radio room. Schuhmchen jumped up, and he patted the dog's head, mumbling comforting noises. With his other hand he snatched a headphone to his ear. A weak ping over background static indicated another ship was operating nearby. Placing both headphones over his ears, he listened intently. There was a distant signal, and he picked up a pencil as the dots and dashes flashed across the airways. The reception strength increased as he noted the letters, signifying the source was approaching. When the message ended, he glanced down at the pad. Translated, the characters formed the familiar pattern of a Cyrillic alphabet. Russian!

'Helmut,' he roared.

A young rating arrived.

'Take this to the Captain immediately.'

He dashed off the note and handed it to the fresh-faced sailor.

> Russian cruisers Pallada and Bogatyr approaching.

The boy turned and ran, forgetting to salute in the rush. The dog barked again, and Bender stroked his head. From the open doorway, officers were ordering the crew to abandon ship.

'Just have to warn V-26 and update the *Augsburg*,' Bender muttered. He grasped the telegraph key.

At that moment, officers bellowed warnings from every quarter. 'Fuses are lit!' Captain Habenicht had decided to scuttle.

Bender had only four and a half minutes to send his last message; the Morse key produced a continuous clatter, sounding like a machine gun in the small space. Two minutes afterwards, an explosion erupted from the forecastle and shrapnel pinged against the cabin walls. Either the Russian warships were closer than he imagined, or some of the scuttle charges had ignited prematurely.

Schuhmchen jumped to his feet, barking furiously. Bender hurried to the doorway. The crew were making for the port side and jumping into the water. A shell landed on the prow of the torpedo boat, blasting several men over the side. He watched as she pulled away, shocked by the force of the Russian shells and the realisation he was being abandoned by his own navy.

Through the maelstrom, one question strove to be answered. Then a shell hurtled into the *Magdeburg*'s wardroom, and the blast forced him to put aside further thoughts. He scooped up the dog and raced to the port gunwale. Most of the men were already in the water. He could see splashes as they waded onto the muddy banks, fifty feet away. More shells landed, one striking the forecastle. A hail of metal fragments whizzed above him, and the deck plates jumped with the power of the detonation.

Still clutching Schuhmchen, he climbed over the rail and gasped in the chill water. As he swam for the shore, Schuhmchen's head bobbed beside him. With their safety assured, he recalled the question that had been bothering him. There were four copies of the codebook on the *Magdeburg*. He had incinerated one in the furnace. Two more were carried to the railings and thrown overboard.

Where was the fourth?

CHAPTER 1

A stiff breeze agitated the trees, rustled leaves and threatened to snatch a sailor's hat. The officer clamped his peaked cap to his head and looked upwards. Dark clouds bustled over Whitehall, and the wind carried the cries of an army Captain. He crossed the road to see a company being drilled on the broad expanse of Horse Guards Parade. With the sound of "Order Arms" following him, he approached the great doorway of the Old Admiralty Building.

Two young soldiers appeared from behind chest-height sandbags, and a burly Warrant Officer emerged into view. He made a quick salute. 'Sir?'

'Captain Reginald Hall, to see Alfred Ewing.'

The officer brought up a checklist, licked a stubby pencil, and ticked off an entry. 'Room 36. That will be the boardroom, sir. Please follow me.'

They entered beneath the portico, turned right

through a stout oak door and into a small vestibule. Out of earshot of the guards, the officer spoke in a stage aside: 'It's *Sir* Alfred, Captain. He's quite particular about that. And he's not fond of anyone calling him by his first name, either.' He regarded Hall for a moment. 'Unless you're already on friendly terms?'

Hall gave the briefest shake of his head, and they walked on. The hallway opened out onto a carpeted marble corridor, and immediately the smell of polish reminded him of his training at HMS *Britannia*, his old naval college overlooking the port of Dartmouth.

They passed an alcove containing a sculpture. 'If you haven't been here before,' remarked the Warrant officer, 'this is the original model for the statue on Nelson's Column.'

Hall vaguely recalled Nelson's body had rested in one of the upper rooms the night before his state funeral. The building appeared to be designed to impress its visitors with past glories.

A curved archway above three steps led to a wide stairwell. At the top, the officer asked him to wait while he went to find Ewing. Hall noticed a lamp suspended in a niche by the corner. The ornate workmanship suggested early eighteenth-century, and he traced the brass filigree with an index finger. Behind the lantern, the marble wall dropped to a smooth sandstone cornice. He followed the coving until his fingers met a coarse section.

As he examined the powdery substance cling-
ing to his fingertips, the officer returned. 'Sir Alfred will see you now.' The man pointed, 'Second
door on the left - please don't forget to knock.'
At the top of the stairs he halted. 'Oh, and good
luck.'

Hall smiled his thanks, dusted his hands and
found the boardroom.

Ewing came towards him, hand outstretched.
'Pleased to meet you, Captain.' The man's accent
held a faint highland intonation.

'And you sir.' He assessed the figure in front
of him: physically, Ewing was short. His silver
hair and moustache were trimmed with precision. The grey wool suit gave an impression of
a gentleman long accustomed to his own emi-
nence.

Hall looked around the panelled chamber. 'An
imposing room.'

Ewing smiled and indicated two great oil portraits. 'This is William IV by William Beechey,
and you'll notice we have Guzzardi's portrait of
Admiral Nelson.'

'Yes, we met downstairs.'

Ewing looked puzzled.

'The statue,' Hall explained.

'Ah.'

Hall's attention was drawn to a large circular
clock above the fireplace.

'That's a wind dial, from the reign of Queen
Anne. There's a series of rods and cogs connect-

ing it to a vane on the roof, and it still works. The limewood carving around it is a famous piece by Gibbons.'

'And is this your place?' Hall asked, pointing to the end of the table where a wide semi-circular section was carved out of the wood.

Ewing chuckled. 'I don't know if I should be offended by that remark! It's where the Secretary to the board sits, so he can be surrounded by his papers.' He studied the curvature. 'A little too big for my frame, don't you think?'

'I didn't mean to suggest…'

Ewing clapped him on the shoulder, 'Come, I didn't take offence.' He waited for Hall to sit, then took his place on the opposite side of the table, underneath the wind dial. 'May I call you Reginald?'

Hall nodded, observing how Ewing's dark thick eyebrows hung over watchful eyes. The appearance was softened by rounded cheeks, hinting at a ready smile.

'Reginald, thank you for coming. I'm afraid I have another meeting in an hour, but we will meet again on Monday when we can go into the detail of the department's work. Today I'd like to acquaint myself with your service record.'

'I am keen to get started, and realise you must be busy.'

Ewing opened a file and peered at the top page. 'Your career has been exemplary. We are lucky to have you at the Admiralty.'

'Thank you, but this was not my choice.'

'No, indeed not.' Ewing picked up a sheet of paper. 'Admiral Beatty was most concerned about the effects of the conditions of the North Sea on your chest. I do hope you are feeling better?'

Hall blinked rapidly. 'I am improving. You need have no worries on that count.'

Ewing smiled, though the impression was one of forced amusement. 'I have some questions about your command - if I may?'

Without waiting for agreement, he carried on, 'I see you brought in several changes during your recent commission. You introduced a three-watch system - unheard of in my day. Why would you want to introduce new notions and designs of your own when the Navy's procedures and methods of operation are already honed to the highest standards and taught in our colleges?'

Hall's gaze fixed on Ewing's lidded eyes. 'I mean no disrespect by this Sir Alfred, but I don't believe you have ever served at sea?'

'No, you are correct. My background has been academia.'

'Then you may not be entirely aware of the practicalities and difficulties in following standard requirements. At the end of a twelve-hour watch, I observed my men were tired. Gunnery accuracy slipped, and the fire rate fell to unacceptable levels. I also considered when German ships might make a surprise attack on our fleet. If I were a German commander, I would engage when our adversary was at its weakest - towards the end of a twelve-hour watch and before the next shift is ready. I found eight-hour shifts were much better - the men were more alert and gunnery statistics improved. My sailors reckoned the new system an improvement.'

'Very well, I grant you Captain. The rest of the Navy is adopting the system. But isn't having a chapel installed onboard a step too far?'

'No,' Hall responded emphatically. 'I am not known for being soft on either my officers or ratings - anyone who has served under me will tell you I am very hard on those who do not pull their weight. But I find I get better performance from sailors out of respect rather than fear. I take care of my crew, and my crew take care of the enemy.'

'Well said,' Ewing smiled. 'It appears you are rewriting the rules of the Royal Navy.'

Hall looked briefly at his hands where minutes before he had grit between thumb and fingers. On an impulse, he had wondered if he could sense the weight of tradition emanating from the stonework and connect with the place where generations of sailors before him had walked. Instead, the damp cement on his fingers was vaguely disappointing. 'Our practice and customs have maintained our Navy's lead over the rest of the world. But if you question the reason we should continue to develop, then you need to look no further than Germany. The Kaiserliche Marine will seek every opportunity to defeat us. We cannot afford to be complacent. We must improve everything we do to beat them. Everything.'

'Quite,' Ewing replied in a tone of mild annoyance. 'As Director of Naval Education for the last eleven years, I am aware of the need to develop improved systems and procedures.'

In the silence that followed, Hall heard the ticking of the great clock on the mantelpiece. 'I meant no offence. Apart from two years at the Royal Naval College, I've been at sea for 30 years, well away from the workings of the Admiralty. It would help me if you could explain your role here?'

'You certainly like to get down to brass tacks. I admire that.' Ewing placed his palms on the table. 'Shortly after the war broke out, Admiral Oliver invited me to lunch. He knew I was interested in cryptography - it was and is a hobby of mine. He brought a stack of encrypted telegrams with him and asked me to head up a section to break the various codes and cyphers the Germans are using.'

His dark eyes rested on Hall, and his lips formed a thin line. 'Sadly, during these momentous times, there is little call for new students in our naval colleges, so I find myself here.' He paused. 'I believe your father was the first Director of the Intelligence Division, as it was called then?'

'He was, but I chose not to follow in his footsteps.'

Ewing raised his hands, palms uppermost. 'No, no, I am not suggesting there was an element of nepotism in your appointment. I see your role as continuing his work.'

'Which is?'

'Receiving notifications about naval operations. For example, the convoys of troopships to France, transferring recruits from the colonies, and so on. That requires good intelligence on the whereabouts of German warships and forces. It's your job to ensure the information is relayed to the right quarters.' He checked his timepiece. 'I'm afraid I have to leave for my next meeting now.' He closed the file.

'May I ask to whom do you report?' He saw Ewing's jaw close, and his cheek muscles tighten.

'Rear-Admiral Oliver. He recently vacated your post to become Naval Secretary to First Lord of the Admiralty, Winston Churchill.'

'And to whom do I report?'

'Oh, I thought that was already clear, Captain. You report to me.'

Count Constantine Benckendorff parted the curtain over his bunk bed. The steady clack-clack of the train and the swaying cot should have been enough to send him to sleep. But while his body reported exhaustion, his brain fizzed with excitement. Had he imagined the stealthy tread of leather-soled boots, or was it an illusion created by his over-active mind? The lead-lined satchel that rubbed against his side was a constant reminder of his duty to protect it.

He reached under the pillowcase and touched the wooden handle of his knife. The pressure of the Bebut Kinjal was comforting; it was a present from his father when he had joined the Imperial Navy as a volunteer. Drawing back the curtain an inch, he glanced along the narrow passageway. If anyone were to steal his bag, they would first have to deal with the Kinjal's seventeen-inch blade of curved steel.

At last, he caught a movement, then exhaled softly in relief. The sight of the retreating uniformed train conductor was oddly reassuring. He laid his head on the pillow; sleep would not be possible until he arrived at the safety of his parent's house in London. His father, the Russian Ambassador to Great Britain, would be at home now, probably in bed. Forbidden to warn his parents, he imagined their surprise when he arrived on the door-step.

The contents of the pouch were too important to risk announcing details of his travel arrangements. His eyes were drawn to its cracked leather exterior and impressive brass lock. He had the key in an inside pocket, but anybody could slit open the flap with a sharp knife. It would have been better if he hadn't known what it contained, yet he had only his own impulsive curiosity to blame.

He closed his eyelids, fighting the drift to sleep by recalling the events that had led to this mission. Three weeks ago he was blissfully unaware of the satchel, its contents, and the responsibility he would be obliged to bear. His most weighty thoughts then were dreams of a new command in the Black Sea. That all changed when a yeoman handed him a signal, summoning him to report immediately to the Flag Captain.

He found him in the chartroom of the *Gangut*, a tall stern-faced officer a few years older than himself.

Captain Mikhail Kedrov indicated a chair. 'When was the last time you saw your parents?'

'Earlier this year, in March, I think.'

'Fine.' The Flag Officer drummed his fingers on the table. 'Perhaps you would like to see them again?'

Constantine inclined his head, 'Of course, Captain. And they would be glad to see me.'

The drumming halted. 'Then we must arrange for you to go.'

'Very well, Captain, I am at your service. Your offer is generous, but I suspect there is something more?'

Kedrov's lips formed a cheerless smile. 'There is.' He hefted a large book onto the chart table. 'I need you to go to London. Meeting your parents is an excellent pretext for a special mission.' He tapped the blue leather cover. 'This was captured from the German cruiser *Magdeburg*.'

Constantine pulled the tome towards him. Though the book was heavy, about 15 inches long by 12 inches wide, and at least 6 inches thick, it reminded him of the codebooks in his own Navy. He inspected the title which was centred in large Gothic type.

Signalbuch

Der

Kaiserliche Marine

'My German is quite good, Captain. It says it is the signal book of the German Navy.' He pointed to the word Geheim which was underlined at the top left-hand corner. 'That means secret.'

'Correct,' replied Kedrov. 'It's the codebook which the German Navy uses to communicate confidential actions to the German fleet. We call it the SKM, for short.'

Kedrov opened the book near the middle and marked the column on the left-hand side. 'This is a list of three-letter code words, and the meaning is provided on the right.' He pointed to the first line. 'LYA' is denoted Lage, which means situation. His finger moved down. 'LYC is given the meaning kritische Lage, meaning 'critical', and the line below, LYD is represented as politische Lage, or 'political situation.'

'You encode the words into three-letter groups?'

'Correct,' answered Kedrov. 'And the message is decoded using an exact copy of the book used to encode it.'

Constantine's eyes widened. 'So with this, we can interpret all the communications from Germany's navy?'

Kedrov frowned, 'No. I wish it were true, but no. So far, we have only been able to understand their weather reports. We think they use some other technique as well as the three-letter codes. We have to work out what that method is.'

Constantine contemplated the problem, 'If the SKM is so valuable to us, why are we giving it to the British?'

'Because they are, let us say, our senior partners in the war.' The corners of his mouth rose in a sly grin, 'And we have two copies of the same.'

Kedrov sat opposite and leaned towards him. 'The reason I'm telling you this is because you need to know the importance of the task. SKM must be delivered to the proper channels.' He gestured to the codebook. 'You will have noticed how heavy it is. The covers have lead inserts. And the satchel you use to carry it also has lead sheets sewn into the lining.' He hefted the leather bag onto the table. 'It mustn't fall into the wrong hands. If necessary, you should throw it overboard. The weights will ensure it sinks.' He placed the codebook inside, folded the flap and closed the clasp. From his pocket, he produced a large brass key and held it up. 'In case you are followed, or anyone tries to take it away from you, defend it with your life.'

Constantine's eyes fastened on the key.

'You must be prepared to die.'

Constantine reached across. 'Then you have chosen the right person,' he said, pocketing the key.

Captain Hall placed his brolly in the stand in the hallway. 'I'm home,' he said, loud enough for his wife to hear from upstairs. He entered the drawing-room and crossed to the drinks cabinet.

'There you are.' Ethel entered as Hall poured whisky into a cut-glass tumbler. 'You're early.' When her husband didn't answer, she sat on the settee. 'Did everything go all right?'

Hall swallowed a mouthful of the Dewar's, then savoured a smaller second sip. 'No. Oliver put Ewing in charge. I'm supposed to report to him.'

'I thought you were to report to Oliver?'

'I thought so too. So now I'm supposed to report to Ewing, and Ewing reports to Oliver. I don't know, Essie, I just can't see it working. The Intelligence department needs the information Ewing supplies, not the other way around.'

'Oh dear. Is there anything you think I can do?'

He slipped one hand in his pocket and felt the crumpled letter. 'I think you've done enough already.'

'What do you mean, Reggie?'

'Your scheme didn't work out as well as you planned,' he said evenly.

She stared at her husband, 'My scheme?'

'You wrote to Oliver behind my back.'

Her voice quavered, 'How did you know?'

'That's not the point. Why didn't you tell me?'

He sat next to her. Her lower lip quivered, and he placed an arm around her shoulder. 'I'm sorry, I know you did it out of the best of reasons.'

'Of course, I did. I couldn't stand to see you cough your way into an early grave. You have asthma and bronchitis. I don't need to be a doctor to see you wouldn't last one winter in the freezing weather of the North Sea.'

Her words stirred a memory, less than two months old. He was standing outside the bridge of his latest battle cruiser the Queen Mary after the action at Heligoland Bight. Across the water, plumes of smoke rose above the Mainz as she sank. Elation surged, then died as his thoughts switched to the men in the water. He wondered how many had been killed on their ships.

He had begun to cough. His chest heaved, and he was forced to grasp the rail with both hands. He had waved away concerned seamen as his chest shuddered under the convulsions. The fit halted when he vomited over the side. A cold wind whipped away the thin, sticky liquid, and the next thought surfaced. This was the first naval battle of the war. With many more engagements expected, how on earth would he survive another victory?

'Reggie?'

Hall returned Ethel's gaze. Her forehead was creased in a frown.

'It's all right, Essie. I'm all right.'

Long before that incident, Admiral Beatty had spoken to Hall about his health. He had hoped to conceal the discussion from Ethel, but she had found out from Beatty's wife, Katrine. Perhaps now was not the best time to reveal he had discovered a copy of Ethel's letter to Oliver in the waste bin of her bedroom.

The anxious lines around her eyes faded. 'What sort of man is Sir Alfred?'

'I suspect Ewing is more than a little uncertain of his position. He saw me in the Boardroom of all places, instead of his office.'

'Maybe he was just trying to impress you?'

'I don't think so - unless his office is like a cupboard.' He had seen that type of man before: supremely confident in his speciality, but lacking any real leadership qualities. 'He comes from academia. He's never been at sea and never seen action. I know he was made a Director of Naval Education, but he's a civil servant, not a serving member of the Royal Navy. I think he was only put in charge of the decoding section because it's a hobby of his. A hobby!'

'Well, dear, what are you going to do?'

Hall's eyes blinked rapidly. 'Do? I have a mind to refuse the post.'

'Reggie, you can't do that.'

'I might be able to persuade Oliver.'

'And be sent back to sea?' Her eyes widened. 'No. You cannot. It will kill you.'

'I don't have much choice, do I,' said Hall, holding the cold tumbler to his forehead. 'To work for someone I don't respect, or to captain another ship. I know which I'd rather do.'

'I forbid it. Absolutely.' She touched his face. 'You have many talents, Reggie. You could put them to good use in that department. You can't win the war single-handedly, but you can develop your men. By doing that you tip the war to our advantage. Germany will meet more than their match when they run into you.'

For a little while there was silence. He said: 'You have more faith in me than I have in myself.'

'Then work for the Admiralty,' she urged. 'At least give it a trial.'

'I don't know - suppose I fall out with Ewing? I wouldn't expect Oliver to support me over my superior.'

'Try it for six months, darling. You could do it for that long. Then if it doesn't work out, I'll have a little talk with Katrine. She could persuade Beatty to have a word in your favour.'

A half-smile formed around his mouth, 'Essie, I'd say you're a better schemer than I am. You should work for the Admiralty.' He had been at sea from fourteen. Since then he had never worked for an incompetent senior officer. Perhaps there was more to Sir Alfred than his initial appraisal suggested.

'Very well, six months.'

'Oh, Reggie, thank you. The war will be over before then, anyway.' She patted his hand.

CHAPTER 2

The sergeant's boots thudded on the oak floor-boards of the first-floor corridor. Hall followed the sound as they passed several closed doors. Drawings for the latest dreadnoughts were drafted only a few years ago in rooms like this, but God alone knew what was going on behind them now.

Up ahead, an elderly messenger was delivering a bundle of papers. Hall slowed his pace, snatching a glance inside the half-open door. The room was large and panelled; the floor covered with a threadbare rug. Behind a sturdy wooden desk sat an older man, bent over a huge volume. He imagined he could hear the scratching of the nib. The whole nation was at war, and yet the Admiralty Building had the appearance of a mausoleum.

The sergeant waited patiently, 'Sir, this way.'

He snatched one last glance at the Dickensian tableau and hurried on. 'It's too dammed quiet,' he muttered.

'Aye.' The sergeant continued his steady stride, speaking over his shoulder as they walked. 'We go right here.'

At the corner, a circle of naval officers were huddled in deep conversation, the gold braid on their sleeves standing out in the half-light. They suspended their whispered discussion as they passed. Hall muttered a muted 'Good morning gentlemen', but there was no reply.

They halted opposite a door with the brass numerals "40" above a "No Admittance" sign. The officer knocked and waited. A short man with hair brushed close to the skull came to the door; eyes beneath a high forehead appraised him dispassionately. Raised voices beyond faded into silence.

'We were told to expect you. Alastair Denniston, pleased to meet you.'

Hall shook his hand, nodded to the sergeant and stepped into the room.

About six or eight men lounged about or sat at desks, awaiting introductions. None were in uniform though one wore a soutane and dog-collar. He stood as he was introduced. 'The Reverend Montgomery.' As they shook hands, Denniston said, 'Before the war, he lectured in history at Cambridge.' He paused for effect. 'Just don't mention Home Rule in conversation.' Montgomery smiled as a groan went up from the rest.

Next in line was Lord Herschell, a smartly

dressed young man with reddish hair and a matching moustache. 'A Lord-in-Waiting, no less. He is helping us to translate captured German documents. I don't expect you to remember all the names, but I'll point them out and leave you to get to know them better. We have Harry Lawrence at the desk, an expert in furniture and art; naval instructors Arthur Parish and Ivor Curtis; and behind them, Richard Norton on secondment from the Foreign Office.'

'Furniture and art?'

'Yes, Captain. It requires a peculiar mix of talents to work on the German codes - and sound knowledge of German is not the most important.'

Hall blinked, 'What would you say is the most important?'

Denniston pursed his lips. 'This is only my opinion, and not necessarily what Sir Alfred looks for.' He hesitated.

'Go on, Alistair. You've no need to fear me.'

'I would say perseverance is the most valuable quality. The ability to keep trying different approaches and never give up until you discover the correct solution.'

'I understand. And is there anyone else working here?'

'Charlie Rotter and Eddie Bullough are away until Wednesday. And I believe Sir Alfred is recruiting others.' He lowered his voice. 'But we only find out when they appear on the circulation list.'

'I see. I suppose appointments are confidential, but there's no point in hiding the fact from the very people who will be working with them. I'll see if there is something I can do about that.'

He turned to address the group, 'Gentlemen, it has been a privilege to meet you. I hope to see more of you over the next days and weeks.' He spoke to Denniston, 'I have a meeting with Sir Alfred in ten minutes. In the meantime please could you show me to my room?'

Sir Alfred's office was a little bigger than a cupboard. As if to compensate for the drab surroundings, Ewing was wearing a mauve waistcoat and a black bow tie with white polka dots. Hall wrested his attention away from the man's attire with difficulty.

'We are calling the department "Room 40",' said Ewing. 'Because that's where we began in the Admiralty. Also, the name itself gives no clue as to what goes on inside. The enemy must never learn what we do.'

'I realise that, Sir Alfred. But isn't there a problem here? How can we continue to use this information if in doing so it reveals our capability?'

'That will certainly be a challenge. But before we deal with that particular dilemma, we have to be able to read German messages.' His voice fell, 'It is going to take time and all our ingenuity to achieve.'

'Why? Is it difficult to come by enemy communications?'

Ewing's face softened into a grim smile, 'Ah, Reginald, that is the one thing we are not short of.' He pushed a pile of papers towards the Captain. 'Some of the traffic we intercept daily.'

Hall lifted a page and inspected the typed heading:

```
12 October 1914. R374   BERLIN to
STOCKHOLM
```

The rest of the page comprised typewritten groups of numbers. Most contained five digits though some had only three or four. The lines were triple spaced and above a few of the figures were German words written in pencil.

Ewing indicated a line. 'We are confident the words above are represented by the number underneath.'

'I see most of the words are missing. Does each number group represent a single word?'

'If only it were so simple,' grunted Ewing. 'Our staff will show you the method - I'm afraid it's very complicated. I've started to recruit some of the best brains from the top Universities to assist, but it's a slow process. I want you to find more men, and women if necessary, to deal with the volume of German signals. The problem will only get worse.'

'How do you go about intercepting German

communications?'

Ewing unfurled a chart that almost covered the table. Hall moved some paperweights to hold down the corners.

'On this map of the world, we have the extent of the British underwater telegraphic cables shown in red. You'll notice they only land on British dependencies or colonies - countries where telegraphic services are under our control. Hence the name The All Red Line.' Ewing placed a well-manicured finger on London, tracing the route as he spoke: 'Going west they cross the Atlantic, making landfall in Nova Scotia in the north, and Bermuda and Barbados in the south. Travelling north and west, across Canada, then reaching the Fanning Islands and Fiji in the Pacific from Vancouver, coming ashore at Brisbane in Australia.'

Ewing pointed to Barbados. 'Going south and east we connect to Ascension island, then Cape Town in South Africa. We cross to Durban, then under the Indian Ocean to the Cocos Islands via Mauritius. Moving north, we reach India from the Cocos; moving south, Perth, where we join up with the western cable.'

'It's an extensive network,' said Hall. 'But I fail to understand where this is leading.'

'Actually, we own many more cables than are shown here - this is a simplified sketch. My point is we communicate with every corner of the British Empire with these undersea links. Our studies show Germany would need to cut over forty of our cables to cause us difficulties. And because we control most of the sea lanes, that would be next to impossible.'

Hall examined the map, 'I still don't see the point?'

'The German network is much less widespread than ours. For example, she has only seven cables from her shores to northern Europe and America. And we've already cut five of them.'

'Ah, I'm beginning to understand.'

'The last two have to pass through our telegraphic centres in London and Porthcurno in Cornwall.'

'Can we intercept them and send the copies here?'

Ewing grunted acknowledgement. 'The plan is working better than the Committee of Imperial Defence could have imagined. Since Germany's telegraphic system is constrained, she is forced to communicate more by wireless. They have a transmitter at Nauen, about twenty miles west of Berlin, and anyone can listen in. We think the Germans have no idea how powerful it is - some days it reaches as far south as the tip of Africa.'

He rose and went to the window. 'Most of the traffic to Europe and the Mediterranean goes via Spain. She is a declared neutral, but there is a lot of antipathy to the British.' He gestured towards the map. 'Orders are encrypted, then transmitted over the radio in Morse code - Morse telegraphy.'

Hall rose to join him and gazed down at the inner courtyard.

'So there you have it,' said Ewing. 'It's our job to discover what's in those messages and pass the information on.'

'And not to make use of the material?'

'That's not my responsibility, Captain.' He glanced at the younger man beside him, 'How do you think you'll fit in here?'

Hall returned Ewing's gaze, 'I'm not entirely certain.'

Ewing registered surprise, 'I appreciate you're not acquainted with this type of command, but I can assure you this division is, and will continue to be, a vital part of the Navy's war effort.'

'I am sure you are correct. I'm just not used to sitting behind a desk.'

'You know my boy, this posting isn't optional.' Ewing regarded Hall. 'In any case, if I'm any judge of character, you won't be sitting behind your desk for long.'

Constantine Benckendorff glimpsed a series of darkened platforms as the train approached the centre of London. Dimly lit pavements came as no surprise when he exited the station; what was astonishing was the quiet. On the last occasion he was here, the streets were busy with the sound of paperboys shouting out the headlines from their newspaper stands, or groups of men or women chatting on their way home after a late-night shift. Now there were few people, motor cars and carriages, and fewer omnibuses.

Constantine lifted the strap of his satchel over his head onto the opposite shoulder. He looked both ways before crossing the road, though there was little need since there was no traffic. He spotted a taxi rank further along.

A scruffy bearded beggar eased himself away from the wall where he had been lounging. He shuffled five paces behind, head down, battered hat tugged low. 'Got a light, sir?'

Constantine whirled round. 'Who...?'

The tramp presented a crumpled roll-up. 'Didn't mean to startle you, sir. But have you got a light?'

Constantine's first impulse was to clutch the belt of his bag. He took in the dirty fingernails and the chap's scraggly beard that looked as if his last meal was still in there. Then an unwashed odour enveloped his senses, and he relaxed. He searched his pockets for a lighter, thumbed off the cap and flicked the wheel. In the glow from the flame, the man's eyes were bloodshot, and he tried to imagine what it was like having to sleep on the streets.

The man drew on his cigarette until the tobacco burned bright red. 'Don't suppose you've got a copper or two to spare, sir? I could do with a nice warm cuppa.'

Constantine shot a quick look towards the taxi.

There were so few pedestrians the chances of it being taken were slim. He hunted in his trouser pockets and looked up at a sudden movement. The tramp had pulled out a short-bladed knife.

Street lights reflected by the blade gleamed along its edge. Constantine's mind froze, but his body reacted without thinking, twisting away from the knife. The man lunged again. This time Constantine was prepared and swerved, about to run. Something stopped him; the vagrant had hold of the strap. He yanked it, but the tramp held on. Light flashed again as the man slashed the canvas band, once, twice.

With a snap, the material parted, and the man grabbed the bag, leaving him holding the other end of the belt. He twisted his arm, wrapping the strap around his wrist. The effect was to bring the man closer, within striking distance of his knife. With his other hand, he reached into his jacket and pulled out the Bebut Kinjal and thrust it at his opponent.

The tramp needed no more persuasion to drop the pack, and he sprinted away. Constantine lent over, hands on knees, taking a lung-full of air. Eventually, he straightened and scanned the street. He was in deep shadow. Neither had made a noise, and no-one had seen the fight. Or if they did, he reflected, they ignored it.

After checking the pack, he stumbled to the taxi stand and told the driver, 'Chesham House, Belgravia.' He placed the bag on the seat next to him. It wasn't until they were passing Regent's Park he noticed his shirt sticking to his side. He withdrew his hand and squinted in the dim light. A dark stain covered his fingers.

'Svoloch.'

'You OK gov'nor?' The driver was watching in the rear-view mirror.

'I'm OK. Some thief tried to snatch my bag.'

'Gawd help us.' The cabby carried on moaning as they passed Marble Arch. Constantine tore pieces of his shirt to make a pad and used his belt to keep it in place over the wound. His parents were in for a bigger surprise than he thought.

Captain Hall surveyed the smoking-room of the United Services Club. A line of slender columns supported the lofty roof, and padded leather armchairs lined the walls. The two chairs they were about to occupy were situated either side of a small table, sufficiently far away from the others so as not to be overheard, but not far enough to avoid the pungent smell of cigar smoke. A waiter deposited a tray of brandy and coffee and glided past.

Hall regarded his colleague. Technically Hall was the senior member of the service though Captain Mansfield Smith-Cumming was at least a decade older. He had a fine head of silver-grey hair compared to Hall's wiry curls surrounding his bald patch. Despite this disparity, watching

Smith-Cumming was like looking at an older version of himself. His nose was less hooked and the cheeks more rounded, but he had the same chiselled, 'cut-water' chin.

It was only six weeks since the accident, and the question of how Mansfield's son had died would still be a sensitive one. Nevertheless, it was necessary to touch on the subject, if only out of politeness.

'How is the leg?'

Mansfield grasped the crystal glass the waiter had left and downed the brandy in one gulp. 'To tell you the truth Reggie, the pain is nothing in the scheme of things. Nothing like the pain of losing your son.'

'I'm sorry to have brought it up - you have enough problems already.'

Mansfield made a dismissive gesture with his hand, 'It's not a problem Reggie. Apart from the French police, I haven't spoken to anyone about what really happened.'

'They're saying you hacked your foot off to free yourself from the car.'

'Let them say what they want. I don't care.' A bleak smile lifted the corners of his lips. 'We were in the Rolls on a long straight road outside Meaux, heading north. Alistair was driving. I remember the line of trees on each side, the wind ruffling our hair. He was having the time of his life.'

He turned to face Hall, 'God help me, I encouraged him to drive faster. We must have met a stone in the road, and the wheel was yanked out of his hands. The car hit a tree and Alistair was thrown up in the air. He landed badly, some distance away.'

Mansfield's eyes drifted aside, and Hall signalled for another drink. When it arrived, Mansfield clasped the glass so hard Hall feared it would shatter. 'I was trapped. Both ankles were broken, and my legs had become jammed under the dash. I could hear Alistair's cries, but I couldn't move. He was moaning - something about the cold. I wanted to go to him, to cover him with a blanket and hold his hand. But I had to stay in the car and listen as he grew weaker. After an hour, he stopped altogether.'

Hall rested the brandy glass against his mouth to hide his anguish. 'I'm so sorry. Bad luck all round.'

'The French police found us several hours later. They brought me to a local hospital, and the doctors removed the left foot the next day.'

Neither spoke for a long period, then Hall began. 'I hope the pain gets better.'

'Thank you, Reggie, it's most considerate of you.' His voice brightened. 'I expect you're wondering why I asked for you. Surely not to listen to my problems.'

'It can't have been easy for you.'

'That's as may be, Reggie. Shall we get down to business? At the very least, it keeps the mind occupied. Do you remember Lieutenant Brandon and Captain Trench?'

'The names are familiar.' Hall paused. 'Yes, I think I have it. They were two of the officers who put on a show during Kiel week. Must be four years ago.' He reached for his coffee, but it had gone cold. 'I was asked to take photographs where the latest ships were being laid. But that part of the harbour was out of bounds.' He recalled the string of German boats the authorities had used to seal off the dry docks.

'I was told you came up with a clever scheme.' He patted Hall's arm.

'Do you recall the Duke of Westminster's motorboat?' Hall smiled. 'She was the star attraction. The papers were full of her beautiful lines. She had the latest engine and steering gear - and her speed! The Bosch couldn't get enough of her. I asked the Duke if we could borrow her the following day. Then I told Brandon and Trench to pilot the boat, and put on an act. After zig-zagging around the harbour, they entered the cordon and promptly broke down. They became the laughingstock of the German navy.'

The corner of Hall's mouth quivered in merriment. 'While they pretended to get the engine going again, another crew member secretly snapped photographs of the installations.'

Mansfield's eyes shone.

'We looked like fools in front of everyone,' Hall continued. 'But we obtained valuable intelligence that day.'

'Then you already know what fine fellows they are. After that successful trip, they were commended by the Admiralty.'

'Only right they should be.'

Two stewards began pulling the heavy curtains together, shutting out the last of the daylight.

'Then perhaps you will help me correct an injustice.' As the lights came on, Mansfield's gold monocle gleamed.

CHAPTER 3

A cloud of cigarette smoke obscured his face as he approached. Karl Smets rested his hand over his coat pocket, feeling the hard edges of his Browning pistol.

The man moved sideways around an intervening table, and Karl glimpsed trimmed silver hair, beard and moustache. The grey woollen suit looked as out of place as a peacock's feather in a chicken coop. The alert blue eyes and lithe figure belonged to a person twenty years younger - quite the opposite of what he was expecting.

'Professor Bernard?' Karl spoke in quiet tones. 'Karl Smets.'

The professor leaned across to shake hands and sat next to him.

'I'd rather you sat there.' Karl pointed to the chair. 'That way, I can talk to you and still keep an eye on the doors.'

'Of course.' The professor inclined his head, then gazed around the bar. Locals faced each other on long trestle tables. Wooden panelled walls surrounded an open fireplace and extended behind his companion. Varnished beams criss-crossed the ceiling, lit by cheap chandeliers. For such a crowded room, the noise was surprisingly subdued.

Karl pushed a glass of Lambic over the table. 'You have not been to A la Bécasse before?'

'No, although I have heard of it, of course.' Professor Bernard studied the cloudy liquid. 'The high point of my week is a small glass of sherry over a game of chess.' A lop-sided smile accompanied the apology.

'Try it,' he murmured, indicating the glass with his chin. 'In this bar, nobody drinks sherry.'

Professor Bernard lifted the glass to his nose and inhaled the sour aroma. 'A little too young for my taste.'

'You should drink some, so as not to appear out of place.'

'Of course.' The professor raised the beer to his lips and sipped cautiously. When he set the glass down, his smile became stern as if contemplating an unpleasant duty. 'I am sorry I was late. This is a difficult spot to find.'

'Au contraire, I was early.' In fact, Smets had arrived half an hour earlier. He had occupied himself by observing the patrons, the patterns of movement, the flow of conversation. It was not unknown for the Germans to infiltrate meeting places like this one, hoping to catch sedition and root out subversives. But if there were any here tonight, they were exceedingly difficult to spot.

'Professor, perhaps you will tell me why you asked to see me?'

'I have taught Physics here at the University in Brussels for the last eighteen years. Every once a while, I see a student whose abilities surpass all those of their generation. I have one now, a young man studying for a postgraduate degree. He is a prodigy and already has five radio patents to his name. He wants to go home, and I thought you might help.'

'That is very brave of you to ask. What makes you think I'm not working for the Germans?'

'I did some research...' The professor's voice tailed off into silence. 'I believe you are in contact with the British.'

'Even assuming I could help,' he prompted, 'why should I put my life at risk?'

'Because, despite the danger, you help others.'

Karl sipped his beer while checking the room. If the professor had discovered a potential link between him and the British, it would only be a matter of course before the Germans found out too. In the meantime, it would be useful to understand why he rated this pupil so highly. He watched Professor Bernard closely as he asked the next question.

'What makes this student so special? I know you have high regard for his academic skills, but it isn't enough to warrant asking a near stranger to spirit him out of the country.'

The professor coloured, 'I understand what you are suggesting, but I only have the boy's interests at heart. The man I mentioned earlier - the person I play chess with - is the boy's father and my best friend.'

'I see.' Karl paused. 'Let's start with the boy's name.'

'Alexander Szek. He is only twenty.'

'And where is his home?'

'Alexander's mother moved to England before the war. That's where Alexander was born. He would be safe with her.'

An argument started two tables away, diverting Karl's attention. Moments later, a burst of laughter signalled the end of the quarrel. Karl frowned at the professor's expectant expression. 'I'm sorry professor, it's too risky.'

A series of deep lines formed around Bernard's eyes. 'I had such hopes you could help.'

'Maybe if you had asked me a month ago, then perhaps.' He lifted his head, indicating the exits. 'Now the German presence is too great.'

'A month ago, I didn't think there would be a problem,' said Bernard. 'Many staff had left, and most of the students had gone. We believed the Germans would have little interest in the rest of us.'

'What happened to Alexander?' A full extraction was out of the question, but he wondered if there was another angle to the case.

Professor Bernard looked at the table as if the events in his mind were being projected onto the flat surface. 'The Germans took him to work on repairing the radio transmitter on Wetstraat. Some of the electricians sabotaged the equipment before they fled.'

'Is he capable of fixing it?'

'Oh yes, he's already repaired it. They started broadcasting a week ago.'

'So what has happened to him?'

'They coerced him into becoming a telegraph operator.' The professor's expression became stern. 'He's sending messages right now.'

Captain Hall held Mansfield's walking stick as he guided him to a seat at the dinner table. He tugged at the carved handle. A sliver of light glinted on the sharp blade below the hilt.

'Satisfied?' Mansfield's tone was devoid of censure.

Hall coughed politely, 'Sorry, I was curious to discover if the rumours were true.' He sat opposite his friend.

'It is one thing to carry a sword-stick, and quite another to know how to handle it.'

'I've no doubt you are an expert in sword-play.'

Mansfield regarded Hall, and his mouth widened in a slow smile. 'And I've no doubt you are an expert in word-play.'

Hall acknowledged the riposte with a grin.

'Have you ever had to use it?'

'No, because it would drill a hole through their heart. It's odd, isn't it - sometimes you only need the promise of a threat. But you must always be prepared to use it.' He chuckled, then raised his arm at a passing waiter. 'The 1905 claret, please. And when you return, we will order.'

When the waiter had gone, he made an apologetic moue. 'The best waiters have left. Most because they were caught and others because they were afraid of being arrested.' He picked up the menu. 'We'd better order unless you're prepared to wait for another hour or so.'

As Mansfield studied the menu, Hall studied him. There was no disguising the bluff, larger-than-life appearance. Yet he couldn't help the feeling at the core lay a steel spine as strong as the blade of his sword stick.

The waiter arrived with the wine. Mansfield ordered Médallion de Veau St. Germain for his entrée, and lamb cutlets with mushrooms and baked potatoes. Hall opted for cold-pressed beef and a mixed grill with Russian salad. When he left, Mansfield raised his glass, 'Fair winds and following seas.'

Hall eyed his glass.

Mansfield leaned forward and lowered his voice, 'What's the matter, Reggie?'

Hall tapped the stem. 'I'm thinking of the men and women who cultivated these grapes. Many of them are dead now.'

Mansfield returned his glass to the table. 'I hope you don't think I'm enjoying this at their expense?'

Hall waved his hand. 'No, of course not.' He raised the glass and inspected the wine. 'Funny how the colour of good wine is so similar to blood.'

'I understand. But both you and I are alive. We are in positions where we can make a difference in this war. I know you're not happy to be without a ship; any Captain would feel the same. But you have a responsibility to do your best.'

Hall drew in a deep breath and let it out slowly. 'Essie told me something similar only yesterday.' He lifted his glass. 'To our men.'

'Our men,' repeated Mansfield and chinked glasses.

They sat for a while in silence, then Hall said, 'You were saying earlier. Something about putting right an injustice.'

'Indeed.' Mansfield placed his napkin over his lap. 'Soon after the affair in Kiel harbour, one of my officers, a Captain Regnart, sent Brandon and Trench on a "holiday" without consulting me. He knew my method was to sign orders with the letter 'C' in green ink. The bugger signed his order in the same green ink, using the initials 'CA'. He told me it stood for 'C's Assistant. What a bloody cheek!'

'A holiday?'

'Not exactly. Regnart ordered them to collect

information about Germany's coastal defences. Anyway, the two were captured and put on trial.'

'I heard. It was in the newspapers, but I wasn't able to follow the case.'

Mansfield looked up.

'I was at sea.'

'Of course.' Mansfield unfolded his napkin. 'In my opinion, the German courts were surprisingly lenient. They received a four-year sentence, but served only two and a half.'

'Why was that?'

'The Kaiser came over to visit his cousin, King George, in May '13. He pardoned them beforehand in a demonstration of his munificent compassion.' Mansfield pulled a face.

'Did they find anything?'

'Not so you'd notice. They were caught soon after landing.'

'So what happened to them after they were released?'

'The Admiralty mistreated them. They claimed captain Ragnart exceeded his brief and was reckless in sending them on the mission. But while that bit was true, Brandon and Trench suffered. I tore a strip off Ragnart, believe me.'

'How did they suffer?'

'The men's stay in prison should count for promotion and pensions, just as if they had been at home. Churchill agreed and stated in Parliament they would be taken care of, but nothing happened.' Mansfield's accusatory stare was interrupted by the arrival of the food. They were silent as the dishes were served.

'I can only apologise on behalf of the Admiralty,' replied Hall. 'If I could find something for them in my department, would that help?'

Mansfield smiled, 'I would be very grateful. Unfortunately, I don't have the budget for them myself, and that won't be changing soon.'

'I'll see what I can do.' Hall's fork remained poised over the salad as an idea occurred. 'At some point, I will need access to your...'. He hesitated, 'network.'

'Spies, Reggie. You mean spies,' chortled Mansfield. 'You shouldn't be afraid to call them by their proper name.'

Hall checked the other tables; no-one seemed to have overheard their conversation.

'Have you anything specific in mind?'

'No, not at present. But it would be useful to have contacts here and abroad who could achieve certain tasks for me.'

'Of course. But you need to realise there are limitations. The first is to do with timing and how we communicate with a spy.' Mansfield wiped his mouth with the napkin and set it beside his plate. 'Getting a message to your spy takes patience. You can't telegraph or radio him directly, because if anyone is watching he will get caught. So we use intermediaries. They have bag drops, chalk marks, or other ways to alert them information is waiting. Your spy then needs to make certain no-one follows him when he re-trieves the drop, or when he meets his go-be-tween. Sometimes it can take a day or two to be sure nobody is following.'

'Understood. You need at least a day's warning, longer if possible.'

'Yes. Then there is the task. The person may not be physically or mentally capable of carrying out something beyond their ability. Not every-one is prepared to shoot someone or able to steal a document from a secure compound, for ex-ample.

'The task must be within their capabilities. I appreciate that.'

'Next, there is motivation.' Mansfield warmed to his theme. 'A spy may carry out a task for many reasons. Mostly this is for money, though some are motivated by other things: love, pat-riotism, hate, revenge, fear of embarrassment from blackmail. It's a long list, Reggie.'

'I understand. You must apply the most appro-priate leverage for the person.'

'You also have to provide a return route for the information you want to receive, and a haven for the spy in case they are spotted. They will refuse to work for you if there is a significant risk of be-coming trapped by the enemy.'

Hall finished his food and arranged his knife and fork on the plate. 'Safe route. I have all that, thank you.'

'Those are three practical pieces of advice I

would give anyone contemplating running a spy or spy network.' He assessed Hall's reaction to his next remark. 'But there is one cardinal rule.'

Hall waited.

'Never become personally involved with your agent. You need to deal with them dispassionately. If you get caught up, you compromise his or her life, the lives of other agents and people who have helped them. You also risk your conscience, and ultimately your own peace of mind.'

Hall was taken aback by the solemnity and felt at a loss how to respond. At that moment the waiter arrived to clear the dishes, and he enquired about sweets. Mansfield chose Tapioca pudding and cream, and Hall asked for a blackberry flan and cream.

Hall gazed at the waiter's receding form. When he judged he was out of earshot, he said, 'So if we have a network of spies in Germany, a German network may exist in Britain.'

'It does - or rather it did.'

'Do you mean you're not sure?'

Mansfield's laugh boomed beyond the confines of the nearby tables. 'Before the war, there were a quarter of a million Germans living and working in Britain and seventy-five thousand of those living in London. Any of them could be spies. Gave Scotland Yard a headache, I can tell you.' He stopped while the waiter returned with their sweet.

Hall asked, 'So we had no idea who was working for Germany's Secret Service?'

'Not everyone, at least to begin with. But Special Branch had a notion who might belong. When Edward the Seventh died, God bless him, a State funeral was arranged. You will remember it, Reggie. Kings and Queens, monarchs and presidents, and their entourages from many counties attended.'

'I do,' said Hall. 'It was only a month or so before the Kiel Regatta. I was Captain of the *Cornwall* then.'

'Special Branch tailed one of the Kaiser's staff, known to them on previous occasions for acting suspiciously. He led them to a barber's shop on the Caledonian Road. A German owned the business. It became apparent he was in the habit of receiving dozens of letters each week, sealed in a large envelope bearing a German stamp. He would open it, then stick British postage stamps on each of the smaller letters and post them.' He finished his sweet. 'Of course, he wasn't to know that before he received his envelope from Germany, section 5 opened it, and all the ones inside. Every letter was photographed and noted.'

'Section 5?'

'What used to be the Secret Service Bureau. Six months ago, the War Office assumed responsibility and renamed it MO5 (G). Headed by a fellow called Vernon Kell. Have you met him?' When Hall shook his head, Mansfield said, 'You should. Good chap. Been in the war and got half his face shot off. We don't always get on, but I have a lot of respect for him.'

'So the smaller envelopes contained instructions to the spies they were addressed to?'

'Correct. There were dozens all over the country. Some even in Scotland and Wales, but most had their own businesses in England. Others were in ordinary jobs: teachers, dock-yard and factory workers, hairdressers, you name it.' He attracted the attention of their waiter. 'Coffee and brandy, when you have a minute.' He caught Hall's expression. 'Make the best of it, Reggie; there won't be any more for a while.'

'What did the police do when they found out?'

'Do?' Mansfield's eyes opened in mock surprise. 'Why they did nothing!'

Hall remained still and considered the information. 'They watched and waited,' he said slowly.

'Absolutely.'

'Until the war broke out.'

'Exactly.' Mansfield beamed at Hall as if he was a particularly bright student. 'Scotland Yard rounded them up in an operation that lasted less than a day.'

'I'm impressed.'

Mansfield checked the tables nearby. 'Gave the Bosch a big surprise from what I heard.'

'But what is there to prevent new spies arriving from Germany?'

Mansfield grew solemn. 'That is my biggest

problem. There are hundreds of refugees landing in Folkestone every day. We have people down there trying to ascertain if they are genuine or not - we can't turn them away. Most of 'em would be shot as soon as they returned home.'

The drinks came, and Mansfield swallowed a large mouthful of his brandy. 'Hopeless task. Unfortunately, we don't know how many are here now.'

'Then how are you going to find them?'

'We do what we've always done. We keep watch. We talk to our informants. We censor the post, telegrams and radio traffic. We also maintain an eye on their favourite haunts: the Café Royal, Oddenino's, the Monico, and so on.'

'Radio traffic? Isn't it encrypted?'

'Most is. That's where your lot come in.'

'Have you found any others yet?'

'No. But we are aware of some. One, in particular, we'd like to catch. He's known as Lieutenant Otto Gratz, also goes by the name Captain Steinhauer. He uses lots of aliases and wears many disguises. I reckon he's the most brilliant spy ever produced by the German Secret Service.'

Hall paused with a brandy half-way to his lips. 'What do you know about him?'

'Well before the war he was the mastermind and chief of the German Military and Naval Secret Service.'

'And he's here now?'

Mansfield shrugged. 'We're not sure. We've

been watching the ports, and our best men in Special Branch and CID are on the lookout in the city. We'll catch him eventually.'

Hall finished his coffee. 'I have to go, but I can't thank you enough for everything.'

'That's fine, Reggie. You know how I like your company. Let's do this again soon.'

'Certainly.'

'And you won't forget about Brandon and Trench?'

'You can leave it with me. I won't forget.'

CHAPTER 4

Ewing bustled through the door.

Hall frowned, 'It would be good of you to knock.'

'Knock?' Ewing's puzzlement gave way to a stern expression. 'We have been summoned by the First Lord, no less, so I suggest you get ready and come with me.'

Hall rose. 'And the purpose of the meeting?'

'We'll find out when we get there.'

He gathered a few papers and followed Ewing onto the first-floor corridor. Once he had caught up, Ewing said, 'He's in block I, so we have a minute. Did you read the newspapers?'

'You mean Antwerp?'

'Yes, Antwerp. Best not to refer to it if possible.'

Hall recalled the piece in the New Statesman. Churchill had been sent by parliament to reconnoitre the city and report, but when he arrived, he found the resistance against the German forces to be ineffective. He assumed control over the remaining defences and attempted to rally them to delay the offensive, but promised reinforcements came too late. He was criticised in the editorial column for his 'foolhardy activities'. Hall had experienced an uneasy feeling about the way Churchill's action had been portrayed. The newspaper was skimpy on the details, yet the condemnation seemed overly spiteful. As a government minister, Churchill could not reply, and to make matters worse Asquith and Kitchener refused to support him publicly.

A sergeant was standing to attention outside Churchill's office. He recognised him as the same man who had escorted him on his first day at the Admiralty. The officer stepped to one side, and they entered a small outer lobby. A harassed young secretary typed on a crowded desk. She plucked up the phone and announced their presence.

As they came in, he glimpsed the silhouette of a man at the far end of the room, peering down onto Horse Guards Parade. The hunched shoulders could only belong to Winston Churchill, whose identity was confirmed when he turned to face them. His broad face was lit with a genial smile. 'Morning, Gentlemen. I believe this is an auspicious day for the Royal Navy.'

Ewing stepped forward, 'Morning, sir.' He lowered his head deferentially. 'How can we be of assistance?'

'Are you acquainted with Nereus?' Churchill's

eyes held an impish sparkle. 'The Greek god of the sea and its rich bounty of fish?' He waved towards his desk. 'This day Nereus smiled on us.'

Hall followed the direction he was pointing. A large book the size of a church bible lay in the centre.

Churchill laid his palm on the green leather cover. 'From the frozen arms of a drowned German sailor, into our hands. The codebook of the Germany navy.'

'Wonderful,' declared Ewing, moving to inspect the prize. 'How did you come by it?'

'Via a courier from the Russian navy,' said Churchill. 'It was rescued from the *Magdeburg* while she was under fire, and brought over by the son of our Russian Ambassador in London.'

They stared at the tome as if it contained the secrets of the ancient world.

'And it almost never arrived,' continued Churchill. 'A tramp attacked our man when he reached London and nearly stole his belongings.'

Hall gazed at his still beaming face. 'So the Germans are aware we have one of their codebooks?'

Churchill shook his head, 'No, I think not. All the other codebooks were thrown overboard. It was only by the greatest fortune this copy survived the water. Besides, they couldn't possibly know when or where our chap was arriving.'

'May I?' Hall lifted the cover and leafed through the initial section. There were no signs the pages had ever been in seawater, and the Captain glanced at Churchill. Was this his idea of a joke, or just his penchant for dramatic effect?

Hall returned his attention to the contents. There were several pages of diagrams showing the various positions of flags for signalling shore and other ships at sea. Another section dealt with semaphore and lamps, and yet another detailed the rules governing the ship's tactical movements during peacetime and war. A much larger segment near the end described the three-letter codes used in wireless telegraphy.

'Very similar to our own,' he murmured.

'Indeed,' said Churchill. 'Take it to Room 40 and let your experts examine it.' He swung round to the window, assuming the same position.

Presuming the interview was over, Ewing struggled to lift the tome while muttering a grateful 'Thank you'.

They had reached the doorway when Churchill spoke in a low voice. 'Captain Hall. Would you re- main for a minute or two?'

The way the remark was made suggested it was more an order than a request, and he closed the door after a disconcerted Ewing.

'I was wondering how your first few days in the job have been?' Churchill went on looking out of the window.

Hall waited.

After a short silence, Churchill shifted his stance. 'Cat got your tongue?'

'No, sir. I didn't want to break into your train of

thought.'

Churchill shot Hall a sharp look, then burst into laughter. After catching his breath, he said, 'I should have known - your father was the same.' He pointed to the chair and sat behind the desk. 'Now you have my complete concentration.'

'I'm afraid it is too early to say how things will work out. First impressions of the staff are...' His voice faded.

Churchill smiled. 'Perhaps the word you are searching for is eclectic?'

'I've no doubt they are a brilliant group of individuals,' said Hall. 'But they don't seem to have any set schemes when attempting to decipher messages.'

'That's because we've never been in this position before. Before the war, the Royal Navy enjoyed one of the longest stretches of unbroken peace in history.' Churchill opened the top drawer of his desk and withdrew a small cigar which had died out. He fluttered a lighted match at the end while inhaling. Between puffs of smoke, he said, 'Now the naval codebook is ours, we have the means. The methods will follow.'

He regarded Hall. There was a pause while he drew on the cigar until the end glowed red. 'You don't seem convinced.'

'Sir, I am a Captain and a sailor. Understanding the processes required to decrypt messages is beyond me. When an enemy ship is sighted, I understand what to do. My men have rehearsed their responses to a wide range of attack. I know when to give an order, and how long it should take to carry out. Every member of my crew knows their place and how they will be judged in their decisions and actions.'

Churchill wafted the cloud of smoke. 'Ah, I see. Well Captain, imagine you are not a Captain but an Admiral. When your opponent is sighted, you may not learn of it until long after the event. What then? Any orders you give could be too late. Worse still, they could undermine the offensive actions of the fleet.' He stubbed the cigar out on a glass ashtray and replaced it in the drawer. 'No. To be an Admiral, you have to be one step ahead of your adversary. You may not out-shoot him, but you can out-think him. You must use all your cunning and guile to out-fox him. Make him believe you are attacking from the flank, then appear behind. Make him suspect you are running away, then draw him into your trap.'

'Then smack.' Churchill brought his fist down on the table with so much force the ashtray bounced. 'Finish him. Swift, clean, quick. That is how to deal with the enemy.'

There was nothing he could disagree with in Churchill's argument. In fact, his ideas corresponded most closely with his sentiments.

Churchill pulled out his fob watch. 'Anything else?'

'Not really.'

'Come, Captain, when you say 'not really' I believe something is troubling you, but you don't wish to trouble me with it.'

'I am a little confused about the line of command.'

'How so?'

'Sir, all the reports I receive rely on good intelligence from agents and informers on the whereabouts of German warships and forces. It's my job to collate the information and relay it to the right quarters.'

Churchill acknowledged with a curt nod.

'From today, Room 40 has a method of decrypting enemy movements. I regard this as a vital input into the intelligence I collect, along with all my other sources. Shouldn't the Intelligence Division be in overall charge of the process?'

'And have Sir Ewing report to you, rather than the other way round?

'Yes, sir. Perhaps I have misunderstood how the system of command operates here?'

'I don't think so.' Churchill stood up and paced behind his chair. 'It was Oliver's idea. Sometimes I reckon Oliver regards it as his own cryptographic unit, God bless him.'

'Then what should be done, sir?'

Churchill ceased pacing. 'It's too soon to say. At present I'm inclined to leave it as it is: see how things develop. I'm confident you and Alfred can work together and sort out any differences. Was there anything else?'

'Actually, there is.' Hall selected a page from his bundle of notes. 'I realise you're busy, so I'll leave this on your table.'

Churchill picked up the paper and scanned the typed text. 'An entry from Hansard?'

'Yes.'

'Dated 4th June 1913,' muttered Churchill as he read the contents.

Hall waited. After a pause, Churchill said, 'Reginald, you have me. What has this got to do with anything?'

'Sir, it is a record of your answer in the House of Commons to a question about Brandon and Trench. You were asked if their incarceration in a German prison would count for promotion and pensions as if they had been at home.'

Churchill tapped the slip. 'To which I replied that it would.'

'Well, more than a year has gone by, yet the two officers have not been compensated for their trouble.'

Churchill flapped the paper. 'I will deal with it, but I still don't know why you are making a case for these men.'

'I would be grateful if you dealt with it,' replied Hall. His eyes blinked rapidly. 'It would be a shame if it was discovered such an omission had gone on for so long, unresolved.'

'Are you threatening me?' Churchill growled.

'No sir, I am about to employ these men in my department. I need them to know they can trust me.'

Churchill approached. 'Ah, I understand.' He placed a hand on the Captain's shoulder. 'Then you also need to know you can most certainly trust me.'

'And the codebook?'

'What about the codebook, Captain?'

'I saw no indication the book had been rescued from the sea.'

'It was discovered in a secret location in the Captain's cabin.' Churchill returned his gaze to the window. His smile faded, and his eyes darkened. 'You must allow for a little poetic licence now and then to leaven the misery of this war.'

Captain Hall picked up a large photograph from his desk. The picture showed a man dressed in the uniform of a vice-admiral of the German Navy, the equivalent to a Rear Admiral in the British Navy. Maximilian von Spee had the appearance of a kindly uncle. Wavy brown hair contrasted with his white moustache and goatee. His friendly expression was more to do with the eyes, which radiated a permanent bonhomie from under bushy eyebrows.

Von Spee's rise up the ranks was as rapid as his own. In other times he could see himself in his company, perhaps at Kiel or at one of the Embassy dinners. Yet for the last two weeks, he had been involved in hunting von Spee across the Indian and Pacific Oceans, determined to find the man and his East Asia Squadron and destroy them both.

Thankfully Germany's main High Seas fleet was bottled up in home ports following a daring raid near the Heligoland Bight in which Hall himself was involved. Altogether three German light cruisers and one destroyer were sunk and three others damaged. Over 700 Germans had died compared to 35 British sailors. When the Kaiser was told the news, he had ordered the High Seas fleet to return to Wilhelmshaven.

Now von Spee's squadron remained the biggest thorn in the British Navy's flank. His flagship was the armoured cruiser SMS *Scharnhorst*, and her sister ship the *Gneisenau* was just as powerful. Three other light cruisers and their colliers made up the squadron - the only German blue water fleet able to roam the oceans at will. The ships were fast; the crews experienced and well-trained. They could shoot further than any of the British naval forces on patrol in either the Indian or Pacific Oceans. Left to their own devices, they would put telegraph stations out of action and sink British commercial ships.

And still, no-one knew where they were.

Hall thumbed through the pile of messages that lay beneath the photograph. There were radio intercepts from ships, from the crews of captured vessels put ashore, and from coastal lookouts with British sympathies. Often the information arrived too late to be of use. Radio reports were frequently jammed, meaning communication with London was restricted to the telegraph stations of neutral counties. Countries supporting Germany refused to accept cables in code.

He examined a report from the Marquesas, a group of islands in the South Pacific. The intelligence received was unreliable. The German cruisers were reported as sailing away from a port on one course, but once over the horizon, they would change direction. They would hide amongst distant reefs, waiting to rebuild their strength before hopping to another island and planning their next raid.

'Like pirates,' he murmured. The East Asia Squadron were opportunistic marauders intent on inflicting the most considerable damage to British commercial sea lanes and activities. In pursuit was Admiral Patey, newly promoted to vice-admiral and on loan to the Australian navy. Fearing von Spee would make for Samoa or New Guinea, Patey brought his squadron to take the German-owned colonies. And still, von Spee eluded him.

Two Japanese cruiser squadrons had joined in the search in the Indian Ocean, but no trace was found. He scanned the dispatches, stopping at one dated 2nd October. The report was from an eye-witness account of the bombarding of Tahiti by von Spee's squadron. Two days later Room

40 had decrypted another note, a radio message from the *Scharnhorst*, claiming the cruiser was 'between the Marquesas and Easter Island'.

The movement east probably indicated von Spee was aiming for America. Information received claimed the German light cruiser *Leipzig* was operating in the area, and he had immediately dashed off a report suggesting the warship would rendezvous with the squadron. That was a week ago, but he had heard nothing from either Ewing or Oliver since. He could only hope his prediction had been considered and they had acted upon it.

He was so engrossed in the correspondence he did not hear a tap on the door. At the second louder knock, he looked up from his papers and rose. The figure of Lord Herschell was framed in the doorway.

'Thank you for coming,' said Hall, indicating a chair. 'This is going to be the first time we've worked together and I wondered how you like to be addressed?'

Herschell smiled. 'There are no airs and graces in these rooms, Captain. You may call me Richard, or Dick if you prefer - everyone else does.'

'Thanks, Richard.' The Captain returned to his seat behind the desk. 'I have some meetings to arrange and being the new boy here I could do with some assistance.'

'I'll do whatever I can to help.'

'First, I'd like an appointment with the Russian

Ambassador - and his son Constantine.'

'Fine.' Herschell flashed a gleaming smile. 'I will make enquiries.'

'Thank you, Richard.' Hall leaned back in his chair. 'Now, for my next request. Take a gander at this message.'

> 12th October 1914. Alexander Szek,
> 20, born London, student at Université
> Libre in Brussels. Father Austrian,
> mother British. Transferred to the Kom
> mandantur on Wetstraat as coding clerk.
> Requested repatriation. H.523

Herschell wafted the onionskin paper, 'Where did you get this?'

'Best not to ask, Richard.' Hall reached out for the note. 'Can you check the Aliens Register for London? Search for the mother, and she may have a sister living with her. I need an address.'

'Of course. Glad to help.'

'Now I don't believe I've seen every one in Room 40. When I arrived, Charlie Rotter and Eddie Bullough were away on business. I've since met Eddie, but not Charlie. Yet I was told he has returned.'

Herschell gave a curt nod. 'He has, but we've been instructed not to speak to him.'

'Why - has he been sent to Coventry?'

'Oh no, nothing like that. He's working on a special project, and Sir Alfred asked us to keep away and allow him some peace.'

'And you don't know what the task is?'

Herschell's lips tightened. 'I'm afraid I don't, Captain.'

It had to be SKM, Hall reflected. Ewing must have assigned Rotter to the sole job of breaking the codes using the codebook from Churchill. 'Where can I meet him?'

'I don't know, sir.'

'But he is somewhere in the Admiralty?'

'Yes, Captain. But I really don't know where.'

Hall rose and approached the young man. 'Look Richard, I don't expect you to know everything. Obviously, Sir Alfred wants to keep the whole thing a secret as much as possible, and I understand Charles might need some quiet space to aid his concentration.'

Herschell made to get up, but Hall signalled for him to remain seated. 'I'm nearly finished, Richard. If Sir Alfred enquires about your absence this afternoon, you can correctly say you are helping me to obtain a meeting with the Russian Ambassador.'

'Understood, Captain.'

'Thank you again. You may go now.'

As Herschell passed him, he murmured, 'No need to discuss the rest of our conversation with anyone else.'

Herschell nodded briefly. 'Of course, Captain.'

CHAPTER 5

It was after eight o'clock in the evening when
Captain Hall closed the door on his office. Most
of the group in Room 40 had departed, and Hall
was certain Sir Alfred had already gone home.
That left a small cadre of code-breakers on the
overnight shift, and Rear Admiral Henry Oliver. Recently appointed as Naval Secretary to
Winston Churchill, Oliver had brought in a camp
bed and worked into the early hours every night.
Although Hall knew to avoid that room, he had
no idea what he would say if he were accosted,
skulking about the upper corridors of the Admiralty.

He had swapped his shoes for some with
rubber soles and began to investigate nearby
offices and rooms. Some were empty, and others
were locked. Near the boardroom, he found Sir
Alfred's office. When he tried the handle, the
door opened. Inside he glimpsed a tidy oak desk
behind which was a bookcase. Fascinated, Hall

was tempted to investigate but remembered he had not yet found the man he sought.

At the end of a corridor, he bumped into someone coming out of the toilets. He was wearing a uniform and Hall said, 'Excuse me, are you Charles Rotter?'

The officer flinched. 'Yes?'

Hall held out his hand, 'Captain Hall, Director of the Naval Intelligence Division. I wanted to have a word.' He checked the corridor. 'Could we go somewhere more private?'

But Rotter was less timid than Hall imagined. 'What would the NID want with me?'

'I've met all your colleagues and just wanted a quick chat because you were away when I first arrived.'

'Oh.' Rotter peered around the empty passageway.

'We could go to your office if it's not too inconvenient?'

'I'm not sure.'

'Sir Alfred and I are contemporaries.' Hall assessed Rotter's reaction and judged a more convincing argument was required. 'I know you are working on decoding SKM if that's what you are worried about. I wanted to get to know you as a person. That is all.'

Hall's argument must have swayed him because Rotter led the way to a cramped room off a larger office. He unlocked the door and stood to one side to allow Hall to enter. A large desk filled most of the space, but what caught Captain Hall's eye was the amount of paper, spread over the desk and stacked in piles on the floor.

Rotter sat behind his desk, and Hall removed a pile of documents from the only remaining chair. He looked for somewhere to put them down, but every inch of the desktop was already occupied.

'Here, let me,' said Rotter, taking the stack and placing it on top of another pile.

'Perhaps we could start by telling me a bit about yourself?' When Rotter didn't respond, Hall carried on. 'I'm not prying into your business, you understand. Until recently, I was Captain of the *Queen Mary*. Understanding my men was crucial to making her the best battle cruiser in the Navy.'

'But I'm not one of your crew,' said Rotter. 'I work for Sir Alfred.'

'We all work for the *Royal Navy*,' said Hall in a friendly voice. 'I only want to discover what you did before coming to Sir Alfred's department.'

'Oh, I see.' Rotter relaxed. 'I was the fleet paymaster.'

'An essential post. And how did you come to be working here?'

'Well for a start I'm fluent in German. If I'm honest, I like the country and the people. I spent most of my leave there.' As Rotter continued, his manner became more confident, and his speech more assured. 'I got on well with German Naval

Officers and came to know their use of colloqui-alisms. Sometimes I felt as if I knew what they were thinking, how they would go about solving a difficult problem, that sort of thing.'

'You could pass for a German officer?'

'Actually, I think I could. I'd often been mis-taken for one.'

'That's excellent.' Hall caught sight of the documents on the floor. 'I see you have a lot on your plate, so I ought to leave you to it.'

'There's no great rush,' replied Rotter. 'I could do with some distraction.'

'Your job must be more difficult than I could imagine,' said Hall. 'I've never had to unscramble coded messages.'

'It's a futile business.' Rotter cast a sour eye over the masses of paper. 'I'm not making much progress I'm afraid.'

As he lit a cigarette, Hall blanched. The match came close to the nearest sheets and Hall had a momentary vision of the whole office on fire.

Rotter breathed out a cloud of smoke. 'To be honest, Captain, I'm not making any progress at all.'

'I'm sorry to hear that,' said Hall. 'Can I call you Charles?'

'Charlie is better.' Rotter exhaled another puff of smoke and sank into a private reverie.

'I heard you already decoded some messages,' prompted Hall, settling into the chair. 'So you must be making some headway.'

'Ah, yes. The weather reports.' Rotter reached across the table and searched among a heap of slips. He grabbed one. 'Here, take a peek - not that there's much to see.'

Hall scanned the typed note.

```
R5063    19th Oct 1914  Grid F4. Wind
light SE. Slight Swell.
```

'F4?' queried Hall.

'Refers to a location off the Baltic coastline,' answered Rotter. 'They divide the map into squares and assign a code to each square.' Rotter held up a hand, 'And before you ask, the Russians sent on copies of the squared maps with SKM.'

'That seems straightforward. Why are the other intercepts so difficult then?' Hall waved to the mountains of paperwork.

Rotter's face twisted into an expression of pain. After a second's pause he began, 'Sir Alfred insists I use the codebook for all communications.'

'Does Germany use other kinds of codebooks?'

'Yes, but as far as we know the German Navy only uses SKM. I believe there are different ones for the army, submarines, the embassies, and so on.'

Hall frowned, 'So you know you're using the correct one in this case?'

'Yes, we're sure about that.'

'Then what's the difficulty?'

'The principle is simple, really.' Rotter tapped

the big codebook lying at the corner of his desk. 'SKM is used by the German fleet to communicate their most important signals. The German Admiralty has the original book, and copies are issued to all naval ships. Orders are coded by the German Imperial Admiralty Staff and broadcast to specific ships or squadrons. When they are received the radio operators look up the codes in their codebook and convert these into proper German words - information or commands they must follow.'

'I see,' said Hall. 'But I don't understand why you can't do the same, now you have a copy of the codebook.'

'Because there is some other mechanism at work,' Rotter explained. 'The process of looking up the codes and turning this into understandable German is called decoding. But I suspect they are also using a different technique called deciphering.'

'Go on.' Hall leaned forward to catch every word.

'Well the Germans are not stupid,' remarked Rotter. 'Like us, they must have considered the possibility one of their codebooks falling into the wrong hands. If all we had to do was decode their messages, we could immediately see everything the German fleet was sending and receiving.'

Rotter pulled on his cigarette and stubbed it out on an ashtray. 'So when they produce a coded message, they use an additional procedure to scramble it further. So-called encipherment. Then, when the enciphered message is sent, it has to be deciphered first before it can be decoded.'

'Ah, I am starting to see the difficulty. So you can't decipher these?' Hall said, pointing to the stacks of papers.

'It's not a case of being unable to decipher them.' Rotter avoided Hall's gaze.

'Then what is it a case of?'

Rotter lifted his shoulders. 'Sir Alfred demands I only use SKM. He believes I will find the answer in there.'

Hall's voice rose in pitch. 'But didn't you explain the business of encipherment to him?'

Rotter sighed and raised his head to regard Hall. 'Many times, Captain. But he ordered me to continue with SKM. I make all these notes,' he indicated the mounds of documents, 'to show him I am carrying out his instructions to the letter. The decoded text is all gibberish.'

Hall's eyes blinked rapidly. 'It doesn't make any sense, Charlie. I can't understand why such an eminent man of science should be so shortsighted. But I'm beginning to realise the difficulty you're in. Supposing you were given a free hand, what would you do?'

Rotter's voice and actions became animated, 'I think they're using a cypher substitution table. Most dispatches start with a call-sign and location, so we group them from the same transmitter. Then we keep trying different substitutions until two messages give us the same beginning.'

Hall smiled at Rotter's evident enthusiasm. 'I'm afraid I didn't understand all of it. By substitution table, do you mean if A becomes J, then B becomes K, and C becomes L?'

Rotter grinned, 'Even the Bosch are not that simple. No, they mix up the letters so you can't guess the next one in sequence. If A is J, then B would be anything but K. They might choose Y or Z. And C would become A or N. It makes the job harder.'

'But not impossible?'

Rotter shook his head.

'I see.' Hall frowned. 'Charlie, breaking this code, or cypher, whatever you want to call it, is the most vital task in the department. It could mean we discover what the Imperial Navy is up to when the fleet is planning to sail, where they call for fuel and when they prepare for battle. It is so important I intend to countermand your orders. Don't worry - you won't be reprimanded. I'll sort out any broadsides that come your way.'

Rotter looked doubtful.

'I take responsibility for my order. How long do you think it will take to find the cypher key?'

'I'm not sure, Captain. But now I've got permission, thanks to you, I won't be wasting my time.'

'Good man,' said Hall. 'Best get to it, eh?'

Rotter beamed.

'Oh, and Charlie.'

'Yes sir?'

'Come and tell me as soon as you make a break-through.' Hall rose and went to the door. 'I need to know the instant you've finished.'

'Yes sir!'

The driver pulled in at the corner of Chesham Place near a large triangular piece of grass which had been given over to allotments. A man in a dark suit, waiting under the portico, escorted the visitor through the entrance.

Between the vegetable plots and sheds oppos-ite, a man in a cloth cap sat on an upturned crate reading a newspaper. He observed the visitor and recognised the sharp chin, curved nose and short stature as belonging to Captain William Reginald Hall. A look of puzzlement passed over the observer's face; Hall was known to be work-ing in the labyrinthine corridors of the Admir-alty, so what was he doing here?

As soon as Hall disappeared, Lieutenant Otto Gratz folded his paper and left the allotment via a wrought-iron gate. His car was parked around the corner, and there he changed his wellingtons for a pair of stout shoes. He drove the car around into Chesham Place, parking at the other end of the street. After switching off the engine, he opened the newspaper once again and resumed his wait.

It had taken several weeks of patient and painstaking work to determine Hall's post and the others who worked with him in the British Navy's Intelligence Division. That he was visiting the Russian Imperial Embassy today would undoubtedly interest Prince Heinrich, the Commander-in-Chief of the Baltic fleet. Otto found it curious Heinrich was held in such little regard by Kaiser Wilhelm II. The prince suspected the codebook had been compromised when *Magdeburg* was found and boarded by the Russian Navy. He speculated they had handed a copy to the British, but the Kaiser dismissed such theories as 'dubious and implausible'. Otto later learnt of two other occasions when Heinrich had broached the subject, only to be snubbed and sent away by his elder brother.

As Otto's eyes scanned the paper, his mind returned to the occasion when he almost had the proof in his grasp. Having had a tipoff from a contact within the Immigration Office in the port of Hull, he had waited outside King's Cross station. A young man was due in London carrying a large leather satchel. Otto wanted to see what was inside the bag, but the unusually aggressive reaction of the man thwarted his efforts.

Since then Otto had staked out the embassy from the allotments, watching who came and went, and which staff left at the end of every day. It made for a boring existence, but the arrival of the Director of Intelligence for the British Navy was interesting enough to offset any tedium. When he reappeared, Otto checked his pocket watch, surprised that half an hour had elapsed.

He watched as the Captain leant in the front window of his car to have a word with the driver. Hall climbed onto the rear seat, and Otto started his car, ready to follow at a respectful distance. At first, they headed for Sloane Square and then the Chelsea Embankment. Otto expected Hall to return to Whitehall, but it looked like he was heading south, which was confirmed when they crossed the river at Albert Bridge. From Battersea, they wound past Clapham Common, Tooting Bec and Streatham. Less than an hour later, Hall's car drew into a side street in the suburb of Croydon. Hall got out and knocked on the door of a semi-detached brick-built house on Moorland Road.

Otto parked on the opposite side some 50 yards away. He looked around, checking he was not being observed. Several children were playing football in the road, and a housewife cleaned the outside of her front-room windows. Satisfied no one was taking an interest in him, he unearthed a pair of binoculars from under a pile of clothes on the rear seat and made a note of the house number.

He reopened the paper and cursed. By the end of the day, he imagined he would know every damn word off by heart. An unread article on page three drew his attention. The battle at

Heligoland Bight had occurred two months before. Why was the paper only reporting it now? The answer was soon forthcoming as the correspondent stated the Admiralty had only just published the naval dispatches. Otto clenched his teeth together at the use of the triumphalist language.

Further on, another piece gave him cause for alarm. Under the title of ENEMY ALIENS, the column claimed over a thousand Germans were being arrested every day. Otto scanned the street then returned his attention to the paper. Most of the arrests occurred in London, but there were reports from Birmingham, Dunfermline, Carnarvonshire, Farnborough, Leeds and Newcastle. As he read, an icy sensation spread between his shoulder blades, and he rechecked the street. No one seemed interested in him, but that could change quickly. He started the engine and drove away at a steady pace.

On the way to his office, Hall bumped into Charlie Rotter. He appeared weary yet elated and tugged Hall to one side.

'Sir, some good news. I found a series of messages transmitted from the Norddeich transmitter. Each one had a sequential serial number before being re-enciphered.'

Hall waited with a bemused expression. 'Do I take it you have broken the code?'

'Broken the cypher, sir. The code...' Rotter halted. Hall was looking straight past him.

When Rotter turned, he saw the reason. Sir Alfred Ewing was trundling down the corridor towards them, sporting a dark blue dinner jacket and a waistcoat adorned with a pattern of gold roses. A purple bow tie topped a starched white shirt.

'Morning,' said Ewing. 'And may I be permitted to know what you *gentlemen* were discussing?'

Rotter eyed Hall. The Captain gave the slightest of nods, and Rotter began. 'Sir, I was about to explain that when I started using substitution tables I...'

Ewing interrupted. 'I believe I asked you to stick to the codebook and to not go off down some other path?'

'Ah, Captain Hall suggested another approach.'

Ewing's face drained of colour, and he glared at Hall. 'Did he indeed? Against my strict instructions! Well, we shall see about that. Captain Hall, I want to see you in my office at nine o'clock tomorrow.'

He stalked off.

Rotter reacted with alarm. 'I'm sorry, Captain. It seems I've got you into trouble.'

Hall reached across and patted his arm. 'I told you not to worry about that, Charlie. Now off you go and bring me whatever you've been working on.'

Hall watched the eager young man hurry away.

'It's better Sir Alfred and I have this out,' he muttered to himself. 'Before it's too late.'

CHAPTER 6

When Hall entered the room, Ewing was behind his desk with Admiral Oliver seated to one side. Ewing indicated a chair, positioned deliberately opposite. It reminded him of when he had been invited to the headmaster's study over some long-forgotten misdemeanour. In the presence of the headmaster and senior master, he had been summoned to explain himself. He had fluffed an excuse which landed him six of the best. The occasion had left him with a very sore bottom and a fervent resolve to be better prepared in the future.

Ewing cleared his throat. 'Captain Hall, I requested Admiral Oliver to be present since I regard this breach of discipline as a serious matter.'

Hall interjected, 'I really think this is a waste of the Admiral's time. If you had asked my opinion...'

Ewing straightened, 'I am not seeking your opinion, Captain.' His gaze swung to the Admiral, then back to Hall. 'Did Rotter put you up to this?'

'No sir, he did not.'

'Then why did you seek to countermand my instructions?' Ewing's cherubic appearance reddened. 'You knowingly flouted my orders for Fleet Paymaster Rotter to be left alone to solve German communications.'

'Decipher, Sir Alfred.'

'What?' Ewing expelled the question like spittle. 'What difference does it make? Don't quibble with me over semantics. You were meddling in the workings of my department.'

Hall waited, letting the silence develop until Ewing shifted in his chair. Before he could explode again, Hall began, 'If he pursued using only the SKM to decode transcripts, he would never have broken them. Now he is making progress.'

Ewing's eyes glittered, 'So you admit you interfered in Rotter's attempt to discover the code?'

'Interfered, no. I have been supporting him.'

'Supporting,' Ewing sneered. 'What is your expertise in decoding German communications?'

'None whatsoever - though I am now better acquainted with the problem and its solution.'

'I gave orders to leave Rotter alone to work on the key. You disobeyed a direct command.'

'Not at all, Sir Alfred.' Hall adopted a conciliatory tone. 'He asked me for help. Not in finding a key, but he was under a lot of strain and only needed someone to talk too. I didn't interfere at all.'

Ewing glanced again towards Oliver. 'I find that hard to believe.'

'I was curious to know why he was under such pressure,' Hall replied. 'All I wanted was to relieve his anxiety so he could be more productive.'

'But what you did, is waste his time and mine by suggesting a course of action he was forbidden to take.'

Hall paused, judging the moment. 'No, Sir Alfred. In fact, it was only because of my involvement that he was successful in decrypting the intercepts.'

For a second there was a stunned hush, then Oliver spoke. 'Has Rotter found a solution?'

'Yes, he has.' Hall reached into his briefcase and pulled out a wad of paperwork. 'Here are the translations from last night's dispatches.' He placed them in front of Ewing. 'He decrypted and decoded the substance of each one.'

Ewing picked up the first slip and started reading.

'You see,' Hall carried on, 'Charlie Rotter knew there was an extra process at work. He suspected once the messages had been coded with SKM, they underwent an additional procedure called encipherment. He discovered this involved a substitution table where one letter is swapped for another. That explains why the Germans are not so concerned when they lose a codebook.'

Ewing deliberately replaced the slip on the pile,

rose and walked out of the room without saying a word.

The Admiral looked thoughtfully at Ewing's receding figure. 'You need to tread carefully Reginald,' he said, turning his gaze on Hall. 'In the meantime, well done.'

Alexander Szek heard something being pushed under the front door. An envelope addressed to him lay on the doormat, and he hastily slipped it in an inside pocket. With two German staff officers billeted in the house, it was vital to intercept all post before either of them.

In his bedroom, he tore open the note.

```
Meet me at six o'clock Au Bon Vieux
Temps, Rue de Tabora.  I have a letter
from your mother. Burn this.
```

The missive was unsigned. Alex reread the passage and scanned the room. It was a ridiculous gesture: there was no-one present, but the unexpected communiqué had raised the fear of... Of what? No matter how hard he tried to rationalise his anxiety, the dread of discovery persisted. Suppose an officer had picked up the message first? At the least arrest and interrogation would follow. The idea brought him out in a cold sweat, and he found a handkerchief and wiped his forehead.

He consoled himself, knowing that until now,

he had done nothing wrong. He had complied with the German authorities in fixing the transmitter and then using it to send messages on behalf of his German overlords. If he had refused, he would have been shot. He reasoned most of his countrymen were helping the enemy anyway.

Then again, it might be a test. The Hun was capable of anything, including checking the loyalty of the non-nationals working for them. But how likely was it they would mention his mother when they believed her to be in Austria? The possibility that made the most sense was his professor had contacted the British as promised.

A tremor of anticipation rippled through Alex's chest. Could this be the start of the escape plan he had so desperately sought? And if so, what were the chances of being caught tonight? He folded the note and placed it in the ashtray while considering the alternative of not going. That was the safest option, but if the note was genuine, he would never know what his mother was writing about. Suppose she or his sister were ill? The prospect of attending the rendezvous was terrifying, yet the desire to discover what was in the letter was irresistible. With trembling hands, he lit a match and watched the slip of paper burn and curl into ash.

Alex looked briefly at the man opposite, then

back to the letter. There was no address, but the script was in his mother's hand, written on a translucent parchment. When he held it up, blue and yellow smudges of colour shone behind from the stained glass windows. He had to hold the flimsy onionskin over a white napkin to read the writing. It was oddly comforting to be in a place that reminded him of a church as he studied her words.

My dear Alex,

We are missing you so much. We miss the sound of your whistling as you toil in the garden and your lovely smile. I hold you in my thoughts and want you to know we are thinking about you every day.

I am so sorry to learn you are no longer at the University. A man from the Gov ernment told me that the Germans are forcing you to work for them. You know your Father hates them for what they did in Austria, and I hate them for what they are doing in Belgium. The papers are full of news of the atrocities they committed, and I am afraid of what might happen to you, now they have invaded Brussels. Please write often to re assure us you are still well.

He could hear his mother's voice as he read. Tears formed in the corner of his eyes, and he looked up to see if anyone had noticed. There were few people in the bar this evening, and no-one was paying any attention.

'There is no rush,' said the man in a kindly tone.

'Can I keep it?'

'I'm sorry, I will have to destroy it when you finish.'

'But I could do that.'

Alex's assertion was met with another shake of the head. 'I can't allow that. But you may have as long as you like to read it here.'

Alex returned his attention to the rest of the text.

> The gentleman asked me to write to you with a polite request to help them. At first, I refused, because I felt if you accepted, it would put your life in danger. But my contact convinced me that if you do cooperate, the war could be shortened, and many lives saved.
>
> The gentleman did not describe what it was he wanted you to do, only that it is something you could easily perform during part of your ordinary duties at work. He also promised that provided you are careful, you wouldn't be discovered or harmed. The person who gives you this letter will explain what they want you to do. I leave the decision up to you.
>
> Isabella sends her love. She has found employment as a governess in an English family. Like me, she is troubled, knowing you cannot escape from Brussels. I

would love to tell you more about our
news, but I only have these two pages on
which to write.

Please look after yourself,

Ihre liebend Mama

Alex straightened. 'What is it you want me to do?'

'Before I tell you, I have two questions.'

'Go on.'

'I need to know if you agree this is from your mother.'

The question hardly deserved an answer, and Alex nodded.

'I need to hear it from your lips.'

'Yes, yes,' Alex stuttered. 'I thought that was obvious.'

'Thank you. The second question may also seem an obvious one to you, but I still need to hear your answer.' He leaned forward and lowered his voice. 'Will you help us?'

Captain Hall stared at the growing mound of messages at the side of his desk. The contents bothered him, but what was more worrying was that no-one in the lofty reaches of the Admiralty saw fit to respond to his concerns. He ran a hand firmly over his head as if by flattening those wiry curls, he could smooth the spiral of politics enveloping the War Staff.

That small coterie was the decision-making core of the Royal Navy. Headed by the First Lord, Churchill, it included the First Sea Lord Prince Battenberg, the chief of the War Staff Vice-Admiral Sturdee, and the Naval Secretary. The problem was that less than a week earlier the press had openly called for Churchill's resignation. Several articles cited "grave doubts" over his ability as an ex-officer in the army to grasp the principles and practice of naval warfare. What worried Hall more was the same paper went on to cast serious misgivings over Prince Louis Battenberg's patriotism because of his family affiliations and connections to Germany.

Hall let out a long anguished sigh. Prince Louis had worked so hard to climb the Navy ladder, from cadet to First Sea Lord. Thought by many in the Navy to be an outstanding officer, Hall knew him to be a fine tactician and fleet handler. He had even occupied Hall's post of Navy Intelligence Director at one stage. But it didn't help that, born in Austria, he remained unable to eradicate his German accent. Before the war, there were several campaigns to oust him, but he survived them all on merit. Now, renewed scuttlebutt circulated about the Prince's loyalties.

And while the War Staff fought a rear-guard action in the newspapers, their collective eyes and minds were missing important problems at sea. Yet what could he do? He drew the pile of papers towards him. The right approach would be to go to Sir Alfred. He closed his eyes. Ewing might be a great engineer and academic, but had no conception of strategic command. What's more, after the business with Rotter, the man hated his guts.

He could meet Admiral Oliver, but he was so busy he had little patience for interruptions. Churchill might listen, but that would be going way over Oliver's head, and perhaps harm his career to be seen doing so. Yet the matter would not wait. Though the correct course would be difficult, he felt compelled to give it another try. He stuffed the papers into his briefcase and left his office.

The Falcon pub in north London sat at the busy junction of the Seven Sisters and Hornsey road. The clientele were mainly men from the nearby factory, or from the notorious slum called Campbell Bunk. As Inspector Edwin Woodhall eyed the pub, he reflected that before the war, German nationals would meet in the swankiest locations. Now they were lucky to be allowed into the seediest of drinking dens.

Detective Sergeant Reid, met him outside. Also known as 'Tich' because of his height, he jerked his head towards the building behind and grunted, 'Otto Gratz. My snout Jimmy spotted 'im in the snug.'

'Did he see you?'

'Nah,' said Reid. 'And Otto doesn't know Jimmy from Mutt and Jeff.'

'Who is he with?'

'Dunno, Inspector. Not seen 'im before.'

'What do you think, Tich?'

'Switch, likely.'

Woodhall surveyed the street. Apart from a customer resting against the doorpost, no-one seemed to be taking an interest. 'We'd better go in.'

The man in the doorway moved to block their path. Woodhall regarded the brawny chest underneath the tight jersey.

'It's OK, Richard,' said Reid. 'He's wiv' me. Special Branch.'

Richard remained doubtful.

'Move,' growled Reid.

The man grunted and stepped aside. Inside the decor was much as Woodhall expected: faded velour covered the seats, and the stink of urine and stale beer caused his nose to wrinkle.

Reid observed his Inspector's reaction, 'Posh ain't it.'

'I'm surprised they let you in. Where's the bar?'

'You go through the door, then turn left past the toilets.' Reid indicated the way. 'Are you sure you want them to see you?'

'No, I don't. Go and check they're still there while I get a drink.'

While he waited, Woodhall scanned the room.

A group of three men sat playing dominoes near the window. An older man nursed his glass, looking as if this was to be his last. A gust of laughter came from the far corner where two men played darts while a middle-aged barmaid looked on with a bored air.

Reid returned after a minute, and Woodhall bought him a beer. They brought them to a table, and Reid briefed the Inspector in quiet tones. 'Identical briefcases, leather, but clapped out. They swap over while having a brew and walk away with each other's. Told you!'

'You've made your point, Tich.'

'What do you want me to do?'

Woodhall mulled over the possibilities. 'Forget Otto, but nab his companion. I don't want Otto to find out, so if the courier leaves first, follow him and arrest him somewhere quiet. If Otto leaves first, detain the messenger outside the pub.'

'Very well, sir. And if they both leave together?'

'Follow discretely. At some point, they will split up. Shadow the courier and arrest him. Can you do that without him giving you the slip?'

'No problem sir, I'm pretty useful with the standard-issue Webley.'

Woodhall looked alarmed, 'Good God, Tich, I want him alive.'

'And you shall have him, sir, if you don't mind the odd scratch mark.'

'Take him down to the station,' said Woodhall.

'Hold him under the Defence of the Realm Act, or the Aliens Act; I don't care which. Then strip him of every item of clothing: shoes, socks, hat, everything. If Otto is as clever as I think he is, then the briefcase might be a blind. Bring the bag and all his clothes to me.' He regarded the detective. 'Got that?'

'Absolutely sir.' Reid grinned. 'Now if you don't mind, I'll finish my drink while our friends finish theirs.'

Admiral Oliver looked up briefly as Hall entered the room. The Admiral's permanently arched eyebrows gave the appearance of a man attempting to appraise and interrogate his quarry simultaneously. He wore a luxurious moustache and beard, but his head seemed disproportionately small when compared to his barrel chest. He was famous for his reticence, and Hall remained standing while waiting to be asked to sit.

Oliver returned to the forms on his desk, occasionally initialling an order or writing a comment in the margins. As the scratching sounds continued, Hall's thoughts wandered. He had never seen such a bare office in the Admiralty. No photographs adorned the desk; no pictures hung on the walls, no flowers decorated the filing cabinets. Instead, the rear wall contained a large map of the world, and a folded camp bed lay tucked in beside a safe. It was reputed the man worked 130 hours a week. In Hall's eyes, the room was as stark and claustrophobic as a prison cell.

The scratching stopped, and Hall's attention switched to Oliver. 'Sir, I need a professional assessment of the latest situation in the South Pacific.' He pulled the papers from his briefcase and placed them on the desk. There were no new bulletins from that theatre, but Oliver was incapable of refusing a request for advice. Hall imagined it flattered the man's vanity to be asked, but any ruse to engage the support of a superior felt justified.

Oliver picked up the first message and read silently. After a few seconds, he replaced it. 'I have seen this before. If this is indeed the latest communique from Kit Cradock, then you are wasting my time.'

'Sir, I am not asking you to review what you have read, but I would appreciate your opinion on what was not said.'

CHAPTER 7

Admiral Oliver regarded Hall with a stern, forbidding expression. 'What exactly are you trying to say, Captain?'

Hall's eyes blinked rapidly of their own volition. 'I've been combining all our communications with Rear-Admiral Cradock, and I've come to a conclusion.' He indicated the world map on the wall behind, 'I wonder if we could take a step back and view the overall picture?'

Oliver pulled a fob watch from his waistcoat pocket. 'You have half an hour, and then I must meet Vice-Admiral Sturdee.'

Hall moved to stand under the map and pointed to a section of the western coast of South America belonging to Chile. 'We know von Spee is heading in this direction. What we don't know is what he will do when he gets there. From the knowledge gathered by the reports of von Spee's attacks, I calculate he's used over half of his ammunition. Also, like us, he may only coal in a neutral port once every three months.' He looked at Oliver, 'He needs to get home before he runs out of either coal or shells.'

'I can find no argument there,' murmured Oliver. 'Go on.'

Hall placed his finger on the map above the capital Santiago. 'He could go north, but the Panama Canal is closed to the Central Powers.' He lowered his voice, 'even though the United States is supposedly neutral.' Hall's finger moved south to the tip of the continent. 'He could use the Magellan Straits into the Atlantic, possibly coaling in the Falklands. If I were him, I'd continue up the west coast, maybe as far as the River Plate, then strike across the ocean to Germany. That way, I'd most likely avoid running into a British squadron early on.'

'That is why he was given instructions to police the coastline.'

'Yes, I was coming to that.' Hall checked a note. 'He has to patrol from Valparaiso on the west coast, south to the Magellan Straits, and up the eastern seaboard to Montevideo.'

'Not quite,' responded Oliver. 'We're forming a new squadron to cover those sea lanes - at Cradock's request.'

'But until that happens, Cradock has been tasked with finding von Spee along a coastline of over three thousand nautical miles!'

'Yes, I grasp the position, Captain. I'm sure the War Staff have discussed all this.' Oliver's tone sounded testy, leaving Hall unsure whether this was because he found the viewpoint indefensible or just plain irritating.

'That leads me to a second issue.' He waited, checking the man was prepared to receive another argument.

The Admiral nodded, and Hall referred to his notes again. 'Suppose they meet, what then?'

Oliver frowned, 'Make yourself clear, Captain.'

'Yes sir. What is Rear-Admiral Cradock required to do if he encounters von Spee?' He passed a lengthy message to the Admiral and waited while he read it.

'Yes, and what is your point?' queried the Admiral.

'At the end of this, Cradock is ordered to *Break up the German trade and destroy enemy cruisers.* I have read and re-read all the telegrams between us and I have found nothing to countermand this order. The Rear-Admiral must still believe he has been directed to attack von Spee when he finds him.'

'If what you say is correct, then I agree.' Oliver's face had lost its long-suffering appearance and developed an air of concern. 'Cradock's forces are no match for von Spee.' He paused. 'I suppose you are aware of the disposition of Cradock's squadron?'

'I made it my business, Admiral,' replied Hall. 'The *Monmouth* was saved from the scrap yards. She's crewed by naval reservists, cadets and coastguards who have had only a month's train-ing. Her guns are mounted too low to the waterline. Even if the crew knew how to fire, they would have to close the gun ports in heavy weather to prevent being washed out. The *Otranto...*'

'Yes, yes.' Oliver held up a hand to stem the flood. 'I see you are up to the mark.' There was a long pause while he contemplated Hall. 'Was there anything else?'

Hall hunted through the stack of papers and picked out one near the bottom. 'There is this.'

Oliver scanned the cable from Cradock dated 26th October and re-read the last sentence.

> Canopus will be employed in necessary
> work of convoying colliers.

'*Canopus*?'

'Yes sir. Another ship destined for the scrap yards.'

Oliver gave him a sharp look, 'She carries four 12-inch guns.'

'She does, Admiral. But those guns are 17 years old - as is the ship. They have a range of 13,000 yards, which is no greater than the 8-inch guns on the *Scharnhorst* and *Gneisenau*.'

'Yes, I seem to remember something about that.' The Admiral's voice drifted.

Hall gestured to the telegram. 'Earlier, Church-ill orders Cradock to build his squadron around *Canopus,* calling her "A citadel". Is it any wonder Cradock ignored the instruction? Did anyone made it clear to the First Lord *Canopus* was then only able to make sixteen knots while von Spee can do twenty-two?'

He waited for an answer as Oliver studied him in silence. 'A week ago,' said Hall, 'we received a report from her chief engineer her maximum speed is now only twelve knots because of the condition of her boilers.'

Oliver sighed through pursed lips.

'So Rear-Admiral Cradock believes he is to hunt for and take on von Spee's squadron,' he said, 'while charged to remain shackled to *Canopus*.'

The room became silent.

'Now I understand why Cradock disobeyed the order,' muttered Oliver, as if speaking to himself.

'There is something else that has been bothering me.'

'Go on.'

'Until a week ago, Cradock was still expecting the arrival of the *Defence*. No-one had seen fit to tell him it had been deployed elsewhere.' For several reasons the battlecruiser had been delayed - not least, Hall considered, because the Admiralty were fooled when von Spee laid a course west, away from South America. 'Cradock must have been counting on the battlecruiser. She is faster than either of von Spee's armoured cruisers and has more powerful guns. In a contest with von Spee, I reckon she would even up the odds for Cradock. Without her, he's no match.'

He observed Oliver's slow nod of acknowledgement. 'When he learned she was to form part of the second squadron on the east coast, Cradock ordered her to join him.'

'So what is your view, Captain?'

'My assessment is the messages to and from the Rear-Admiral are too vague. There's room for misunderstanding, and in such a serious confrontation with Germany, I would want the Admiralty to feel they have given Cradock as much support as he needs to do the job. We need to communicate clearly what that job is.'

'I see what you mean, Captain.' The Admiral considered his next words. 'And I'm afraid I agree with you.'

Hall spoke as if thinking out loud, 'At some stage, Rear-Admiral Cradock and von Spee may meet. What do you think Cradock would do then?'

Oliver stared at the desk as he mulled over their discussion. After several seconds his lips moved and Hall heard him murmur, 'I know him well. He will fight to the death.'

Inspector Edwin Woodhall stood with hands on hips and surveyed the room. Perhaps this morning, feeling fresh after a sound night's sleep, he might discover what he had missed yesterday.

On his desk, a newspaper, letters of introduction and a passport sat neatly to one side. The rest lay scattered over the cheap pine top: a battered leather suitcase, a pair of dusty boots and black woollen socks. On the floor were brown baggy trousers, a smelly pair of long johns, a stained white shirt, a black jacket and a flat cap.

Every item of clothing had been examined minutely, but so far, Woodhall had found nothing suspicious. The heels from the boots were removed and pried apart. The lining of the hat was razored off. The turn-ups on the trousers, the buckle on the belt, the collar of the shirt: all revealed nothing. He had even examined the seams of the long johns with a magnifying lens the previous evening, a job he never wanted to repeat. But none of the man's apparel showed the smallest hint they contained a secret communication.

The Inspector had gathered some information from the assorted items. The man's name was Max Boxler, and he liked to read The Times. The Inspector retrieved the two-day-old paper, opened it out and scrutinised the columns again. There were no pencil or pen marks highlighting keywords of a message and all the pages were in their correct sequence. Woodhall had obtained a copy from the printers, checking that pages from another journal had not been inserted. When he warmed the paper over a lantern, no secret ink magically emerged in the margins. Blowing carbon dust over the pages produced no tell-tale indentations where a hidden message had been scrawled.

The letters were similarly unforthcoming about their owner. Written on plain white paper, they felt rough to the touch. The first was addressed to a hospital in France, introducing Boxler as an exporter of medical equipment. A pamphlet gave details of the types of antiseptics available, including sodium hypochlorite, and a small range of blood transfusion apparatus. Several others were to London hospitals, advertising the same products.

According to his passport, Boxler was Swiss, which gave the Inspector a problem. If true, Boxler could not be treated as an enemy alien and interned. Boxler's documents might be authentic, but how could he be sure?

Woodhall's eyes strayed to the briefcase, the only identical object which both Otto Gratz and Boxler possessed, according to his Sergeant. Inside was a thin black lining which proved easy to remove, leaving a clean matt surface of leather underneath. He drew the scruffy case towards him. There was no hidden floor, and the leather was stitched around the edges and looked perfectly normal. True, the edging was so worn it had become frayed. When he brushed a thumb over a corner, he saw the casing comprised two thin layers of leather.

The Inspector grabbed a magnifying glass and inspected the binding. Using a razor knife, he carefully sliced the stitches until he was able to grab the two layers with his hands and tug them apart. With more slashes of the knife, he exposed the inner of one side of the case.

Still nothing.

Woodhall closed his eyes and cursed under his breath. Yet there was still the other side panel left, and he made short work of removing the stitching and opening out the interior.

Inside lay a single sheet of paper, and the normally composed Inspector let out a whoop of elation.

'Alleluia!'

A brief knock and the door opened to reveal the unusually sombre face of Lord Herschell.

'Morning, sir. May I have a minute?'

'Certainly.' Hall indicated the chair in front of his desk.

'I brought this.' Herschell slid a folded piece of paper over. 'It was sent by an Inspector Woodhall from the Special Branch. He had a tip a German national called Otto Gratz was meeting a courier in a pub in north London. The courier's name is Max Boxler, and he was about to leave for France. Woodhall apprehended him before he got as far as the ferry. When he searched his things, he found this note secreted in his briefcase.' He indicated the paper on the desk. 'Trouble is, he can't make head nor tail of the message.'

Hall unfolded the sheet and scanned the contents. There were three lines on the page, with letters grouped into a familiar pattern of five characters per word.

'Where is the courier now?'

'The Inspector is holding him in the cells on the pretext of checking his documentation.'

He returned the sheet. 'Take this to Sir Alfred. Tell him it's urgent, and I need a translation by tomorrow at the latest.'

'Right Captain.' Herschell paused at the doorway. 'By the way, did you hear the news about the First Sea Lord?'

Hall looked up, 'What?'

'He's resigned - or he was asked to leave, I don't know which.'

'I'm very sorry to hear that. Battenberg was a good man.'

'I was told Admiral Fisher is to take his place.'

'Oh.' Hall wasn't surprised - bringing back old warhorses to fight again was not an uncommon occurrence. Fisher had been a regular visitor to Downing Street since the war began, and the newspapers had captured several photographs of the great man with Churchill on the steps of number ten. 'Thank you, Richard,' he said. 'Don't forget to have that message decoded as fast as possible.'

When Herschell left, his thoughts shifted to the War Staff at the Admiralty. They had been issuing Cradock's rag-tag squadron with confusing and contradictory orders. It would take a while for Fisher to acquaint himself with details of the German and British Navy's deployment and operations. Meanwhile, Kit Cradock and von Spee could meet, and he hated to think about what would happen then. A knot started to twist in his stomach, and he set off for Oliver's office.

In the corridor outside, navy officers scurried to meetings or were conferring with colleagues. *Like ants in a nest*, he thought, *stirred up by a big stick.* Halfway along, he met Oliver hurrying towards him.

'Admiral.'

'Not now, Captain,' said Oliver side-stepping.

He faced the Admiral. 'I was coming to see you about Admiral Cradock.'

Oliver pivoted. 'What about him?'

'With all these changes, will he still get *Defence*?'

Oliver's face froze. 'No. Winston has countermanded Kit's latest request.'

'But...'

'I am busy, Captain. We can talk later.'

Hall tried the key to his office but found it was already unlocked. Ewing was waiting for him. He closed the door behind him, recalling this was the second instance when the man had entered his room without asking. In the past, when a junior officer made a blunder, it was his manner to conceal the hot rush of his blood. Now he must make the same effort when a higher rank-ing officer did likewise.

'Sir. What can I do for you this morning?'

'Yesterday you sent Lord Herschell to me with a request to decode a message.' Ewing's Scottish accent seemed to lend weight to the accusation.

'It was not a request.'

Ewing's face froze, and his voice held a hard edge. 'You appear to lack a basic understanding of the chain of command. I am senior to you and Head of Room 40.'

'With respect, Sir Alfred, the message I sent needs to be decrypted by tomorrow. The transla-tion is vital to the war effort.'

'*I* shall decide what is and isn't vital to the war effort. If you need something doing, you must come to me directly and explain the circum-stances of your request. *I* will then determine the priority.'

Hall moved around his desk. He drew a large diary towards him and opened it at today's date. 'Sir, the intelligence department doesn't func-tion like that, and it will not. It is not up to you to decide the importance of the work that passes my desk. If you cannot agree to that, then I will have no recourse but to approach your senior officers.'

'I have been informed you have already done so,' Ewing breathed. 'You have had meetings with Admiral Oliver without speaking to me first. If that happens again, then we shall see who goes and who remains.'

Hall waited several seconds before responding. 'Sir Alfred, I have no wish to leap-frog the chain of command, but I have a job to do, and it is sometimes essential to short-circuit naval bureaucracy. I appreciate decoding transcripts can take time. All I was asking for is this note - which is only three lines long - be given top priority.'

Ewing paused as if signalling acceptance of an unspoken apology. 'On this occasion I agreed to give the intercept the priority you requested.' He pulled a piece of paper from an inside pocket and placed it on Hall's desk. 'But if you want any further messages decrypting, you *will* have to come to me personally.'

'Thank you, Sir Alfred.'

Ewing clamped his lips together.

Hall could swear he heard a hiss like steam escaping a boiler as Ewing left the office. The door closed, and in the stillness, there was but one single thought. Managing an entitled superior was like pouring treacle: sticky when spilled. Life at sea was an ocean away from the petty self-important bureaucracy at the Admiralty. Why on earth should he remain? Already he could hear Essie's objections in his mind. *You promised; you said you would stay at least until Christmas.* She would not accept him leaving because of some office quarrel. He had made a promise to his wife, and he must keep it.

He let out a deep sigh and picked up the note

Ewing had left. A chill developed on the back of his neck and spread slowly up into his scalp. He massaged the muscles while contemplating the contents.

The first revelation was that he was being followed. He sensed the stealthy presence of the enemy, as surely as the sight of smoke on the horizon. How could he, the head of the foremost Intelligence Division in Britain, not know of a German shadow? The idea was both sinister and shocking.

The second shock was they knew about his meeting with the Russian Ambassador. What would the Germans make of that? Even more importantly, how would a spy go about discovering the subject of the meeting? He attempted to put himself in Otto Gratz's position. Perhaps he could approach a junior member of staff. But the personnel at the embassy were not present at the meeting, and nothing would be got from them. The only two people attending were the Ambassador Aleksandr Benckendorff, and his son Constantine. The ambassador would be well protected by staff, both at home and at work. However, he remembered from their conversation, Constantine had been given various permits to inspect London's aerial defences. His stay in London had been extended for a fortnight, and no doubt the young man would want to visit other attractions in the capital before returning to duty on the Black Sea. Hall suspected this was a small reward for delivering the SKM codebook safely.

He tapped the note. If he were a German spy, he would find a way to extract information from Constantine. And when he knew the truth and communicated with the Fatherland, the usefulness of SKM would be lost. The German Navy would issue a new book to the fleet, and Britain would once again be unable to discern the substance of their communications.

The third shock was equally disturbing. Gratz had followed him to the house of Isabella Szek. When knowledge of his connection to her circulated within the Imperial German Army, it wouldn't take long for them to realise Alexander Szek, their coding clerk in Brussels, was related to Isabella. The link would prove to be a fatal one for Alex and another blow to Britain.

He held the slip up to the light and examined the message again. Was there a way to turn such damaging information around, and put it to his own use?

CHAPTER 8

Hall re-read the cable the Admiralty had sent to Cradock the previous evening.

> *Defence is to remain on east coast under orders of Stoddart. This will leave a sufficient force on each side in case the hostile cruisers appear on the trade route.*

From Cradock's point of view, the one ship that could make a difference was being denied him. And not only did the Admiralty claim the squadron on the west coast sufficient, but also implied Cradock's own rag-tag unit was too.

Perhaps Cradock would not receive the message at all. Connections to South America were notoriously difficult. It usually took three days, sometimes longer, for Admiralty messages to reach the southern oceans. First, a telegram was sent via the undersea cable network to Cerrito in Montevideo, Uruguay. The contents were then re-transmitted by wireless. For ships in the southern Atlantic, it would be picked up by a station on the Falkland Islands. Reaching the west coast where Cradock had assembled his squadron, was more challenging. The intervening barrier of the Andes prevented wireless transmissions and cables had to be re-sent over landlines to the nearest port. Telegrams were then collected by ship, and the whole process could take several days.

Hall fervently hoped the fleet had sailed out to sea, or bad weather prevented the timely retrieval of the message.

Two days later, on the evening of 31st October, the seas off the coast of Chile were relatively calm when the light cruiser Glasgow entered Coronel harbour. The Glasgow was the fastest ship in Admiral Cradock's squadron. She was used to being the lead in the hunt for Von Spee; at a pinch she could outrun every one of the enemy ships.

Her captain, John Luce was in his mid-forties, having had several years experience as a captain of the *Hibernia*. The light was fading, and he checked his pocket watch; it was 6:42 pm. He observed a boat pull away from a German merchant ship, and shortly afterwards a beacon burst into flame on a nearby hill.

The British Consul was piped aboard, and Luce welcomed him. During the discussion, Luce learnt about the extent of German intelligence operations in Chile. News of his visit would already be on its way to the German consul at Valparaiso, and then on to von Spee.

Amongst all the letters the consul brought was a telegram from the Admiralty. Luce turned the envelope over in his hands. A sense of tragedy hung over the ship's officers and ratings alike. Ominous mutterings had been going on for a while. The Glasgow, though small, was the quickest ship in the squadron. Sailors on the other vessels whispered she would be the only one fast enough to escape von Spee when they met. The rest, they said, were done for.

In exchange for the note he held, Captain Luce passed a message from Cradock to the consul, for onward transmission to the Admiralty. The Rear Admiral had shown him the text, and a single sentence stood out:

> I intend to proceed northward secretly
> with squadron after coaling and keep out
> of sight of land.

Luce was not sure how the Admiralty would interpret the plan, but to him the intention was clear. Cradock had decided to find von Spee and fight.

Already the wind was strengthening from the south. He estimated it would take the best part of ten hours to decode the various cables and to leave any coded responses at the port. He hoped the weather would abate, but his experience in these latitudes convinced him the squall would only increase in strength. A glance over the bow towards the shore revealed dark forests behind the town and shadowy mountain tops beyond. Although it was still warm, he shivered and drew his coat around him.

Lord Herschell lounged in Hall's doorway. His smile was a tad too smug, decided Hall. 'Come in and close the door behind you.'

The young Lord was unable to contain his news any longer, and Hall smiled. 'You'd better sit down before you explode.'

'We've got another codebook.'

'Oh?'

'It's the HVB or Handelsschiffsverkehrsbuch, for short.'

Hall chuckled.

'Yes,' said Herschell. 'I was told HVB was in use before the war. Now it's used by German warships to signal merchantmen. It's been adapted so naval shore commands, coastal stations and patrol boats can use it.' Herschell's smile grew, 'And I've heard some German warships use HVB to communicate with each other!'

'So what have we learnt?'

'Ah, too soon to say.' Herschell's grin faded. 'It only arrived off the boat from Australia yesterday.'

'And how did they come by it?'

'The short version says it came from the *Hobarth*, a German-Australian steamer. Shortly after the war began, she attempted to dock in a small port near Melbourne. The Captain had hidden secret documents in his cabin, but he was found out. The HVB was amongst the papers.'

'But that was nearly three months ago! Why the delay?'

Herschell shrugged, 'Maybe they didn't realise how important the codebook was. And when they did, they dispatched a copy by steamer to London.'

'Or they decided to copy the book first,' muttered Hall. 'It wouldn't surprise me if they wanted a crack at the codes first.' He glanced at Herschell. 'Perhaps when they realised they weren't making any progress, they sent it by the slowest possible route, to allow them more time.'

'Perhaps,' said Herschell noncommittally. 'Anyway, we have it now.'

'Agreed,' said Hall. 'I'm glad you called. I need another meeting with Constantine Benckendorff. Could you arrange that soon? And tell Inspector Woodhall I'd like to see him here tomorrow at 9 o'clock if that is convenient.'

The weather had broken, and thunder rolled around the heavens as if seeking a way to earth. The stained glass windows of the Au Bon Vieux Temps were dark, and Alexander Szek scanned the room for any sign of his contact. Meetings made him nervous. Even in his student days, he was reluctant to enter a pub with his friends. There was something about the smoke, the flow of alcohol and the raised voices that still scared him.

A man sat down next to him, and Alex's heart raced. He wore a hat pulled down over his forehead and spoke in a low voice. 'Don't turn round. Drink your beer and pretend as if you belong here.' The man was known to Alex as Karl, but that might be a false name.

Alex continued to perspire. His mother had asked him to follow these instructions, but she did not understand how much stress this was creating for him. Each lunch break, he would have his sandwiches at his desk. When he was alone, he would copy out the contents of the codebook he used in his job as a telegraph operator. He used a soft pencil to inscribe the columns of letters and numbers onto a special paper which he hid in his clothing. At any point he could be spotted and asked to account for his actions.

'What have you got for me?'

Alex shot Karl a brief glance, then remembered and picked up his glass. 'I - I haven't brought anything,' he said, avoiding eye contact. He knew he sounded weak and frightened, but he couldn't do anything about that.

'What?'

'I had an idea. Copying the codebook will take months. Why don't I steal it?'

Karl was already shaking his head.

'I'm often last to leave at the end of my shift. I'd conceal it in a bag. No one would know.'

'No.' Karl's emphatic tone ruled out the possibility. 'They would all realise at the start of a new shift. Then you'd be for the firing squad.'

Alex flinched. 'You could take me to London.'

Karl swivelled to face him. Though Karl's eyes were shaded by the brim of his hat, specks of light glimmered in both. 'And what do you think the Germans will do when they find you and the book are missing?'

Alex's mouth went dry.

'And I thought you were a University student,' muttered Karl.

'I'm only trying to help.'

'You can help by giving me the pages you've copied.'

Alex hesitated. The act of handing Karl his copy of the notes would commit him to carry out the subterfuge for a year, or maybe longer. That meant risking discovery every day until it was finished.

'Could you get me a miniature camera? I could photograph a lot more pages.'

'It's possible.' Karl didn't sound positive. 'But that will take ages. In the meantime, I need your copies.'

Alex put his hand inside his coat.

'Under the table, lad. Slowly does it.'
Alex passed him a brown envelope.

At 9:15 am the Glasgow slipped her moorings and made for the sea on a northerly course. Through his glasses, Captain Luce glimpsed the peaceful harbour for the last time. The wispy fog that wrapped the hilltops would soon disappear. Tin shacks lined the shore and a dense forest encroached on the shanty houses like a belligerent army.

Out of sight of land, Luce ordered a turn to the south-west to rendezvous with the squadron. The ship began to pitch and roll in the short swell and mounting seas. Wave tops, beaten into egg-white spume, spilt over the foredeck. *Glasgow* staggered under the assault but made good progress until a lookout sighted smoke at one pm. Forty miles west of Coronel Bay, Cradock's flagship the *Good Hope* came into view. Soon the elderly light cruiser *Monmouth* was sighted, followed by *Otranto*, a converted ocean liner.

It was not possible to transfer the mail to the *Good Hope* by boat, and Luce gave the order to trail a waterproof cylinder containing the messages across the bows of the stationary flagship. Seamen caught the line with grappling hooks and hauled the tube on board. About an hour later, the wind calmed enough for a boat to be launched, and Luce transferred to the *Good Hope*.

'John, welcome aboard.' Kit Cradock's hand-shake was firm.

Luce followed him to the Admiral's quarters.

'It was good of you to come.' Cradock's tone was warm and friendly. 'Do you have any more news for me?'

'Yes sir, last night we heard many messages from the *Leipzig*. They started around two in the morning.'

'Just the *Leipzig*?'

'Yes sir, my radioman says her Telefunken signals are distinctive, a kind of high-pitched sound.'

'Wonderful. Then if we find her alone, it will be one less problem to worry about.'

'Suppose she is not alone, what then?' Luce's voice carried his concern.

'Then we will see what develops.' Cradock paused. 'How are the men?'

'Well sir, my intelligence officer Hirst did the rounds before we visited Coronel. As he was collecting the mail, he told me two officers on the *Monmouth* had given him personal letters to their wives.' Luce studied Cradock's wide-set eyes. 'They are afraid they will not survive an engagement with von Spee.'

Cradock brought out a telegram from his pocket. 'Take a look,' he said, handing the paper over.

The Captain scanned the text.

'You will notice the phrase,' said Cradock,

pointing, *'...sufficient force on each side'*. The Admiralty believes we have sufficient force to see off Von Spee.' He leaned towards the Captain and lowered his voice. 'Not a word to anyone else, but personally I do not.' He straightened. 'But after forty years at sea, I will not be accused of cowardice like my friend Troubridge.'

Luce knew the name. Rear-Admiral Troubridge was due to be court-martialled for "failing to engage the enemy during the pursuit of *Goeben* and *Breslau*".

'But sir, the court-martial hasn't taken place yet. He could be exonerated.'

'No, Captain Luce. I will not stand before any court to justify my name to a service I have given my life to.'

Luce's eyes switched to the telegram which lay on the table between them.

'I understand your apprehension, John.' Cradock lowered his voice once more. 'And your concern for your officers and men. If we engage, and there is nothing more you can do, you must leave.'

The Captain's eyes fixed on the Rear-Admiral.

'That is an order, Captain.' The Admiral inspected the view out of the porthole. 'I see the glass is falling again. You should hurry back to your command.'

'But sir?'

The Rear Admiral gave the young man a friendly pat on the arm. 'Go and do your best.' His smile, though not fulsome, was encouraging. 'As we all must do.'

Inspector Woodhall surveyed the interior of Captain Hall's tiny office. 'So the Navy has offices even smaller than Special Branch.'

Hall smiled and nodded to the staff sergeant, 'Thank you Tom, he'll be safe with me.'

The Captain rose and shook hands with the Inspector. 'Thank you for coming, Inspector.'

'Call me Ed. Everyone does except my staff - though God knows what they call me when I'm not there. I expect this is something to do with the Boxler case?'

'It is indeed.' Hall arranged a small pile of papers on his desk. 'I am about to take you into my confidence, Ed. You'll know all about that, I suppose, but the information I have could have international repercussions if it falls into the wrong hands.'

'Very well, Captain. You can count on me.'

'Thank you.' Hall picked up the first item from the pile and passed it across the desk. 'This is a decode of the message you found in Max Boxler's briefcase.'

> 28 Oct 1914. Director of Naval intelli
> gence Cpt Reginald Hall met with Russian
> Ambassador. Attempting to discover
> subject of meeting. Also DNI interest
> in British woman Isabella Szek residing

25 Moorland Road Croydon.   Steinhauer

The Inspector scratched his head. 'Looks like you're being followed.'

'Correct. It gave me a touch of the collywobbles, I can tell you.' He passed across a second message. 'This is a translation of the note I want putting back into Boxler's briefcase.'

> *28 Oct 1914. Director of Naval intelli gence Cpt Reginald Hall met with Russian Ambassador. Attempting to discover subject of meeting. Steinhauer*

'Of course,' said Hall. 'The words will be encoded and encrypted, so the Bosch thinks it's an original message. I don't want my visit to Croydon to be known. Can you do that?'

Woodhall frowned. 'Getting an identical briefcase would be a big problem. Most people are familiar with their own, down to the last scratch. Anything out of the ordinary will be spotted.'

'Perhaps you could track down a master cobbler to stitch up the old one with identical stitching? Tell me, how is our friend being treated?'

Woodhall shrugged, 'The same as any other potential enemy alien. He claims he's Swiss and we've found him a comfy cell until we verify his documents.'

'Excellent.' Hall relaxed. Once you've returned the note and stitched up the case, you may let him go.'

'Just like that?' Woodhall's astonishment was

plain.

'Just like that. Don't follow him - he may become suspicious. He must find his own way to his masters and deliver the message.'

'OK, I can do that. But what about the Ambassador? We wouldn't want anyone to interfere with him - now that would cause an international incident!'

'I'm not worried about the Ambassador.'

'You're not?' Woodhall's face assumed a puzzled expression.

'No, Ed, I'm not. Because you'll let slip you're putting on a man to follow his son, Constantine.'

Woodhall raised his eyebrows. 'His son? What's he got to do with anything?'

'I'll tell you later.' Hall regarded Ed. 'While Boxler is getting his things together, you receive a call from the next room with orders to tail Constantine. Only by accident, you leave the door open a fraction, so Boxler overhears. When he has left, telephone me straight away.'

'OK, I've got that. It makes little sense, but I understand what you're asking.'

'Splendid.' Hall blinked for several seconds. 'It will make more sense when I explain. The Germans will want to talk to Constantine when they find out you're taking an interest in him rather than his father. They are desperate to know if he delivered a secret codebook from Russia to us. I wish to exploit the position, without Constantine or his father coming to harm.'

'How will you manage that?'

'You mean, how will *we* manage that?' Hall replied.

Hall chuckled at Woodhall's incredulous stare; the situation would be comical if it weren't so serious. 'We are scheduled to meet Constantine at the embassy in half an hour from now. I have a taxi waiting, and I'll tell you on the way.'

As they left the room, Hall locked the door behind him. Outside on Horse Guards Road, they climbed into the taxi.

Hall continued his instructions. 'You explain you are assigning a man from Special Branch to watch Constantine. The Boche will try to find out from him what I was doing at the embassy. I intend to brief him with an alternative story, that we are working on a plot to have Prince Heinrich, the Kaiser's brother, killed.'

Woodhall's eyebrows had reached a peak. 'Blimey. I only came about Boxler.'

'I need you there, Ed, to convince Constantine how important it is to pass along the false report. Once Boxler tells Otto, I expect Otto will attempt to befriend Constantine. Perhaps in a bar or a pub, at the theatre or in one of his clubs. He'll probably try to get him drunk, then ask him lots of questions. Then he'll drop my name into the conversation, pretending he knows me. Ply him with more drink and get him talking. I want Constantine to go along with the charade before you give him the fake story.'

'So we don't nab Otto then?'

'No. I know he's your biggest fish Ed, but we have to let him contact Germany and deliver the report.'

'Is it because you want them to believe we are plotting to murder the Prince, or to divert attention away from the codebook?'

Hall regarded Woodhall with a sly smile. 'It's both, Ed. Let's put the cat amongst the pigeons.'

CHAPTER 9

Captain Luce stood on the bridge, the words of Rear-Admiral Cradock echoing in his thoughts. *'Go and do your best. As we all must do.'*

Months ago when they were coaling in Port Stanley in the Falklands, Kit Cradock had paid Luce a courtesy visit. He reminded Luce of a stern yet fond father figure; stern because he would rebuke anyone he felt deserved it, fatherly because of his paternal affection of his fellow officers. When Luce suggested they had dinner in his cabin, Cradock preferred the officer's wardroom so they could all enjoy each other's company.

Over dinner, Luce discovered a decisiveness about the man he found attractive. Not only was he a fine leader but also one of the most highly decorated officers in the navy. Whatever decisions he made, he would follow them as well as he could.

While he brooded, a rating handed him a message.

> Strong wireless signals from Leipzig.
> Not far north of our position.

For the last few weeks, they had only heard wireless messages from the *Leipzig*. He believed she was operating alone, perhaps as a scout for von Spee. If they could catch her isolated from her squadron, they stood a decent chance of eliminating one of von Spee's Bremen-class cruisers.

When the next communication arrived, he checked his fob watch, which registered 1:50 pm.

> Form line abreast, 15 miles separation.
> Glasgow nearest coast, then Monmouth,
> Otranto and Good Hope. Head north at
> 10 knots. Report earliest sighting of
> Leipzig. Cradock.

The hunt was on.

Constantine found his seat in the stalls before the lights dimmed. Underneath the stage a small orchestra began the overture for "A Country Girl", and he settled back to watch. Seconds later, and before the curtains opened, a young woman sidled past to sit in the empty seat on his right. He snatched a glance, more out of curiosity than irritation, to see who had been so discourteous as to arrive so late. She looked to be in her early thirties with long curly brown hair, clasping a wide-brimmed straw hat on her lap. At that moment, the curtains opened.

He must have seemed more irritated than he imagined because she leant in close to whisper an apology.

'That's quite alright,' he murmured, and both sat back to enjoy the show. During the song "When the birds begin to sing, out we go a-harvestin" he glimpsed her reaction. Bathed in the glow from the stage lights, she was smiling and tapping her foot in tempo. She had smooth skin and curls which bobbed on her shoulders with the music, but his gaze lasted a fraction too long, and her eyes met his. He directed his attention towards the stage, hoping the darkened hall would hide his embarrassment.

'You enjoy musical plays?' She kept her voice low.

'Ah, yes.' To remain focussed on the performance, he felt, would be rude, so he faced her steady gaze. When he recalled the events of the evening, that was the point he knew he was in love.

In Russia, it was always his intention he would meet someone, fall in love and marry. But he had not counted on the rigours of life in the Imperial Russian Navy where duty came before romantic entanglements and career came before passion. When he had command of a ship, there would be many opportunities to meet someone who knew the form. The daughter of an Admiral would be preferred, but an aristocrat or land owner's daughter would be equally satisfactory. He had visited London before, but this was the first occasion he had ever encountered such a beautiful specimen of womanhood.

His reply lacked the detail and accuracy he wanted to convey. She was so lovely he felt the need to start again. Yet her beauty caught his tongue. His reply sounded overly formal and stilted to his ears. 'This is my first visit to a London theatre. We have nothing quite like this in St Petersburg. I am enjoying the production very much.'

The lady smiled. 'I'm so glad.' She held out her hand. 'Evie Brown.'

He held her fingers in his hand. 'Count Constantine Benckendorff, at your service.'

A voice from behind shushed him to silence. He leaned back, trying to suppress a grin. There were twelve songs altogether in the first half, and whenever he looked at Evie, she would acknowledge his glance with a brief smile.

At the end of the first act, he shuffled to the centre aisle, expecting she would follow, but she had gone the other way. In the press of people making for the bar, he lost sight of her. He searched the entrance hall where a few people lingered around an ornate American logwood stove. In case she had left, he opened the outer doors and looked both ways along Cranbourn Street. When he couldn't see her, he re-entered the theatre and walked up to the first-floor foyer.

Many of the theatre-goers were standing around a polished wooden handrail which overlooked the marble stairs. Dry potted palms stood at either end of a chaise lounge. A few lucky individuals were seated by the far wall, but most were standing and conversing. Constantine shouldered his way through the crowd, overhearing odd snatches of conversation: 'I told the maid to...', 'Pride of Scotland in the four-thirty...', 'Devil of a job getting the right...'.

As he pushed past a couple, he saw her across the room. One of her gloved hands rested on the railing while the other held a cigarette holder. He moved to get a clearer picture of her only to discover she was conversing with a man in his early forties. The man sported a luxurious moustache and wore a brown suit and flat cap. His eyes were half-closed in an expression of mild amusement.

Constantine hesitated. Was this an old friend she met by chance or was he a suitor? Perhaps they were married? He recalled Evie wore no rings, and if they were married, surely they would have sat together during the performance. A bell signalled five minutes before the start of the second act. Whatever their relationship, he didn't want to intrude as they were about to retake their seats. He found his way to the stalls and a few minutes later stood to let her into her place.

The second half contained ten songs, but Constantine's attention was no longer on the play. He speculated about the man he had seen, and the relationship with the girl by his side. Towards the end of the show, he admitted to himself there was more than a sliver of jealousy in his interest. He became so self-absorbed he missed her remark and apologised.

'I was saying how stern you appear to be. This is supposed to be a happy ending!'

'I'm sorry, Evie. May I call you Evie?'

'Of course. Perhaps your mind was on something else?'

Applause drowned their whispered conversation, amid calls from the audience for an encore.

When the play finished, Evie and Constantine rose to their feet. This time he would keep an eye on her, and he leant closer.

'Actually, I was wondering if you were doing anything after the show? Perhaps you would like to go for a drink, or I could walk you home?'

She grinned. 'Well it's very kind, I'm sure. But I have to work tomorrow, and I need an early night.' She half-turned in the gangway, and her smile grew. 'And as for walking me home, I don't think you would be so generous if you knew where I lived!'

An elderly couple were struggling to leave their row of seats, and Constantine moved to the side to let them out. On the steps down to the entrance, the crush intensified, and somehow the distance between him and Evie increased. When he reached the exit, she had disappeared, and he clasped his head in frustration. He could see several taxis moving off into the street, but he couldn't make out if she was in one of them.

He spotted a doorman helping the elderly couple into a taxi.

'Excuse me, did you just call a taxi for a young lady? Long dark curly hair. Very attractive. She was wearing a hat with lace and had a kind of shawl wrapped in a knot about her shoulders?'

The doorman hesitated.

Constantine fumbled in a pocket and withdrew a five-pound note. 'I need to know where she went. She dropped a handkerchief.'

The doorman had the sense not to roll his eyes. 'Oxford Gate, Brook Green. I don't remember the number.'

The note disappeared.

The first hint of the enemy's presence arrived as the sun arced over the western sky. A lookout shouted 'Smoke on the starboard bow!' and Captain Luce lifted his binoculars, searching towards the coast. On his second sweep, a black smudge appeared in the glasses.

The lookout called, 'Three funnels. Light cruiser!'

The Captain breathed a lungful of air; could they have found the *Leipzig* alone? 'Turn towards her,' he commanded. 'Full speed. And signal the

Good Hope.'

They closed within 24,000 yards. The ship's outline became clear - there could be no doubt she was the *Leipzig*. Seconds later, his hopes were crushed. The lookout called again, 'Two more ships. Four funnels!'

Luce spotted smoke belching from von Spee's most powerful battleships. He didn't need the lookout's advice: these were the armoured cruisers *Scharnhorst* and *Gneisenau*, running south at 20 knots. His stomach contracted in a ball, yet he kept a straight face and an even voice. 'Signal the *Good Hope*.'

Cradock ordered the rest of the squadron to close in on the *Glasgow*. As Cradock's ships gathered, Luce estimated von Spee was about twelve miles away. His warships were closer to the coast and both his armoured cruisers were making 20 knots towards them.

Cradock's squadron turned, coming beam on to the steep waves. Luce was not concerned about his own ship the *Glasgow*, but when he focussed the binoculars on the *Otranto*, he became alarmed. The combined force of the wind and waves drove against the sheer sides of the converted liner, and he estimated she was rolling over the vertical by up to 30 degrees. Not that the *Otranto* would play any part in the battle, he mused. Her slow progress, light armour and immense size marked her out as a liability.

The notion crossed his mind; this was not her

fight - Cradock should let her go. But he may have calculated she would be protected by the remaining ships in the line. He swivelled the glasses onto von Spee's flagship, the *Scharnhorst*. *We will have enough to do, without having to protect Otranto,* he thought.

It was tempting to swing the glasses south to look for *Canopus*. She might be old and slow, but her 12-inch guns would give von Spee something to think about. Instead, he placed the binoculars on the chart table and checked the map. *Canopus* was over 250 miles south, steaming north at 12 knots. The Captain made a rough calculation; she would take over 18 hours to arrive.

Reluctantly he let go of the idea of *Canopus* coming to the rescue. The next suggestion crept upon him like a fog at sea, a treacherous, traitorous scheme that crawled from the dark and spilt over the deck. Faced with an overwhelming force, Cradock could leave the encounter and return another day. But if he allowed the raiders to escape, they would round the Magellan Straights and reach the Falklands before Stoddart's fleet could form up. They would shell Port Stanley and plunder her coal stocks and disrupt British commercial shipping. They could then flee across the Atlantic to their home ports.

He squinted through the glass windows of his bridge; the Pacific Ocean presented a vast area to hide a whole armada. Their escape would also come at the expense of losing Otranto. Von Spee would catch her easily, and she was in no shape to fight. Confirmation came in the following message from Cradock:

> I cannot go down and engage the enemy at
> present, leaving Otranto.

He checked his watch; it was 5:05 pm and almost dusk. At last, he understood Cradock's tactic. The bright sun, low above the sea, would dazzle the German gunnery crews and prevent them from focusing on their target. But the manoeuvre was a double-edged sword. Once the sun sank below the horizon, for a short period Cradock's squadron would be highlighted by the last rays of the dying sun. Not only would their silhouettes stand out to the German gunners, but von Spee's ships would blend in with the dark contours of the coast and become invisible. Cradock must have realised that time was running out, because five minutes later his decision arrived in the form of a flag hoisted on the forward halyard of the *Good Hope*.

> Engage the enemy.

Captain Luce and the rest of the squadron struck a course to narrow the gap with their adversary. The first problem became apparent soon after the turn. He observed the enemy's ships moving away, closer to the coast. Von Spee had seen through their ploy, and he had the speed to keep out of harm's way. Even if they could draw nearer, they would be broadside onto the waves, and any advantage in the accuracy of their guns would be lost.

For the next fifty minutes, the two squadrons maintained a steady distance 12,000 yards apart. Captain Luce inspected the opposing forces. He picked out the *Scharnhorst's* dull grey sides against the dark background of the coastline. Her oddly shaped bulbous prow shouldered the seas aside, while each of her four funnels threw out thick oily smoke. These were bracketed fore and aft by tall wireless antennae, giving the whole a pleasing symmetry. Pleasing to some, maybe, he considered, but deadly nevertheless. It was not her eight 8.3-inch guns and six 5.9-inch guns that worried him, as much as her crack gunnery teams. Von Spee's squadron had been commissioned two years earlier. His gun crews had plenty of practice and were highly trained.

In the lead, the *Leipzig* ploughed on. There was little to fear from her; the light cruiser had no big guns, only a pair of 105mm cannons and a few torpedoes. The *Gneisenau* was *Scharnhorst's* sister ship, a year older but equipped with almost identical armour and armament. She followed the *Scharnhorst*, and behind her came the *Dresden* and *Nürnberg*. The *Nürnberg* was a light cruiser with ten 4.1-inch guns, similar to the *Dresden*. In the days before the war, she had accompanied Royal Navy warships on protection duties during the revolution in Mexico. Now, they faced each other like duellers destined to fight to the death.

Small armaments aside, only the range and accuracy of the gun crews on both cruisers caused unease. As a general rule the larger the guns, the greater the range. But *Scharnhorst* and *Gneisenau's* eight-inch guns had a similar range as Cradock's ten-inchers, simply because they were much newer. He left the bridge to stand by the forward lookout. They were running in line formation with *Good Hope* first, followed by *Monmouth*, *Glasgow* and *Otranto*. *Last and least*, he reflected, then pondered what Cradock's next move would be.

He didn't have long to wait; the next signal arrived at 6:18 pm.

> Follow in the Admiral's wake am going to attack the enemy now.

Apprehension gathered like a rain cloud. Cradock had already tried that ploy once, and von Spee had declined to engage. What would a repeat of the manoeuvre gain? Then, a glimmer of Cradock's plan emerged. By forcing von Spee ever closer to the shore, there was a risk one or more of his ships would run aground on a rocky outcrop or sand bar. Von Spee didn't have enough speed for his entire squadron to break free of Cradock's stranglehold without engaging, so he would have to split his force.

Captain's Luce's face relaxed. Cradock intended to divide and conquer. The man was a genius!

There was only one problem, and he frowned at the unwelcome idea: the conditions would last only until the sun went down.

The Captain rechecked his fob-watch; Cradock had 40 minutes to implement his strategy.

CHAPTER 10

Captain Luce observed von Spee's ships moving nearer the coast. Both squadrons were steaming south, but the gap between them had widened to 18,000 yards. At over 10 miles distance, they appeared no longer than the width of a fingernail. As the sun edged the horizon, Luce observed the time: 6:50 pm. The opportunity to land a fatal punch on the enemy had slipped away; they had lost the advantage of the light. Von Spee's squadron faded against the dark coastline, and the sun sank below the horizon, throwing Cradock's four ships into sharp silhouette against the sky.

Luce picked up his glasses and scanned the line to the shore. A grey smudge that might be the *Scharnhorst* emerged. She appeared to be drawing closer though the distance was well outside the range of his 6-inch guns. Only *Good Hope*'s two 9.2-inch weapons could bridge the gulf, but Luce comprehended the difficulties Cradock faced; nine-tenths of his crew were reservists and untrained. During their brief meeting off Coronel, Cradock confirmed he had only time for one practice shoot before leaving Portsmouth. To attempt a hit at this distance would be a waste of ammunition.

Even with his own trained and accomplished sailors, Luce knew to inflict real damage on the German squadron would need a miracle. Experience told him if he could get close enough to von Spee, only three in a hundred shells would hit the mark. When fired, each round took over 30 seconds to reach the target, and the warship would have moved by four hundred yards or more. And in these heavy seas spray constantly obscured the gun sights. Hitting a ship over five miles away while on a platform moving through a vertical height of eight feet would appear impossible to a land-lubber.

And any that landed may not cause any damage. Some shells failed to explode, others would smash against heavily armoured sections, while others struck non-vital parts of the enemy's ship. But, reflected Luce, his adversary was under a similar set of constraints. Two things would decide the outcome of the encounter and von Spee had the upper hand in both. His experienced gunnery crews had won prizes before the war, and though his largest guns were only 8.3-inches, their range was at least as great as Cradock's two 9-inch guns.

Luce's face creased into a mask of thoughtfulness. With the loss of daylight, Cradock's strategy had weakened. Despite the odds against them, it was still possible for him to damage von Spee's squadron. Perhaps he hoped von Spee would use up most of his ammunition during the fight, leaving him defenceless when attempting to make for his home port. Maybe he was hoping to buy enough time for *Canopus* to reach them and weigh in with her 12-inch guns. But one thing was sure: Cradock could not hope to win.

Luce switched his attention to the German squadron which had now closed to within 12,000 yards. At 7:04 pm, the first flashes of light sparked from the *Scharnhorst*. From his position third-in-line, Luce marked the spot where the opening salvo splashed, 500 yards short of *Good Hope's* port bow. A second round created a fountain 500 yards to her starboard, and Luce gritted his teeth, waiting for the third shot. Though he was expecting it, the explosion on the *Good Hope's* foredeck was shocking in its power. The detonation blew the turret off her mountings, and the boom reached Luce as a curtain of flame ran along her deck. The precision of *Scharnhorst's* 9.2-inch guns was staggering.

Now the other ships in von Spee's squadron opened up, concentrating their aim on the target opposite: *Scharnhorst* on *Good Hope*, *Gneisenau* on *Monmouth*, *Leipzig* on *Glasgow* and *Dresden* on *Otranto*. Not only was the rate of fire so much higher than their own, but the efficiency of the German gunners was also incredible. Luce spotted hundreds of pockets of white water around his ship caused by exploding ordnance. Within minutes *Monmouth* was struck, and fires started on her upper deck.

So far *Glasgow* had received no hits. Like the *Good Hope*, she encountered the same difficulties with her 6-inch guns only eight feet above the waterline. The gun crews could not see the *Leipzig as* tall waves obscured their gun-sights, and spotters on the upper decks had difficulty seeing the splashes to pinpoint their shots. Short of a direct hit, spotting where a shell landed in the sea was the most critical guide for the gun layers, the seamen whose job it was to alter the elevation and direction of their guns. On the highest deck, they searched for the splash a gun's shell made, then shouted detailed instructions on how to improve the shot. In the growing darkness, the enemy was fading, and it became increasingly difficult to tell where their shots landed.

Onboard the *Glasgow*, the gun crews directed their attention to the *Dresden*. But so far, Luce observed neither the *Dresden* nor *Leipzig* had yet taken a direct strike. Both were returning fire with their 4.1-inch guns, but their flight fell short. As the distance between them narrowed, it wouldn't be long before they came within range.

The *Good Hope* swung towards von Spee. The German ships were beyond the reach of all but her remaining rear-mounted 9-inch gun. If Luce were in his Admiral's shoes, he would turn to starboard, dowse the flames and use the darkness for cover. The *Good Hope* steamed at reduced speed towards the enemy, and Luce couldn't tear his eyes away. Her forward deck continued to blaze, and he guessed Cradock wanted to close the distance to enable her 6-inch guns to come into play. But the barrage from the *Scharnhorst* was inexorable. As the *Good Hope* drew close, more blasts battered her superstructure. Her masthead glowed incandescent in the dark, reminding Luce of a fiery cross, held bravely before the gates of hell.

Now it was *Otranto's* turn to come under fire. Luce realised why the Germans were targeting the lightly armed liner. Her bulk presented a large target, and once the Germans had found her range, they would use the elevation to zero in on the remaining ships. After taking several hits, she moved out of line and headed west.

And still, the *Good Hope* sailed ever closer to the enemy. At 6,600 yards the *Scharnhorst* and *Gneisenau* lowered their gun sights, and more shells found their mark. At 5,500 yards, the *Good Hope* shuddered under the onslaught of broadsides from both ships. Flame immersed her upper works, and she came to a juddering halt.

Captain Luce peered through the bridge windows of the *Glasgow*. A strike on the *Good Hope* blew a sheet of flame above her foredeck, closely followed by another detonation from her after decks. A column of fire hurtled upwards, ejecting a shower of sparks and debris like a volcano. A round must have hit one of her magazines, and Luce realised this was a turning point. He heard a double-boom over the sound of exploding ordnance, the shouts and screams of men. The keel broke in two, and the whole of the forward section heeled gracefully into the sea. Mercifully, her fires were extinguished as she sank and Luce could no longer see her slip to her final resting place.

It was 7:50 pm, less than an hour since the battle had begun. The instant Admiral Cradock and his crew of nine-hundred men died was the time Captain Luce became the senior naval officer of the remainder of the squadron.

On *Monmouth*, the fires from an earlier blast continued to smoulder. Now that *Good Hope* no longer posed a threat, *Scharnhorst* and then *Gneisenau* trained their guns on the second capital ship. A shell from the *Scharnhorst* found her forward mount, blasting the turret overboard, and *Monmouth's* rate of fire faltered.

Shortly afterwards, Luce caught a second explosion as flames reached her ammunition stores. *Monmouth's* forecastle crumpled with the force of the detonation, completely devastating her upper structure. More shells from *Gneisenau* landed and the light cruiser listed to port. She lost speed and veered to starboard, away from the action.

Still, the German guns spoke. Small flashes in the darkness were followed half a minute later by the whistle of a shell. There was no point in gritting your teeth in the silences, hoping they wouldn't find your ship. Luce soon realised every time the *Glasgow* fired, the German guns would target his ship.

At eight o'clock, the moon rose to give an intermittent view of their opponent. A lookout spotted one of *Glasgow's* shells bursting on the *Gneisenau*, putting her forward 6-inch gun temporally out of action. Captain Luce scowled; it was a lucky shot. What surprised him most was *Glasgow* had survived unscathed for so long.

With both his capital ships incapacitated, it was essential to disengage. The *Glasgow* was hit five times, lightly wounding four seamen. Only one of the five shells had caused real damage when one watertight compartment became flooded. She could still make a top speed of 24 knots, and Luce gave the order to search for the *Monmouth* and see what help she required.

They found her twenty minutes later in the west. Her fires were out, and she was listing heavily. After a brief exchange of messages, Luce realised the seas were too rough to attempt to rescue the crew. The moon had risen, and the lookout spied von Spee's squadron on the far horizon, searching for them in line abreast. Soon they would be discovered and attacked. Sadness descended as silently as nightfall.

'Turn northwest,' he ordered. 'Full speed.'

On their way, they came close to the *Monmouth*. He heard cheers from the crew of the wounded vessel. Fifty minutes later, they turned south, and the lookout stepped into the bridge.

'Captain, I think you should see this.'

Luce accompanied the young man to his lookout station and followed the pointing finger. The moon was hidden, yet towards the north, a silvery flicker reflected against low clouds. He visualised the searchlights focusing on *Monmouth* as the rumble of distant guns increased.

Then there was silence.

Constantine's stomach rumbled. On the right, the shopfront displayed trays of scones, iced fingers and chocolate-covered sponge cake. On the left, a range of teas, creams, honey and jams were laid out. Above was the sign J. Lyons & Co Ltd.

He hesitated in the doorway. If he entered the tea shop, she would realise he had followed her. A couple pushed past, and he decided no matter how hard he pretended the meeting was accidental, she would know immediately he had engineered the encounter.

With a sharp intake of breath, he grasped the handle and strode purposely through the front door. To the right was a counter with more mouth-watering cakes, bread and muffins. The smell of freshly baked dough drew him further inside where he was met by a waitress. Her black uniform was offset by a white apron and cream headdress, a lacy equivalent of a tiara.

His eyes swept around the spacious dining room; there were many more tables than he expected though most were empty. There was still no sign of Evie, and he wondered where she was. He asked to be seated by the wall to keep an eye on the counter and ordered a large pot of breakfast tea and a scone.

He shivered. From six o'clock this morning he had been watching Oxford Gate, the street Evie Brown had been dropped off the previous evening. He had found a bench in a stretch of grass in Brook Green. After twenty minutes he regretted he hadn't brought a warmer coat. When she appeared, it was nearly eight o'clock, and his body felt like he had endured a month in Siberia.

The waitress arrived and placed the teapot and a scone on the table. 'May I take your coat, sir?'

'No thank you,' he muttered through chattering teeth.

'Perhaps sir would like a blanket?'

He looked up, expecting a sly grin, but her face expressed only concern.

'We do keep a supply for our elderly customers, but you are quite welcome.'

'No, no, thank you. The tea will warm me, I'm

sure.'

In fact, the tea was delicious, and he felt better by the second cup. He spread butter and jam over a portion of the scone and bit into the crumbly texture. As he savoured the taste, he looked up and saw Evie standing across from him. Unlike the other waitresses, she was wearing a floral dress.

He almost choked and used the napkin to wipe away the crumbs from his lips. 'Oh, I'm sorry. I didn't know you were there.'

She seemed amused yet distant. 'You must have known I worked here - it's too much of a coincidence otherwise.'

Constantine stood and covered his mouth with the napkin while trying to swallow. 'That's not quite what I meant,' he mumbled. 'Would you mind joining me for a minute while I explain?' He gestured to a chair.

She looked around the almost empty room, then sat opposite him. 'I see you like our English scones. Don't you have anything similar in Russia?'

'Ah, no. This is the first time I have been to an English tea house.'

'Lyons Corner House,' Evie corrected. 'Or you could say tea room. Tea house sounds Japanese.'

'Sorry.' Constantine glimpsed her wry smile. 'I still have a lot to learn.'

Her eyes sparkled. 'It's perfectly acceptable. Now, perhaps you can tell me how you found me here.'

'It's quite simple. I followed you.'

'Followed me?' The sparkle disappeared. 'Whatever for?'

'There's a revival of Miss Hook of Holland at the Prince of Wales Theatre starting on Wednesday. I thought you would like to see it.' He studied Evie. 'That is if you haven't seen it before?'

'No, I haven't. But going to the theatre twice in two weeks is a little expensive, wouldn't you say?'

'No, I wouldn't say because it will be my privilege to take you.'

As Evie considered the idea, he leaned towards her. 'I can pick you up next Monday at six-thirty. The doorman told me you lived in Oxford Gate, but couldn't recall the house number.'

Evie's cheeks dimpled. 'It's 37.' Her face assumed a stern air. 'Very well. But next time I think you should wear something warmer.' She leant across the table to straighten his coat lapels. 'I don't want you to catch your death.'

Churchill was in a bad mood. Hall could tell immediately he heard him bark 'Come in!'

When he entered the room, Churchill was pacing behind his desk using a black walking stick. As he strode towards one wall, he talked. 'Not less than a week ago, I asked you to give me all and any updates from Belgium concerning their possible use as staging posts. I made it clear Germany could use those ports to launch an invasion on England.'

'Yes, you did, Mr Churchill. You specifically asked I should pass all agents' reports emanating from Belgium to you, quote: "as and when I receive them".'

'So you are responsible for this.' Churchill tapped a piece of paper on his desk.

Hall picked it up.

```
2 Nov 1914.  Many submarines under con
struction in Germany, location unknown.
Intended to deploy approx 200 along Zee
brugge coast.  H.673
```

'Yes. I passed this to the Chief of Staff yesterday, straight after I received it.'

'Did you not question the veracity of the report at all?' Churchill regarded Hall over his glasses.

'Of course, privately, I did. However, you asked me to bring you all the reports immediately, and I complied with your order.'

'Did you consider how many personnel would be required to operate this fleet of submarines? How many officers would need to be trained to command an armada this size? What resources would be required to transport these vessels to the coast?' As he spoke, Churchill's voice rose in pitch. 'Before the war, the total number of submarines in the German inventory was only twenty-seven. How were they able to ramp up the production to over two hundred in a little over three months?'

'Sir, this agent doesn't mean submarines. Invariably he refers to anything manufactured for under the sea as a submarine.'

'So what the bloody hell does he mean?'

'It should be obvious, Mr Churchill. He means mines.'

'Well, it's not bloody obvious to me!' Churchill cracked his walking stick across the table. 'You should inform me of the meaning of these bloody reports.'

'At the risk of disobeying your specific orders?'

Hall's rapid blinking caused Churchill to halt his tirade. In a softer tone, he said, 'I expect you to use your intelligence when you present accounts from unreliable agents. A brief note would have been acceptable.'

'I have been giving that issue some consideration, Mr Churchill.'

'Wonderful. And what about the decodes of our German friends?' He handed Hall another slip of paper. 'Since when do ships *run*?' He pointed to a recent message. 'And when do ships return to port *athwartwise*? Such lack of basic naval knowledge and procedure is driving their lordships mad. How can we rely on information like this?'

'You must appreciate the staff who decipher intercepts are mainly academic scholars. They probably know more than anyone else in the world about their particular subject. But next to nothing about the German navy, or any other navy come to that.'

'Then perhaps they should,' Churchill retorted.

'No, Mr Churchill, I disagree.'

Churchill's glasses nearly slid off his nose. 'Reggie, here's a report on the recent movements of the German cruiser *Ariadne*. How is it possible when she sank two months ago? You should have known she capsized after the battle of Heligoland Bight.'

'That brings me round to the same problem.' Hall reckoned that now Churchill's temper had subsided to the point where he had started to call him by his first name, he could do the same. 'No-one in my department is allowed to see the transcripts. The volume of messages arriving means I'm unable to vet and analyse every one that passes across my desk. It's not possible.'

'You're going to tell me you need more staff.'

'I have always wanted an experienced naval officer - someone who has actually been to sea, to read the transcripts, analyse the contents and report in a language their lordships will understand.' Hall paused. 'I have also been giving the whole matter my consideration: how the intelligence is sifted, scrutinised and evaluated. We need a system to attach a level of trustworthiness to the information we receive before it ever reaches the decision-makers.'

'It sounds as if you have someone in mind.'

'Yes,' replied Hall. 'There is a Commander Hope already in the intelligence division. At present, he compiles German ship movements in the chart room. I think he'd make an excellent chief of staff for the code breakers.'

'I dislike widening the circle of people who know our little secret.' Churchill's stern voice didn't match the twinkle in his eye.

'There are only nine people I am aware of in the inner circle,' responded Hall. 'Unless you have previously informed the Prime Minister and members of the War Council?'

'The less said about that, the better,' said Churchill. 'Let's make it ten people for now, and I will review the arrangements around the flow of information.' He regarded Hall over the rim of his spectacles again. 'With a view to tightening up security.'

CHAPTER 11

The note was hand-written in black ink and headed *Exclusively Secret*.

"An officer of the War Staff, preferably from the Intelligence Division should be selected to study all the decoded intercepts, not only current but past, and to compare them continually with what actually took place in order to penetrate the German mind and movements and make reports. All these intercepts are to be written in a locked book with their decodes, and all other copies are to be collected and burnt. All new messages are to be entered in the book, and the book is only to be handled under direction from Chief of Staff. The officer selected is for the present to do no other work. I shall be obliged if Sir Alfred Ewing will associate himself continuously with this work."

Captain Hall scanned the bottom of the page. Churchill had initialled the order in red ink, and the First Sea Lord Admiral Fisher signed in green.

He let out a sigh of relief. On an initial reading, Churchill was confirming his request for an experienced naval officer to screen the messages from the code-breakers in Room 40. But on the second examination, he became dissatisfied about how the information they obtained would be employed. Churchill was enforcing so much secrecy Hall wouldn't be able to share the decrypts with his staff. And since Commander Hope would report to Hall, he would likely inherit the same restrictions and be prevented in communicating with the code-breakers.

He tucked the secret charter into an inside pocket. As he was about to get up, Oliver entered his office without knocking.

'Morning, Admiral. I was coming to see you. I wanted to discuss Churchill's approval for a liaison person for Room 40.'

The Admiral seemed not to hear Hall's words. His eyes had drifted to the tiny window from where low grey clouds sped across an overcast sky.

'Admiral?'

Oliver's attention switched to Hall. 'It seems your intuition about Cradock's predicament was correct.' He unfolded a yellow telegram form and passed it over the desk.

Hall scanned the text. It was a short cablegram

from the *Canopus*.

> At 8.45 p.m. received first intimation
> that squadron had been engaged from
> GLASGOW.

His eyes leapt to the next line where they read
and then re-read the sentence.

> Fear GOOD HOPE lost, our squadron
> scattered.

The cable had arrived from the Falklands earlier that morning, the 4th November. He presumed the *Canopus* had sent the message ahead of her rendezvous at Port Stanley.

Both men were silent as they contemplated the news.

'Do we have any other information to confirm the situation?' Hall asked.

'The German papers are full of the battle and the success they achieved in the South Pacific,' said Oliver. 'I didn't believe any of it at first. Then this came.' He indicated a telegram.

'What are they saying?'

'Von Spee and his squadron are coaling in Valparaiso. There're celebrations on the streets. The city is giving them a hero's welcome, and a special dinner is being laid on in honour of the victory.'

Again there was a long pause. Hall spoke at last, 'So no official notification yet of the extent of the casualties?'

'No, none. Admiral Fisher has ordered *Defence* to join the squadron, but I fear it is far too late for that.' Oliver cleared his throat. 'I ought to apologise Captain.'

Hall's surprise was apparent in his voice. 'Whatever for?'

'For not taking you seriously enough. For not insisting on issuing a clarification. For not sending *Defence* earlier. We made a lot of mistakes.'

'Sometimes sir, it can be a good thing, provided we learn lessons. What do you think Fisher will do?'

'I expect he will want to send a squadron down there to make sure von Spee isn't allowed to do any more damage.'

'That might weaken our Grand Fleet when we have the rest of the German fleet boxed in their home ports.'

'That might. But if we are to restore confidence in our Navy, then we must do it.'

Hall nodded. 'I agree.'

Count Constantine Benckendorff held the taxi door open.

Evie Brown accepted the outstretched hand and stepped onto the pavement. 'Thank you.'

For a second there was an awkward pause, then he bowed. 'Shall I send the driver away?'

'Oh.' Evie's eyebrows arched. 'Of course, you must come inside for a drink.'

They continued to hold hands while mounting three steps to the front door. As she inserted the key, she said, 'My mother, Elise, is away this week.'

They exchanged surprised glances, and Evie laughed. 'Sorry, I didn't mean it the way it sounded. What I meant was, she is visiting her sister in the country. She has an insatiable curiosity, so her nosy questions won't bother us.' She opened the door, and they entered the hallway.

'For a second, I'd hoped you meant it the way it sounded.' A cheeky grin accompanied Constantine's words. 'But I would settle for a drink if that's all there is.'

'Very well,' she said, entering the drawing-room and crossing to an Edwardian cabinet. 'I imagine a fine young gentleman from Russia would want something stronger than tea.' She lowered the top section and pointed to an arrangement of bottles, glasses and decanters. 'We have wine, sherry, ale and whisky. I might even have vodka if I can find the bottle.'

'Perhaps I can help,' he said, moving closer. 'I have an excellent nose for vodka.'

'I thought vodka didn't smell?'

Constantine murmured in her ear. 'Any young gentleman from Russia can distinguish a quality spirit.'

Their lips touched. He smelt her perfume, the scent of wildflowers. He kissed her and their arms wrapped around each other. For a minute, he held her until she broke away.

'I don't know what came over me. Count, I think you'd better sit over there where I can keep an eye on you.' A smile removed the edge from her words. She busied herself with pouring the drinks. 'Vodka, for the fine Russian gentleman,' she said, handing him a large measure. 'And a small sherry for the lady.'

She sat in an armchair across from him. 'I'm dying to learn about you and your life in Russia. Tell me what you do and how you arrived here.'

He observed Evie. She was wearing a long skirt for the evening, but the hem rose to reveal a slender ankle and a shapely calf as she crossed her legs.

He cleared his throat, 'I'm a commander in our Imperial Navy. My father is the Russian Ambassador to Britain, and I sometimes courier documents to him.'

'My word, what an exciting life! How often do you see him?'

'Not as often as I would like. I was here earlier this year during the winter, but could only stay for a couple of nights. Sometimes I'm allowed to stay longer. On this occasion, I'm here for a fortnight.'

'So are you enjoying the sights of London?'

'The sights, yes. And the people. I find Londoners quite friendly when you get to learn their little ways.'

Evie chuckled. 'And in what little ways do you

find us so amusing?'

'Everyone is so polite. You are taught to say "please" and "thank you".' He inclined his head. 'Now it's my turn. I want to know so much about you.'

She opened her palms, 'Ask away.'

'I know your name and where you live. I know you live with your mother, but where is your father?'

Evie's smile faded, and her eyes fell.

'What is the matter? Have I said something wrong?'

'No. I normally tell people he is dead.'

'What? He's not dead?'

'He's not dead, no. I tell people that because it's easier.' She straightened and returned his gaze. 'My parents are separated.'

'Oh.' He paused. 'It happens a lot these days. Married people fall out of love. Maybe the man takes a mistress, and his wife finds out. There are lots of reasons marriages break up.'

But she was shaking her head. 'No, it's worse than that.' Her shoulders slumped. 'He was, and still is, German.'

Constantine pondered her remarks. 'I see how that could be a problem if he were here.'

She stood to refill their glasses and sat next to him. In a quieter tone, she said, 'Mostly he was at sea. I haven't seen him for years, ever since they parted company.'

'I'm sorry.'

'Don't be.' She waved her arm. 'We never got on well, and mother doesn't miss him at all.'

'How come you and your mother are living in London?'

'She is British. They met in Germany and got married there. Our family name is Braun. When they separated, Elise brought me to London. She had no wish to return home, so she changed our name to Brown. You see, I was born in Germany, but because my mother is British everyone assumes I am British too, including my employer.'

Her eyes flicked to one side. 'I was always afraid the police would find out. Especially now, when they are rounding up Germans every day and sending them to the detention camps. Elise would die, and I couldn't bear to be in prison.'

He put his arm around her shoulder and gave her a gentle hug. 'They will never find out from me.'

She responded with a nervous smile. 'Thank you. I knew you were a gentleman.'

He glanced towards the door. 'Is there anyone else living here?'

'No, only me and my mother.'

'But you have friends who could help you if you were in trouble?' His voice held his concern.

'There is an aunt who has a cottage in the Cotswolds. It's where mother is now.'

He sipped vodka while pondering Evie's problem. 'Since you arrived in England, did you or Elise tell the authorities about your father?'

She pursed her lips. 'No, I don't think so. She changed our family name partly because she saw what was happening between England and Germany. But also to make it difficult for my father if he ever came looking for us.'

'Does your mother have a British passport?'

'Yes, she never gave it up when she moved to Germany.'

'Then I don't see why you or your mother would experience any trouble from the authorities.' He thought for a moment. 'Has your father ever come looking for you or your mother?'

She shook her head, 'I don't think so. If he did, he never found us.'

'You said he was at sea. Perhaps he might not be able to make the journey to England.'

She shrugged. 'He was the first officer on the *Augsburg*. As far as I know, he still is.'

He lifted his glass, intending to finish his drink. His hand stopped half-way to his lips. 'Wait, you said the *Augsburg*.'

'Yes? Is there something wrong?'

'The SMS *Augsburg* was a sister ship to the *Magdeburg*.'

'What does that mean?'

'It must be a coincidence, that's all.' He rubbed his forehead with the tips of his fingers. 'I remember. Two months ago the *Magdeburg* ran aground near the coast of Finland. The *Augsburg* was with her, but left when two of our ships approached. Maybe your father was there when it happened?'

Evie regarded him. 'It's possible. What happened?'

'To the *Augsburg*? She escaped unharmed, I think.'

'Oh. And what about the *Magdeburg*?'

'She was shelled, and the crew were eventually rounded up. That's really the reason I was sent to London - to bring some documents they found on her to my father.'

'Oh.' Evie remained puzzled. 'Well, I'm grateful for whatever brought you here.'

'Thank you. I have taken up enough of your evening already.' He looked around for his coat.

'You don't have to go.'

He returned her gaze and reached over to caress a strand of her curls. His hand moved to touch her cheek, and he drew her close.

For the second time that evening, he experienced the piquant fragrance of her perfume.

Captain Hall waited in the corridor outside the meeting room as the board members filed in. Churchill and Admiral Fisher were talking as they jostled to be first.

Churchill stood to one side, his eyes sparkling with humour. 'Age before beauty,' he said, arm outstretched to allow Fisher before him.

Lord Fisher refused to take the bait and remained opposite. 'Brawn before brains,' he replied, with a barely suppressed smile.

They both made a dash for the doorway and became jammed between the posts. Like two schoolboys, they tittered at the ridiculous situation before both burst through.

Rear Admiral Oliver rolled his eyes and entered the room, followed by Vice-Admiral Sturdee, Chief of the War Staff. Then came Rear Admiral Sydney Fremantle, President of the Signal Committee. To Hall's mind, he was the only man who looked the part of a traditional sea captain. Fremantle's splendid white beard and moustache gave him the appearance of an Arctic explorer.

Rear-Admiral Arthur Leveson, Director of Operations Divisions of the Admiralty War Staff, preceded him into the room. Hall didn't know him well, except they had both been to the same gunnery school, though at different times.

It crossed the Captain's mind he was last in the queue. At sea, he had given no regard to the competence and leadership qualities of their Lordships, and his place in the pecking order. But now he was this close, he'd had to stifle disloyal thoughts several times. Did they have a full grasp of the complex and difficult decisions they would need to make in the months ahead? Past evidence suggested otherwise.

Once the door closed and everyone was seated, Fisher scanned the group. His gaze alighted on Sturdee, and Hall sensed a change in mood. He was aware of some background to the long-running quarrel. Before the war Fisher, the arch reformer, clashed with the traditionalist Beresford. Fisher wanted to sweep away many old and out-of-date naval customs and introduce new technology, but was opposed by Beresford and Sturdee. Fisher had marginally higher seniority and won the argument, but the disagreement rankled long afterwards. It was rumoured he had stepped in to prevent Sturdee from becoming a First Lord of the Admiralty, and he could see the resentment remaining in Sturdee's fixed stare.

Fisher distributed papers, walking around the table as he gave them out. 'You'll notice a new item on the agenda, the shelling of Great Yarmouth.'

He sat. After receiving a nod from Churchill, he began to explain. 'Yesterday there was a raid on Great Yarmouth by a German Squadron led by Admiral Franz von Hipper. There were three battlecruisers, an armoured cruiser and four light cruisers, a sizable force. I'm told a minesweeper challenged her, but I'm wondering why our Fleet didn't put to sea?'

The Director of Operations, Rear Admiral Leveson, coughed. 'On this occasion, I believe the commander of the Grand Fleet was returning to port.'

'So no action was taken because Admiral Jellicoe was on a train?'

Silence fell.

'I find it hard to understand what has happened to our Navy in the three years since I retired,' said Fisher. 'Luckily, there were no civilian casualties, the bombardment was short, and the shells only reached the beach. But how was it we were not informed about their presence?' He regarded Hall, 'Only when the first rounds rained down on the shoreline?'

'We had no warning, Admiral,' responded Hall. 'If the German squadron maintains radio silence throughout the action, as appears in this case, we cannot give any notice.'

'Then what is the point?' Fisher's voice assumed a hectoring tone. 'We only lost one submarine when it hit a mine. But suppose the entire German Imperial Fleet had put to sea? We wouldn't know until it was far too late.'

'No sir.' Hall returned the Admiral's fierce gaze. 'Combined Fleet movements are not possible without some radio contact. The reason this action occurred without the use of radio was that the raid was highly organised beforehand, and with limited objectives. We think the purpose was to lay a minefield off the coast.'

Fisher looked across at Churchill. 'I don't like the idea of the enemy being able to sneak up on us.' He faced Hall. 'Don't you have spies to keep watch on German shipping movements?'

'There are a few, but not enough,' Hall responded. 'We have to rely on intercepting their communications without their knowledge.'

'Speaking about communications,' interrupted Churchill, 'can we move on to the main business of the meeting? I now have the full text of the telegram from *Canopus*. We need to decide on a plan to rid us of this troublesome commander von Spee. What do you say, Jackie?'

'I say this.' Fisher made sure he had everybody's attention before continuing. 'In all my days in the Royal Navy, I have rarely encountered such badly constituted orders to a squadron. The cablegrams are full of errors, contradictions and ambiguities. I have a lot of sympathy for Kit. The Navy has lost not only many fine men but also an outstanding officer because of our mistakes.' He regarded Sturdee. 'As Chief of War Staff, the blame lies with the person responsible for framing them.'

Sturdee's face grew red, but before he could speak, Churchill interrupted. 'Thank you, Jackie, but now is not the time to play that game. Besides, you should take into account I was partly liable for directions to Cradock.' He straightened. 'No, we must consider our failings later. Today we have to put right the situation if only to honour Kit Cradock's name.'

The words sounded like a prayer, and Hall had a vision of them being delivered by Churchill from the pulpit. The effect was to calm the meeting and focus attention. Churchill carried on, 'So what do you propose?'

'I have already ordered the battlecruisers *Invin-*

cible and *Inflexible* to be detached from the Grand Fleet and readied to join Admiral Stoddart's squadron on the east coast of South America,' said Fisher. 'This time, there can be no mistake.'

'And when they get there?' enquired Churchill.

'It all depends on what von Spee does next,' interjected Fremantle. 'As far as we know, he is in the southern half of the Pacific. There are only three ways he could go, north towards the coast of North America, east across the Pacific, or south to the Magellan Straits and into the Atlantic.'

'If he goes north or east, he is bound to meet up with Australian and Japanese warships,' offered Fremantle.

'Remind me what those ships are, would you?' asked Fisher.

Leveson checked his papers. 'At present, the squadron comprises the light cruiser *Newcastle*, the Japanese cruiser *Idzuma*, and the small battleship *Hizen*. There is the battlecruiser *Australia* at Suva on Fiji, which could be ready to join them in a few days.'

'Order her to do so,' commanded Fisher. 'They're not a match for von Spee.' He stared at Sturdee. 'Please be so kind as to make it clear they are to search southwards for von Spee, but not to engage his ships under any circumstances, merely to report his position.'

Hall observed Sturdee as he returned Fisher's stare. For several seconds the room was quiet again, and he waited, fascinated to discover who would blink first.

CHAPTER 12

After a long pause, Sturdee nodded agreement, but kept his eye on Fisher.

'There are other options.' The interruption came from Fremantle. 'He could find some place to hide after coaling, and hop islands until he spots an opportunity to inflict more damage. Or even chance to make for the east coast and disperse, making it much more difficult for us.'

'Then we must keep searching.' Fisher rapped the desk as if to return everyone's attention to the main issue. 'I understand the course of action we take depends on what von Spee does next, so we now need to work out the most likely route and plan our strategy accordingly.'

'In the action off Coronel, von Spee will have expended most of his ammunition,' said Hall. 'I estimate he has less than forty per cent of a full load remaining. If he stays in the Pacific, he risks losing most of that if he encounters the Allied squadron. Even if he wins another battle, his squadron is lost without enough shells. I think he will go south and into the Atlantic where he has a shot at making for home.'

'Good point, Captain,' said Churchill. 'Jackie, what is your estimate?'

'Von Spee has kept us guessing for the last two months. The Captain's logic is sound, but we should expect von Spee to make us think he will do something else.'

Churchill surveyed the meeting. Most were nodding in agreement, except for Stoddart, whose face remained inscrutable.

'Very well, we anticipate von Spee will sail through the Magellan Straits. What then?' Churchill asked. 'Let us imagine we have rounded the Horn. There are two thousand miles of coast-line to the north, and another two thousand miles or more of open water to the north and east.'

'He must coal before making it across the Atlantic. There is a lot of support from German nationals in Argentina, so it wouldn't surprise me if he headed for the River Plate,' observed Admiral Leveson.

'I calculate it would take another four or five days, at 12 knots,' said Fremantle. 'Assuming he survived off Coronel relatively unscathed.' The Admiral's last few words brought a brooding quiet to the assembled men.

Hall felt reluctant to interrupt, wondering briefly if he ought to bring up such an obvious

DOMINIC HAYES

point. 'There are the Falkland Islands, and Port Stanley is practically on route.'

'If he believed there were any British warships there, he would avoid it like the plague,' commented Leveson.

'Supposing he knew there were none in the area?' Churchill's eyes gleamed.

'Then he would attack,' said Leveson. 'He could coal there, then destroy the rest of the stock which would deny it to us later. He would destroy the wireless station to prevent direct communications with our squadrons.'

Churchill regarded Hall. 'Well Reggie, do you think you could convince our German commander Port Stanley is open and free from enemy ships?'

As Hall considered the request, a couple of ideas leapt into mind. He would need to give them careful consideration, but they were definitely worth examining in detail. 'I think I could, with careful planning. The outcome can never be certain, but I will try my best.'

Churchill beamed. 'That's all I ask for Captain. See what you can do, eh?' He gathered up his papers, and gradually everyone made for the door.

'Frederick, would you mind staying for a minute?' Fisher's voice was so quiet, it went unheard by the departing officers.

When they had all left, Fisher faced Admiral Sturdee. 'I am sorry for my outburst earlier. We've had our differences in the past, but it shouldn't prevent us from working together now.'

Sturdee didn't appear convinced by Fisher's change of tone. 'Admiral Fisher, you have done much to prolong the antagonism between us. I wish it were not so, but I cannot find it in me to forget. Forgive, possibly. But forget, no.'

'Sometimes disagreements can sour relations for long periods,' observed Fisher. 'It was never my intention to be constantly at war with you. There is a real live enemy who requires our enmity. Whatever I said about your position as Chief of Staff, I have always had high regard for your command at sea.'

Sturdee's face relaxed, but his eyes remained wary. 'I sense you have an order for me.'

'It's a request, not an order. During the meeting, I was reviewing who should take the flag for the two battleships we're sending.' Fisher lowered his voice. 'I couldn't think of anyone better than you.'

'You're positive that's a request and not an order?'

'I am.'

'Then I accept.'

'Thank you, Frederick.' He held Sturdee's arm as they walked to the door. 'I know I've chosen the right man.' He watched as Sturdee strode down the corridor. His back seemed straighter, and his stride seemed lighter.

A flicker of a smile crossed Fisher's lips.

Elbows on desk and head in hands, Captain Hall, pondered the question on how to persuade von Spee Port Stanley would be free from British warships. The vice-admiral would no doubt have informants reporting enemy ship movements all along German-friendly ports on both the east and west coasts of South America. But information about British ships crossing the Atlantic would be more difficult to come by. Admiral Fisher had stipulated utmost secrecy over the provisioning of the *Invincible* and *Inflexible* at Portsmouth, and throughout the crossing, they would maintain radio silence.

Would it be possible to bribe a local reporter in Valparaiso? In the city, rumour and gossip would spread around the streets like the bubonic plague. Most accounts would concern von Spee's success, but there were also bound to be stories predicting a British reprisal. Perhaps he could sow a false trail.

If the British squadron were not based out of Port Stanley where else could they be? He approached the wall map behind his desk and traced the coast of South America northward. Though neutral, Argentina's relationship with the Allies was complicated. Given the rule under such an administration, they could find no lasting support there. His finger travelled along the coast of Uruguay. They sided with the Allies when war broke out, so the port of Montevideo was a possibility. Further north was the extended coastline of Brazil, so the same neutrality rules would apply, making any port there problematic.

His finger carried on its northward journey past Rio de Janeiro and halted at Nova Vicosa. Opposite the town was a group of small islands some 15 miles off the coast. The Abrolhos Rocks were uninhabited islands with shoals extending beyond the three-mile limit, meaning they were outside Brazilian territorial waters. The anchorage was narrow and exposed to trade winds and storms, but *Any Port* reflected the Captain. His thoughts were interrupted by the telephone.

'Captain Hall?'

'Speaking.'

'Inspector Woodhall. Sergeant Reid has made his report.'

'I'm quite busy. Could I call you back?'

'No Captain. I think you'd better hear this straight away.'

Hall noted the alarm in the Inspector's voice and sat behind his desk. 'Go on.'

'Last night, the Count stayed at a woman's house. Her name is Evie Brown, and she is the manageress of the Lyon's Corner café at 213 Piccadilly. My sergeant had a funny intuition about this one.'

Hall frowned, 'I see nothing funny about that.

He's a young man, enjoying a visit to London.'

'Sergeant Reid followed them from the theatre. The Count stayed the night at her house.'

'So?'

'Sergeant Reid tailed the woman in the morning. Instead of going straight to work, she called by a café stall in Regent Park. There she met a chap, a down and out. Dark beard, scruffy clothes, wearing a scuffed bowler.'

'What happened then?'

'Reid managed to get a photograph from behind some trees. They parted after a five-minute chat. She went straight to her tea shop and remained there, at least until two o'clock when Tich left.'

'Tich?'

'Sergeant Reid. He's so tall we call him Tich.'

'Ah, I see.' Hall became pensive. 'I'm still not convinced the Count gave away any secrets, but I will find out. Thank you Inspector.'

'You're welcome, Captain. Will there be anything else?'

'Yes, I think it would be an idea to find the chap in the scruffy clothes. Get a better description if you can and circulate it to all police.'

'I'll do that, Captain. But supposing the man knows some confidential material and uses wireless to get the message out?'

Hall hesitated. 'There are ways to detect an illegal broadcast. The army has listening posts which can locate a transmitter using three aerials. He would not be likely to get away if he tried to contact Germany while he is here. Not many know this is possible, Inspector, so I want you to keep it under your hat. If the man is Otto Gratz, he will be aware we can trace him this way. I believe he would rather try to leave the country with the intelligence.'

'I understand Captain.'

Hall thanked the detective and put the phone down, then dialled the number for the Russian Embassy.

Captain Hall was leaning on the railings over-looking the Thames when Constantine arrived. The Count joined him, and they both watched as a barge went past.

'Morning Captain. I'm wondering why you chose to meet here?'

'Smell that,' replied Captain Hall, gesturing to the busy waterway.

'I smell petrol fumes, fish, and the sewers.'

'This river is the mightiest in Britain. It brings in goods to the city and the country and sends goods to the rest of the empire. I asked to see you here because whenever I come, I can smell the sea.' He studied Constantine. 'I thought you would appreciate that, as a fellow sailor.'

'I do appreciate it, Captain, but I fail to see why you wanted to meet at all.'

Hall returned his gaze to the river. 'How to put

this as delicately as possible?' he mused. 'You spent last night in the company of a lady?'

Constantine stiffened. 'Yes, what of it?'

'You remember our talk at the embassy? When I impressed on you to keep secret your government's gift of the German codebook?'

'Oh.' Constantine seemed to shrink a little.

'I am hoping you refrained from divulging the secret, and instead discussed the cover story we prepared for you.'

'Ah, not quite.' Constantine's crestfallen expression betrayed the denial.

'So you told the lady you delivered SKM to the British government?'

'No, not in so many words.'

'Then what exactly did you tell her?' He swung round to observe Constantine's reply.

'I merely said I had delivered some documents to my father.'

'Secret documents? You didn't mention SKM?'

'No.' Constantine shook his head. 'I'm positive I didn't say that.'

'And you didn't say where you obtained them?'

'Ah.' Constantine stopped. 'I did mention they were from the *Magdeburg*.'

'Then it wouldn't take a genius to work out the documents included SKM.'

Constantine paled, and he remained silent.

'Right now we're scouring the country for the person she talked to, and can only hope we get to him before he leaves the country.'

'She's a working girl, not a spy.'

When Hall continued to stare, Constantine muttered, 'I trusted her. She works in a corner tea shop, for God's sake.'

'Oh, my dear boy. You are more naïve than I imagined.'

'You told me it would be a man. He would try to get me drunk - and I was never drunk with Evie.'

'I'm afraid you've made a huge mistake. And now the information is on its way to the continent. You have given away a state secret, and there will be hell to pay.' Hall blinked rapidly. 'If you were a British national, you could be put on trial and hanged.'

Colour drained from Constantine's face. 'I am very sorry. What can I do to make amends?'

'Don't see her again.' He moved to go when another idea occurred to him. 'I will ring you later. In the meantime, I suggest you stay in the Embassy.'

He had only ten minutes before he was due to meet Mansfield Smith-Cumming. Nevertheless, he decided to walk to the United Services Club rather than take a taxi, hoping the fifteen minutes exercise would help clear his mind. All along Northumberland Avenue, he worried the problem. Germany might soon become aware the Royal Navy had possession of one of their codebooks; he should tell Oliver, but what exactly would he say?

After five minutes of dodging other pedestrians, he arrived at two options. He could simply not tell anyone about the problem and hope the Inspector caught Otto Gratz before leaving England. Or he could tell Oliver he had spoken to Constantine and warned him about divulging the information, but Constantine had let the secret slip. Hall could say once he knew about the indiscretion he had instructed Inspector Woodhall to begin a man-hunt. There was no need to mention the briefing they had both given Constantine about promulgating an alternative story.

Neither option was ideal. If he said nothing and Otto escaped to Germany, Churchill's dire predictions would come true. If he told Oliver the secret was no longer a secret, Churchill's fire would incinerate everyone in his path. Though he had little to do with the matter, Hall would be bound to be caught in the gun-sights. He might have to face the humiliation of going back to sea, and his wife's silent condemnation.

'Bloody hell.' Without thinking, the words escaped his lips.

'Excuse me!' A lady in a three-piece suit, bonnet and umbrella had stopped abruptly. 'Are you swearing at me!'

'Sorry, ma'am.' Hall removed his peaked hat and held it against his chest. 'Not at you, ma'am. Just life in general.'

She gave him a withering stare and moved on.

Lunchtime at the club was no different from the evening. Members would come and go in a variety of suits, but the number of men in uniform was on the increase. Captain Hall left his hat and coat with the doorman while his membership was checked against the register. Though silence was encouraged, there would bound to be the odd muted exchange between acquaintances in the great hall. But once in the reading room, quiet was the order of the day. To hold a conversation, it was best to meet in the dining hall. Hall found his colleague and friend already seated at a table for two in the furthest corner.

Captain Mansfield Smith-Cumming stood with evident difficulty.

'Thought I'd be seeing you again,' he said with a flash of cheerfulness. 'Just not so soon. '

'The pleasure is all mine,' said Hall dryly. 'I'm sorry I'm late.'

'Then you don't mind, I've ordered for us.' Mansfield lifted the decanter and poured a glass of wine for Hall. 'How is life in room 40?'

Hall checked the nearby tables.

'Don't worry, no-one can hear.'

'I do worry Mansfield, there's been a leak. That's partly why I'm here.' Hall clasped his hands together in an appearance of composure. 'Your friend Otto has managed to wheedle the truth from Count Benckendorff. Otto Gratz knows we have SKM.'

'I assume you warned Benckendorff. How did it happen?'

'A young filly named Evie Brown.'

'Ah,' said Mansfield, arranging his napkin. 'The old honey trap.' When he caught Hall's puzzled expression, he carried on, 'We used to have a saying: the way to a man's heart is through his stomach. The way to a man's head is through his..'.

'Yes, yes,' interrupted Hall. 'I understand.'

'How do you know it was Otto and not anyone else?'

'We had a sighting from Sergeant Reid.'

'Ah.' Mansfield held back while the waiter delivered the first course. 'I heard Woodhall had signed up?'

'I've no idea. The thing is Otto knows and is on his way back to the Fatherland.'

'Which is where I come in.' Mansfield raised a knife and fork to attack his food. 'Give me her details before you go and I'll see to it.'

'Thank you, but you said the man was a slippery character and a master of disguise. He's likely to get to Germany.'

'He may,' said Mansfield, dabbing his lips with the napkin. 'So we need a stern anchor.'

'I'm not sure I take your meaning.'

'Only a figure of speech, Reggie. Means I need to take additional precautions.' He laid his knife and fork together on the plate. 'You said that was only partly the reason for our meeting. What is the other part?'

'I expect you heard about Kit Cradock's defeat?'

Mansfield threw his napkin onto the table. 'I did, Reggie. Couldn't help wondering how the Admiralty let that kind of thing happen.'

'I can't tell you,' Hall replied. 'It's bad enough fighting a war thousands of miles away, but the biggest battles are happening right here in the Admiralty.'

Mansfield's mouth curled. 'Politics.'

There was silence as the second course arrived. 'Anyway Reggie, what can I do to help?'

'I need a spy in Valparaiso.' Hall toyed with his knife. 'I want him to persuade Vice-Admiral von Spee the Falklands are free from British warships, but I have no idea how to go about recruiting one.'

'Is that all?' Mansfield was grinning.

'That's all for now. It's worth at least a dinner.'

'If you are thinking of recruiting, you must understand it will take money and a lot of patience. Your vice-admiral will have left long before you can get anyone there.'

'Damn, I imagined it would only take a few days.'

'No, there's a much quicker way,' said Mansfield, eyes twinkling. 'It helps we already have someone in place at our embassy. You cable some money, tell them what you want, and Bob's your uncle.'

'You have someone in Valparaiso?'

'Two actually. And one is a naval attaché.'

'Good grief, I never believed it could be so simple! I suppose Germany has spies in all their embassies?'

'As do we all,' nodded Mansfield. 'But before you get too excited, a word of caution. You must use them carefully and only when it is vitally important. Most host countries turn a blind eye to the doings of foreign embassy staff, but if they misbehave, they are sent home.'

'Well this is vital - may I use him?'

'It's a her.' Mansfield smiled at Hall's astonishment. 'I imagined it would surprise you. But Germany has already used a woman against Count Benckendorff. There's a kind of satisfaction to be had in using another to strike for Britain, don't you say?'

'Absolutely, Mansfield. I knew I had come to the right man. So I'll give you details about my Evie Brown, and you let me have details about your mysterious female spy.'

The two men jotted down particulars on their table napkins, then ceremoniously swapped them.

CHAPTER 13

Constantine halted outside number 37 Oxford Gate with Captain Hall's dire warning still resounding in his ears: 'Stay in the embassy and don't see her again!' But with only one night left before his return to Russia, the compulsion to visit Evie again was overwhelming. He mounted the three steps to her door and rapped the knocker.

There was a long silence, and he feared he was too late. He knocked again. After a shorter wait, the door opened.

'Oh, darling!' She wrapped her arms around him.

He checked the street over his shoulder. 'May I come inside?'

In the hallway, she caught his troubled expression. 'What is it?'

'We'd better go in. I've something serious to tell you.'

She led the way to the living room. 'Drink?'

'No!'

'What's the matter, Constantine? I only asked.'

He sat and clasped his knees. 'I'm sorry, I didn't mean to be rude. Do you remember when we first met?' He carried on, 'You arrived late to the theatre and sat in the seat next to mine. I thought then how pretty you were.'

Evie tilted her head, 'You were rather dashing too. Is that what you wanted to tell me?'

He raised his hand, 'I'll come to that in a minute. At the interval, I looked all over for you. Eventually, when I found you on the first floor, I saw you talking to an older man.' He looked at her directly. 'Who was that?'

'Oh.' Evie frowned. 'He was just someone I knew.'

'Who was he, Evie?'

'I can't tell you,' she said at last.

'Shall I tell you who I think he was - he was your contact with Germany.'

'Please, don't...'

Constantine interrupted her protestation. 'I've been a fool. You used me to get information about the documents I brought to London. I wasn't aware we were being followed, and now the authorities know what has happened. And you are involved!'

'Oh, God.' Evie rose and glanced towards the window. 'Are they here?'

'No. Not yet, anyway. I came to warn you to get away.'

She turned. 'Why?'

He hesitated, 'Because I'm in love with you. And I think you are in love with me.'

The silence lingered. At last, she said, 'Yes, it's true. I do love you.'

'You must leave now if you don't want to go to prison. You can write to me care of the Russian Embassy.'

'I will, I promise.' She hurried to the bureau, wrote briefly, and passed him the folded slip of paper.

As his fingers closed around the note, she kissed him briefly on the mouth.

'Now I have to pack.'

Constantine followed her into the hallway and watched as she rushed up the stairs. For a while, he could hear the sound of drawers opening above as she threw clothes into a suitcase. He closed his eyes; in his heart, she had already gone, and there was nothing more he could do. His shoulders slumped and he slipped out the front door without another word.

Inspector Woodhall watched from the relative warmth of his car as the Count descended the steps to the pavement. The Count halted and turned to gaze up at the front door. As he moved, Woodhall glimpsed a long, pale face with eyes fixed somewhere in the distance.

The Inspector consulted his pocket watch,

picked up a pad and made a notation. He wouldn't have much longer to wait.

Further down the street, Otto Gratz folded his newspaper into a neat square, and walked in the opposite direction.

The following day, as Admiral Fisher hurried to his next meeting, he spotted the agitated figure of a young man with red hair. He was carrying a sheaf of notes and looking up and down the first-floor corridor as though lost. Fisher frowned and asked gruffly if there was anything the matter.

'I have some urgent messages for Commander Hope, but I don't know where to find him,' said Lord Herschell.

'Commander Hope?'

'Yes Admiral. He vets all the messages from Room 40.'

'Well if he's not in room 40, he might be in the map library. Come with me.' Fisher pivoted on his heel and returned the way he had come; Herschell had to hurry to keep up. Fisher opened an office door and proceeded through the outer vestibule into a large room. A man lent over one of the tables, engrossed in a map of the North Sea.

'Commander Hope, I found this young man waiting to deliver messages.' The Admiral indicated Lord Herschell.

As Herschell approached, several sheets of paper slipped from his pile of papers and Fisher stooped to pick them up. He scanned the first message.

'This looks interesting,' he said, handing the slip to the Commander.

Hope glanced at the text. 'Actually, I wouldn't pass this one on to the Director.'

'Why not?'

'See how the message starts, Admiral. I know from experience this is a movement report. These types of cablegrams all begin the same way.'

'So the information gets lost?'

'No, Admiral. I plot the coordinates on the map over there.' Hope nodded to where a large map of the world hung from the opposite wall. On the adjacent wall, a series of long pigeon holes had been built housing other rolled-up maps.

'And what happens then?'

Commander Hope led the way to the wall map where black lines criss-crossed almost every ocean and sea. Herschel slipped quietly away.

Before explaining the method, Hope inspected the note Fisher was still holding. 'This one's from the SMS *Bremen*. She's a German light cruiser. Launched ten years ago, if memory serves, and she's the lead ship of her class. At the last notification, we placed her in the Baltic, attempting to block the Russian navy with the rest of the fleet. I take the decoded map references, compare them with the gridded sheets we obtained with the codebook, and plot them on the map. This confirms she has not moved out of the Baltic and therefore poses no danger to us.'

'And that's it?'

'Not quite.' Hope removed a map from a pigeon hole. 'We keep the wall map up to date with German ship movements where there is little threat to our navy and interests.' He unfurled the sheet and placed it on the table. 'Nearer home, we plot movements on larger scale maps. Here's one of the English Channel and German bight.'

He stood back to allow Fisher a better glimpse. There were many more black lines crossing the map.

'And what is in these areas?' Fisher pointed to several empty spaces.

'We think the Germans may have mined those regions and hence avoid them. That information is broadcast to our ships at sea, and we send them updated charts. New movement reports are continually compared with the German gridded charts to make sure the report we give remains accurate. It also helps our code-breakers spot areas where the Germans plan to mine next.'

'That's excellent, Commander. Well done.'

'It's all right, as far as it goes.'

'Whatever do you mean?'

'When I receive decrypts, I'm not permitted to speak or otherwise communicate with the people who deciphered them.'

'How is that a problem?' Fisher's curiosity appeared genuine.

Commander Hope picked the next message from his desk and handed it to the Admiral. 'Here's an example. A German ship is asking for harbour lights to be switched on.'

'Usually means the ship is planning to enter the harbour,' responded Fisher.

'Yes, normally that would be correct. But I have logged a note from the same ship only three days before, asking for coal in the Mediterranean. Given the ship's engines and specification, it would not be possible for her to have made the voyage, even at top speed. There is obviously a mistake somewhere, but because I don't have access to the original intercepts, I can't say where the mistake lies. I can't even talk to the code-breakers because of the restrictions in place.'

'I see. And how often is this sort of thing happening?'

'Frequently, Admiral. It's not such an issue with the regular movement reports, more so with important communications. I always pass those on to the DNI. Those are the messages you and the War Staff see, and I have to say I'm always concerned the intelligence is not sufficiently accurate.'

'I see, Captain. It appears excessive secrecy is causing a muddle. I want you to see all the messages, and feel free to discuss the contents with anyone in room 40. Also, now that young man knows where to find you, I want him to bring you copies of the decrypts twice a day, and to ensure there is an as little delay as possible in assessing them. I will make sure everyone understands the importance of this change to the procedure.'

Fisher checked his watch. 'I'm afraid I'm too late for my meeting now, but I suspect our accidental encounter was even more important.'

As Fisher hurried out, Commander Hope noted the Admiral had emphasised the word *accidental*. Perhaps he was more perceptive than people gave him credit.

Inspector Woodhall frowned at the interruption as his desk telephone rang. A restless night meant he missed the alarm and had arrived late to work. He lifted the earpiece with a sigh; the paperwork would have to wait.

'Reid here, governor.' Carried by a scratchy line, his sergeant's voice sounded miles away.

'Speak up Tich, I can hardly hear you.'

'Yes sir, is that better? I'm calling from the Burlington Hotel, Dover.'

'Yes. What progress?'

'Some, Inspector. I followed some information received and found a B&B in Dover. Our quarry is supposed to have stayed there one night. I flashed my police card, and the landlady let me in to inspect his bedroom. Found nothing there, but some hairs in the sink, and a dark stain.

Could be a hair dye, by the looks of it.'

'So you think Otto has another disguise?'

'Yes sir. The landlady didn't see him go, but she wasn't worried 'cause he'd paid the night before.'

'So we've no idea what he looks like now?'

'No sir. I went straight to the ferry port and asked around.'

'When did the ferry leave?'

'The first sailing is at nine-thirty. I got there at about eight o'clock. No-one recognised the description, not that it's much use, anyway.' Sergeant Reid hesitated. 'There was one thing, though. As I was talking to a member of the public, I happened to see a taxi draw up at the rank. A family got out, and the husband paid the driver.'

'Yes, go on,' urged the Inspector. Reid often slowed down at the point things were getting interesting.

'The man had a large black beard and was wearing a heavy overcoat and bowler hat. The wife was much smaller, demure. They had a young boy with them.'

'Yes?' The Inspector's grip on the telephone tightened.

'Well, as I carried on talking, it occurred to me.' Reid paused.

'Yes, yes. What?'

'Well, at first I thought the chap wasn't my man - why would I? We know Otto travels alone, and it's not possible to suddenly acquire a wife and child - even Otto can't work miracles.'

Woodhall briefly imagined his hands around the sergeant's neck, shaking the words from his throat. 'What was it that made you think it was our man?'

'Well sir, it wasn't until later I realised how warm it was. I began to wonder why anyone should be wearing a woollen overcoat. And then I thought maybe the wife and child weren't his. Suppose he'd offered to give them a lift to the ferry?'

'So, what happened?'

'Well, Inspector, if he was indeed our man, then I'm afraid he's gone.'

The Inspector banged the earpiece against the stand so hard, it nearly broke.

On an open stretch of grass in St James' Park, a company of the King Edward's Horse regiment drilled under the directions of a rather loud Sergeant. The newspaper Captain Hall held under his arm was full of the fighting on the western front and lists of the wounded and dead. His thoughts of the war in France and Flanders overrode unhappy considerations of the navy battle fought at the other end of the globe in the South Pacific.

He found an empty bench and surveyed the scene. So much had changed in the three months since war had been declared. Long queues had formed outside army recruiting stations and men in uniform strolled around the lake. If the rumours could be believed, the lake was to be drained to make way for the Ministry of Shipping buildings.

Since the meeting of the War Staff, Hall had received several visitors to his room, including Walter Page, the American Ambassador with whom he had developed a close relationship. Other visitors, such as senior naval officers, civil servants and junior MPs would complain about the lack of information from the South Pacific, while others bemoaned the lack of support given to Cradock. He had listened to their grumbles and made sympathetic noises, but it was too late to change the course of history.

As he opened the paper, his stomach twisted in a taut knot. The British public was about to discover Britain no longer ruled the waves, and they would bay for blood. Part of the discomfort was a kind of collective guilt he shared with Oliver and others, and part, his individual responsibility in the failure. His wife Essie had reminded him he had no share in the decisions of the War Staff, but that was no consolation. He should have done more.

Skipping past the personal columns on page one, he scanned the money markets and financial situation on page two. On page four, there was a short piece about golf, a reminder that despite the war, life went on. He found the editorial on page eight with the headline 'Battle at Sea'.

Below was a sketch map of the coast of Chile, with the town of Coronel marked.

The piece continued: 'Various worrying reports from nationalistic sections of the German press were confirmed yesterday with the release of a statement from the Admiralty late last night. Six days after the Battle of Coronel, German stories of a naval victory by Vice-Admiral Graf Maximilian von Spee have been confirmed. His East Asiatic Squadron met and defeated the 4th Squadron of the Royal Navy led by Rear-Admiral Sir Christopher Cradock.'

'In gale-force winds and mountainous seas, the two sides clashed and a titanic battle ensued. Within five minutes of the encounter, the flagship *Good Hope* was struck, and minutes later, the light cruiser *Monmouth* suffered a devastating blow which set fire to her upper decks. Despite the failing light, the *Good Hope* made a brave and spirited attempt to close on the German squadron, but she was crushed by the sheer firepower of the enemy.'

'The *Monmouth* left the scene, having been holed below the waterline and taking on water. Listing to starboard, and down by the bow, she was discovered by the German light cruiser *Nürnberg* two hours after the battle began. *Nürnberg* placed a shot across her bows and waited for a response. When none came, she shone a searchlight on her ensign, making it clear to the sailors on board she should hoist the flag of surrender. Instead, the gallant commander faced his tormentor, gathered speed and tried to ram him. The *Nürnberg* opened fire, sinking the *Monmouth* at 21:58. Six-hundred and seventy-eight men lost their lives.'

Captain Hall's hands shook, and he let the newspaper fall. In all his years at sea, he had rarely cried. He had known the substance of the engagement for days. But the article brought home the reality. This morning in the park, seven-and-a-half thousand miles from the battle scene and a week after the event, the tears came freely. He made no effort to dry them, gazing instead at the blurred sky through brimming eyes. After a while, he withdrew a white handkerchief and mopped his face. He drew a deep breath, picked up the paper and resumed the account.

'Rear-Admiral Cradock went down with his flagship, along with 899 officers and men. It was not possible to rescue any sailors because of the darkness and roughness of the seas. Cradock was one of the most highly decorated officers in the Royal Navy, and his bravery is not in doubt. However, when this paper studied the resources and capabilities available to both sides, it became clear that notwithstanding the heroism of the British commander and sailors, they were beaten by a superior force. The German squadron was faster, better equipped and had better guns. We have serious doubts about the strategy employed by the Lordships at the Admiralty in forcing an engagement with von Spee's squadron.'

'Our readers may be assured that though this was an important battle, the vast majority of the German High Seas Fleet remains confined to their home ports. The strength of our Grand Fleet will continue to see to that. It is this paper's expectation the balance will be restored when their Lordships send a force to deal with von Spee.'

Captain Hall crumpled the paper and placed it in a nearby bin. He left the park with only one thought; he would make the Germans pay.

CHAPTER 14

Inspector Woodhall greeted Captain Hall from the other side of his office. 'Morning, Captain. You might need to take a seat.'

Hall sat on the bench against the wall. 'I'm ready.'

Woodhall filed his papers and turned to the Captain. 'I'm afraid we've lost Otto Gratz. My deputy thinks he's taken the ferry to France.'

'How did it happen?'

'It appears Otto was in disguise and accompanied by a wife and small child. Tich wasn't expecting that, and it didn't occur to him until Otto was long gone.'

'We'll never find him now; the whole of France is in turmoil.'

The Inspector nodded agreement. 'But there is some good news. I have Evie Brown.' He caught Hall's startled expression. 'While Tich was in Dover, I took over surveillance duties outside her house. Last night I caught her trying to leave the country.'

'Good God, man. Well done. Where is she now?'

The Inspector nodded towards the rear of the police station. 'In the cells. I thought a night on a hard bench might help to make her more accommodating. And I found this on her dining room table.' He handed the Captain an envelope.

The flap had been opened and then resealed. He opened the envelope and withdrew the letter.

```
Dear Mama,

I have had to leave urgently.  Please
return to Aunt Margarete and stay there
until you hear from me.  There is noth
ing to fear.  I will be safe, and you
need not worry.

All my love.

Evie
```

'Where is the mother?'

'We're making enquiries Captain. In the meantime, I have the house under observation. Do you want to interview the daughter?'

Hall tapped the letter against his chin. 'How long are you able to detain her - legally, I mean?'

'The court would allow a reasonable period to investigate and gather evidence.' He studied Hall. 'What are you planning?'

'Oh, nothing yet. I'm trying to work out how she could be useful to us, but with Otto already in

France, I'm afraid we're already too late.'

'Too late for what may I ask Captain?'

'To stop Otto reaching his objective.'

'Which is?' The Inspector lifted an eyebrow.

'To inform his commander we possess a code-book that belongs to them.'

Evie Brown wound her index finger around a curl of hair and pulled. Tears from over-full eyes trickled down her cheeks.

Captain Hall entered the room and set eyes on the forlorn figure, seated behind a metal table. She was far from the beautiful woman he had been told to expect. Her rouge was smudged, her eyes swollen and her clothes were crumpled. He closed the door behind him, sat in the chair opposite and pulled out a clean handkerchief. While she dabbed her eyes, he fished out a packet of Player's Navy Cut and a box of matches and placed them on the table.

'Help yourself.'

She lit a cigarette with a shaking hand, drew deeply and began to cough.

He grinned, 'Not used to the strength?'

She shook her head and removed a fleck of tobacco from her lower lip.

He eyed the young woman. Despite an unnerving experience of a night in the cells, her voice was firm. He looked beyond the dowdy exterior, at the long dark curls that surrounded her oval face, and at her brown eyes that possessed a depth he had rarely seen in another woman.

'I resent being held here, only to be stared at like an exhibit in a museum. Why have I been arrested and imprisoned?'

Her words roused him from his reverie. 'Actually, you're not in prison, merely in detention. And strictly speaking, you have not been arrested. The Inspector here,' he inclined his head towards Woodhall, 'is investigating whether he should arrest you.'

'Why, what is it I am supposed to have done?'

'He could arrest you under the regulation which prevents persons from communicating with the enemy or obtaining information for that purpose. The Defence of the Realm Act gives him that authority.'

Her eyelids narrowed, and her mouth set in a line. Only the swift darting movement of her eyes indicated she had been affected by his aggressive attitude. She drew a deep pull on the cigarette. 'Nonsense. You'll be claiming I'm an enemy German national next. I'm British, and I have a British passport to prove it.'

Hall held up his palm. 'Oh, I know you're British,' he said softly. 'We checked with Lyons. But your friend here is German.' He placed a blurred photograph on the table which showed a middle-aged man with a beard. His clothes and bowler hat were dirty, giving the impression of a gentleman who had fallen on hard times.

Evie's eyes widened fractionally. 'That's just some tramp that stopped me on my way to work one day. I gave him some change, that's all.'

'Evie, you're a superb actress. I will leave you with the cigarettes.'

Her performance was so remarkable, a tentative idea began to take shape. He rose and nodded to the Inspector. At the door, he paused.

'Oh, by the way, Evie, your mother will be well looked after when she returns.'

When Captain Hall returned to the Admiralty, he found Sir Alfred pacing outside his office.

'Where have you been?' Ewing's aggressive stance left no doubt the man was furious.

'I had important matters to attend to. What can I do to help?' He replied as calmly as he could.

The response infuriated Sir Alfred. 'I have been waiting outside your office for the last ten minutes. Why am I not able to unlock the door?'

'I had the lock changed.'

'On whose orders?' Ewing's face grew crimson.

Hall removed a key from his pocket and unlocked the door. 'Why don't you come in?'

As soon as Ewing entered, Hall closed the door firmly behind him and gestured to the chair.

The man seemed to be on the verge of apoplexy. 'I repeat, on whose orders?'

'On my orders.' Hall crossed his leg, his relaxed posture in stark contrast to his senior.

'This is outrageous,' Ewing spluttered. 'I order you to hand over the spare key.'

Ewing waited. 'Are you refusing to obey an order from a senior officer?'

'Not at all, Sir Alfred. I haven't been given a spare, and as far as I am aware I hold the only copy. Obviously, we couldn't have a situation where I'm locked out of my own office, so I am unable to help. You should talk to the quartermaster.'

'I will do no such thing. I shall speak to Admiral Oliver and get this whole mess sorted out.'

'In the meantime, is there anything I can do for you?' Hall's voice remained quiet and professional.

'Most certainly. I gather you persuaded Winston to employ Commander Hope in room 40?'

So this was what was annoying him. 'We both reached the conclusion it was necessary to have a person to vet the decrypts before they reach the War Staff.'

'But that's not what is happening. Commander Hope has been talking to the codebreakers, questioning the information. Information they've already gone to great lengths to get.'

Hall leaned forward, masking treacherous thoughts with an impassive face. 'But that is precisely the problem. We are not making the best use of the information by just passing the text on. That's what Commander Hope is being asked to do - challenge the intelligence. Where there are any discrepancies, he can sort it out before it gets to the War Staff. If anything he's improving the credibility of your office.'

Ewing's face showed signs of reverting to its former puce colour. 'Credibility?'

Hall interrupted before the explosion. 'Intelligence needs to be analysed and interpreted. It requires the attention of someone who understands navy procedures. Someone who can summarise decrypts in the language their lordships understand. They must have confidence in the reports they receive, both in its importance and its accuracy.'

He placed his elbows on the desk and clasped his hands together. 'You must know the War Staff regard all your reports as suspect. There have been too many errors in the movement reports, too many claims the German fleet was coming out, only to be reversed the next day. If Commander Hope can prevent mistakes being made, surely you can see how valuable that is to us?'

'You misunderstand, the Captain is taking over and he doesn't even speak a word of German! The men are beginning to look up to him. He's acting like their chief of staff.'

'Well, it's because he is. It would appear he's doing his job well.'

'I think you are deliberately failing to understand.' Ewing's speech slowed. 'I run the department, and I can't have anyone taking charge who undermines my authority.'

'Sir Alfred, I do see. No-one is setting out to undermine your authority.'

'Maybe no-one is setting out to do that, but it's happening all the same. Sometimes I'm in the office, and the men hardly acknowledge I'm there.'

'I understand Sir Alfred. I'm bound by the same rules. My staff are not permitted to see any intelligence originating from your department. Yet they know I have access to the information and that causes resentment. It's very frustrating to be unable to share information and talk it over with, frankly, people who are more qualified to assess and verify the source and quality of the data.'

'Because you are in the same boat doesn't resolve the problem.'

'No, but I do sympathise with you. For my part, I just get on and do my best.'

Ewing made to rise. 'Well, I will not give up.'

'What will you do?'

Sir Alfred's brows lowered. 'Do? That's something I'm not going to discuss with you.' He reached the door and paused. 'But I wouldn't get too fond of your impregnable office if I were you.'

Most men on the ferry were in army uniform though there were some women and older men who were seeking family members or loved ones.

Otto had overheard one woman talking non-stop to a group of others. She had discovered too late her son had joined up. He was only sixteen years old, and she had brought his birth certificate to demonstrate the proof to his CO and return the boy to his home in Manchester.

He felt sympathy for her in the beginning. However, she seemed to have an inexhaustible fund of stories about 'her son', and his attention faltered. After a quarter of an hour of incessant chatter, he left the warmth of the stuffy seated section to stare over the rail at the murky water of the Channel. After eight months living with the possibility of discovery, it felt good to be on his way home.

When the ferry docked at Calais, Otto walked down the gangway, hidden behind a gaggle of passengers. Orderlies directed the arrivals into separate lines to have their papers checked. It was doubtful they would stop him - the best craftsmen in the Abteilung IIIb, a division of German military intelligence had created his documents. But it was likely his description had been telegraphed ahead. He found a large pair of black-rimmed glasses inside his coat and put them on. Rummaging in the knapsack, he retrieved a worn boater and placed it on his head when no-one was paying attention.

British Army and French customs officers sat behind wooden trestle tables, and the column gradually decreased. When his turn came, the officials scrutinised his passport and Swiss canton identity card and allowed him through without a pause.

If the first hurdle was easy, the second - finding a room - was more difficult and expensive. All accommodation in the centre of town was booked, and he had to travel to the outskirts. On the way, a French gendarme stopped him to inspect his papers. Eventually, he saw an advertisement in a window of a small terrace in a warren of streets behind the Boulevard la Fayette.

The owner, a wrinkled woman of indeterminate age, demanded a week's rent in advance.

'But Madame, I only wish to stay a night.'

She shook her head and held out her hand.

He counted out the notes, and she led the way through the front door. In the hallway, the smell, a combination of stewed cabbage and urine, made him pause. He followed her retreating figure up the stairs to a box room. She opened the door, waved him through and left.

He soon found out why: the reek of rotting food hit him at the doorway in a wave. He held his breath and examined the tiny space. There wasn't much to see: a single bed, bare floorboards, damp patches of wallpaper and rat droppings in the corner.

Otto slung his knapsack on the floor and sat on the bed. Springs groaned under his weight. He lay down to more protests and lifted his weary feet onto the bedspread, boots and all. A sleepless night was the least of his worries, and he considered whether to steal a radio set tomorrow and send a message in secret. Detection was unlikely this side of the Channel; the real problem would lay with the Kaiser. Otto was duty bound to report to his superior in the German Naval Intelligence Department, but the issue would only be resolved by the highest level, the German Emperor and King of Prussia.

Impulsive, impatient, imperious: Otto's assessment of the Emperor was of a man of many faults. During one of his earliest audiences with the Kaiser, a minister arrived with a folder of telegraphic cables marked Urgent. Distracted, the Kaiser broke off his conversation to sift through the top half-dozen messages. Someone interrupted, and the Kaiser handed the file to the minister and waved him away. To Otto's mind, a cable from France would not do; he had no choice but to seek a meeting. Even being present was no guarantee the man would agree to a proper course of action. The Kaiser had been warned several times before about the codebooks falling into the wrong hands, yet he still affected unconcern.

No, his best bet would be to involve Prince Heinrich, the Kaiser's brother. He still carried influence and would ensure his brother took Otto's information seriously. But Heinrich was a stickler for evidence, and Otto had no direct proof the SKM codebook had been jeopardised - only the word of a 'trollop' who worked solely for money. He would have to convince Heinrich of the facts: that she had wormed her way into Constantine's affections after he had brought the codebook to London. It was inconceivable she could have made up all the details of that encounter.

Otto closed his eyes. He needed to see Heinrich, but he was probably at sea in the Baltic. To reach him, he would first have to go to Berlin. With considerable effort, he opened his eyes and reached for his knapsack. Inside was a schoolboy atlas that was grubby and torn in places. He swung his feet onto the floor, flipped the book to a double-page spread of Europe and poured over the map.

Going overland would present insurmountable difficulties. The French Army and British Expeditionary Force were attempting to oppose the German advance along a front from the north coast of Belgium all the way to Switzerland. Heading through the lines would be impossible. He might persuade the British on one side, and the Germans on the other, but the no man's land between would be mined and bombed with artillery, not to mention assaulted by both sides in a series of attack and counter-attack. Potentially he could get to Switzerland, and from there across the border, but the journey would be long and fraught with danger.

No, the best route would be by sea. But even that had its problems; the British Navy were stopping and searching all ships destined for Dutch ports, looking for contraband. He wasn't sure if this applied to fishing vessels, but if so, it was possible they would discover him. Possible, but not likely, he thought. The other problem was large sectors of the sea were mined. But that was something he could resolve by getting details from naval command.

Once more he closed his eyes. Now all he needed was a poor fisherman prepared to smuggle him into Holland. Having swapped his British currency for Francs, money was the least of his problems.

Downstairs, the landlady looked upwards and scowled as the sound of her tenant's snores shook the thin ceiling.

CHAPTER 15

Captain Hall laid his head against the leather seat of the taxi as they sped past a throng of pedestrians. They were gazing into shop windows and walking the streets as free citizens. Sadly Evie Brown would not be so lucky. At best, she would not gain her liberty until after the war. At worst, she would never be free because he intended to order her on an operation, an assignment so dangerous it could end in her death.

He lifted a palm to cover his eyes as if trying to hide his face from the crowds. There was something else still bothering him; the reason he had invented the scheme in the first place. He had told no-one at the Admiralty about Otto's flight to France. His only motivation was to get himself off the hook. It was cowardly, but while his reason remained undiscovered, he felt compelled to take the risk.

Other questions elbowed their way to the front of his thoughts. Would he have been so troubled if she were less attractive? The answer made him squirm - he would not. She was both young and beautiful. In a moment of personal candour, he would admit he was too preoccupied with her.

He should have talked to Essie; she would have understood and guided his thinking. But at the same time, she might have discovered how taken he was with Evie. Last night he had hardly slept for thinking about her. He remembered the way she had brushed the hair from her eyes with such a delicate movement of her arm. When he dreamed, he saw her face. And when he woke he imagined her dark eyes were still on him. He had been married to Essie for twenty years, yet this was the first occasion he felt unable to admit his views about another woman to his wife. His fascination for Evie easily overcame the alarm at his own dishonesty and hypocrisy.

The taxi pulled up in Great Scotland Yard. A press of men queued along the pavement, waiting to sign up. Since the start of the war, many public buildings had opened their doors to draft young men into the army and he directed the driver around to the front entrance.

Inspector Woodhall was in his second-floor office, scrutinising case files from behind his desk. 'Morning, Captain. You look like something the cat's dragged in.'

'Thank you, Inspector. I didn't get much sleep last night.'

'Aye. I bet you're up to your neck at work.'

Reluctant to reveal the real reason for his disturbed night, Hall remained silent.

'Did you want to interview Miss Brown?'

'Yes Ed. But before I do, I'd like a quick word, if I may?'

'That's fine, fire away.'

'What do you make of her?'

Woodhall lit a cigarette. 'When we brought her in, I imagined she was a typical socialite. Parties, lunch with girlfriends, airy notions of voting rights for women. I changed my mind when I learnt she was the manageress of the Lyon's corner shop at such a young age. And between you, me and the gatepost, she's such a good-looking lass.'

'And how is she this morning?'

'She seems better. We gave her some new clothes, and she's had a wash. She's been asking about her mother.'

'And what did you tell her?'

'Only that we would wait for her return.' The Inspector stubbed out the cigarette. 'Do you want to see her now?'

'Not yet, Ed. I have a suggestion about how we might use her. Set a thief to catch a thief if you know what I mean.'

Woodhall checked the clock on the wall. 'By my reckoning, Otto's had a 48-hour start.'

'I've had an idea about that,' said Hall. 'But what I wanted to know was if you felt she has sufficient intelligence and wit to find him.'

'There's nothing wrong with her brains. She's clever and knows how to play a situation. What are you expecting her to do if she finds him?'

'I think it would be better if you didn't know, Inspector. I'm grateful for your assessment, but now I need to talk to her.'

The interview room looked shabbier than ever. Light seeped through a single grimy window; the bars on the window spoke of a prison cell. Faded cream walls were stained with the odd splash of tea, and green paint from the metal table had peeled away, revealing a rusty surface.

Evie was composed. She was wearing a blue striped dress, belted at the waist, falling above her ankles. When she sat, her hands were folded on her lap in a relaxed pose. Hall sensed his heart beating a little faster.

'Good morning, Captain. I hope you are here to tell me it has been a great mistake, and I can go home now.'

He let the silence linger, noting how her smile faded and the doubt crept back into her eyes.

'I'm sorry,' he said at last. 'There is no mistake.'

She raised a hand to cover her face in a gesture that mimicked his own ten minutes earlier. 'You are not going to release me?'

'No.'

'What about my mother?'

He shrugged, 'She will be looked after during

the trial.'

Her voice rose in alarm, 'Trial - what trial?'

'We know you have been collaborating with Otto Gratz, an agent of the German Secret Service. We have the evidence to prove it. I'm afraid the penalty is severe, and the outlook for you is not great.'

'What evidence?'

'We have witnesses who are prepared to swear in court.' He witnessed her dejection in the fall of her shoulders and the dipping of her head.

There was a long pause before she spoke. 'So I will go to court?'

'Evie, you are lucky. Collaborators in France and Belgium are being shot without a trial.'

Her eyes widened. 'Oh, God. My mother will die.' She became thoughtful. 'If I go to court, will I be investigated and questioned?'

'Of course, that is part of the legal procedure.'

Evie's eyes closed, and she remained still.

He breathed slowly, 'I could help you avoid prison. But it would mean giving me your full cooperation.'

'What can I do?'

He leaned forward. 'I could speak with the Inspector.' He gestured beyond the walls of the room. 'I could persuade him to drop the case if you agree to assist me.'

He held up his hand as she was about to speak. 'Before I answer any of your questions, I must tell you in helping me, you might get caught. If you do, you are likely to be shot.'

Evie considered his offer. 'And if I don't help you?'

'You go to trial. I can't say what punishment the judge will give, but I imagine you would be in jail for several years.'

She paused for a long spell. 'And what happens to my mother in the meantime?'

'We have nothing against her. She could live her life as normal.'

'Except it will be without me.'

He nodded.

She breathed. 'What do you want me to do?'

He assessed her response. The tone of her voice held the smallest hint of hope. 'We think Otto is on his way to Germany. We want you to go to Berlin and stop him before he can relay the information you gave him.'

She rolled her eyes towards the ceiling. 'And how do I do that?' She regarded him with a fierce stare. 'Kill him with my bare hands?'

'Yes, if necessary,' he replied mildly. 'We will give you some training and a firearm.'

'But Otto left two days ago. He will arrive in Germany long before I do.'

'So you admit you met Otto and gave him the information?'

A frown of resignation crossed her face. 'Yes.'

'Very well. I need you to think carefully before you tell me your decision. You can have an hour to mull it over.'

She breathed deeply. 'I don't need an hour to think about it. You give me no other course. I will do it.'

'Including killing Otto? I don't know what the relationship is between you, but could you bring yourself to kill him?'

She hesitated, and her eyes hardened. For the briefest moment, he thought she was going to say something different to the question she uttered.

'If I fail, what will happen to my mother?'

'We would make sure you never see her again.'

Her eyes closed, and it pained him to see the effect of his words.

'Then, I will do it.'

A streetlamp illuminated a patch of grey cobblestones in Lombardstraat. A figure in a cloth cap and greatcoat emerged from the dark into the soft pool of light. Alexander Szek looked the other way along the empty street; at the far end, another figure stepped into the road. A quick glance around confirmed there was no obvious means of escape.

Abruptly he brought up a hand to cover his mouth, but the attempt to staunch the nausea was unsuccessful, and he bent over and vomited onto the pavement. When he straightened, the man under the streetlight was beckoning. Alex's shoulders slumped, and he advanced reluctantly.

The shadows underneath the stranger's hat were so dark that even up close, he wasn't able to make out all the details of the man's face. Yet some characteristics, the narrow eyebrows, a silver thread of a scar along one cheekbone and the stranger's height and build suggested they were acquainted. As the man wrapped an arm around his shoulders, he knew this was Karl Smets, the spy who had coerced him into copying details from the German's secret codebook.

'You're shivering,' Smets said in the now familiar gravel voice. 'There's no need to be afraid.'

If the words were meant to comfort, they had the opposite effect. 'I have given everything you asked for,' Alex whined. 'More than you were expecting. I'm keeping my part of the bargain.'

Smet's large hand gripped Alex's arm. 'You are. I'm not going to hurt you, believe me.'

They had moved away from the lamp, and Smet's face was unreadable in the darkness.

'Let's go for a walk.' Smets released his hold and led the way.

Further along the street, Alex glimpsed the doorway to his house and hung back. A hundred thoughts streamed through his brain.

But Smets had paused too. 'You will go home before the curfew. But only after we've finished our little chat.'

Alex shuddered, then matched the slow ambling stride of the older man.

'By now you must be familiar with forwarding

messages to Berlin for onward transmission.'

'Yes.' The surprise was clear in his reaction; perhaps he would not be punished after all. 'I get a few to send every month.'

'Is there a special format?'

'Yes. They begin with who the cablegram is from and to and their respective ranks, and the date and time. A code represents the destination country. The message body follows, and it is signed off by the initials of the sender.'

'So you know the code to forward a message to South America?'

Alex kept his curiosity from showing. 'Of course.'

'What happens to the original signal?'

'I place it on the pile. At the end of each day, they are bound up and filed.'

'And have you ever sent cables to the Consul-General in Valparaiso?'

Alex considered the question. 'I think so. Maybe one or two last month.'

'What route does the cable take?'

'I code the text and send it to Berlin by Wireless/Telegraph. Nauen recodes the signal and transmits it to Valparaiso. Valparaiso re-sends the note to wherever the vice-admiral is.'

'Suppose he is at sea?'

'Then the cable is sent to the nearest port. The admiral sends a ship to collect his messages, perhaps every few days.'

'I see. So it could be a week before he receives

the cable?'

'Yes, or more.' When Smets didn't respond, Alex elaborated. 'Bad weather at sea will delay the collection.'

'Right. I want you to dig out a previous cable from a high-ranking officer who has recently sent a cable to Valparaiso and make a note of the sender and receiver. Of course, it's vital you are not caught.' Smets halted. 'Do you think you can do that?'

'Actually, I know I can. The others go early, and I have to tidy up at the end of my shift. I often have to file the original messages and transcripts. Sometimes I need to retrieve a particular message when they ask for it to be re-sent.'

'Then I want you to send a cable to the Consul-General, to be forwarded to Vice-Admiral Maximilian von Spee, commander of the German East Asia Squadron. Mark the message Urgent and from your high-ranking officer. If you can, reference his earlier cable. Say something like this: Further to my cable dated 5th November to such-and-such, etc.'

'What's the message?'

Smets drew Alex into the shadow of a doorway and pulled a note from his pocket. 'Here. Send this, then eat it.'

'Eat it?' Alex could not keep the surprise from his voice.

'Eat it. It's very thin paper and easy to swallow.' Smets paused, then repeated the words for emphasis. 'Eat it.'

'All right. What happens then?'

'Then you leave no trace the cable was ever sent. It's unlikely anyone will ask about it, but if they do, make a show of searching for it, but say you cannot find it.'

Alex chewed his upper lip.

'I know how scared you are Alex. But if you do this, I will let you have a letter from your family. Think of that.'

Alex let out his breath slowly. 'All right. Karl, could I ask *you* for a favour?'

'Depends on what it is.'

'Please, could we meet in a pub next time?'

Smets grinned, pulled his cap down over his forehead and strode into the shadows.

It was dark when Captain Hall turned the starting handle on the car. The first drops of rain splashed on the windscreen, and he switched on the wipers while rehearsing the direction he would take. The easiest way to get to Blackdown House was via the boroughs of Richmond and Twickenham. But the concerns of the day intervened before he could mentally run through the route.

News that the battlecruisers *Invincible* and *Inflexible* had left port under the command of Rear Admiral Stoddart should have lifted his mood. But he learnt later they could only make a maximum of 10 knots to conserve coal stocks. To add to the difficulties, the ships were still being fitted for the expedition when they sailed. Several artificers and craftsmen remained on board to finish the work. Hall banged the wheel in frustration.

It was already late, and if he didn't start soon, everyone would be in bed when he reached his destination. Blackdown Camp had been set up by the War Office over ten years ago near the village of Deepcut. The main house was renamed Blackdown House when the army took over and was now occupied by the 2nd Battalion of King's Royal Rifle Corps.

He reread her note with a grunt of annoyance.

Dear Captain Hall, please may I see you before I go?

Evie

Undercover of darkness, he was setting off on a journey to meet a spy. He should be at home, resting in front of the fire with a glass of sherry. The war seemed to have the power to thwart everyone's best intentions.

It was his own fault. If he admitted he had let Otto Gratz escape, carrying the knowledge the British navy had found the key to the German codebooks, he would not be in this situation now. He might have lost his post at the Admiralty, but he would not be involved in a hare-

brained scheme to commit another spy to intercept Otto Gratz before the secret was discovered.

And to make matters ten times worse, he was
forced to send Evie Brown on the mission. No-
one else had the knowledge she possessed about
the chameleon-like Gratz. She was not only
beautiful, but also a sensitive woman with only
thoughts for her mother and family.

He scowled in the dim interior. Something had
changed in him, he wasn't sure what exactly. He
inspected the view out of the side window to
take his mind away from increasingly bitter re-
flections. The black silhouette of Twickenham
stadium loomed ahead. The rugby games ended
three months ago when the ground was given
over to graze cattle and sheep - another change
brought about by the war, but one that was
strangely affecting.

Two missed turns and an hour later, he arrived
at the Blackdown Barracks. There were half a
dozen barracks scattered over acres of land with
Blackdown House at the centre. He had wanted
to avoid placing Evie in any of the barracks -
apart from the fact she would stand out amongst
the thousands of men - her training sessions
were being conducted in secret.

Hall braked to a stop on the stretch of concrete
outside a large isolated mansion. An imposing
figure stood to attention at the top of the stairs.
His shadow spilled over the steps in a jagged rep-
resentation of a soldier at arms.

CHAPTER 16

Alex worried his upper lip. Anxiety caused his forehead to feel clammy, his stomach to writhe, his head to turn dizzy. His fingertips developed pins and needles, and he rubbed them together to dispel the inescapable experience of fear. Today he had resolved to send the telegraph.

He exhaled slowly. He sent hundreds of telegrams every day, so one more should not cause so much distress. But this would be an unofficial message he had composed himself. If he were found out, there would be only one outcome. Two - he corrected himself - they would torture him for information before taking his life. The idea caused another bout of nausea to ripple through his intestines.

'Are you all right, Alex? You look faint.' Günter was the youngest and most sympathetic of his three colleagues.

'I'm fine. Just a touch of diarrhoea.'

'Well, if you're sure...' Günter placed his last

completed transmission on the day's pile. 'We're going to La Fleur En Papier Doré for lunch. Mind the shop while we're out, won't you?'

Alex nodded, hardly daring to speak. While he waited for the three telegraph operators to finish up, he busied himself with filing the previous day's signals. After they left, he lingered for five minutes to ensure no-one returned unexpectedly and then removed a slip of paper from an inside pocket. His hand grasped the telegraph key, and he tapped out the prepared note. He was the fastest sender amongst the four operators, and his finger tapped the key so rapidly it sounded like the staccato beat of a drum roll. Within a minute, the telegram had gone, and it was necessary to get rid of the paper. He found a box of matches and set the slip alight, allowing it to burn over a nearby ashtray.

As Alex poked the ashes, he imagined the telegraph operator at Nauen taking down his dots and dashes. He would find the numbers in the codebook and convert them to a series of letters which he would check against a table to produce the final message. From there, the words would be handed to another employee for retransmission over the wireless network. The text would have to be encoded and encrypted in the reverse process before the communiqué could be broadcast over the airways to South America.

'What are you doing?' Günter's usually friendly smile had changed to puzzlement.

Alex sat up smartly, colour draining from his cheeks. 'I ah.'

'Well?'

'I've started smoking,' said Alex, fumbling in his jacket. He produced a packet of Eckstein cigarettes. 'Would you like one?'

'No wonder you're so pale,' Günter laughed. 'I'll have one now for later.'

'Em, how come you're back so early?'

Günter scowled. 'Madame Jacobs has closed down because of the food shortages.'

'And where are Dieter and Hans?'

'Gone to find somewhere else to eat. I never thought it would be so difficult to get food in Belgium.'

Alex remained silent, but he couldn't help thinking. *We were fine until you came.*

'Anyway, to work,' said Günter.

A few minutes later, Alex realised he had offered Günter a cigarette from an unopened packet. Yet another muscle spasm twisted in his stomach. Would Günter remember he was supposed to just have smoked one?

Hall declined the offer of whisky and watched while the man opposite poured a stiff drink for himself.

Army Ordnance Corps Sergeant Aled Evans spoke quietly with a light Welsh inflexion. 'Evie Brown? First-class spy material, I'd say.'

'How is that?'

'Quick learner and she fights like a tiger. In the short stretch she's been here she's already proficient with a range of handguns and the rifle. I wish we could keep her for the front.'

'What else?'

The Sergeant eyed Hall steadily. 'Captain, most of our recruits spend up to six months before we send them to France. Three days is a ridiculously brief period. I wouldn't want the responsibility of her death on my hands.'

'It's not in your hands,' Hall replied gruffly. 'Strictly speaking, it's not in my hands either. She has to go tomorrow.'

'Well, I hope she returns safely, that's all I can say.'

'You could tell me about the other training she's had.' He heard the terseness in his voice, but there was nothing he could do about it.

'We trained her in hand-to-hand fighting on the second day,' replied the Sergeant. 'And we tested her with a variety of non-explosive weapons - knives, batons, kitchen utensils, that kind of thing. She nearly broke the instructor's arm with a rolling pin, would you believe?'

Hall exhaled, 'I imagined she would pick things up quickly. She was a manageress of a coffee house.'

The sergeant hesitated, 'There's only one thing, in my opinion. It's something that could easily be put right, but you should know.'

'Go on.'

'She's so pretty; she's bound to attract the attention of the Bosch.'

'Of course, Aled. And I'm sorry I sounded so brusque. I'm damned annoyed we have to send such an inexperienced woman on this mission. And, as you say, such a beautiful one as well. I'll mention it to her. Now when can I see her?'

Hall waited outside at the top of the steps and stifled a yawn. It was dark, with a crescent moon. From the surrounding barracks, sounds of shouted commands and replies carried over the still air. Even at this late hour, the army doesn't sleep, he pondered. Then why should anyone from the Navy?

Her footfalls sounded on the wooden veranda. 'Captain Hall?'

She stood in the shadow of the half-open doors, dressed in over-large dungarees that concealed her shape; she could be an aircraft mechanic or an ambulance driver. When she moved, the light fell across her face, and her eyes sparkled with animation.

'Evie.' He let the word settle. A moment later, he started towards her, and she stepped back. He stopped, ashamed at how the gesture had appeared.

She raised her head and looked him in the eye. 'You don't want to send me to Germany, do you?'

'No.' He coughed to cover his embarrassment. 'Unfortunately I have no choice; you're the only person I know who can identify Otto Gratz.'

An awkward pause followed. Hall's voice assumed a brusque note. 'The Sergeant reminded me of your attractiveness earlier. He pointed out that when you are in Germany, you should not draw attention to yourself. You must try to appear ordinary, let yourself go a little. Don't wash your hair, and definitely no rouge. The idea is to become faceless - one plain housewife going about a normal housewife's business.'

Evie cocked her head to one side. 'I see the sense of that.' She carried on in a light-hearted vein, 'Yes, I will remember to cultivate the appearance of a nondescript, uninteresting hausfrau, who only wants to live a nondescript, uninteresting life.'

'It could save your life, Evie,' he said sombrely. 'I don't want you to die.'

Evie's smile disappeared. 'If you don't want me to die, you would let me go.'

Hall hesitated. 'I can't.'

'I'm tired, Captain. Have you any more advice?'

'I'll only keep you ten minutes, and then you can rest.' He observed the soldier, standing guard twenty feet away. 'Let's go for a stroll.'

They walked in silence. There was light enough to see a path that led into the side garden.

'How are they treating you?' he inquired at last.

'All right, I suppose, If you don't mind being

woken at four-thirty in the morning and shouted at whenever you're too slow or just too dim. I have been ambushed with surprise attacks during the day *and* at night when I was sleeping. Surely that's not part of basic training?'

'It's no different to being in the Navy,' he said in a sympathetic tone. 'An attack can come without warning. Basic training comes as a shock to most people, especially those from the cities.'

Her shoulders rose and fell.

'What's the matter?'

She remained staring at something unseen in the shadows. 'The war has never been far from me, however much I've tried to avoid it. Now I'm forced to see it because it's right in front of me. It's like an animal, watching me, waiting for me to move.' She quivered. 'Waiting to pounce.'

'Have you considered what you'll do when you return? Are you planning to continue working at Lyons?'

'No.' She started to walk again. 'I can't think beyond today.'

He caught up with her as they rounded the path. 'How are you finding the new clothes?'

'They're fine - how did you get them?'

'We still have a few German tailors left in London. They were very accommodating.'

'I can imagine.' She paused, 'How is my mother?'

He handed her an envelope and watched as she fingered the flap. It had been opened, and no attempt had been made to stick it back.

She drew the page close to her eyes. As she read by the faint light of the moon, he regarded her carefully, noting the smooth skin and glossy curls of hair resting against the collar of her overalls.

When she finished reading, she said, 'Thank you Captain, this is reassuring.'

He waited. When she didn't speak, he said, 'You asked to see me?'

'Yes. I want to write to her.'

'Of course.'

'And will you deliver it personally if I don't return?'

He inclined his head. 'I promise.'

'Thank you.'

The silence stretched out. Eventually he said, 'Is there anything else I can do?'

She drew her head slowly from side to side. 'No, my mind's too full to think properly. I can't help wondering how I'm to get to Germany though - I keep worrying I'll arrive too late to be of any use.'

'I don't believe that will be a problem.'

'Very well, Captain. Can you tell me where I am to go once I arrive in Berlin?'

A cloud passed across the moon. 'Tomorrow. Everything will be explained tomorrow,' he murmured.

The car bounced over the ruts on the road, and Evie checked her Junghans pocket watch, noting the time. It was 7:32 am, not yet sunrise and a lingering fog hung over the low ground like a layer of smoke. She shifted in her seat for a better view of the countryside. 'Am I permitted to know where I am going?'

'Yes Miss Brown,' Sergeant Aled Evans responded in a rich Welsh lilt. 'We're on our way to Farnborough.' He changed down while concentrating on the track. 'Should be there in ten minutes.'

'My name is Braun,' she chided. 'You should know better than that.'

He smiled, and the car bumped over another rut.

After a minute, she darted a glance at the driver. 'So how am I getting to Germany?'

He raised a forefinger and tapped his nose.

They made the rest of the journey in silence, passing through the village of Farnborough before coming across a broad expanse of level ground, surrounded by a wire fence. In the distance, an orange windsock fluttered from a pole. They drew up alongside a hut, and the guard came out, examined the Sergeant's pass, and waved them through. The car rattled and jolted over the grass to a large hanger and stopped.

Outside the building stood a biplane with wings above and below the fuselage. There was an engine at the front, boxed off in a vertical grill which bore a single propeller. The two wheels below the cockpit reminded her of the wheels she had seen on children's tricycles. Her breath formed a mist on the windscreen.

The Sergeant was already out, bending over to peer through the driver's window. 'Well Miss Braun, are we ready?'

She opened the passenger door, without taking her eyes off the biplane and followed him towards the cockpit. He crooked an arm around a strut and lent against the wing. 'Impressive, isn't she?'

Evie stood facing the aircraft and reached out to touch the propeller. She slid her fingers over the highly polished wood, following the line of the curve up to the sky.

The Sergeant nodded in approval, 'Mahogany.'

'And these?' She indicated the wooden struts, spaced vertically between the wings.

'Aye, those too.'

She ran her fingers over the nearest, enjoying the silky varnished surface and admiring their elegant tapered shape. Through the tension wires, she saw a young man in uniform walking towards them.

'Morning, Miss Brown. Captain Morgan of the Royal Flying Corps. At your service.' The Captain dashed off a salute.

Evie glanced at Sergeant Evans, who regarded her critically.

'Mein name ist Fräulein Braun,' she said in an

annoyed tone. 'Ich weiß wenig Englisch.'

The Captain smiled his apology. 'Let me tell you about the aeroplane, as you are about to fly in her.' As they circled the machine, he gripped the wing surfaces, prodded the fuselage and tugged the rudder at the rear. 'Isn't she beautiful? She's an Avro 504 with an eighty horse-power engine. My wife says I spend more time with her than I do at home - which is probably true.'

He brought up a map case and showed her a map of southern England, the channel and northern France. 'When we leave here, we head for Fareham near Portsmouth to top up the tanks. Then we take off again and cross the channel. If my navigation is accurate, we will reach this airfield in northern France where you will be transferred to another aircraft with a new pilot.'

The Captain looked up from the map. 'Are you ready to begin?'

'Yes, thank you.'

The Sergeant saluted, and Evie reached up for a brief hug. Momentarily startled, he patted her shoulder. 'You'll be fine, Miss. Remember what we taught you, and you'll be fine.'

On top of the pile of the day's dockets was a letter, addressed in vaguely familiar handwriting. Captain Hall rolled up his shirt sleeves, grasped the vellum envelope and inspected the hand-written address. In the three months working at the

Admiralty, the number and type of letters he received had increased. Some came from the public, but most were from colleagues or senior staff. A growing number of ministers were also writing to him, and on one occasion he had received a letter from King George V.

The memory brought a brief smile. The King had written regarding a suggestion on improving training for naval cadets, and he promptly acknowledged the message and passed it on to Sir Alfred. Though George wasn't the brightest of the royals, Hall respected the King's naval experience. He had spent fourteen years in the Royal Navy and toured most of the world.

Unable to determine the author of the letter by the handwriting, Hall slit open the envelope and read. The message was from Constantine with an apology for disobeying orders and a heartfelt request for forgiveness. In an apparent gesture of reparation he had included a sheet of paper, which had an address written in Evie's own handwriting. Constantine's stated wish was to return to England in the near future, and his need to show "good faith".

The note did little to appease Hall's ire at Constantine's actions. But looking on the bright side, he had been able to 'turn' the woman into becoming an agent. She might yet stop Otto Gratz from reaching the ear of the Kaiser.

He picked up the phone and dialled Inspector Woodhall's number. 'Morning Inspector, Captain

Hall here. I trust you are well?'

Woodhall gave a guarded response.

'I wondered if there was any news about Evie Brown's mother, Elise?'

'Yes Captain, she has returned. I met her to break the news. Very upset she was, but she's settled down now.'

'You said nothing about where her daughter was going?'

'No, I didn't. I only told her the government required her for a short period as they needed more German translators. I think she believed the story.'

'Perhaps it would be best to put her under a 24-hour watch, Inspector?'

'Unnecessary Captain. The Home Office removed her passport. I explained it was a routine precaution while Evie is helping us.'

Hall flicked the corner of Constantine's letter. 'In connection with Miss Brown, I've come by an address in Berlin. There's nothing else on the paper, only an address.'

'From Evie?'

'Yes, indirectly.'

'I don't know, Captain. Could it be her parent's old house? When we detained her, she was about to flee the country, presumably to Germany.'

Hall nodded, 'Thank you, Eddie.' He replaced the handset. So the Inspector confirmed what Constantine was thinking: Evie had wanted Constantine to keep in touch with her when she returned to Germany. That could only mean she had feelings for him.

The thought sat like a stone in his gut. She was probably in love with Constantine, but there was no doubt Constantine was in love with her. In that relationship, there was no room for a middle-aged, balding Captain. He had been stupid beyond the point of all reason. Though he had sent her on a dangerous mission that could end in her death, the notion still lingered they might become close sometime in the future.

Captain Hall cradled his head in his hands.

CHAPTER 17

Captain Morgan handed Evie a cap and woollen gloves. 'Your hands will be frozen up there,' he advised. He helped her up onto the lower wing, and then into the front seat.

'Are you sure? Surely this is where the pilot sits?'

The pilot chuckled, 'You wouldn't be able to steer - there are no instruments!'

She settled in and realised the cockpit had not been designed for a woman - at least not a passenger as small as her. The sides of the frame rose above her shoulders, and her head only just cleared the fairing. Ahead, two struts supported the wings on either side, and she glimpsed the underside of the wing above her. She was too low down to see clearly through the tiny windshield. Across the tarmac, she spied a ground technician in overalls striding towards them.

Behind her, Captain Morgan laughed, 'We'll soon be away!'

But that proved to be more of an aspiration than a reality. The mechanic grasped the top edge of the propeller and yanked downwards, putting all his weight into the attempt. The engine wheezed. Again and again, the engineer tried and sometimes the cylinders would turn a few times, but they never started. A second technician joined the first, and together they heaved on the rotor, then stood back. The motor coughed once, twice, belched a mixture of oil and smoke and chugged into operation.

Captain Morgan adjusted the throttle, and the motor's revolutions increased, reaching a snarling hum. The rush of air almost blew Evie's cap off and brought a thrum of excitement to her midriff. One mechanic removed the blocks in front of the wheels and waved them off. They hopped over the grass towards a strip of tarmac while Evie's stomach began a series of slow turns, and she regretted the full English breakfast she'd had earlier.

Once they reached the airstrip, the airframe shivered, as if it knew what was expected. Gathering speed, Evie sensed the craft rise after a short take-off. It felt as if she had left her stomach behind, and for a second, she realised how fragile the aircraft was. The pilot had told her most of the fuselage was covered in fabric and offered no protection in a crash.

They ascended in clear cold air. The wind had strengthened, and her hair streamed away from her face. She peered over the side. Well-ordered fields, bounded by hedges, grew smaller. As the altitude increased, the aircraft responded with a sureness that contrasted with its lumbering progress on take-off. The vulnerability she had experienced before was gone, raising the possibility she might enjoy this new phase of her assignment.

The pilot yelled, pointing at the many army buildings dotted below. Over the sound of the engine, she heard him shout 'Aldershot Barracks'.

When she resumed her view of the horizon, an immense sense of freedom, of being above all her worries, calmed her racing pulse. She'd had no time to think about the future, only about the present. Whatever the fates brought, for now, she would experience this surprising and unexpected change in her life.

Reluctantly, Hall reached for the next docket on the pile. It was a partly decrypted telegram, dated a week earlier on the 5th November 1914. The text that had been decoded prompted a recollection; he had read something similar before but in a different format. He scanned the lines again, then opened the door and asked for his secretary to step in.

When Lord Herschell entered, he gave him the cable. Herschell scanned the top line:

> *"Further to xxx orders, xxx xxx supplies*
> *and xxx. Xxx to return to xxxxxx."*

'Seems familiar,' murmured Hall.

Herschell beamed. 'The code-breakers haven't determined all the terms, but I think it's the one you sent.'

Hall lifted expectant eyes.

'Well Captain, this is a guess, but not much of one. If we fill in the blanks, it might go something like this:

> *Further to previous orders, restock on*
> *supplies and ammunition. Prepare to re*
> *turn to homeport.*

'Ah, the orders we sent to Admiral von Spee. I'm curious - how did we obtain this copy?'

'The original was forwarded by encrypted telegram from Brussels to Berlin on route to von Spee in Valparaiso. We can tell that from the header information at the beginning of the message. To reach South America, they broadcast from the transmitter at Nauen. It's so powerful, we pick up her signals from the station in Hunstanton.'

'And we haven't filled in all the blanks for these types of messages?'

'No sir. This is a new code, and the finest people in the department are trying to do just that. But it is slow going. Take this message, for example.' He tapped the slip. 'If I'm right, then they discovered eight additional words.'

'That's excellent, isn't it?'

Herschell grimaced. 'Not really. If this latest codebook is anything like SKM, it will have over thirty-four thousand words.'

'I see.' Hall kneaded both temples with his fingers. 'Well, keep trying. I don't suppose there's any better system for discovering the codes?'

Herschell's forehead creased in a frown. 'The best course would be to find an original copy of the German codebook. There is another way, but it's so tenuous it's not worth mentioning.'

'I'm listening.' Hall smiled encouragement.

Herschell sat on the chair opposite the desk. 'Radio reception in the southern regions is often haphazard because of fluctuating atmospheric conditions. We think the operator sends important messages by a second, more reliable but slower route, employing a different code.'

'Telegraph?'

'Yes, sir. We would do the same in similar circumstances. But we still don't know what route they are using since we cut Germany's transatlantic cables at the outbreak of the war.'

'Could they be coercing a neutral state, somehow? Maybe they made a deal with a country such as Argentina? We have contracts with them for beef, wheat and grain, and it wouldn't surprise me if Germany had similar deals with her. They could use Holland or one of the Scandinavian countries to get around the blockade and secure their own supplies.'

'It's possible. We need to continue looking.'

Hall handed the note back. 'Richard, at times like this I believe we will win. I only hope that the message finds its way to von Spee.' He paused. 'Oh, that reminds me. I came across this yesterday.' He pulled out the middle drawer of his desk and withdrew a slip of paper. 'It appears to be a distress call from the Cocos Islands. It reads *Under attack from SMS Emden.* You'll see it's dated four days ago.' He passed it over the table.

Herschell studied the text, and his mouth tightened. 'I know the ship - she's a Dresden class light cruiser. Ten 4-inch guns and eight 2-inch guns if I remember; a well-known commerce raider. Commander Hope used to track her when he was in the chart room.' He stroked an ear-lobe. 'She was part of von Spee's original East Asia Squadron, but she disappeared soon after he sailed west.'

'We've all heard about her Captain, Karl von Müller. He's often spoken of as a gentleman.'

'You're correct. He's famous for sinking 25 ships with the loss of only one enemy sailor.'

'The Cocos ring a bell.' Hall rose and inspected the world map on the rear wall.

Herschell joined him. 'There Captain, in the Indian ocean. North-west of Australia, and south of Malaya. It's very remote. They had a telegraph relay outpost with undersea cables linking Britain with Australia and Asia.'

'I remember, the All Red Line. I assume those links were cut. How long before we can reinforce the station?'

'I would imagine a few days, at least. I will find out.'

'OK, thank you. I want to learn a great deal more - it would help me to understand how our telegrams are sent around the world.' He paused, 'how is it going in Room 40?'

'Sir Alfred hardly comes out of his office these days. Seems to prefer to leave the men to get on with their work. They're a rum bunch, most of them. Seem to sit about for ages, then suddenly there'll be a flurry of activity, and the pens and pencils will fly over their papers. One of them arrives on a bicycle and rides it along the corridors after hours.'

'So long as they work out the codes, I don't care if they come in on a pony.' Hall smiled. 'May I ask you a personal question?'

'Of course, Captain.'

'Are you happy working as my assistant?'

'Absolutely. I wouldn't want to change.' A worried expression crossed Herschell's face. 'Why do you ask?'

Hall held up a hand. 'No need to be anxious, Richard. You're not going anywhere, you're too valuable to me.' He placed his elbows on the table and clasped his hands together. 'When I was asked to join the group here at the Admiralty, I worried about my lack of connections. I'd spent all my life at sea, so the only people I knew were navy officers of the same rank and below. In my family, there were few links outside the service, and that was one reason I chose you to be my assistant. You have ties in royal and political circles. Are you still Lord in Waiting to George V?'

'Yes, Captain.'

'Also I understand you have a friendship with King Alfonso XVIII of Spain? That may become important in the coming months.'

'Yes, I do,' said Herschell.

'The reason I'm telling you is because of Turkey's intervention in the war. If I could use some trade argument to convince them to withdraw, it would make our task of defeating the Central Powers easier.'

'I'm not sure how I can help, Captain.'

'Not you personally, Richard. I'm considering enlisting another aide - a person with contacts in the city. If they have language skills, so much, the better. But they must be able to keep secrets and be very diplomatic when negotiating amongst the top men in their profession. I wondered if you knew anyone?'

Herschell pondered the issue. 'There is someone who might fit the bill. I have a partner in my stockbrokers firm, Cazenove & Akroyds. He's got a quick mind and loves entertaining. You'd like him.'

'Excellent. Please, could you arrange for us to meet him?' He eyed the stack of papers on his desk. 'Meanwhile, I've a lot more to do.'

A wintery wind blew across the platform of the Mannheim Hauptbahnhof, obliging the soldiers to pull their collars higher and well-wrapped Frauen to tighten their scarves. Evie Braun shivered. She had thirty minutes to wait for her train, but instead of using the time to plan, her thoughts flitted over the experiences of the past twenty-four hours.

Her elation at flying faded as the bitter cold invaded the cockpit. She could not move in the confined area, and after landing at Fareham, she asked for more clothes. When she returned from the toilet, she discovered two blankets on her seat, which she arranged around her shoulders and lap. Their protection helped keep her warm as they passed over the channel. She recalled the endless grey waves and her apprehension of crashing into the sea.

Before long, the coast of France materialised from the mist. Passing over dry land, however, didn't lessen the anxiety. It wasn't until half an hour later when they were circling the landing strip the knot in her stomach relaxed. When the aircraft trundled to a halt, time itself seemed to rest. She remembered the silence, the soft swish of the wind ruffling the grass and the quiet ticking sound the engine made as it cooled.

The next section of her journey sped by. A

tight-lipped young Frenchman hustled her into a car and drove her to an airstrip twenty kilometres away. There a similar biplane waited, painted in a different colour and with strange markings. She wrapped herself in the blankets and prepared for a lengthy flight.

As they flew over the French countryside, the fields and hedges below seemed untouched by the war. Farmers worked their land, and tiny cows and sheep grazed, giving a semblance of normality. Another brief touchdown and change of aircraft and they were on their way again. She imagined Captain Hall like a spider at the centre of a web, working behind a desk in a grey building in London, organising the logistics of refuelling and the rota of pilots.

But now the roads were filling with horse-drawn carts and motor cars. At one point she spotted a London bus and several taxis that would be more at home in the city. They followed the road for a while, watching as the traffic grew, flowing ever eastwards. A large encampment materialised, and she identified a white flag with a small red cross, fluttering outside a wooden building. The garrison resembled a village, stretching for half a mile in all directions, and she wondered how many men and women were housed there.

The plane gained height. She assumed the pilot wanted to avoid being shot at by soldiers at the front. He had explained earlier their aircraft, a Fokker, was an unarmed German mono-plane used for observation only. The plane had suffered engine failure over French lines and was captured and repaired by the Aéronautique Militaire. She supposed it was a miracle the French soldiers below hadn't recognised the craft and tried to shoot them down before now.

Then they were over the trenches, a network of ragged slits like the teeth on a saw. The enemy ditches were located a hundred yards distant. In between the blackened stumps of trees and blasted earth, a broken field gun surrendered to the elements. Small khaki figures lay scattered in no-man's-land. She stared at their crumpled forms, willing them to move, but none did, and tears welled in her eyes.

The flight lasted another hour until they set down in a farmer's field. The pilot gave her hurried instructions to the nearest village before leaving. From there she caught a bus and then a train to Mannheim where she waited, hunched against the chill in her thin coat and scarf.

A soldier sat at the other end of the bench and glanced in her direction. 'Sie sehen so kalt aus, Madame.'

She assured him she wasn't cold and declined his offer for a tot of Schnapps. Although this was the first occasion she had spoken German in years, she found the words easily, aware she had retained her Berlin accent. *That should not be so surprising* she reminded herself, *Germany had been her home for sixteen years.*

The soldier moved on, and Evie checked her handbag. The British had given her 3,500 Marks, the equivalent of one hundred and seventy pounds sterling - more than she would earn in two years at the coffee house in London. She touched the folded notes in the bag; they might buy her way out of trouble if she was careful.

Her fingers brushed the German passport they had made for her. The cover was formed from flimsy cardboard with an unflattering picture of her inside. All the pages were well-thumbed and stained to give the impression of age. The irony surprised her - Captain Hall didn't know she still had her original.

Captain Hall. He was so clever, but he was unable to conceal his affection for her. She detested him for exploiting her connection with Otto Gratz, but he had made sure she was looked after throughout the journey. When she entered Germany, she would send him a telegram containing only two words: *Tiberim traiecit.* He would understand the meaning of *Crossing the Tiber.* On reaching Berlin, she would send him a further message to let him know she had arrived: *A caelo usque ad centrum* - from the sky to the centre.

Waiting passengers started towards the platform's edge, anticipating the train. As she rose and smoothed her coat, a moment of dizziness overcame her, and she reached out to the bench to steady herself. She was thinking of Otto

Gratz. The Captain believed he had to blackmail her into finding Otto. But she had agreed to the mission for an entirely different and more compelling reason: one Captain Hall would never comprehend.

The sound of the train's arrival drew her from her daydream. Here in Germany, she was playing a part in the war, a minor role to be sure, but an important one. A cloud of steam enveloped her, and in the half-light her lofty convictions leaked away, to be replaced by a more disturbing emotion. The closer she advanced towards her objective, the greater her fear.

CHAPTER 18

The chartroom was one of the largest rooms in the Admiralty. There were a dozen large-style desks and despite this being a Saturday, there were many officers present. More were bent over the maps or regarding the maritime charts pinned to the walls. Some smoked pipes while others talked on the telephones. A few boys from the telegraphy branch darted in and out of the room carrying sheaves of paper and distributing them to their recipients. The steady hum of conversation portrayed an air of organisation, and Hall imagined their thoughts like clouds of smoke rising to the ceiling.

Commander Hope rose and came towards him. 'Good afternoon, Captain. Are you ready for the briefing?'

'No need for ceremony, Herbert. Before we discuss the Cocos, do you have any news about von Spee?'

'No Reginald.' Hope's despondent expression

was all the clue Hall needed. 'We know that von Spee and his crew were in Valparaiso until 4th November. They were seen leaving and the Consul-General relayed the account to us.'

'Where did they go?'

'Possibly Más Afuera. That's the most westerly island in the Juan Fernández Archipelago.' Hope hesitated. 'That doesn't mean to say it's their eventual destination. They were reported sailing ten days ago; even if they called at Más Afuera, they could have left for some other port since.'

'Blast!' What Hall's explosion lacked in volume, it made up for in forcefulness. 'I trust our telegram reaches von Spee in time. And what about the progress of *Invincible* and *Inflexible*?'

'Captain...'

'Reginald will do, Herbert.'

'Well Reginald, they only departed three days ago. Are you aware of their speed limitations?'

'Aye,' Hall muttered. 'I heard they must not exceed 10 knots. When are you expecting them to arrive?'

'Not before the twenty-sixth.'

'I suppose they need to economise on coal,' he said at last. 'Now I'd like a report on what's happening in the Cocos Islands.'

'We know quite a bit. We've re-established communications.'

'So soon? I thought they were waiting for a supply ship?'

'Ah, there's more to tell - shall we?' Hope led

the way to a chart table where a large map was spread out. A pile of transcripts rested on the top. 'Remember the location of the Cocos Islands, sir?' He indicated an insignificant speck in the Indian Ocean. 'And the All Red Line?'

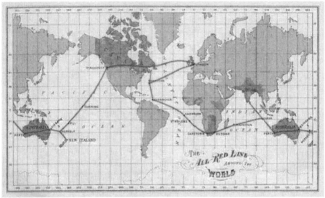

'The Cocos are a collection of small islands, the largest of which is Direction Island. That's where the telegraph outpost is situated. He pointed to a spot north-east of Australia. It's an atoll in the shape of a horseshoe.'

'I'm sure we'd all like to visit for a holiday, but what's your point?'

'Bear with me Reginald. The undersea cable from London goes to Capetown, then across land to the east coast. At Durban it enters the sea and comes out again at Mauritius, having briefly made landfall again on Madagascar. From Mauritius the cable goes undersea, rising on the eastern edge of Direction Island. At the opposite side of the island, one link goes north to India, the other runs south to Australia.'

'I see,' said Hall. 'One cable goes in, and two come out.' He pointed out the red line at the eastern end. 'So that's where I'd go. To stop communications, I'd only have to cut one cable, not two.' He contemplated the map, 'but how are we already in contact with the island?'

'There are several reasons, Captain. Don't forget, telegraphic cables work in both directions. Provided the Germans didn't cut the cables to India and Australia, we can reverse the route. We use the transatlantic cable from London to Canada, over the whole of that country, then across the Pacific with booster stages at Fanning Island in the middle of the Pacific, then on to Norfolk Island, east of Australia, before making landfall at Brisbane. From there we go overland to Perth on the east coast, and then undersea again onto the Cocos.'

'Bloody hell.'

'Yes, Reginald. It can be done, but you must understand this route takes a lot longer to get there. At each post, the telegram has to be recorded and the header decoded. Before resending to the next station, it is re-encoded. Some relay stages don't operate during the night, and as the signal crosses different time zones on its way around the world, it could be a week or more for a cable to arrive. A response could take as long to receive.'

'Fascinating. But you said there were other

reasons we're still in touch?'

A young lad arrived with a message which he handed to Hall. 'It's urgent, Sir.'

He took the folded slip and nodded to the boy. Turning to Commander Hope he said, 'Give me ten minutes, would you?'

Hall decided to read the note in his office. As he walked along the corridor, his heart beat a little faster, and he breathed deeply to curb the tension. Entering the room, he went to the window and unfolded the telegram. The brief content was dated yesterday.

Tiberim traiecit.

When Hall re-entered the chartroom, he found Commander Hope sorting through a sheaf of telegrams.

'Sorry to break off like that, Herbert.'

'That's fine, Captain.'

'Reginald, Herbert. Call me Reginald. Now, where were we?'

'I was about to take you through the order of events.' Hope reached for the message on top. 'First, some background. The operators on Direction Island were on the alert - don't forget, they received all the latest news from London and around the world. They knew the SMS *Emden* was a German raider and had already caused material problems in the Indian Ocean. She had sunk twenty-one vessels in the previous two months, and more than a dozen allied ships were hunting for her - but with no success. They were expecting a visit.'

He handed the cable to Hall. 'Here's their first urgent query to London. *Unidentified ship off the entrance*. You'll notice the date - the night of 8th November. They had spotted a warship. Four funnels would suggest a British cruiser, but they couldn't discover her name or establish her class. It was only when she sailed into the lagoon they realised the fourth funnel was false.'

He handed Hall two new slips, 'More panic messages to London, though the islanders shouldn't have been so surprised. The next morning a launch with nearly fifty crew on board landed on the beach, under the command of First Lieutenant Hellmuth von Mücke.'

'From the *Emden*?'

'Correct Reginald. It later transpired some of those were expert wireless operators. The landing party made straight for the base. The station commander, Superintendent Darcy Farrant, ordered his men to welcome them. When von Mücke arrived, there was a polite exchange and the First Lieutenant asked the station staff to leave.'

'Farrant handed over the keys to the broadcasting room,' Hope continued. 'There was no resistance, and the Germans smashed up the wireless sets and telegraph equipment. They were about to wreck the generator, but Farrant complained to von Mücke. He told him their ice machine would no longer work. They had to go on living on the island, long after the Germans left - might they allow them to keep it? And while they were at it, Farrant expected they would take down the radio mast. As their tennis courts were underneath, he asked if they could do it in such a way as to keep them clear?' Hope's eyes widened in mock astonishment. 'The Germans complied.'

Hall chuckled.

'After felling the mast, they set about cutting the cables.' Hope indicated the map. 'This shows a simplified view. Three cables enter from the east and more leave on the western side. As the Germans began at the eastern end, their ship, the *Emden*, came under attack from the HMAS *Sydney*. She had been part of a convoy bringing Australian troops to Egypt for training. They had picked up the island's earlier calls for help and sent the *Sydney* to investigate.'

He sorted through a handful of messages from the pile and summarised each. 'Von Mücke, his men and station staff, watched from the station - some climbed on the roof for a better view. According to witnesses, the *Emden* fired first and found her target, but the *Sydney* retaliated. She was more powerful than the *Emden*, and her shells pounded the *Emden*'s decks and superstructure, forcing her onto the rocks. Eventually, the *Emden* capitulated, and the remaining crew were taken on board the *Sydney*.'

Hall pictured the scene. The *Emden*'s Captain was one of only two enemy captains he admired - the other being von Spee. Both were independent spirits and knew how to command and inspire. Both accepted calculated risks, yet remained charitable to those they had defeated. And both exhibited the highest qualities of men at sea. His eyes rested on Hope's final cable. 'What happened to von Mücke's party?'

'They discovered the Governor used to own a wooden-built schooner called the *Ayesha*. They found her, but she was in bad shape, having been deemed unrepairable. Von Mücke ordered his crew to take half of the island's provisions and loaded them aboard. When the *Sydney* returned, the *Ayesha* had sailed.'

'How many onboard?'

'Three officers, six sergeants, and thirty-eight sailors.'

'You said there were other reasons the station could receive and broadcast soon after the Germans departed?'

Hope's mouth stretched in a wide grin. 'Superintendent Farrant kept a buried stash of equipment amongst the trees. He also laid extra dummy cables - two were cut by the Germans, thinking they were the real thing. The one genuine cable was spliced together by a supply ship which arrived a day later.'

Hall lifted his chin towards the maps and the pile of telegrams. 'I have to admire Farrant. Another resourceful commander, just where we need resourceful officers. I could do worse to become more like him.'

'Ah, sir?'

'Reginald to you, Herbert.'

'No disrespect intended, Captain, but I think you are more like him than you know.'

Hall smiled. 'Thank you, Herbert, that's been illuminating.' He inspected the last telegram. 'This may appear disloyal, but I hope the crew of the *Ayesha* survive.'

Except for the glow from the window on the first floor, number 36 Curzon Street appeared empty. Hall entered the house and listened. Normally the housekeeper would be rattling pans in the kitchen to prepare for tea. Sometimes there would be the murmur of conversation from the drawing-room as Essie, and her lady friends discussed their volunteering efforts. This evening there was only silence.

'Essie?'

His eyes flicked towards the stairs. When there was no reply, he mounted the steps in twos. Their bedroom was in darkness, but some light spilled onto the landing from the spare bedroom. He pushed the door open.

'Essie?'

She was sitting on the side of the single bed, with a large handkerchief pressed to her face.

'Whatever's the matter?' He sat beside her.

She blew her nose and faced him. Her eyes were red, and her cheeks blotchy.

'Essie, what's happened? Is it the children?'

She shook her head. 'Tell me, who is Evie?'

Hall's jaw went slack, 'How did you come by that name?'

She turned away. 'It doesn't matter. I've been thinking these last few weeks. Your air of distraction, the late nights. At first, I put it down to the demands of work, then on Wednesday I smelt her perfume on your clothes.'

'What?'

'You must have come home in the early hours. When I collected the washing, I noticed her perfume on your shirt.'

'Oh, I see.' Hall's eyelids blinked rapidly. 'It isn't anything, Essie.'

'Then what about this note?' Ethel picked up a folded slip of paper resting on her lap. 'The maid checked your pockets before the wash. She found this.'

Dear Captain Hall, please may I see you before I go?

Evie

'Essie! You really have got hold of the wrong end of the stick!'

Ethel stared at the far wall as Hall explained why he had visited Blackdown camp. 'So you see,

Essie, there's nothing to be worried about. She's only a spy.'

Her eyes dropped to the floor. 'Is she pretty?'

The question took his breath away. 'Essie, nothing happened between us.'

'But she is beautiful, isn't she?' Ethel faced him again. 'We've been married twenty years, Reggie. I know how you are. There's more to this than you've told me.'

'All right.' He paused. 'Yes, she is pretty. In fact, she's a stunner. The sergeant at Blackdown said she was *too* pretty, and I had to advise her about making herself more plain, so she wouldn't attract attention.'

He held Ethel's hand in his own. 'It's also true she is going to Germany, and almost certain she will die there. I sent her; if I really loved her, would I do that?'

Ethel searched his face. 'No, the man I know wouldn't. But you were torn?'

He clamped his lips together, then said, 'Yes, if I'm honest. She is a clever bewitching woman, and I was attracted to her.' He held both of Ethel's hands. 'Any man would be the same. But she's twelve years younger. Do you think she would give me a second glance?'

Ethel's mouth softened. 'If she had any sense, she would.' She drew close to him and placed her arms around his shoulders. 'Any woman would.'

The train drew to a stop with a squeal of breaks and a gush of steam. Evie gripped the door handle and lifted her newly bought suitcase onto the platform. It was remarkably light as it contained no clothes - just the two blankets that had staved off the freezing air while flying. To passers-by, the bag would lend support to her appearance as a seasoned traveller.

Other passengers swept around her making for the exit, and she removed a miniature mirror to examine her face. She had never dreamed the journey could be so exhausting. The earlier dab of powder and rouge failed to conceal the weariness she felt; her eyes were raw and puffy and limp curls dangled from beneath her hat. Captain Hall would approve.

As she strode along the platform, she saw soldiers boarding her train. The image of no-man's-land returned, a reminder of their likely destination. 'Arme Kerle,' she muttered, handing her ticket to the collector.

'Pardon?'

She flicked a hand towards the men, 'Die Soldaten,' she said, letting her grim expression give meaning to the words. 'How many of the poor buggers would live to return home?'

The man shrugged.

There was only one thought on her mind as she left the station. She would go home and sleep. Tomorrow she would buy enough provisions from the corner kiosk to keep her going for a week. She remembered where Otto lived and hoped he would call there before reporting to his commanding officer. After a rest, she would break in, hide and wait for him.

What happened after that would be down to her. The British sergeant had offered her a small handgun which she had declined. She knew she was a poor shot and would likely miss. The biggest issue though was the distinctive sound of it going off. Before long she would have to deal with nosy neighbours and the police.

Darkness was descending as she stepped out of the taxi. She had parked short of her street, and already the sights, sounds and smells provoked sharp memories from her younger life. At this time of the evening, there was no traffic, only a few locals walking in the unlit gloom. She rounded the corner where a line of large houses ranged either side. On the left, Mr and Mrs Fischer owned the sweet shop closer to town. Mrs Weber, an elderly lady when Evie was young, had occupied the bungalow opposite. And Mr Schneider, who lived alone next door, didn't like callers.

She spotted her old house, a spacious two-story detached building with a steep, pointed roof. Mock external timbers adorned the first floor, and in front was a narrow garden, now over-grown with shrubbery. The place was empty:

no lights glowed from the many lead-lined windows, and all the curtains were pulled close together, though not closed.

She checked over her shoulder. No-one was paying attention, and she opened the latch on the gate. She shielded her eyes, approached the bay-window and peeked through the glass. By moving to one side, she could make out the features of the drawing-room; it looked the same as when she had left, an old rug on the floor, an oak sideboard and armchair against two walls, and the same Haller mantel clock sat above the marble fireplace.

Her father must still be using the house during shore-leave. She followed the path to the rear garden. In the far border, she found a weathered bell from her father's ship, the *Augsburg*. She discovered a key underneath.

But as she placed the key in the lock, the door gave way, and she crept inside. The interior was in darkness, and a musty odour of neglect rose to her nostrils. Her immediate instinct was to switch on the light, but whoever had broken in might still be nearby.

The only illumination came from the transom window above the front door. She passed down the hallway, feeling her way. Her fingertips brushed the doorway to the drawing-room. When she was little, she was only allowed in when she practised the piano. She peered in, but there was no-one there. The next on the right was the living room which she recalled had an open coal fire and leather armchairs her father liked to lounge on when he was home from the sea.

Facing her, at the end of the hall was the kitchen. Through the gap, she saw a great enamelled sink on one wall and a table on the other. She remembered where she was standing when her father showed in a man and introduced him as Captain Steinhauer, the person she later came to know as Otto Gratz.

She whirled at a sound. Against the light in the hallway was the silhouette of a large man wearing a raincoat.

It was Otto.

CHAPTER 19

A rush of blood pounded her temples, and she gasped.

'What are you doing here?'

'I might ask you the same question.' Otto's voice sounded dry and ironic.

She didn't answer, and Otto carried on in a quiet, matter-of-fact fashion. 'After you told me your Russian Count was the courier for secret documents, I kept watching your house. I saw he was also under observation by a policeman from the Special Branch. That could only mean you were under suspicion. Either they would apprehend you and take you away, or you would leave. But where would you go? They are rounding up Germans and German sympathisers every day. You wouldn't be safe anywhere in Britain. But you were brought up in Germany, and your family home is still here.' He gestured at the surrounding walls. 'So it was only natural I visit to check.'

When there was no reply, he carried on, 'Answer me. Did I not help you and your mother travel to England?'

At last, she spoke. 'At what price? Even after we arrived in England, I couldn't move without looking over my shoulder.'

'That was the cost of accepting my assistance to move to England. Your mother agreed, and you understood all that.'

He took a step towards her, and she backed away. 'But there is one thing I do not understand,' he said, advancing again. 'How did you get here so quickly? Travel is difficult. There are countless obstacles.'

She retreated into the kitchen, keeping her eyes locked on him.

'Millions of British and French soldiers are trying to march into Germany. Many are dying in the attempt, yet here you are as if spirited through the ether.' Otto's frame filled the doorway, blocking most of the light.

She sensed the corner of the sink behind her and put a hand out to steady herself. 'You managed to get here, despite the difficulties.'

As he crossed the threshold to the kitchen, a shaft of light from the window illuminated his eyes. They were large and dark and fixed on her. 'After crossing to France, I had to pay for a place on a fishing boat. A bribe that cost a lot of money.'

She slid her palm to the edge of the table. There

was nothing on the surface.

'You have little cash. I know that' he said in the same low tone. 'Not enough to secure a passage on a ship, however small.' He waited. 'Unless you got the funds from somewhere else.'

Her hand dropped and came to rest on the handle of the drawer. The touch triggered a memory - it was where her mother used to keep the kitchen utensils. She remembered the wooden rolling pin and a few kitchen knives.

'To be here so swiftly, you must have had money.'

He lunged for her, arms outstretched, hands circling her neck. Her left fist, still gripping the handle, pulled the drawer out and the items inside clattered to the floor. She fell to her knees under his weight, bringing her right arm around with claw-shaped nails, raking his cheek. For a split second, he turned his head aside. Her mind went blank, powerless to recall any of her training. Only one element remained, not a move or a defence, only a principle: hit hard and fast.

Already he had the advantage. His weight forced her onto the ground. The grip around her throat starved her brain of oxygen, and she sensed her thoughts drifting. He moved again, kneeling over her, legs either side and ripping the buttons of her coat. He tore at her dress.

'No,' she wheezed.

With one fist around her larynx, his other hand ripped her undergarments.

She felt the chill air, and her voice faded into a whisper. 'No.'

He unbuckled his belt one-handed and cursed when the leather caught on the pin. Unable to free the strap, he let go of her throat. She sucked in air, and her flaying arms encountered an object on the floor above her head. Her fingers encircled the knife.

With a grunt, he freed the buckle, opened his trousers and thrust against her.

She brought her arm around in a fast scything motion, feeling the tip penetrate his side. He roared, but before he could snatch the weapon, she had yanked the knife out. As she prepared to strike again, he moved to grab it, and she stretched further out of reach. Her fist made contact with her other hand, and the touch gave her the strength she needed. She grasped the handle with both hands, bringing the knife down in a short arc with startling, savage power. The point entered beneath his shoulder blade, and his head fell forward onto her chest.

His breath felt hot against her neck.

As they stood on the steps of Number Four Grosvenor Gardens, Hall studied his wife. Essie's radiant smile communicated her anticipation of the evening ahead; a reception at the American Embassy was a first for both of them.

The doorman arrived, dressed in a waistcoat,

wing-collared shirt and bow tie. 'Good evening sir and madam. May I see your invitation?'

Hall handed over a thick card, and they followed the man along a wide hallway. Essie nudged him and pointed upwards to an imposing crystal chandelier.

'Stay aboard Essie,' he grinned. 'This Captain is going up in the world.'

A steward opened the double doors on the left with a flourish, revealing a party already in full swing. A butler with a tray of champagne offered them a glass. He hesitated. Didn't the Americans know about the rising cost of food prices in Britain? It would be insensitive to be seen with such an expensive drink.

Essie must have read his thoughts because she whispered into his ear. 'Every sailor is entitled to his daily tot of rum. When was the last time you were invited to a party?'

She had a point. His attention wandered around the large room: in the far corner, Captain Mansfield Smith-Cumming was giving forth to Walter Page, the American ambassador. Nearby, a small group of British politicians stood talking to Edward Bell, the embassy's Second Secretary.

'Oh, there's Lina,' said Essie. When Hall looked blank, she explained, 'Admiral Arbuthnot's wife. You don't mind if I leave you for a minute, do you?' Without waiting for a reply, she threaded her way through the guests towards her target.

Page spotted Hall and waved him over. 'Come

DOMINIC HAYES

and defend me from these hoodlums, Reggie! They're badgering me to ask Wilson when is he going to lend Britain a hand and join in against the Bosch.'

'You're well able to defend yourself, Walter. Besides, your president is a confirmed advocate for peace. I can't see him changing position because these gentlemen are hounding you.'

'Except we're not gentlemen,' said Herbert Kitchener with a playful smile.

'I was being tactful,' Hall murmured.

For a second, there was a shocked silence; then the men burst into laughter. Kitchener pretended to wipe dry eyes. 'They said you were a sharp one, Reggie. Nearly as sharp as your chin.'

'There's no need to be so personal,' announced Hall in tones so cold the conversation stopped. 'Unless I can retaliate against that bush you call a moustache.'

As the laughter resumed, Lord Herschell appeared by his elbow. 'Excuse me for the interruption, but can I have a word?'

They moved out of earshot. 'I found this telegram when I was going through the communications file.' Herschell handed him the form.

Hall studied the three lines of text. 'I'll need to think about it, Richard. Have you mentioned this to anyone else?'

Herschell shook his head, 'No, no-one.'

He leaned in close. 'Then in the meantime please can you keep quiet about it? I don't want anybody to know apart from you and me.' He stuffed the note into an inside pocket. 'And when do I get to meet my new assistant?'

'He's here, Reggie. I'll introduce you now, but afterwards, I must sing for my supper.' Herschell pointed towards a black baby grand piano resting on a raised platform. He brought forward a short man, a few years younger than himself.

'Captain Hall, may I present Claud Serecold?'

'Pleased to meet you, Claud,' said Hall, shaking his hand as Herschell strode to the piano. 'Has Richard said anything to you?'

'A little,' said Serecold. 'He told me you're in the intelligence section of the navy, and the war needed men like me to work for you because you're probably a genius.'

'Only probably?'

Serecold laughed, 'I'd prefer to make up my own mind.'

'I'd like you to have the opportunity,' Hall whispered as the room went quiet.

Herschell was sitting in front of the piano, hands raised above the keys. When the first chords sounded, Hall knew the piece immediately: Clare de la Lune by Debussy. He was surprised at Herschell's delicate touch and sensitivity and in the way he allowed the top notes to sound over succeeding arpeggios.

The melody brought a recollection of his honeymoon in Paris when they were first married: strolling along the Champs-Élysées, the

Eiffel tower at night and a visit to the Louvre. But the most memorable experience occurred when they were sitting on one of the pavement tables on Rue de Belleville. They heard the same piece on a gramophone machine from inside, and the combination of his wife's company, the location and the music became a special memory for both of them.

He looked across the room for Essie, but she was already smiling and looking in his direction. He raised his glass, and she acknowledged by raising hers. As the final chords faded to silence and before the applause, each sipped their champagne together.

After crawling out from under Otto's dead weight, she had paused for a while, staring at the wreckage of their fight. Her gaze was drawn to the knife above his coat, protruding above his left shoulder blade. A frost descended in the room, encircling her shoulders and arms. Her body trembled. She wanted to scream, but a voice within warned her of the consequences. Instead, she cried. She wept for herself, the trauma she had endured and the hapless fate that brought her back to Berlin.

She had not slept for the last twenty-four hours, and she wrapped her arms around herself. If she didn't sleep soon, she wouldn't be capable of planning for what lay ahead. She found her suitcase in the hall and ascended the stairs, one slow step after another. In the box room dust covered every surface. Her old bed stood in the corner, stripped of sheets. She removed the blankets from the suitcase, stretched out on the mattress and pulled the scratchy woollen covers up.

Sleep wouldn't come. Her mind roved over her childhood. Images of Otto kept appearing like a scene in a thunderstorm, illuminated by intermittent flashes of lightning. He had been a friend of the family since Evie was a little girl and hadn't married. She recalled her dad, teasing him about his lofty intention to remain footloose. Yet she had never seen Otto with other women. Instead, whenever her father was away at sea, he visited more often, sometimes staying over and sleeping in the spare bedroom at weekends. When she was twelve, she noticed him taking more of an interest in her. They would go for walks, and he would hold her hand when no-one was looking.

Things changed dramatically when her father returned home from his ship a day early. Then, she hadn't known why he and mother were so angry towards each other. But now she understood. Between the shouting matches and the bitterness, Evie's bewilderment turned to anger when Elise announced she would leave and take Evie with her. They were to live with her cousin Hildegard who was married to a farmer outside the village of Werder.

She recalled the day she left her school and friends behind, the tearful embraces, and her father's stony face as he saw them off from the train station. For four months they lived with Hildegard and her surly husband Bruno, a big-boned and boorish man. When she went to bed, she would hear arguments below between Bruno and her mother. Most nights, she would cry into her pillow before sleep came.

A week later, Elise summoned Otto. Evie had a clear picture of the moment he arrived at the farm. She was in the hay barn and had a clear view of the two, talking in the yard on upturned crates. He would throw glances in her direction, and each time her mother shook her head. She couldn't hear what was being said but had the distinct feeling she was the subject of their conversation.

After an hour, her mother came over. 'Darling,' she called. 'Can we talk?'

Evie's stomach was fluttering, but she pretended to be studying and flicked through the pages of her exercise book. Her mother sat on the bail beside her, smoothed out her skirt and regarded her with a long, searching look.

'I am very sorry,' Elise began.

'Why, Mama? You have done nothing wrong.'

The weak twitch of the muscles around Elise's mouth could hardly be called a smile. 'I have fallen out with your father. And because of that, we had to come here.'

'But it's not your fault. It's nobody's fault.'

'You are a lovely girl, Evie. Do you know that?'

She glimpsed Otto in the distance, smoking his pipe and pacing up and down. Occasionally he would glance in their direction.

Elise smoothed the wrinkles of her skirt, brushing over them again and again. 'I'm afraid we can't stay here with Hildegard. I have run out of money, and Bruno insists we must pay for our food and lodgings.'

'Why is Bruno so mean?'

'Because they only have enough food for the two of them. They share what they are able, but that can't go on forever.'

'Why can't papa pay? You always said he was well paid in the navy.'

'He is Evie. But we are getting a divorce. In the meantime, he will not pay a Pfennig towards our keep.'

She considered the statement. 'Is that why Otto is here? Can he pay for us?'

'No, it's not as simple as that. I am planning to leave Germany and take you with me. Otto is going to help.'

'Where will we go, Mama?'

'To England, to your aunt Margarete. She will take us in until we get back on our feet.' Elise stopped, and lines gathered about her eyes. 'There is only one problem.'

'What is it, Mama?'

'Otto demands a price for our tickets.'

'What price, Mama?'

Elise caressed Evie's cheek. 'After we arrive in England, he wants you to…'

Evie's dark pupils shrank, 'To do what Mama?'

'To run certain errands for him. They will be small tasks which you can do.'

'They why are you so scared, Mama?'

Elise stroked her hair and brushed a lock behind her ear. 'Because if you are found out, you might have to go to jail. What Otto is asking is not legal, but I will do anything I can to help you.'

'What sort of things?'

'We won't know until we get to England. At the moment, we have no money. And without his help, we won't be able to leave.'

'How could he be so cruel?'

Elise regarded her hands, folded neatly on her lap. 'I'm sorry, Evie, we have no choice.'

Evie's eyelids opened over eyes that rasped like sandpaper. She closed them quickly, struggling to catch the echo of her mother's words from her dream. 'We have no choice.'

But she was no longer on the farm. She sat up and looked through the window of her small bedroom. The street below and the neighbour's houses confirmed she was home in Berlin. Perspiration sprang on her forehead as she recalled the horrors of the night before: the shock of meeting Otto and their fight.

The bedsprings protested as she rocked on the tiny mattress. After a minute, she slowed and was still. There was no point in giving in to the feelings of horror and revulsion. She had to do something; there was a body to be got rid of. She would have to plan how to do that and escape.

She swung her feet off the bed and rose unsteadily in the grey morning light. Her dress was in tatters, and she clasped the ragged ends together as she tottered towards the landing. Down the stairs, the sense of dread increased with every step. As she descended the last stair, she darted a look along the hallway. Signs of their scuffle were obscured in the half-light, and she mentally prepared herself for the sight of his body. The kitchen door stood ajar, and her eyes narrowed to pierce the darkness cast by its shadow. She paused, puzzled and uncertain.

Otto had gone.

CHAPTER 20

The knife had a brown wooden handle. Her mother had used to use it to cut apples and peel potatoes. It wasn't sharp, but at four inches it should have been responsible for mortally wounding Otto. As she turned it, the light glistened from the congealed blood on the blade, a reminder that her effort to kill him the night before was a pathetically weak one. When she returned to England - if she returned, Captain Hall would regard her with eyes that saw through her. He would listen to her stutter as she recounted the fight with Otto and ask her why she had not finished the job after stabbing him. But she was exhausted from all the travelling and wasn't expecting Otto to arrive; the shock of his appearance gave him the upper hand. If she had considered it before, her old house would be the first place on Otto's list to visit. If she had been prepared, she would have given a better account of herself.

Hall's eyes would blink, in the way they sometimes did, but he would not respond - a soundless invitation to continue to fight her corner. Would he accept the argument that in those last shocking moments, Otto was unconscious and unable to defend himself? How could she bring herself to slit Otto's throat when she believed he was no longer a threat? Hall would remain impassive and ask why, given all the effort and expense in getting her to Berlin, she did not finish the mission when she had the chance.

There was no answer. She placed the knife on the table and wiped beads of sweat from her forehead. Stepping around the pool of blood on the floor, she followed the smear marks along the hallway and through the still-open door. Dawn was breaking as the trail carried on down the path and onto the road where it vanished. Perhaps someone in a car had spotted Otto and taken him to hospital. She scanned the street in both directions. Relieved there was no-one about, she dashed into the safety of the house.

Captain Hall's voice continued in her head. *You should not draw attention to yourself. You must try to appear ordinary, let yourself go a little. Don't wash your hair, and definitely no rouge.* She regarded herself in the mirror in the hall, surprised she already looked the part. In fact, her torn dress and dishevelled appearance made her appear more like a tramp than a plain housewife. One sniff of her clothes confirmed she was starting to smell, and she was starving, having not eaten anything in the last 24 hours. Now Otto was still alive, there was always the possibility of a police investigation. They might already be on their way. The thought propelled her into action, and she raced up the stairs to fetch her battered suitcase.

Vice-admiral Maximilian Johannes Maria Hubert Reichsgraf von Spee stood and raised his glass to the assembled guests. 'I hope the German people and the united Empire will be victorious, with God's help,' he said, reciting the Kaiser's toast from three months earlier when the Emperor announced the start of the war.

'With God's help,' echoed the crew in the wardroom. There was silence as the sparkling wine was drunk in honour of the occasion.

When von Spee sat, the Consul-General wobbled to his feet. 'Gentlemen, I am privileged to receive your invitation tonight aboard this fine warship.' He staggered and almost overbalanced in an ostentatious gesture to the four walls of the room. 'I would like you to raise your glasses to the SMS *Scharnhorst*, and all those who sail in her.'

'To all those who sail in her!' The toast nearly blew him back into his seat.

Honour satisfied, it was the turn of the German Minister. He had attempted to pace his drinking during the evening but had surrendered early to the uneven struggle. 'My friends.'

Cheers sounded around the table.

'My dear countrymen.'

Applause erupted amongst the men.

'My fellow comrades.'

They stamped their feet and banged their glasses.

'I am honoured that your Captain, a national hero in our homeland, has invited us to share in your feast.' He raised an almost empty glass. 'To victory.'

'To victory,' roared the assembled crowd. 'To victory, to victory.'

'Sir,' a quiet yet insistent voice sounded at von Spee's side. 'Sir, I have an urgent cable.'

For a second von Spee considered sending the messenger away until he caught sight of the telegram in the servant's hand. 'Very well,' he said, removing the message from the man's grasp. 'You may go.' He nodded to his First Officer to take over and headed for the deck. Standing against the rail, and with the massive barrels of the forward gun turrets behind him, he gazed across the waters of the bay of Bahia San Quintin. It was humid, and a waning moon silvered the water. On the distant hillside opposite, lights from houses glittered like stars in a black sky.

Home was six thousand miles away. Although born in Copenhagen, he had been brought up near the banks of the Rhine. Since then he had regarded Germany as his true homeland. It was clear from the many messages he had received she now wanted him and his Squadron to return. But at what cost? After the humiliation of Coronel, the British would send an overwhelming force to crush him. He recalled the scene when a lady had presented him with a bunch of Alum lilies in Valparaiso, over a fortnight before. The pro-German crowds that greeted him and the crew were jubilant; he had given the enemy their most significant naval defeat in over a hundred years, and the people rewarded their heroes with gifts, music, parties and dancing in the streets.

But his mood then did not match the delight of his admirers. Instead of thanking the lady for her generous gesture, he recalled the phrase he had uttered: 'These will do nicely on my grave.' Her expression changed to one of surprise and dismay; this was not how a conqueror should behave.

Since then some of his humour had returned. It was reasonable to suppose the British would exact revenge, but he could still outwit or outthink them. The biggest problem was the many conflicting reports of the whereabouts of British battleships. He turned the envelope in his hand and extracted the telegram. Here was yet another missive, but one that needed to be treated with care. He noted it was sent four days before to Valparaiso from a senior officer based in Belgium with information about the dispersal of British warships along the South American coast.

The light from the stairwell was sufficient to see the text and his lips shaped the words as he read.

> Further to existing plans, restock on
> supplies and ammunition. Prepare to re
> turn to homeport. Intelligence reports
> suggest British ships HMS Defence,
> Cornwall and Carnarvon stationed in
> the River Plate. No British warships
> at Stanley when recently visited by a
> steamer.

He folded the paper, stuck it in his pocket and pondered the contents. The note was odd: there was a misspelling, and unusual use of the words *komm nach Hause* instead of *Rückkehr zum Heimathafen*. It was conceivable they were caused by telegraphic operators as they re-keyed the message and relayed it from one station to another. Here, at this remote location, it might yet be possible to determine whether the directive was authentic, or posted by the British in some nefarious scheme.

He returned to the wardroom where the men were still in high spirits. Standing at the head of the table, the vice-admiral lifted his glass and waited until every one stood in silence. 'To the memory of a gallant and honourable foe.'

'To the memory of a gallant and honourable foe,' repeated the assembly.

'Oberfähnrich Zur See, please accompany me,' he ordered. 'The rest of you carry on and enjoy the evening.'

Back on deck, von Spee spoke to his Chief Petty Officer. 'I want you to verify my orders from a recent cable.'

'Yes, Admiral.'

'Contact our naval attaché to confirm the intelligence I've just received.'

'The naval attaché in Valparaiso, Admiral?'

'The one in Valparaiso, yes. You know him already. Speak to him directly about the location of British warships *Defence, Cornwall and Carnarvon*. Can you do that without letting anyone else know?'

'Yes Admiral, but it will take days by train to get there. I could easily telephone him from the port.'

'No, I prefer you to meet him in person. When the attaché has found the information, return without speaking to anyone else. If anyone asks you about your orders, refer them to me.'

'Yes Admiral. When do you want me to go?'

'Immediately. We have no time to lose.'

Von Spee watched as the man executed a salute, spun on his heels, and disappeared towards his cabin.

Otto heard a groan and caught a scent of blood. Moments passed before he realised the sound came from him. More seconds ticked by before the realisation dawned the blood was his too. He was face down on the floor, his nose above a sticky congealed puddle. Pain radiated over his back, centred just below his shoulder blade. Instinctively he stretched his left arm around, searching for the locus of hurt and encountered a kitchen knife. Fatigue weakened him, forcing him to rest. Should he try to extract it if it caused more bleeding? Would he be better off to leave it where it was?

His body needed relief from the agony, and his fingers grasped the handle and teased it backwards and forwards as he eased the blade out. The effort was exhausting, and he rested his head against the floor when it was done. Now the torment had diminished a little he detected another well of pain, on the side of his left thigh. She must have stabbed him there too, the vixen. The ache in his back and the throbbing in his leg were considerable, but she was only doing what any other person would do to defend themselves against attack. It was unlucky she had discovered a knife, and yet more unfortunate for him she had found the strength to use it.

Even though he lay motionless, his mind whirled with thoughts and speculation. He was convinced she had been sent to Berlin to kill him - but why? The British authorities must know he had eluded their grasp in Dover and was carrying the knowledge the Royal Navy had access to one of the German codebooks. Soon the Admiralty would break their coded messages. Then they could read Germany's secret communications to the entire fleet of the Kaiserliche Marine. A loud grunt escaped his lips as he placed his hands either side to lever himself into a kneeling position. He was still alive, and while he was conscious, he would use every fibre in his exhausted body to reach the Emperor.

But the attempt to stand defeated him, and he slipped full length to the ground. The only option was to crawl towards the front door and stop someone on the street, or flag down a motor car to help. Evie would have fled by now, he realised, so he would ask the police to track her down. The idea of meeting her once again, on his own terms, spurred his efforts. At the door, he gripped the handle to lift himself into a half-way crouch and lurched along the path. He paused at the gate to fiddle with the latch, all the while sensing his power ebbing away. Once through, he staggered to the pavement. With his eyes closing, he used the remains of his strength to stumble onto the road. He fell to his knees, unable to hear the rapid approach of an automobile. The last thing he felt was an immense blow to his side.

From Evie's vantage point in the window of her café, the broad boulevard of Invalidenstrasse stretched towards the east entrance of the Lehrter Bahnhof train station. The city had changed so much since she and her mother left sixteen years before. There were many more private cars on the roads, and she had already seen several electric trams. The women wore colourful clothes, set off with vibrant scarves or feathered hats. Above some buildings hung electric advertising signs. There was a throbbing pulse to the place, a sense of a people who knew where they were going and wouldn't stop until they got there.

And I know where I want to go too, but I can't get there, she thought. The rendezvous point was to be the port of Flensburg at the border with Denmark. Captain Hall had arranged for someone to meet her there. But he didn't have to risk buying tickets under the watchful eye of the police.

Earlier, she had bought a new dress, underclothes and a coat, and slipped into the station to purchase tickets. That was when she spotted several police officers, checking the papers of everyone intending to travel on the two outbound platforms. Behind the glass counter, a young and harried man looked up as she approached.

'I'd like a single ticket to Hamburg please.' There was no point in letting him know her eventual destination. She passed the correct money over. As the man retrieved the ticket, she asked, 'I'm wondering why the police are checking everybody's papers?'

The man paused and shrugged, 'Just routine, I think.'

With over an hour to wait, Evie sought a café to consider the journey ahead. She was travelling under the pseudonym of Elise Meier, her mother's maiden name, and her documents were in order. The fact that Otto was still alive changed everything. Her one chance of escape would arrive in an hour, but if Otto had spoken to the authorities and given them her description, she would be picked up and questioned. She stared at the steam rising from her coffee, once more, contemplating the war and its consequences. Her disguise would not last long, and when she was found out, she would face a summary execution, or worse.

But was Otto well enough to alert the authorities? He had crawled from the kitchen onto the street, so it was reasonable to suppose he would talk. Even if she could get as far as Hamburg, the police would stop her when she changed trains. Faced with the prospect of train guards also on the lookout, the likelihood of making the three hundred mile journey to the port seemed hopeless. And travelling would be as difficult tomorrow, or the following day, the two alternative days the Captain had allowed as a fall-back. Captain Hall had explained that if she hadn't found Otto by then, it would be too late as he would have gone to the authorities.

She considered taking the first section of the route by bus. Perhaps bus stations were less well patrolled? But if the authorities knew about her, the journey would prove equally challenging. However long she pondered the problem, there seemed to be no solution. Yet staying in Berlin for another day would be as dangerous.

As she sipped her coffee with an unsteady hand, a taxi pulled up to the station, and a passenger got out. She quashed the notion almost as soon as it arose: any taxi driver would suspect a fare when offered enough money to go to Hamburg, let alone Flensburg. But the idea persisted. Suppose she made for a town or village a short distance away. She could rest there until the search died down, then board the train further along the line. The suggestion also had the advantage of taking her out of the city. But where would she stay?

There was only one place where she could hide out for the required period - her aunt's farm near Werder. Would Hildegard still be there? If so, she would have to put up with her morose husband. Her options were limited: try to find somewhere to shelter in Berlin and be caught sooner rather than later, or lie low at Werder and attempt to manage the situation when she arrived. Evie swirled the coffee dregs and drank them down. The crockery rattled as she replaced the cup on the saucer.

CHAPTER 21

The taxi dropped her off at the bottom of the track to the farm. The suitcase bumped against her legs as she set off along a meandering rutted drive, trudging past fields belonging to the farms on either side. Unusually for mid-November, a skylark sang, high over a youthful green carpet of sprouting winter wheat. Evie drew in a deep breath, taking in the clean country air and the loamy scent of earth. This was what it felt like to be out of the city, away from the prying eyes of strangers and beyond the reach of police.

In a shallow dip ahead lay a group of grey stone buildings. Bruno had owned the farm for as long as she could remember. At the thought of him, her anticipation subsided. As she neared, she spotted a figure coming to towards her. The woman was dressed in wellingtons and an old raincoat. A drab scarf covered her head.

'Evie? Ist es Evie?'

The woman gazed at her for a moment, then

held her arms out and enveloped her in a hug. Evie felt her throat catch. Was this her mother's sister? Could this person, whose lined face was the colour of the soil, whose greasy hair rubbed against her neck and whose breath carried her surprise and pleasure at the meeting, really be her aunt? It had been over sixteen years since they had seen each other and she accepted, at last, this was Hildegard, a woman who had suffered deeply at the travails of time.

She drew back. 'Aunt Hildie. How lovely to see you.'

'Meine kleine.' Hildegard stepped forward to stroke Evie's hair. 'How are you? You have grown into such a beautiful young woman! Come, you must be starving.' She took the suitcase from Evie, swinging it as though it were empty and looping her other arm through Evie's. Together they walked, steering a course through the gate, across the yard and into the house.

'Sit down, and I'll get you some rabbit stew.' Hildegard cut a generous wedge of bread on the table and placed a steaming bowl in front of her. 'I am so happy! How is your mother? Tell me what has brought you to Werder?' She laughed. 'Sorry. I'll let you eat in peace.'

Evie dipped her bread into the thick soup and glanced around the kitchen. It was a large room, the largest in the house, she recalled, set in the centre of the home. She sat at a sturdy oak table which stood before an open-hearth fireplace, big enough for two people to sit underneath. A log fire burnt in the grate and the floor was flagged in flat-topped stone. Several rooms led off to bedrooms, and she glimpsed a utility room containing empty milk churns and tack for the horses. Nothing much had changed in the intervening years.

Hildegard could restrain her questions no longer. 'I hope everybody is well in England?'

'Yes aunt, everyone is well. Mama sends her love. I came to Berlin on business, and I couldn't go without seeing you.' She paused. 'Where is Bruno?'

'Oh, probably feeding the pigs, this time of day.' She touched Evie's arm. 'Don't worry. Now I expect you will stay awhile.'

'Just a few days, I'm afraid. Maybe a week.'

Her aunt lifted her head at a sound. 'Oh, there you are Bruno. Guess who's come to stay.'

A tall bearded man, wearing a discoloured overcoat, baggy trousers and boots, entered. 'And who might you be?' he said in a rumbling deep-pitched voice.

'Bruno,' Hildegard scolded. 'This is your niece, Evie. Don't you remember her?'

Bruno removed his hat, placed it on the hook behind the door and turned to Evie. 'Did I hear correctly? You intend to stay for a week?'

Evie looked across at Hildegard. Her aunt jumped to her defence. 'Bruno! She can stay as long as she likes.'

Bruno picked up the newspaper lying on the table and brought it to the stool near the fire. He opened it with a flourish and bent his head in the middle pages.

Hildegard regarded Evie and raised her eyebrows. 'Actually my dear, I had an inkling you might be visiting us. Wait a minute.'

Hildegard left and returned a minute afterwards, bearing a letter. 'It's for you,' she said as she handed it over.

Evie lifted the envelope to the light, recognising the flowing script with a jolt. 'Thank you, Hilde.' She cast a glance at Bruno. 'I think I'll open it later.'

That evening, Bruno and Evie sat at the table, while Hildegard bustled about the kitchen preparing the meal.

'You've not told us what brings you here,' said Bruno gruffly. 'Must be a dammed important visit during a war.'

Hildegard glared at her husband.

'Actually, it is,' Evie replied. 'I made the journey on behalf of my mother.' She regarded both of them. 'You know my parents divorced a while ago.'

Her aunt placed a large pot on the stand and shot a look at her husband. 'Sometimes I think it may be worth it.' She nodded encouragement towards her niece. 'It must have been hard for you and Elise.'

'It was. There was a divorce settlement, but none of the money due was returned.'

Hildegard dished out the Spätzle and pushed a bowl of Sauerkraut towards her. 'Go on, eat up, child.'

'Thank you,' said Evie. 'There were many complications. We were told the problems began after the war started. Getting in touch with father was difficult when he was posted to the Baltic. What with Britain and Germany at war with each other, nothing seemed to be happening. Normally, Elise would wait until the war was over, but she has...' She hesitated, searching for the right words, 'Financial difficulties.' She carried on, 'I hoped by coming over I could speed up the repatriation of the money.'

Having rehearsed this scene several times in her mind, she waited for their reaction. The argument seemed convincing then, but now she wasn't so sure.

Her aunt made encouraging noises. 'Oh, your poor mother. Fancy you having to come all the way to Berlin! But I expect you have sorted something out for her?'

'I have started. I had a meeting with the lawyers, and the wheels are in motion. I'm waiting for confirmation. In the meantime, I wanted to pass on my mother's regards.'

Bruno's newspaper rustled as he looked up, 'Which lawyers?'

'Which lawyers?' Evie struggled to mask her

surprise.

'Yes, which lawyers?' Bruno continued. 'You said you visited your mother's lawyers in Berlin. Which firm did you go to?'

'Ah, the one on Kaiserdamm. I forget the name.'

'Möller Partners?' he offered.

Evie suspected a trap, 'I don't think so. I don't recall.'

His voice grew heavy with scepticism. 'You came all this way to meet them, and you can't remember the name?'

'Bruno,' interrupted Hildegard. 'You brute, Evie is tired after her long journey! Let her rest, for goodness' sake. And put another log on the fire. Can't you see she's freezing?'

Bruno glowered and wiped his mouth with his sleeve. He moved to the stool by the hearth and made a show of selecting the smallest piece and threw it on the grate. The paper lay on the floor, and he sat and opened it, burying his head in the inside pages.

For several seconds there was silence, then Hildegard spoke. 'Don't mind him. His manners are not so good these days. He has to work longer hours, and it doesn't make his temper any better.'

'I'm sorry, auntie. I've come at a bad time.'

'No, you haven't. It is always a pleasure to see my niece.'

Evie caught the glance Bruno threw in Hildegard's direction. Rather than suffer another brooding longueur, she said brightly, 'May I help with the washing up?'

The stone sink lay in the utility room. She washed, and her aunt dried the crockery as they chatted. 'Bruno always seems to be busy, Aunt Hildie. Even when I was little, he was constantly out on the farm. We hardly saw him when we came to visit.'

Hildegard rubbed a plate vigorously with a tea-towel. 'Bruno has been a farmer all his life. He inherited the land from his parents after they died, and when we got married, we decided to make a go of it.' She paused to reflect. 'It was hard work then. We had sixty morgen, about a hundred of your acres, which is a lot for one man to harvest and till. And Bruno had ambitions to do more. He bought some cattle, and after a while, some pigs.' She smiled. 'And I had my chickens.'

Evie's thoughts shifted to the question of why they never had children, but she judged it too early in their newfound relationship to mention.

Hildegard carried on, 'You know our farm is almost entirely surrounded by others. There was a lot of pressure to sell up and move to the city. But Bruno was determined. He always said as long as we were together, we could make a success of it.'

She stacked the plates in the cupboard below the sink and brought out cups and saucers. 'Put the kettle on, would you, and we'll have some tea.'

Night had fallen during the meal. As they

waited for the water to boil, Hildegard's eyes strayed to the window. When she spoke, Evie had the impression she was not looking through the glass, but into their shared past. Her voice assumed a gentler tone as if relating a folk tale. 'We had two horses to pull the plough. And we had enough money left over from the last harvest to buy a seed sower. We were doing well.' She flashed a look of pride towards Evie. 'Oh, you'll never be rich as a farmer, but we worked hard, and we were happy.'

'What happened?'

A rustle of paper preceded Bruno's re-entry into the conversation. 'The war, that's what happened. As soon as the blockade of our ports began, everybody started hoarding, so groceries became scarce. The price rose, and only the richest businessmen and shopkeepers in Berlin can now afford to buy food.' Bruno folded the newspaper and tucked it behind the woodpile. 'Then the government fixed ceiling prices on grain. Most local people abide by the ruling, meaning I have to travel further to find buyers. And with the restrictions in place, I can't get fertiliser or I have to bargain for it on the black market.'

Hildegard nodded in agreement. 'Corn is so hard to come by: the government is allowing bakeries to substitute potato flour to make bread. We're lucky to be living on a farm - at least we can use some produce to feed ourselves. I feel for everybody in the cities, especially for families with children.'

Evie's eyes widened, 'Oh auntie, I had no idea everyone was suffering so much. Everywhere looked so normal in Berlin.'

'Well dear, it might appear normal, but every day we hear people are worried sick when they'll find their next meal. And no-one can tell us when the situation will get better.'

Evie got up abruptly and went to her room. When she came down, she deposited a pile of notes and coins on the table, a total of one hundred and fifty Marks, the equivalent of a month's wages in England.

'No,' Hildegard protested. 'We can't take your money. You're our guest.' She looked to Bruno for support, but none was forthcoming.

'We're very grateful,' he said in a gravelly voice. 'In ordinary times we would refuse, of course.' He stared at Hildegard, daring her to contradict him. 'But these are not normal times, and we are thankful for your generous gift.'

Hildegard remained silent.

'Now I have an early start tomorrow,' said Bruno, 'so if you don't mind, I will be away to my bed.'

The floorboards squeaked as Captain Hall made his way to Room 40. The staff had grown in the past few months and spread out into surrounding rooms, though everyone still referred to the section as 'Room 40'. A perfectly nondescript name, he thought, for what was the most important department in the building.

The atmosphere inside was very different from when he first came to the Admiralty. Two elderly men were posting messages into 'pigeon holes' set against the rear wall, and he saw a new pneumatic tube mail system had been installed. A capsule arrived with a startling rattle and dropped into the receiving basket with a loud hiss. The messenger unscrewed one end of the cylinder and read the message. After making a note in the register, he hurried out of the door.

Sir Alfred Ewing's office was tucked around the corner, almost hidden behind his secretary's desk. Mountstephen looked up at Hall's approach and beckoned him on. Mindful of Ewing's last sneering remarks about his locked room, Hall knocked on the great man's door and waited. Across the room, two younger men were pouring over a telegram between them with an air of intense concentration. He recognised one of them as Alastair Denniston. Rather than disturb their thoughts, he waved, but they paid no attention.

Today Ewing was wearing a black waistcoat over a brilliant white shirt with the sleeves rolled up above the elbows. A light-green bow tie provided the only splash of colour, and Hall suspected someone had asked him to moderate the flamboyance.

Ewing indicated the seat opposite. 'Glad you

could spare the time from your busy schedule.'

Hall wondered at the man's even tone. Was he being sarcastic, or genuine?

'I wonder if you could enlighten me,' he went on. 'We've intercepted a couple of messages that appear to be directed here. We only want to ensure they are being delivered to the correct department.'

'I'll do what I can to help, of course.'

Ewing pushed two slips of paper across the desk.

Hall picked up the first which said *Tiberim traiecit*. His stomach twisted as if an indigestible lump of food had caught in his gut. He read the second: *A caelo usque ad centrum*. 'Thank you, these are for my section,' he said, struggling to match the same even quality of Ewing's voice.

'Are you all right Captain? You seem a little lightheaded.'

'Yes. I'm fine,' he replied. 'I suffer from a chest problem. Nothing I haven't seen before.'

'They're on the cryptic side, wouldn't you say? There's no sender or recipient information, so it's reassuring they have reached the correct destination.'

'Yes, thank you. We have already received copies. Is that all?' He stood up to go.

Ewing remained seated, 'I expect they relate to a current operation?'

'Yes.'

'The earlier note: *Crossing the Tiber*, would appear to be a message from someone who has made it across the border. But which border?'

'It's best not to speculate Sir Alfred. The operation is secret.'

'It's in my nature.' Ewing shifted in his seat. 'And the nature of this office is to take an interest in all messages, especially as enigmatic as these. And in the second telegram: From the sky to the centre. I'm taking an educated guess here, but one would imagine an agent has crossed into Germany and made it all the way to Berlin.'

'I cannot say, Sir.'

'Well I'm sure you have everything in hand, so there's no reason I shouldn't mention them to Admiral Oliver?'

The knot in Hall's stomach tightened, and he pondered his reply. If he agreed, Ewing would go to Oliver. If he asked Ewing to keep it quiet, he would interrogate Hall and still might go to Oliver. On balance, he decided, it was worth asking the question.

'The mission is at a critical phase, Sir Alfred. Of course, you can speak to the Admiral, but if the operation were to be aborted now, several lives would be lost.'

'So Admiral Oliver is not aware of the details of this assignment?'

Hall drew in a long breath. 'No, Sir Alfred. My department is responsible for many sensitive operations, and it is not always possible to keep the Admiral up to date on all of them.' He gazed at

Ewing. 'And there are some assignments where it is better not to ask.'

'Ah.' Ewing regarded the telegrams lying on the desk. At last, he said, 'I see.'

'Now I really do need to get on.'

Ewing waved him away. 'Of course.'

In his office, Hall locked the door and threw himself into his chair. During the day, other, more pressing matters had caused him to put Evie to the further reaches of his thoughts. The whole episode with Ewing had brought her to the front of his mind again. He could visualise her face as if she were sat across from him: the knowing brown eyes that saw past his pretence of officialdom; lips that suggested sensitivity beyond her age.

But dreaming about her would not help now that Ewing knew about the mission. He would speak to Oliver, and Oliver would summon him to clarify the meaning of the telegrams. He couldn't evade scrutiny; the Admiral would get to the bottom of the escapade and discover he had sent an agent into Germany. He would want to know why, and Hall would have to explain how a German agent had come into possession of the Admiralty's most closely guarded secret - the British were reading all the Kaiserliche Marine fleet signals.

Once Oliver had exploded and calmed down, he would enquire why Hall hadn't seen fit to inform him and the First Lord of the Admiralty.

He would also want to know why he hadn't prevented the German agent from escaping England and conveying vital information to his superiors in Germany.

Hall rested his head in his hands. A court-martial was inevitable.

CHAPTER 22

Admiral Oliver caught Hall in the corridor outside his room. 'Ah, Captain. What's all this about
messages in Latin, eh?'

Hall lifted his eyebrows as if the question was
too trivial to raise, let alone answer. 'I have an appointment at the Foreign Office, sir. Can it wait?'

The Admiral remained motionless. 'Pop in before you go, Captain. Shouldn't take long to clear
up the mystery.'

Hall nodded.

On the way to his office, he popped in to Claud
Serecold's room. Only five days had elapsed since
the dinner at the American Embassy, when Claud
had agreed to become his assistant.

'Phone Mansfield Cumming, would you Claud?
Tell him to expect me in an hour.'

Back in his own office, Hall closed his eyes.
Oliver, now Chief of Staff following Sturdee's de-
parture, had more influence than ever with the
War Group. The interview with him could be the

first step in what could be a lengthy enquiry, ending with Hall's discharge from the Royal Navy. Dishonourable discharge, he corrected himself. Essie will be mortified when I tell her, not to mention the hierarchy in the Admiralty, and the high-powered politicians and civil servants he had met in his short term at the Admiralty. He could hear them whispering: 'Ran a spy, you know, female by all accounts. All quite hush-hush, but she came a cropper, and now the Hun knows we cracked their codes. They changed all the damn codebooks, so we go back to the beginning. Only it will be much harder, and so-and-so says we don't stand a chance in hell of breaking them.'

Hall's eyes snapped open; he had to face the consequences.

He found Oliver behind his desk, scrawling a note in the margin of a memo. 'Sit down and tell me about this business of the Latin signals. I heard they are in some sort of code?'

'They are, Admiral. A simple communication between my agent and the department.'

'I appreciate that, Captain. But Sir Alfred believes he knows the meaning. Is he correct in thinking one of your agents is in Berlin?'

'That is a reasonable interpretation.'

The Admiral raised his eyebrows. 'I only ask because if Sir Alfred can grasp the significance, then the Bosch will also understand.'

'That is Sir Alfred's reading of the cables, yes.

However, the message cannot be comprehended without understanding the context. Of course, we know the whereabouts of our agent, and therefore the information only makes sense to us. The Hun is completely unaware we have a spy in Berlin, and they have no grounds on which to interpret the cable.'

'I see. Is it also true our agent is...'. The Admiral was cut short by a loud knock. 'Yes, what is it?'

The door opened to reveal Claude Serecold, clutching a cablegram. 'Sorry to interrupt gentlemen, but I have an urgent message for the Captain.'

'Oh, very well.'

Serecold advanced into the room and handed over the folded slip. Hall examined the note and was soon engrossed. 'I'm sorry, Admiral, but this requires my immediate attention. May I have your permission...?'

Oliver raised his chin. 'All right, Captain, but I want to revisit this topic when you are less busy. Shall we say next week?'

Hall acknowledged and followed Serecold out of the room, closing the door after them.

'You took your time,' scolded Hall. 'Oliver was about to tug the noose.'

'Sorry,' replied Serecold. 'It was hard to judge the right moment.'

'Here,' said Hall, passing the cablegram to Serecold. 'Take this and get rid of it. I'm due at

Whitehall Court. Back after lunch.'

Serecold watched Hall's receding figure, then peered at the blank piece of paper before crushing it into a ball.

Although the weather was mild for the season, Hall was wearing his winter coat - a legacy of a cold spell from the previous week. His mind, still occupied by the narrow escape from Oliver, didn't register the short route.

Number Two Whitehall Court was one of several entrances into the grand 19th-century building which housed the Foreign Office, amongst other, less conspicuous departments. The Foreign Section of the Secret Service Bureau had offices on the seventh floor, adjacent to a suite of rooms which Captain Mansfield Smith-Cumming called home.

The lift squealed as it started its slow journey towards the top of the building, giving Hall the space to ponder his next move. Right now, it felt as if he was lurching from one crisis to another.

Mansfield was waiting for him, arm outstretched as he stepped out. 'Reggie! So pleased to see you.' He stepped back. 'You look like you've lost a destroyer and found a dingy!'

Hall glanced around the marbled landing. 'Not here, Mansfield. Could we go inside?'

'Of course, Reggie. Follow me.'

Mansfield led the way into his apartment. The

move was so unexpected, Hall paused at the doorway. 'We're not meeting in your office?'

'No, no. Colleagues to the left, friends to the right. Besides, I've got a special bottle of McKechnie's Old Scotch stowed away. Just been waiting for you to pop over for a taste.'

They walked into the sparsely furnished flat. The large carpeted room was dominated by a bookshelf lining the length of a wall. Opposite, two chairs were tucked under a gate-leg table and a lumpy settee squatted in the corner. On top was a folded copy of The Times, with the casualty list from East Africa uppermost, under the title "Roll of Honour". A pen lay near a half-completed page of a notebook.

Mansfield disappeared through a doorway, and Hall was drawn to the bookcase. There were several stacks of brown files from his office, books on warship construction, yacht design, engineering and cars. One tome was entitled Practical Port Defences, and he recalled that before the war Mansfield was in charge of protecting Southampton harbour. A single shelf contained photographs, and he picked up a silver-framed portrait of his friend, standing with a younger man in front of a Rolls. Both were smiling.

'That was Alistair before the accident,' said Mansfield from over his shoulder.

'A fine young gentleman.'

Mansfield handed him a crystal tumbler, half full of whisky. They clinked glasses with the toast: 'To our men.'

Mansfield indicated the chesterfield and reversed a straight-backed chair to face Hall. 'You don't seem to be quite your normal self, Reggie.'

Hall swirled the whisky but didn't drink. 'No. Something's happened at the Admiralty. I can't tell you what exactly, but I'm likely to lose...' He paused and reached across to place the glass on the table. 'Well, I'm about to be court-martialled.'

'Good God, Reggie. What on earth?'

'I made a mistake. It didn't seem important at the time, but now it's become a serious matter.'

'Is there anything I can do to help?'

'Thanks for the offer, but no.' He looked up, noting the concern on his friend's face.

'But surely, there is something...'.

'Actually, I came about another problem.'

But Mansfield wasn't to be distracted. 'Does Essie know?'

'No, I've not told her anything. It's a little complicated.'

'Ah.' Mansfield lifted his tumbler to draw in the whisky's aroma. 'Do I sense a woman in all of this?'

There was a long pause while Hall considered his reply; eventually, his lips formed a thin smile. 'You're very perceptive, but there is something even more important.'

'Very well. I'm listening.'

'Five days ago, I sent an agent to Berlin on a particular mission. They didn't show up at the rendezvous, or on subsequent days afterwards.'

'Five days - it's not enough time to be worried yet, surely.'

'Ah.' Hall regarded Mansfield. 'This particular assignment had to happen quickly, or not at all. The fact that she hasn't reported back in time is concerning.'

'A woman?'

'Yes, a woman. I wondered if you had heard if the police are looking for a British spy?'

Mansfield drew a notebook and pen towards him. 'Description?'

'Age thirty-two. Height five foot eight. Blond hair. Attractive.'

'How much experience has she got?'

'None.'

Mansfield's pen remained poised above the paper. 'You sent an inexperienced agent into Berlin?'

'There was no one else to do the job.'

'How much training did she have?'

Hall hesitated. 'Three days.'

'Three days?' Mansfield's voice rose in disbelief. 'You gave her three days and sent her to Berlin?'

'Must you always repeat what I say? I told you no one else could do this particular operation. I want to find out if you had any intelligence about her. Has she been caught?'

Mansfield closed his notebook. 'This much I can tell you: if there is an ongoing city-wide hunt for a female British spy, I would know. But she might have been detained already. Perhaps the secret police are keeping it quiet so as not to panic the public.'

'It's important I get her back.'

'Why?'

Hall didn't reply, but the agonised expression on his face was enough for Mansfield. 'Do you remember the conversation we had at the club?'

'Yes, I do.'

'Then you will recall the first rule of running an agent: *do not get involved.*'

'But there were no other options open to me. I just want to know what I should do.'

Mansfield folded his arms. 'An inexperienced female agent with only three days training wouldn't last a day in Berlin. Forget her Reggie. She's gone.'

Near the centre of the Parque General Cruz in Valparaiso, the Chief Petty Officer of the SMS *Scharnhorst* sat on an unoccupied bench, reading a newspaper. He was dressed in a wrinkled off-white linen suit whose creases had softened in the humid air. The officer was more interested in his pocket watch than the headlines; it was 4:45 in the afternoon, making the person he was meeting three-quarters of an hour late.

He folded his paper, deciding to take one last circuit of the park before leaving. He would ring the embassy tomorrow to discover what had happened, a delay Vice-admiral von Spee would find intolerable. As he rounded a corner, a man in a grey suit and Panama hat joined him, walking by his side.

The man doffed his hat and inclined his head. 'I am happy to make your acquaintance again. You may recall we met at the German Embassy when you were last in port.'

'I do, indeed. But I've been waiting - you're nearly an hour late.'

'Strictly speaking, I was early. I arrived before you to ensure you were not followed.'

The officer halted in surprise.

'Please,' said the attaché, 'let us keep moving. We are two gentlemen, talking a walk in the evening air. You see there?' He pointed to a life-size statue of a lady draped in a Grecian style robe. You may have seen several dotted about - they were moved here from the Victoria Theatre, following the earthquake eight years ago. The local authorities in their bureaucratic officialdom seemed to have forgotten to return them.'

'I've not come all this way to listen to a history lesson,' snapped the officer.

The attaché leaned in close and whispered, 'There are spies everywhere. I need you to give the impression we are simple tourists, only interested in culture.'

The officer gasped in exasperation, 'I'm in a hurry. Just let me have your report.'

'Of course.' The man pointed along the path.

'But please, let us walk.' He removed his hat and covered his mouth with the brim. 'We could not confirm the whereabouts of the warships *Defence, Cornwall and Carnarvon*. However, the embassy *has* confirmed there are no British ships in Port Stanley.'

'Thank you,' replied the officer. 'That is all I needed from you. Good day.'

The man in the Panama hat watched him go, then walked up a steep cobblestone street away from the park. Perspiration flowed, and when he reached the café, his clothes were damp. He ordered a coffee, and after a few minutes, a female customer entered the gloomy interior and sat opposite. She wore a wide-brimmed hat which cast a deep shadow over her face. From her handbag, she removed a brown paper envelope. She passed it under the table in a move so well practised, nobody would notice.

The attaché opened the flap and squinted at the contents below table level. At a rough guess, there were 500 pesos in old, used notes. He smiled and stuffed the envelope into an inside pocket, finished his coffee and left.

The amber liquid clung to the sides of the glass as Hall swirled the whisky. He lifted the tumbler to sniff the aroma, as he had seen Mansfield do. Unfortunately, neither the fragrance nor the flavour was on a par with McKechnie's Old Scotch; the alcohol burnt a raw course down his throat and left an acrid taste in the mouth.

His wife paused by the door. 'Reggie?'

'Yes, Essie.'

'I'm on my way to bed. Will you be coming soon?'

'You go up, Essie. I've some things to straighten out.'

She leaned against the doorjamb. 'You seem on edge these last few weeks. Is there anything I can do?'

'No, Essie.'

'If you tell me what's troubling you, I might be able to help.'

Hall expelled a long slow breath before replying. 'It's not something I can discuss with you, dear. You know I would if I could.'

'It's about the Evie girl, isn't it.' She said it like an assertion.

He stared into his glass. 'Partly.'

'You told me she might be killed. Is she dead?'

'I don't know, Essie. We haven't heard from her.'

'When you have recovered, Reggie, I am always here if you want to talk. Remember that.'

'I will, dear. Goodnight.'

He listened as Essie mounted the stairs and the bedroom door opened and closed behind her. And then there was silence. In the quiet of the living room, his thoughts bounced around the inside of his head like an echo in a church.

He heard Mansfield's voice again, grave with the warning: "Forget her Reggie. She's gone." Essie was right - he needed help from someone, but who?

His first thought was Inspector Woodhall from the Special Branch, but he had recently enlisted into the 1st Scottish Rifles. Mansfield had already dismissed the possibility Evie was still alive, so he should not expect support from that quarter. But if not Mansfield, who else? Perhaps a colleague at the Admiralty? He could discount Ewing, as the man was set against him. But should he? If he explained the position from the beginning, he might be persuaded to see the dilemma from Hall's point of view. Working against that assumption was the man's temperament, his rigid adherence to the rules and the mentality he was always right. No, he could not confide in Ewing.

Hall recalled persuading Oliver to reassess the situation regarding the Admiralty's communications with Admiral Cradock. He appeared to be a reasonable man. But when Oliver knew the full story, he would not want to get involved in any scheme to return Hall's agent. In all likelihood, he would assign a portion of the blame onto Hall. Hall would nevertheless have to undergo a court-martial, though the outcome under Oliver would not be as catastrophic for his career as any other chairman.

Hall could do worse than speak to a member of the War Group. The problem there was that all, with one notable exception, had very old-fashioned views - not only on how the war should be conducted but also on the conduct of the poor buggers waging it. Even after so many deaths on the battlefields, this was a game played by gentlemen under gentleman's rules. That kind of thinking was at odds with his own attitude to the serious business of gathering and using intelligence. Surveillance and espionage required cunning and deception, subterfuge and misdirection. Not one of his superiors was in favour of these attributes, so none would treat Hall's request seriously.

Except one. Churchill was a force on his own. He would grasp the issue immediately and throw out suggestions on how it could be resolved. There was a rather significant drawback. The burden of obsessive secrecy had originated with Churchill. It was Churchill who had written the *Exclusively Secret* memo which limited the number of people with access to the intercepts. More than anyone else in the Admiralty, Churchill would come down most heavily on those who allowed confidential information to leak to the enemy.

Round and round the whisky swirled, and round and round his thoughts circled. At a quarter past two, his chin dropped to his chest, and the glass fell to the carpet. He woke with a rush and the sudden realisation most of the contents of the bottle had gone. The answer to the question he had been struggling with all evening still eluded him. There was no-one he could turn to.

CHAPTER 23

Sunlight slanted through the kitchen window, and Evie moved to observe the courtyard. At the far side of the cobblestone square, a few bales of hay were stacked against the wall; dung stained the gaps between the pebbles and half-a-dozen hens pecked for fallen grain. The peaceful scene was broken by a tall man dressed in a black coat and wellingtons as he strode across the yard, oblivious to the chickens scattering in an eruption of flapping wings and raucous clucking.

In some ways, Bruno was more intimidating than when she was a young girl. Then, he was merely a figure in the background. He would often be out in the fields when she and her mother visited. Even when they ate together at mealtimes, he would leave the table first, claiming some job called for his attention: the fence needed mending or his growing herd of cows required milking.

Now he was agitated and angry. He had

avoided eating with them in the evening. She presumed he was elsewhere on the farm, attending to a never-ending list of tasks that drew him away from them.

After her first uncomfortable encounter with Bruno, she became grateful for his extended absences. His wife was his antithesis, warm where he was uncaring, generous and interested where he was rude and abrupt. It always concerned her why she should have married such an insensitive boor. Her mother avoided answering questions on the topic, and she wasn't prepared to ask Hildegard.

This morning, the fourth day of her stay, she climbed the stairs to her bedroom to fetch a book Hildegard had lent her. She stopped at the threshold; something had changed, but she wasn't able to pinpoint what. Perhaps her aunt had been in to tidy up, but the bed remained unmade, as she had left it earlier. She glanced towards the rough wooden wardrobe. Her suitcase was out of sight on the top, but someone taller might have spotted it.

She lifted a rustic chair from the little washtable, dragged it over to the wardrobe and reached down the suitcase. It weighed the same, but she needed to make sure. Placing it on the mattress, she opened the catches and sifted through the contents. Inside were her two 'lucky' blankets, the change of clothes she purchased in Berlin, and the remaining money from

England. She counted the notes - two thousand eight hundred Marks remained, so nothing had been stolen.

Underneath it all, she found Constantine's letter. The envelope was addressed to her in precise, loopy handwriting and as far as she could tell the contents were undisturbed. She unfolded the sheet, and a frisson of excitement rippled inside her belly as she re-read his note.

Dear Evie,

I sincerely hope this letter finds you well.

When we met at your house in London, we expressed our love for each other. I wanted to say more then, but there was not enough time. Now we are countries apart I want to remind you that no matter how long we are separated, I will love you. I love you deeply and think about you every day. When I wake at night, my thoughts turn to you, and I wonder if you still feel the same way about me.

My love is like a hunger, always present, reminding me that until I see you again, I can never be fulfilled.

Keep well, my darling and write when you can.

Your eternal servant,

Constantine

The paper fluttered in her hands, and she rose to close the window. So much had happened since they were together. In her hand was a constant reminder of those beautiful moments; his words seemed to call to her. But the relative safety of the farm and Hildegard's comfortable presence had persuaded her to remain awhile before continuing her travel. Perhaps now she should plan her return route to England.

She rested on the bed. The days at Werder had passed so swiftly, and she had settled into a pleasant rural routine. Hildegard would rise at six o'clock to prepare breakfast for herself, her husband and Evie. At six-thirty, Bruno would leave to milk the cows. After washing up, she would help feed the chickens and bring in the still-warm eggs. She hoped the longer she stayed, the more likely the search would be scaled down or even halted altogether.

She prowled the room. The table held an enamel bowl of water for washing, a comb and a brush. A thin towel hung from a hook on the wall. Opposite stood an iron bedstead with a straw mattress. On the stool beside the bed was a cloth, a candle and Hildegard's book. There were so few items it should be easy to spot if anything was disturbed, but everything was tidy. She tucked the chair under the table. When she first came to move it, it was positioned further out. *Such a little thing*, she thought. *But her life could hang on small details like that.*

Hall was late to work the next day. Although he drank spirits in his earlier career, the headache this morning was a salutary reminder he could no longer shrug off the after-effects like he used to.

Serecold popped in with a mug of piping hot tea. 'Good night, sir? Thought you needed something to wake you up.' When he saw the glare Hall gave him, he made a rapid exit.

Hall rubbed his temples and eyed the pile of paperwork on his desk. There was no point in feeling sorry, he reflected and picked up the first document. Five minutes later, as he reached for the next file, an envelope dropped to the floor. He bent to retrieve it and recognised Constantine's distinctive handwriting. It was a contrite letter he had written after leaving London and returning to Russia. Idly, he scanned the contents:

Dear Captain Hall, I am writing to thank you for your hospitality and under standing during my sojourn in London.

Please forgive me for not visiting you before I departed. I am afraid I left under a cloud and wish to apologise. You may recall your command to remain at the embassy and not to see Evie Brown. Against your strict instructions, I met her the night before my departure to advise her to leave England. I have no regrets about my actions since I wanted

Evie to have a chance of a life outside of prison. Once the war is over, I hope to meet her again. Maybe then I might be forgiven for disobeying your orders.

Should you wish to contact her, I enclose a slip of paper which she gave me on our last evening. You will see it is an address in Germany where I could keep in touch. I hope this gesture will go some way to making amends for my in discretions, and I may soon be permitted to return to England in the perform ance of my courier duties. Once again, please forgive the errors of my youthful inexperience.

Your eternal servant,

Count Constantine Benckendorff

PS Should you want to contact me, you can do so via my father at the embassy.

He recalled Constantine's expression of infectious enthusiasm and his positive outlook. A plan began to form, and after some thought, he decided the idea was worth pursuing. He would reflect on it without the distractions of the office, during his forthcoming train journey.

As seagulls swooped and called over the chilly waters of Grimsby harbour, a draught of cold air crept underneath Captain Hall's coat and squeezed his ribs. He coughed, and the tickle provoked a series of hacking rasps.

'Can I help ye?'

To ease the pain, Hall leaned over the iron railings, signalling there was nothing to be done. A minute later and the convulsions eased enough for him to speak. 'Sorry. Bad chest, you know.' He pulled his coat around him.

The man eyed him for a second and gestured to a teashop across the street. 'We should go indoors where it's warmer,' he said in a light Scottish drawl.

They crossed the busy road, and the man held the door open for him. Inside the air was warm and humid with steam coming from a huge urn that sat on the counter. A couple of tables were occupied near the door, and Hall led the way to take a seat at the far corner.

They ordered tea, and the man removed his bowler hat and set it down on the placemat next to him. Hall observed a shock of curly red hair and two blue eyes as clear as a tropical sea. The man held out his hand. 'Captain Alex Youngson.'

'Captain Reginald Hall.' He raised his cap and placed it opposite his companion's.

Alex regarded the two hats. 'They look like they're holding a conversation.'

'Captain to Captain. Though I'm glad I'm not wearing yours.'

Alex's eyebrows lifted.

'Small boat; big seas.'

'I'm glad I'm not wearing yours,' Alex responded. 'All that gold would give me a pain in the neck.'

A large lady came with their teas and plonked the cups down in front of them. She stared at Hall's cap, did a quick curtsy in her pinnie, and retreated.

'We've both come a long way, Captain,' said Alex. 'May I ask why you wanted to meet?' The trawler-man peered over the rim of his cup. 'Only the person who telephoned was 'na very forthcoming.'

'I came because I saw your name in the paper.'

'Oh, that! Suddenly I'm famous because the papers printed my name.'

'There's more to it than that, surely?'

Alex lifted his shoulders. 'Not really. I've no idea where the reporters got their story. Certainly not from me. Och, they talked to me all right. But what they printed bore little resemblance to what actually happened.'

Hall put his hand inside his coat and withdrew a newspaper. Moving his teacup, he spread it on the table and turned to page fourteen. 'It says here a U-boat attempted to sneak into Scapa Flow, where the Grand Fleet was anchored.'

'Aye, that bit is true. We discovered later it was U-18, a new boat by all accounts.'

'It reads here you were the first to spot her by identifying her periscope in the water.'

'Well, that's a lie.' Alex wagged his finger. 'It was

'na me or anyone on the *Dorothy Gray*. The U-boat had reached the Hoxa Sound by late morning and lay there for a while. I expect the Captain was waiting for a warship to come out. Are ye familiar with the geography?'

'Not in detail. But I imagine this would be at the southern end of Scapa?'

'Aye, above a large expanse of open water we call the Pentland Firth.'

'Oh, I know that stretch.'

'Then you'll also be aware it's one of the most treacherous places for currents, cross-winds and the like.'

'Aye,' said Hall in imitation of his colleague.

Alex regarded him sharply, but when he glimpsed the half-smile on his lips, he chuckled. 'I expect you do; she's not called Hellsmouth for nothing. Anyway, a steamer on minesweeping duties saw the periscope and gave the alarm.'

'And where were you then?'

'We had problems with the engine and put into Longhope to have it fixed. That's at the south end of Hoy, at least eight nautical miles north-east from where the U-boat was first spotted.' He sipped his drink. 'When Action Stations sounded, half my crew were ashore, and we had to sail with only five men.'

'And the patrol hunting the U-boat?'

'Oh, aye.' Alex's blue eyes drifted to one side at the memory. 'We tried to follow them, but the engine held us up. Before long, we lost them.

I thought then, that was it. What use was a trawler that could only make three or four knots? They would find the submarine and alert us on the return.' He set his cup down. 'That's when the sub commander surfaced, and we ran into him.'

'You didn't attempt to ram him?'

'No, Captain. It was more by accident than on purpose. Gave the sub Captain an awful shock though. He'd been lying low. I suppose he'd heard the flotilla pass overhead and reckoned he'd waited long enough. I guess he didn't hear us - our propeller was making slow turns because of the engine problem. As soon as he popped up, we were into him and rolled him on the beam end. I found out later it put his hydrophone motor out of action and broke his reserve steering gear.'

'So, what happened next?'

'The sub disappeared beneath the waves, and we blew our siren to attract the attention of the destroyers. We steered in circles and kept a lookout in case he surfaced again. The fleet was a long way off and we had a long while to wait. I can't imagine what the sub captain was thinking. We had knocked him to the bottom, about one-hundred-and-sixty feet. He could 'na see a thing because his hydrophones weren't working, and he had a posse of destroyers circling overhead.'

'German subs are a lot tougher than I imagined. How did you catch him?'

'He tried going east, creeping just above the

seafloor. He would have been blind at that stage. What with the currents and tides around Hellsmouth, the boat struck a rock and surfaced again. This time he was unlucky enough to be facing the *Kaphreda.* She's another trawler on minesweeping patrol, and she rammed him. Back down he goes.' Alex jerked his thumb towards the tablecloth. 'The destroyers were soon on station, but blow me, the sub almost escapes again.'

Hall waited, knowing there was more of the tale to unfold.

'The canny Captain was still trying to escape to the east,' Alex resumed. 'But the currents dragged him north, onto the Skerries. Anyway, the next thing we heard, she had breached her hull and had to make to the surface. When she came up, she was flying a white flag. They picked up all the crew, bar one man who drowned before they could reach him.'

'So, if you hadn't damaged U-18, she may have got clean away?'

Alex lifted his cup in silent acknowledgement. 'Now, perhaps you can explain why you wanted to meet me? It can't have been to verify a story in the newspaper?'

'In part, maybe. Tell me, Alex, what sort of fish do you trawl for?'

'You mean, before the war? Mackerel in the winter, and herring in the summer. Why do you ask?'

'How much experience do you have of bottom trawling?'

'Some. If you could be more forthcoming, I could give you a more precise answer.'

Hall dug out an envelope, placed it on the table and rested his fingers on top. 'This is a ship-to-shore telegram from HMS *Undaunted* to the Admiralty. I shouldn't be showing you this, or to anyone else for that matter, so I'd appreciate it if you could keep it to yourself.'

Alex moved to pick it up, but Hall's fingers remained, pinning the envelope to the table.

'Alex, this means no mention to your crew or your friends. Not even your wife.'

Alex paused. 'Right Captain, I understand.' He extracted the note and read it.

```
15:16 17 Oct 1914   Undaunted. to Adty.
Reliable information.  Sailor observed
throwing trunk overboard SS19 following
action off Texel 53 17'21"N 3 28'27"E.
```

'I'm beginning to see why you arranged to meet,' he said. 'You want me to recover the chest.'

'How likely would that be?'

'You tell me - how big is it?'

'We're not sure, Alex, perhaps something this size.' He held his arms about three feet apart. 'It will have a lead lining to ensure it sinks.'

Alex tapped the telegram. 'She went overboard four days ago. I'd need to check the charts for currents.' He looked up. 'How did it happen?'

'A British patrol encountered a flotilla of German torpedo boats off the Dutch coast. The Germans were on their way to lay mines off our shores. We sank all four of them.'

'If we trawled in that area, we might attract attention from a German patrol.'

'You might,' said Hall evenly. 'I'll make sure you have adequate protection.'

'You realise this could take a long time? The chest may never be found.'

'I'd still like to try. What else would you need?'

'Another three trawlers would help. We would divide the search area into squares and cover a lot more sea.'

Hall pursed his lips. 'I can arrange that. Tell me which ones you want, and I'll see to it.'

'Thank you.' Alex's eyes dropped to the note. 'You're not going to say what's in that box are ye? It must be very important, but ye din'na need to tell me. But what I would like to know is: why me? You've heard I'm not the hero the papers say I am.'

'No, that's true,' murmured Hall. 'But you're the luckiest fisherman I know.'

CHAPTER 24

A groan emerged from Steinhauer's lips. The sound encapsulated his boredom and constant pain. He had been waiting to see the Director of the German Naval Intelligence Department, and the intense ache in his back was a continual reminder he should still be in a hospital.

He had swallowed twice the recommended dose of Codeine before the appointment with his commanding officer, and the black-and-white patterned floor of the Bendlerblock building only reminded him of his incarceration in the Charité. The infirmary had one redeeming feature. But if he had to weigh that against the smell of excrement and decaying flesh and the bright lights of the surgical theatre glinting from the scalpel blade, he would have preferred to forgo the attentions of the pretty nurses.

Police Officer Gustav Steinhauer was known to Special Branch in England as Otto Gratz. And to Evie Braun, he corrected himself; she always called him Otto. He could recall her body beneath him, her bare midriff where he had torn her dress, the sense of an impending climax. But the outcome was both unexpected and shocking. His back throbbed as he recalled her words when she stabbed him the second time: 'No,' she had whispered. 'Please, not again.' The rest of his memory was blank until he came round in crisp linen sheets to the sounds of groans and cries of wounded soldiers in the nearby beds.

'Gustav, so happy to meet you again.' Captain Isendahl held out a hand to assist him to his feet. Unusually, Isendahl was clean-shaven. His alert eyes missed nothing, though his hair, parted in the centre, gave the impression of a haystack after a storm.

Steinhauer rose with difficulty.

'You appear to have improved since our last meeting.' Isendahl led the way towards an anteroom.

Steinhauer reached for his stick and followed the retreating form one painful step after another.

Isendahl waited patiently, holding the door open for his subordinate. Before the war, Steinhauer was one of the best police officers in the force. Isendahl had recognised his talent and moved him into section 'N', the Naval Intelligence Department under the Secretary of the Naval Office, Admiral Alfred von Tirpitz.

Isendahl's estimation of Steinhauer grew when

he discovered his gift for disguise and his ability to speak fluent English. He could worm his way into the company of the highest echelons of British society and the intelligence gleaned was always exciting and pertinent to the thinking of their politicians and peers. But the information he had imparted at their earlier meeting was not as momentous as he imagined. It was up to Isendahl to humour his intense and passionate colleague, a job he was glad to do if only to keep him loyal.

Steinhauer spoke first before either of them was seated. 'May I enquire what response you received from Admiral Tirpitz?'

Isendahl held his hand up. 'Gustav, you must know how these things are. I passed on your report about the possible loss of SKM..'.

'It's a matter of fact,' interrupted Steinhauer. 'The British already have SKM.'

'But there is no proof,' Isendahl responded smoothly. 'If I recall correctly, your exact words were *secret documents* had been given to the British Admiralty by a Russian courier. There is no evidence they possess the actual codebook, or the documents are German in origin.'

'These are from the *Magdeburg*. What else could they be?'

'You have documentary proof? A statement from someone who has seen it, perhaps?'

'I may not have physical proof.' Steinhauer's back straightened, and his voice grew louder with conviction. 'But I am *certain* they have it.'

'Therein lies the problem. I was about to tell you since your last visit I've exchanged cables with Lieutenant Commander von Müller and Admiral von Tirpitz. While they appreciate your diligent efforts and the sacrifices you made, neither of them wish to commit to changing the book until furnished with positive proof.'

A long silence ensued. Both men had been standing, and to break the tension Isendahl bid Steinhauer to take a seat.

'So there is nothing more I can say to convince you otherwise?'

'My dear Gustav, I am inclined to believe you. But without the support of my superiors, I cannot issue the necessary orders.' He relaxed into the chair. 'You do understand how long is needed to publish a new codebook - not to mention the problems associated with distributing it to our fleets all over the world?'

'I do, of course, I do.'

'From the Admiral's perspective, it's a monumental task that demands too great an effort when our concentration should be on winning the war. Also, Tirpitz made the point that if the British had broken our codes, they would exploit their knowledge of our fleet's movements and intercept our ships. There has been no sign of that, and until then, the book will remain in use.'

Steinhauer grabbed his cane and attempted to stand.

'However.'

Steinhauer remained seated and waited.

'However,' Isendahl went on. 'I offered a compromise that keeps our superiors happy and should satisfy your concerns over the security of our directives to the fleet. In fact, Tirpitz has already agreed to it.'

'And what is that?'

'I proposed we change the encipherment mechanism. You know we add this extra layer of protection to all our messages. It's considerably easier for us to produce a single page of substitutions than a whole book. I am expecting the new cypher to be issued in the next week or two. You should be pleased. In the meantime, I suggest you get some rest and get better.'

Steinhauer stood with visible effort. 'I have done my duty in bringing this to your attention. I only hope you never live to regret my advice.'

The timid knock could only have been made by one person - his new personal assistant Claud Serecold.

'Come in!'

Claud peeked around the door. 'Just wondered how your trip to Grimsby went?'

'I would prefer if you would stand where I can see you,' said Hall.

'Right, sir.' He strode in and stood facing Hall's desk, performing a casual salute while his face registered a cheeky grin.

'Claud, if I didn't know better I would say you have some good news for me.'

'Actually, Captain, I don't. Or rather, I have some news, but it's not good.'

'You'd best sit down and explain.'

'I contacted Ambassador Benckendorff, as you requested. He didn't want to talk to me. I was fobbed off by several underlings until I made it clear I wanted to speak to him on your behalf.'

'Carry on, Claud.'

'Eventually, I had him on the telephone, but he was very reluctant to give me any information at all. I offered to call at the residence in case he was concerned about speaking on an insecure line, but he told me it would be pointless. He had no idea of the whereabouts of his son.'

'Most unusual,' Hall murmured. 'Did you discover anything at all?'

'Nothing from him, sir. So I went through the Aliens Register and found Constantine was already in the country.'

'Unbelievable,' he spluttered. 'So where did you find him?'

'That was the problem. The Aliens Officer I spoke to at the Home Office said Constantine's passport had been endorsed with a red stamp, but not with a black stamp.'

'Meaning he had entered the country, but not yet left.'

'Precisely.'

Hall rubbed his forehead between fingers and thumb. 'Thank you, Claud. I'll take over from here.'

He dialled the operator and asked to be put through to the Russian Embassy. Half a minute later he was speaking to Ambassador Benckendorff.

When the pleasantries were over, Hall's voice assumed a more serious tone. 'Aleksandr, I am struggling to trace Constantine on an important matter. You may be aware he had to leave London suddenly. He had let slip details about a highly confidential subject to an enemy agent.'

'I know of the broad circumstances, but not the detail.' The ambassador's deep voice resonated down the handset.

'Only we've had some difficulty in getting in contact with him; it would be helpful if you could assist us.'

There was a slight pause on the line. 'He is here on official business. I'm not at liberty to say what. I can only tell you he is acting as a courier to deliver some sensitive and extremely confidential documents.'

'Thank you, Aleksandr. Please give my regards to your wife and accept my apologies for disturbing you.'

'Not at all, Reginald. I heard you enjoyed the ball at the American Embassy. I must invite you and your wife to *our* next one at the Russian Embassy.'

Hall placed the handset on the holder and lifted it immediately. For the next two hours, he rang round all his contacts, enquiring if they had any word about recent Russian diplomatic correspondence. At the end of that time, he pondered the result. Not one person knew about any new Russian initiative to do with the war, trade or commerce. He contemplated the conversation with the ambassador and smiled at the thought of Essie's reaction when she heard about an invitation to another ball. But how did Aleksandr know they had been to the American Embassy? He supposed the various embassies had their networks and passed along tit-bits of information. Nevertheless, it was a little out of keeping for Aleksandr to mention their attendance at the American ball. Perhaps he was dropping a small clue for Hall to follow?

He visited 'the library' on the first floor of the Admiralty, taking down and skimming several tomes dealing with Russian - American treaties. After half an hour, he came across an entry referring to the abrogation of the U.S. - Russian Commercial Treaty in 1911, regarding the cancellation of America's 1832 Treaty of Commerce. The original dealt with trade agreements between the two countries but was rescinded when Russia refused to recognise passports issued to Russian-born Jews who had become naturalised American citizens. Was it possible Russia was making a fresh proposal, and Constantine was conveying this initiative to America?

The suggestion was paper-thin, but it was the only pointer he had. Back in his office, he paused before picking up the handset again. If Constantine was travelling to the U.S., he would most likely embark in Liverpool. Hall's next call was to the port authorities; he waited while they checked the register.

The clerk came on the line. 'Sorry Captain, there's no record of anyone called Benckendorff on any ship sailing to America for the rest of this week.'

'How many ships left today?'

There was another silence. 'Two, sir. The Alcantara departed at eleven-fifteen.' A pause. 'No-one by that name on the passenger list.'

'What about the second liner?'

'Wait a second, Captain. The Adriatic should have sailed, but she's been delayed with a boiler problem. Port engineers are trying to fix it.'

'And Benckendorff?'

'Hold on, Captain... Yes, his name is here. Benckendorff, C. Count.'

'Right, thank goodness! Now get me the harbour master, quickly!'

'Yes sir.'

He heard the phone being dropped on the clerk's desk and listened to the sound of other telephones ringing and the voices of other clerks answering them. After a short wait, the clerk returned to the phone.

'Captain Hall, I am putting you through now.'

There was nothing quite like a ship leaving the dock on a long ocean voyage. The sound of the gulls and the noise of the crowd filled the dockside with an air of lively expectation. Bunting fluttered, and the occasional blast of a ship's foghorn amplified the mood of excitement.

Constantine leaned over the railings to observe the movement of the crowd below. With departure so close, the jetty remained thronged with well-wishers, stevedores and sight-seers. While he enjoyed the spectacle of so many people engaging in such a grand send-off, he was impatient to depart. When he was last in England, his visit had ended abruptly, and he had no wish to hang around longer than necessary. The prospect of a week at sea, bracing air and delicious food would help to put that behind. Now he could relax in his first-class cabin and look forward to visiting America.

A young ship's steward pushed through the crush on deck, repeating an announcement in a loud voice: 'Sailing in thirty minutes. Non-passengers, please make their way to shore.' Already the two gangways were lined with departing guests and relatives seeing off loved ones.

Down below, the multitude swelled with the influx of people leaving the liner. While he watched, two men on the fringe caught his eye.

Both wore police helmets and were making a route through the throng. They were heading for the gangway, sparking a tickling sensation between his shoulders. It was possible they were here on a different matter, but he couldn't help feeling they were coming for him.

He spun around and made rapid progress along the companionways and staircases onto the uppermost deck. Inside his cabin he opened the wardrobe and searched in the dark recess at the back, retrieving a leather satchel. It was still locked. He touched the cracked exterior, remembering other occasions when he had delivered the contents to their intended recipients. This would be another first for him, a predicament about which he shouldn't feel ashamed. Nonetheless, the circumstances would leave a lasting stigma.

He grasped the handle, locked the door behind him and worked his way down on the opposite side of the ship, arriving at the aft section of the main deck. Most passengers had either retired to their cabins or disappeared to the lounge or restaurant areas. He seized a moment when no-one was looking in his direction, and threw the bag as far out into the river as possible. There was a muted splash, and the lead-lined briefcase sank.

When he returned to his quarters, the door was unlocked. Inside the two policemen stood, legs astride, waiting for him. They were big men, broad-shouldered, and both wore moustaches.

His eyes swivelled towards the bed. Hidden beneath the pillows was his knife, but it would take far too long to retrieve.

The nearest policeman raised his warrant card. 'I am Sergeant O'Connor, and this is Constable Fosse. Are you Count Benckendorff?'

'Am I under arrest?'

'Please answer the question.'

'Yes, I am.'

O'Connor held out his hand. 'Identification please.'

Constantine found his passport and handed it to him.

O'Connor flipped through the document. 'We have orders to accompany you to a different location.'

'Whose orders?'

The policeman shook his head. 'We're not permitted to say. Please gather your things for the journey.'

'So I am not going to America after all?'

'No sir. Please hurry. They are keeping the ship back until we disembark.'

Constantine packed his suitcase and noticed the other man standing in front of the door, blocking the only exit.

'There, I'm ready,' he said.

'Let me see.'

As he held up his case for inspection, O'Connor slipped a handcuff over his wrist and clipped the other end around his own. 'Apologies for the ruse, sir. It's only a precaution until we reach our destination.' Constable Fosse grasped the suitcase, opened the door and stood to one side.

Constantine shrugged his jacket sleeve down to cover the manacle, and he and the guard left together. All the well-wishers had gone, hurried along by a blast of the ship's foghorn. As they stepped on the quay, he heard the orders to pull up the gangplank. He stopped to regard the stately liner. Dark smoke billowed from both funnels while the passengers on board waved farewell with hands, hats and handkerchiefs. Mooring lines were uncoupled, and a deep-seated rumble from the engines agitated the water.

'Where is Constable Fosse?'

O'Connor pointed to the second gangplank in time to make out the Constable hopping down onto the quay.

'Come on.' O'Connor nodded towards a black car.

The police car was waiting at the rear of the dock. Constantine was made to sit on the rear seat with the policemen either side. A short drive brought them to the side of Lime Street train station where he was ushered through a door guarded by an official. On the platform, he was waved through the ticket inspection and escorted into an empty carriage. Less than a minute later, the whistle blew, and their train pulled away.

The sun had set long before Constantine's train pulled into the terminus. They had been travelling all day, while his two guards remained tight-lipped for most of the time. At last, a whiteboard with tall black lettering slid by, spelling the name of the station: Folkestone.

He inspected his pocket watch, which registered nine-thirty. Even this late in the evening, the platforms were crowded. Men and women stood, packed into a formless mass of humanity. He supposed they were refugees from the continent, fleeing from the German army's advance. Some ladies wore bulky clothes and coats with fur-trimmed collars. Older men, some with walking sticks, regarded those around them or stared at the ground. There were very few children, and he wondered where they had gone. He hoped they were with their mothers, awaiting a different train to take them to a new home. Three British Bobbies kept the crowd away from a group of injured Belgian soldiers. Stretcher-bearers led the way to the exit, followed by the walking wounded, aided by their pals. He presumed they were making for a line of ambulance cars and motor buses he had glimpsed earlier.

Still cuffed to his escort, he stepped off the coach. The plight of the disabled and the displaced became apparent. Compared to the relative tranquillity of his carriage, the scale of the activity around him came as a shock. The noise of the throng was overpowering, like the muted roar of a wounded lion. Above the background clamour, he could distinguish the shouted commands of the orderlies and the cries of maimed soldiers.

In stark contrast, at the furthest platform, a cordoned off area was almost deserted. A single light shone on the door plaque: Stationmaster. As a stretcher party hurried past, O'Connor tugged him towards the office.

A short man in a naval officer's uniform greeted them. After a few muttered words, O'Connor undid the handcuffs. Constantine rubbed his wrist while surveying the exits. The policeman caught the look and shook his head, indicating he should follow the officer.

The man opened the door and entered; O'Connor and Fosse remained outside. Inside, the room was dimly lit. At the far end, a brass lamp illuminated a large circular patch of a rosewood desk. He could make out the silhouette of a person sitting behind. Beneath the light, the silver buttons on the man's jacket gleamed. Above the edge of the shade, his features were in shadow.

'Constantine, so glad to meet you again.'

Constantine recognised the voice immediately. It was Captain Hall.

CHAPTER 25

Hall regarded the man standing in front of the desk. He was tall, with broad hunched shoulders and dark hair. His eyebrows protruded, casting deep shadows and making the eyes unreadable. Lines surrounding the mouth, suggesting a wry and entertaining character, were now tightly gathered. While his posture marked him out as a sportsman, the overall impression this evening was of a wary and impatient athlete, about to erupt.

'Before you say anything, please listen to me.' Hall held his palm up in the light. 'You were detained before sailing to America and brought across the country. I know you have been travelling many hours and are angry at being under the restraint of your guards. You've had little to eat or drink, but most seriously, you had to abandon your assignment to deliver secret documents to the Wilson administration.'

'Am I under arrest?'

'No, you are not.' Hall leaned forward so his face could be seen in the glow from the lamp. 'In fact, after our conversation here, you are free to walk out of that door and resume your mission. We will not stop you.'

Constantine glanced behind. The small naval officer stood out of earshot at the rear of the office, away from the exit. 'I find that hard to believe.'

'It's true. There are some questions I need to ask, and if your answers are satisfactory, I may have a proposal. If you answer them and listen to my proposition, you will then be free to leave.'

For several seconds there was silence in the room. 'Very well, Captain. Let's have your questions.'

'I understand you are a bit of a linguist?'

Constantine's forehead creased in a frown. 'Yes, I speak five languages.'

'Including German?'

'Yes.'

'Fluently?'

'Yes, Captain. May I ask what is the purpose of your interrogation?'

'How long have you known Evie Brown?'

There was a pause. 'Three weeks.'

'When did you last see her?'

'Two weeks ago. She left England before I returned to Russia.'

'Have you heard anything from her since then?'

'No.'

'Have you written to her?'

Constantine didn't reply. 'Well, did you send her a letter to this address?' He produced Evie's note and the slip she had enclosed.

Constantine picked up the letter. As his eyes scanned the writing, Hall witnessed the muscles around his jaw clench. When he had finished, he looked up. 'Is she all right?'

'Would you be concerned if she were in danger?'

Alarm crossed Constantine's face, 'Is she in danger?'

Hall pursed his lips. 'We're not sure. I want to take you into my confidence, but I'm not sure I can rely on you - not after last time.'

'If Evie is in danger, I will do anything in my power to help her.'

Hall weighed up his words; they were said forcefully and with utter conviction. 'Constantine, I will be completely frank. I asked for you for two reasons: one, I believed your affection for Evie would provide a powerful motivation to complete this task.' He regarded Constantine directly. 'And two, I can't afford to send anyone else.'

After a short silence, Constantine said, 'I understand, Captain.'

'You must promise me never to repeat anything I say now to anyone else. Do I have your word on that?'

Constantine nodded.

'I need to hear you say it - do I have your word as an officer?'

'You do. I promise not to repeat anything said here.'

'Very well. Nine days ago, I persuaded Evie to travel to Berlin on an important mission. She was to meet up with a person who we believe discovered a state secret and intended to pass this information onto German high command.' He glowered at the man opposite. 'A secret which she had extracted from you.'

'Ah, I'm beginning to understand. And what was she supposed to do when she met this person?'

'Stop him. Kill him, if possible - before he passed the information on.'

'You are not serious. She isn't capable of killing anyone.'

'How well do you know her?'

'Well enough to know she's not a killer.'

Hall hesitated. The next question was the fulcrum to the discussion and would determine whether the plan went ahead or not.

'Do you love her?'

Constantine recoiled but refused to answer the question.

'Would you be prepared to go to Berlin, find her, and bring her home?'

In the silence, he heard the tick of the Station-master's clock on the far wall.

'Yes.'

'Thank you. We will give you some help, of course.'

Constantine straightened. 'Now it's my turn to ask the questions. You sent her to meet someone in Berlin. What is his name?'

'A police officer called Gustav Steinhauer. When the war started, he began working for the Admiralstab, using the alias Otto Gratz. We think he assumed a disguise to enter Britain and he travelled widely. We were aware he was in Scotland when he contacted Carl Lody - another German spy who was subsequently caught and shot in the Tower. Gratz was much too clever to be captured so easily.'

'You said you sent Evie to Berlin. If I am to locate her, where exactly is she?'

'We instructed her to visit the house belonging to her estranged father.'

'How was she to meet Otto?'

Hall didn't reply. After a lengthy pause, he began, 'We had no idea where to begin looking. We only knew Otto would arrive at some stage. Since we couldn't give her a location, we told him where to find her.'

'I don't understand - you told him where to find her?'

'Yes. We passed coded messages to Otto from someone he trusted.'

Constantine stood abruptly, knocking his chair to the ground. 'You told him where to find her?' He moved towards Hall.

Claud Serecold had been standing near the exit and ran forward to intervene. 'Please, Count. The Captain isn't your enemy.'

Constantine continued to advance on Hall, as Serecold pulled his arm. Constantine shrugged off the restraining hand and glared at Serecold. 'He's just sent my Evie to Berlin to kill a spy! If he isn't my enemy, then who the hell is he?'

'Sit down *Count*, and remember your manners.' Hall's sharp rebuke sounded like a whip-crack. 'Unless you wish to be confined to barracks.'

'I thought you said I was free to go.'

'You are,' said Hall evenly. 'The door's behind you.'

Constantine's large frame heaved. 'Where can I find her?'

'We don't know; she may be on the run. You could start here.' He pointed to the note Evie had written.

Constantine pocketed the slip. 'How do I get to Germany?'

'You return on the boat that's just arrived from Holland. You'll be met by a contact who will take you to a crossing point. The Germans are building an electric fence all along the Dutch border, but I'm told it's still possible to cross in many places.'

'And after that? How do we get back?'

'The same way. My contact will wait for you there.'

Constantine lowered his eyes to the floor as if

the threadbare carpet offered a solution. After several seconds, he raised his head and looked Hall in the eye. 'OK. I'll do it.' He marched towards the door, stopping at the sound of Hall's voice.

'You are forgetting something.'

He returned to the table. The object Hall had placed underneath the lamp was familiar. He bent over for closer inspection. It was the knife he had left on board the liner: his dependable Bebut Kinjal.

A biting wind lifted spume from the swell and carried it over the deck, damping the Admiral's uniform and moistening his face and hands with a fine spray. It was bitter above, but Admiral von Spee preferred to be in the open air than in the stuffy smoke-filled atmosphere of the wardroom.

He liked to believe he could glimpse beyond the dark shutters of the night, out across the vast body of water where his squadron was anchored. Yet even in daylight, he couldn't see the shore, so big was the Gulf of Penas. The enveloping arms of the mainland provided no protection from the west where a series of anticyclones appeared with unrelenting regularity. And when the weather came from the opposite direction, the wind would rake the ice of the San Quintín Glacier, and bring unwelcome freezing conditions like a cat depositing its catch before its master.

He shivered. They had endured four days at St. Quintin Bay since his remaining two cruisers *Dresden* and *Leipzig* re-joined the squadron. It was pointless, staying longer. To prepare for the lengthy and hazardous journey around Cape Horn, the fleet had topped off coal and the rest of their supplies. Now, there was nothing else to be done, except to decide about when and how to re-turn to homeport.

As he opened the door to the wardroom, the warm air made his cheeks tingle while his ears were buffeted by the raucous voices. Sat around the table were the commanders of the *Gneisenau*, *Emden*, *Nürnberg*, *Dresden* and *Leipzig*, their first officers and his own chief petty officer.

'Only an Admiral would be brave or foolish enough to be out on a night like this!' The com-ment came from Captain Maerker, commander of the *Gneisenau*.

Von Spee smiled, then sat and rubbed his numb hands together. 'Let's hope I am brave enough to beat the enemy and not foolish enough to allow you to accept the honour.' He grasped the proffered wine glass and raised it towards the ceiling. 'To a safe voyage.'

In the silence that descended, he guessed their thoughts had switched to their families and loved ones. Most of the men under his command here had been at sea for four months, and it was only natural they would be thinking of home.

'So we are leaving tomorrow?' Maerker's executive officer Pochhammer enquired.

'There are no favourable omens,' the Admiral responded. 'But I can't stand another westerly.'

One by one, the officers tapped their glasses. The beat grew and together they lifted their glasses and called upon the patron saint of German sailors: 'St Nicholas, St Nicholas, St Nicholas!'

'We sail tomorrow; the most dangerous stretch of waters anywhere: round Cape Horn into the Atlantic.'

'And straight for home,' said Pochhammer, glass still raised in celebration.

'No.' The single word was sufficient to silence the men for a second time that evening.

'No,' the Admiral repeated. 'We will make one break before heading across the Atlantic.'

'You're not considering the Falklands?' Captain Maerker scanned the men's faces. 'We've received lots of rumours the British are marshalling their forces there.'

'That's exactly what they are - rumours.' Von Spee focussed his attention on his own first officer. 'Tell us what you have discovered, Günter.'

'Yes, Admiral. Like the rest of you, I'd heard the gossip about the British fleet. A week ago the Admiral ordered me to confirm the location of Royal Navy ships on the eastern seaboard of South America. He asked me to travel to Valparaiso to meet the attaché at the German Embassy for the latest information surrounding the enemy's whereabouts. The reason for contacting him personally, rather than by telephone, was to ensure we were not being misled by someone pretending to be who they were not.'

Günter looked around the men and saw he had their rapt attention. 'I met the attaché three days ago. He told me he didn't have the location of some British ships, but there were no enemy warships in Port Stanley. A steamer visited recently and had relayed the details to the embassy.'

'Which ships?' enquired Captain Maerker.

'*Defence, Cornwall and Carnarvon.*'

Maerker studied von Spee, gauging his reaction. 'They are gathering like vultures over a carcass. I say we leave the Falklands and find the quickest way home.'

'We may have no choice, Julius,' von Spee replied in a calm voice. 'Don't forget we have a long voyage ahead, and we will need to coal and resupply after Cape Horn.'

'That will take about seven days,' said Maerker. 'And when we reach Port Stanley, the British could be sitting and waiting for us.'

'That is true, Captain. Which is why I recommend we review the situation once we round the Horn. Is there anyone who objects to this plan of action?'

No-one lifted their hands in opposition. 'Thank you, gentlemen. I suggest you return to your ships tomorrow and make ready for sail at noon. Now is there any more wine in that bottle?'

Before knocking on Oliver's door, Captain Hall inspected the cuffs of his uniform and straightened his tie. There was no point in giving the Admiral another excuse to find fault. Knowing how the naval minds worked at the Admiralty, he was certain they would bring a court-martial; the only uncertainty about the outcome was the severity of the punishment. Whatever they decided, his career at the heart of the British Navy's organisation was over. His eyes blinked furiously, uncontrollably, only stopping when he heard the Admiral's order to enter.

He marched stiffly to stand in front of the desk, hands by his side, his body at attention. 'You wanted to see me, Admiral.'

Oliver frowned. 'Yes, the business of the Latin cables. Sit down, my boy.'

It seemed he had caught the Admiral in a good mood, but it wouldn't last long he reasoned. He had kept his cards too close to his chest, and that alone would be enough to hang him.

'When we met a week ago,' said Oliver, 'I was concerned if Sir Alfred could understand your telegrams without having to resort to a codebook, their meaning might be easily deciphered by the Bosch. You were saying...'

'Before we were unfortunately interrupted, I was attempting to make the point the German high command is unaware we sent anyone to Berlin. Even if they intercepted the cables, they could not relate them to any of their activities.'

'But surely they would then know they had a spy in their midst?'

Hall's stomach reacted with a sharp twinge; he had walked into that one. 'Yes Admiral, that is correct. But it is also true they are already aware several spies are operating, not only in Berlin but in all their major cities.'

Oliver looked puzzled, 'Then why have none of them been captured?'

'I regret, some were arrested and jailed. No doubt you recall Brandon and Trench, who are currently working for me?'

'Ah, yes. Now that you mention it, I believe they were found snooping around some German harbour defences at Bremen or Wilhelmshaven.' He peered at the paperwork on his desk and sighed. 'Very well, I think you know what you are doing. Just keep me informed, will you?'

'Of course, Admiral. Thank you.' He rose and walked to the door. As his hand rested on the handle, Oliver spoke again.

'There was one more question, Captain. Apologies, I've only just remembered. What was the purpose of sending your spy?'

Hall turned. 'We received information a master spy called Otto Gratz was working in

London. Special Branch had been keeping an eye on his whereabouts. They became concerned when they learnt he was returning to Germany with secret intelligence. I suggested we sent an agent to track him down before he handed on any material.'

'Ah, I see,' responded Oliver. 'And this secret intelligence?'

Hall gave a discrete cough. 'I was told Otto used an attractive woman to approach the Russian courier who delivered the SKM codebook to us. We understand she extracted some information from him and passed this on to Otto.'

Oliver stared open-mouthed. 'You mean, Germany knows we have SKM?'

Hall inclined his head. 'It is possible.'

CHAPTER 26

Admiral Oliver stared at Hall. When he spoke, his speech was brittle with emotion. 'I cannot believe my ears. You are telling me the Admiralstab know we possess the SKM codebook?'

'I said that it was possible, Admiral, not certain.'

'Do you realise how serious this is?'

'I do, sir.' Hall stepped towards the desk. 'Special branch and I have been working day and night to retrieve the situation.'

'To retrieve the situation.' Oliver's voice was distant. 'Then why in God's name didn't you apprehend the Gratz person when he was in London?'

'The police have been bending over backwards to capture Gratz before he escaped to Germany. They almost had him in Dover, but he gave them the slip.'

'This just sounds like one calamity after another!'

The Rear-Admiral was right, thought Hall. But for an officer with his credentials, he seemed fixated by the present crisis. Four months ago Oliver had led a group on a clandestine mission to blow up almost forty German merchant ships in Antwerp harbour. If he were such a capable leader, he would understand that things could go wrong on any operation. Instead of dwelling on the problem, he should be working to find a way around the obstacle.

'I said earlier Otto is a master spy. There are two reasons we could not catch him. The first is no-one knows what he looks like.'

'Yet you know his name and the fact he was connected with the courier?' It was clear from his expression Oliver had not adapted to the set-back.

'This is the only known photograph the force has.' Hall pulled out a print from his pocket and laid it on the desk. It showed the blurred picture of a man with his back to the camera, framed by the branches of trees. He was wearing a dark beard, scruffy clothes, and a scuffed bowler. 'This was taken while they were following him. You can see his face is to one side, but it's still not possible to make out his features.'

Oliver scrutinised the picture. 'And the second reason?'

'He is an expert in disguise. He changes his appearance, by dying his hair, or shaving his moustache, and wearing different clothes depending on the circumstances. One day he may be a workman, the next an Army officer.'

Oliver let the snapshot fall and his face screwed into a grimace. 'Why didn't you tell me about this earlier?'

'At first, the detective was unsure what had taken place between the courier, the girl and Otto. It was only when Otto attempted to leave the country it became clear he was carrying vital secrets.'

'That's when he evaded the police and boarded a ferry to France?'

'Yes.'

'Good grief, man. You should have come to me straight away. Not doing so could put you in a difficult position, if you understand my meaning.'

'I do, and I considered updating you on the details. But...'

'But what?'

'I wasn't able to see how you might help resolve the predicament, Admiral.'

Oliver was about to speak when Hall carried on. 'And it seemed to me there was only one viable plan.'

'Which was?'

'To send someone after him. To find Otto Gratz and ensure he does not relay the secret to the German high command.'

'And who did you send?'

'A young woman called Evie Brown. She was

the go-between the courier and Otto Gratz.'

Oliver's countenance registered shock. 'You sent a woman? Captain, how is this going sound to the War group? Not only did you send someone who was already implicated in the plot, but you assigned a woman!'

'Yes, I know,' Hall said quietly. 'But in this war, I believe you must use every weapon to hand. And as you pointed out, she was previously involved in the conspiracy.'

'I am astonished, Captain. And what do you think the papers will make of it?'

'I would strongly suggest this affair is kept well away from the newspapers.'

'But why send anyone patently mixed up in the business?'

'There *is* a reason. She is the only person in England who has seen him and can identify him.'

Oliver remained silent for such a long time, Hall thought he had been forgotten. After a minute, Oliver fixed him with a glare. 'I see, and I understand why you did what you did. However, I find your conduct in this case high-handed. The fact remains you didn't inform me until now. And you sacrificed a young woman to redeem your and the police's incompetence.'

It was as he feared: Oliver's reaction was as predictable as a dinosaur's. But he hadn't finished.

'I must warn you, you will have to answer these and other questions before an inquiry. In the interim, I will make an order to stop the mission.

You cannot bring the Admiralty into disrepute.'

'Admiral, you must do as you see fit. However, I ask you not to issue the order straight away. It is conceivable she might still be successful.'

Oliver picked up the papers and tapped them on the desk. There was a new edge to his voice. 'This farce has gone too far. Be prepared for a proper inquiry.'

Hall softened his tone. 'Sir, she may have removed the threat already. Can I propose a simple method to test whether she was successful? If she failed, the German navy would be forced to change the codebook. If not, the codebook remains, and Room 40 will continue to decode the Kaiserliche Marine's messages.'

'Abandon the mission. That is an order.'

'Yes Admiral, I would if I could. But we have lost contact with her.'

The Admiral's eyes locked onto Hall's like the barrels of two twelve-inch guns.

'I suggest we wait for seven days,' Hall continued. 'At the end of that period, if Germany has not changed the codebook, they must still be unaware of our ability to unscramble their messages.'

'It may take longer than a week to produce a new codebook.'

'Very well. But you agree it wouldn't be more than two weeks if they knew?'

Oliver paused for a moment, then nodded agreement.

'If the German authorities are still unaware after that period, then the secret is safe.'

Oliver considered Hall's argument, then said, 'Agreed. You have fourteen days. In the meantime, try to contact her.'

'Yes, Admiral.'

'And keep me up to date on developments!'

Evie surveyed her small bedroom: the iron bedstead where she slept, the plain table with a washbowl, a wardrobe and a wooden stool that stood in for a bedside table. Such rustic furniture would be ridiculed in London's fashionable society, but here it was in keeping with the surroundings. For nearly two weeks, she appreciated the simplicity of her room and its crude yet natural furnishings. She would miss it.

She began to gather her few things together. A quiet tread of footsteps on the stairs caused her to pause and listen. Hildegard's voice was followed by a soft knock. She opened the door and stood aside as her aunt entered.

'Oh, darling. Leaving so soon?'

Hildegard settled on the bed next to the suitcase and regarded the contents. 'I'm sorry. It's Bruno, isn't it?'

'I hadn't planned to stay so long, aunt Hildie. It's been nearly a fortnight, and I have to get back to England.'

'Of course, you do. Elise will be missing you.'

She stroked the folded clothes. 'I never imagined I would see you again after the war started. It was such a pleasant surprise when you arrived.'

'For you, perhaps. But not for Bruno.'

Hildegard patted the space beside her. 'Sit with me for a minute. I know he can be very withdrawn, and his manners leave a lot to be desired. But he has much on his mind.'

Evie sat next to her.

'When we were young,' Hildegard began, 'Bruno was a quiet, shy lad. He was tall and had dark hair, and many of the girls found him attractive. Elise and I were close and used to do most things together, including going to the dances.' She faced Evie. 'I think I should not be telling you this, but your mama also liked him. Nevertheless, he only looked at me. Compared to your mother, I was the plain one, the girl with the sad eyes and downcast spirit. Elise was not only beautiful, but she was also so full of life. You take after her, dear. He should have fallen in love with her, but he only wanted me.'

Evie studied her aunt's face. 'Did you quarrel with her?'

'No.' She giggled and touched Evie's arm. 'Your mother took it all in good humour. She had many suitors in those days, so it wasn't a hardship for her.' Her tone grew more serious. 'I had no-one except Bruno. He was wonderful to me, then. We were married when I was twenty-five.'

'And were you happy?'

'Yes.' She sounded hesitant, 'At least, at the beginning.'

'Something happened?'

'I fell pregnant before the wedding. Your grandparents were strict Catholics and dis-avowed the union. There was a lot of ill-feeling.' Her voice faded, and she stared at the sunlight slanting through the window. 'Then, my baby girl died during birth.'

Evie held her hand and waited as Hildegard sifted through the memories. 'They were painful times,' she said at last. 'My parents told me it was God, taking out his anger on my sins.'

Evie put her arm around her.

'That wasn't the worst part.' Hildegard's wan smile hinted at more pain. 'Bruno became quiet and reserved and didn't appreciate I was suffer-ing too.' Her eyes filled with tears. 'There were complications with the afterbirth. When it was over, the doctor said I wouldn't be able to have another baby.'

Evie gathered her aunt into a hug. 'I'm so sorry, Hildie.'

After a minute, Hildegard straightened and wiped her cheeks dry with her apron. 'When Bruno found out, he blamed me.'

'But that isn't fair!'

'Nothing in life is fair, Evie. Expect nothing from people, because people aren't fair.'

They remained side by side, quietly holding each other. When her aunt spoke again, her voice had assumed its usual tone. 'Elise was a great comfort. She stayed with me for several weeks until I was well enough again. You were about three then, and your father was at home from the sea. He cared for you. Afterwards, when Elise visited, she brought you. That had a bad effect on Bruno. He wouldn't talk about it, but I thought when he saw you, he felt the loss of our baby more keenly. He would go into town and start drinking. Sometimes he wouldn't come home for two or three days. There were heated arguments between us. After a while, it would settle down, but in the end, I had to tell Elise not to come. I visited her instead.'

'Mother never told me about this. I suppose she didn't want me to worry.'

Hildegard reached out to caress her niece's hair. 'No. We both agreed not to say anything until you were older. And then the years slipped by, and neither of us found the right time to tell you.' She let her hands drop onto her lap. 'Are you still intending to leave today?'

'I'm sorry, Hildie. I have to go.'

'At least have some lunch with me before you set off. Bruno's gone to the market and won't be back until later.'

After she left, Evie took a last look around the room, closed her suitcase and lugged it down the creaky stairs and into the kitchen. While Hildegard chopped vegetables, she helped stir the pot hanging above the open hearth. She added a log to the fire, and hot sparks flew out. When the stew was done, Hildegard ladled a large spoonful of the broth and tore a crusty loaf in two. 'You'll need something for the journey.'

As Evie dipped the warm bread into her bowl, the farm dog Dieter barked. Hildegard rose and peered out of the window. 'It's Bruno,' she said with a trace of alarm. 'I wonder why he's so early?'

Bruno strode through the doorway, and Hildegard stood. 'Darling, whatever's the matter?'

He gazed at Evie, then regarded his wife. 'We should talk privately.'

'Please let me know if this concerns me,' said Evie. When he didn't reply, she rose. 'I'll be in my room.'

Hildegard watched her leave, then turned to Bruno. 'You've been drinking again.'

He waved his hand as if this was of no account, and sat on the stool by the hearth. 'It's in all the newspapers; the police are on the lookout for a young woman. They've been inspecting the train and bus stations, stopping everyone and checking papers.'

Hildegard covered her mouth. 'Did they stop you?'

'Yes. They didn't say why they are searching for her, but it's obvious she has committed something serious. There's a rumour she tried to kill a man, and she's on the run. I've been giving this some thought. Whatever she's done, we don't want to be implicated in her crimes. If they find out we are harbouring a criminal, we will be sent to prison.'

'What are you saying, Bruno?'

'We should hand her over to the police.'

She stared open-mouthed at her husband.

He forestalled her objections, 'I know what you are going to say: Evie is your niece, your own kin. But she has come to Germany for a specific reason.'

'She came because of her mother - my sister!'

'Surely you don't believe that tale about collecting her mother's divorce settlement?' He spat in the fire. 'She didn't even know the name of her solicitor!'

In the silence, Hildegard heard the spit sizzling on a log. 'Whatever the reason, it must be an important one. And isn't she paying you handsomely?'

'Yes, but at what cost? Do you want to go to prison?'

'If you turn her in, they would charge you too.'

'I could drop her off in town and leave her to find her own way.'

'She would be found immediately,' Hildegard snapped. 'And where do you think the police would go next?'

He fell silent.

'No, we have to find somewhere to hide her,' said Hildegard. 'Until the dust settles.'

'But where? There's nowhere on the farm.'

'What about the Sheperd's hut you use when you move the sheep to pasture?'

'Yes, it's possible, I suppose.'

'The hut is so far out of the way, they'll never think to search there. And it has a fireplace and plenty of dry logs to keep her warm at night.'

'And what then?'

'You leave her there for a few days, a week maybe. When the authorities give up the hunt, you collect her and take her to the nearest train station.'

Creases formed across Bruno's forehead. 'What about the farm?'

'I'll look after it while you're away. God knows I've had enough practice.'

Bruno spun at a sound. Evie was standing at the foot of the stairs.

At the top of a gentle rise, Constantine lay on the ground, full length amongst a field of winter wheat. From his vantage point, he could see the farm below, with the farmhouse nearest to him. Beyond, the milking shed and other outbuildings cast long shadows across a rectangular courtyard. A five-bar wooden gate led from the yard into a meadow where cows grazed.

He reached for his knapsack, removed a leather case and flipped open the lid. Inside was a pair of British-made prismatic binoculars. As he adjusted the thumbscrew, the stonework of the nearest building leapt into his field of vision. Panning away, he spotted some hens pecking in the dirt.

Reversing direction, he trained the glasses on a downstairs window and caught a shape passing behind. Abruptly there was a flurry of movement, and a figure left the house and crossed the yard. He was tall and wore a dark overcoat and heavy boots. Several moments passed before he could focus on the man: a fleeting impression of a long, pale face with a black moustache and untrimmed beard before he disappeared into one of the sheds.

The sound of conversation drifted in the still air, preceding the appearance of a woman, in her fifties or sixties. She spoke to someone closer to the house. Constantine shifted to get a better view, but the other person remained out of sight, hidden by the roof.

For a while, Constantine strained to catch the discussion and identify the mystery character. An agonising wait followed before two women moved to the centre of the courtyard, and his heart thudded with recognition. They were hugging each other. But he could recognise the second woman, even without his binoculars.

CHAPTER 27

As the afternoon faded into evening, Hildegard watched two figures tramping away from her across the muddy field. Bruno led the way, his tall figure silhouetted against the orange light. Evie followed, her suitcase an awkward encumbrance. When she swung round to wave, Hildegard's throat tightened and her eyes blurred with incipient tears.

Soon they were out of sight, and she crossed the yard to the kitchen. The remains of their last meal lay on the dinner table, and she set about washing up. When she finished, she made a mug of coffee and sat by the table, savouring the heat from the fire. Her mind wandered as she fretted over the journey her husband and niece were making. In normal times the hut was half a day on foot, but because they had started late in the afternoon, she calculated they would arrive after midnight. Bruno had brought his electric torch and knew the paths well. Even in the dark, he was unlikely to lose the way.

She sighed and said a quick prayer for their safety. Bruno's newspaper caught her eye, tucked behind the pile of logs. She turned the pages, scanning the dense text until she arrived at the back page. When she didn't find what she was looking for, she spread the paper on the table and scrutinised every column inch. There was no mention at all about the authority's search for a young woman, let alone one who had murdered a man.

Dieter barked, and Hildegard raised her head, confusion etched along the lines of her face. He was barking against the five-bar gate, and when she arrived, she stared into the sunset, trying to glimpse what had disturbed the dog. A subtle movement in the distance held her attention. It appeared to be a person, travelling in the same direction as Evie and her husband earlier. She put a hand up to shade her eyes against the low sun, but the individual had gone.

On first seeing Evie, Constantine's heart thudded and his veins pulsed as if injected with a shot of vodka. She was dressed in a greatcoat and wore wellington boots. He trained the glasses on her, surprised to see a tanned face glowing with health. His initial feelings - grateful to find her still alive - gave way to admiration. In her short time in Germany, she had thrived.

But it was apparent she was leaving. She carried a small suitcase; maybe the farmer was taking her to a train or bus station? When they left through the five-barred gate into a field, Constantine's curiosity peaked. He watched the farmer's wife go inside the house and he waited until he could move unobserved. But every minute's delay meant a greater distance opened up between him and the couple and he got up from his observation post.

As he pushed through the gate, another notion occurred to him. He could catch up with the couple and join them and be reunited with Evie. But Constantine's cautious nature intervened; the man might be escorting Evie out of the country, but until he was sure of his intentions, it was best to follow at a discreet distance. Evie would not be aware she had a guardian angel.

After three fields, Constantine realised Evie and the farmer were sticking to the path. He could see the tufts, flattened by the passage of humans and animals, suggesting it was well used.

He pulled out the binoculars. The light was fading, and the couple were about two hundred yards ahead, moving slowly up a grassy slope. At that instant, the farmer turned in his direction, holding up his hand to shield his eyes from the setting sun. Had he caught a reflection from the lenses? Constantine lowered the glasses and hid behind a tree. A minute later he moved out, looking towards their last position, but they had disappeared.

After several kilometers, Evie had fallen behind and Bruno had to wait for her to catch up.

'I could help you with that.' He reached for the suitcase.

Before he grasped the handle, she yanked it aside. 'No, it's all right, Bruno. I can manage.'

'I'm only offering to lend a hand.'

'I know.' She brushed her hair out of her eyes. 'It's not that. I can't stop thinking about Hildegard. She will be alone when the police arrive.'

Bruno seemed surprised. 'Oh, she'll be fine. She's a lot stronger than you think.' He glanced at the sky. 'The night's drawing in and we need to go.'

'I can't keep up with you.'

'Then give me your case.'

'No. I want to carry it.'

Bruno shrugged. 'It's your decision.'

They carried on, but the gap between them lengthened again. Shortly afterwards he halted near the crest of a hill. She had almost caught up with him before he started off again. The ground became more uneven, and she tripped and fell headlong. She slid, her thick coat breaking the worst of the impact, but the suitcase went flying. Bruno reappeared, but instead of helping her up, he made straight for the case and picked it up.

'I told you it would be an encumbrance.'

Evie sat up. 'Aren't you going to help me up?'

'A young girl like you?'

She saw his lips curl.

'Come on,' he snarled. 'We need to go.'

She rose with difficulty. 'Whatever's the hurry? We're miles away from civilisation.'

But Bruno's only response was to continue walking.

She followed, struggling to maintain the pace. His sudden change in mood was unnerving. Was it possible he was trying to get her lost? In her head, the questions framed themselves without answers as she lifted one tired leg after the other. The weariness rose up her legs, arms and chest until her mind became numb with the effort. Time was no more, only the constant strain of moving through a dark and unfamiliar landscape.

At some point, he switched on his electric torch, and she could spot his progress in the distance. She drew several deep breaths and picked up speed. Five minutes passed before she realised Bruno's lamp was stationary. She broke into a run, only to fall again. Why had he left her alone in the fields?

The lamp cast a yellow light over the scene. Propped up by a rock, it shone on her open suitcase and the shadowy figure of Bruno kneeling over it, examining the contents. Already her clothes had been thrown out, and her blankets discarded in the grass.

He caught her startled expression. 'I told you to get rid of the case. You don't need dresses where we're going.'

'Where are we going?'

Bruno spat. 'This is all we need.' He held up the tobacco box. 'Money! With money, you can buy as many clothes as you like. You can return to England, and I can run my farm the way it should be run.' He shoved the tin into his coat pocket. 'Come on.'

Evie scrabbled to retrieve her clothes and jammed them into the case. She had to half-run after him to keep up, and at that point, it started to rain. In ten minutes the headwind strengthened and the rain, almost horizontal now, beat into her eyes. Bruno's lamp grew faint and eventually disappeared. She tripped again and couldn't find the strength to get up. Physical and emotional exhaustion overwhelmed her, and she cried out in fear and anger.

Constantine removed his knapsack and greatcoat, squatted on his heels and drew the thick material of the coat over him to form a tent. In complete darkness, he felt in his bag and withdrew a torch and switched it on. His experience gained from naval training was a light, no matter how dim, could be seen over great distances at night, provided it wasn't obscured by natural

elements of the landscape. He was not yet prepared to let Evie and her guide know he was
following; there were too many odd questions
about their haphazard expedition that didn't feel
right.

He brought out two more items from the bag:
the first, a map in a transparent map-case containing a pencil, was followed by a British military compass. To locate his present position, he
checked how long he had been travelling. He
converted the duration into an approximate distance from the farm, making an allowance for
the heavy going underfoot. Next, he fixed the
compass over the marked farm buildings, align-
ing the edge along the north-easterly direction
he had taken when following the couple. He
drew two marks representing the minimum and
maximum length he had travelled.

To confirm his location, he removed the compass and scanned the line on the map, noting the
features he had already met on the ground. He
recalled a small stream at the bottom of a valley
and an outcrop of rock near a stand of trees. He
estimated they had covered sixteen kilometers
over rough ground, mostly during the dark. The
next task was to estimate the couple's ultimate
destination. He extended the blue line with
dashes, then inspected his work. The problem
was they were going... nowhere. There were no
roads or farms on the course they were heading.

He checked his pocket watch again. It was

nearly midnight, and the longer he spent on his calculations, the less chance he would have of catching up. Before removing his coat, he placed the compass on the ground and rotated it to point north-east. When he put his coat and knapsack on, he checked the bearing. While he marched, he could not use the torch, but thankfully the northing needle had a luminous tip. It would mean he would have to follow the course, regardless of the conditions underfoot - either that or stop every hundred yards or so to make a fresh bearing.

On balance, the second method would be the slowest. Constantine clenched his teeth. A few minutes later, with his ankles deep in mud, he sighed with exasperation. Both ways would be as slow as each other.

There were other obstacles he encountered: a copse presented a thicket too dense to penetrate, forcing him to go around, take a new bearing and adjust for the deviation to the route. A boundary wall was too difficult to scale, but he found a section where some of the stone wall had crumbled. After a while, with no sight of Evie and the farmer, he suspected they had changed direction. If that were the case, no amount of casting about in the dark would find them.

A drizzle fell, and the doubts grew. The task was hopeless; he would have to resume the search at dawn. The rain became a downpour, and water dripped down his face and off his nose. He must stop and search for shelter. As he moved to the edge of the field, he imagined he heard a cry. He stopped and listened.

The cry came again, beyond the wall. He hurried towards the source, clambering over the stones. The sound now was softer, closer. Almost by accident, he stumbled over a suitcase.

At seven-thirty in the morning, Lord Herschell was Hall's first visitor of the day. 'There's a Captain Alex Youngson outside. He has something for you.'

'Well, send him up Richard, I've been expecting his call.'

Herschell hesitated. 'He says he will need several people to assist with a heavy sea-chest.'

Hall regarded his assistant with interest. 'Take Claude with you and ask the Sergeant at the entrance to round up a couple of squaddies to help. Let's see. You'd better bring it up to the library. I'll clear the table. Oh, and you'll need some tools: a cold chisel and a sledgehammer should do.'

When Herschell left, he resisted the temptation to rub his hands together. 'At last, some good news,' he murmured. 'We could all do with a bit of that.'

The library was empty when he arrived, and he set about clearing a desk of books, charts and papers. Five minutes later, the arrival of Captain Youngson was announced by a commotion in the corridor outside. A series of shuffles and grunts were followed by the piping voice of a young man: 'Here, let me get the...'

The door flew open, and a group of men appeared, struggling with a long box. They might have been carrying a small coffin - one filled with bricks, to judge by the effort they were making. As they shuffled into view, Hall directed their efforts to position it on the table.

Captain Youngson approached, hand outstretched. 'Good morning to ye.'

'Welcome.' Hall clasped his hand and shook it warmly. 'I wondered if you had caught anything.'

'Aye, it took us a while, but I think we found what you were after.' The trawler-man peered at the carpet. 'But are you sure you want to open it here? She'll be full of seawater.'

Hall's gaze swept around the portraits hanging from the panelled walls. 'The distinguished alumni of the Admiralty crossed more seas and oceans in their time than anyone here. A few drops of saltwater won't upset them.'

'Well said, Captain,' commented a voice from behind.

He turned to view the speaker. 'Sir, I see the word has got around. I sincerely hope you won't be disappointed.'

Churchill waved his cigar in the air, causing the end to glow. 'Whatever's in that trunk, I'm confident we're in for a grand spectacle.'

More people entered the room, including Admiral Oliver and Sir Alfred Ewing.

'I think we're all here now, Reginald,' said Churchill. 'Shall we begin?'

Hall addressed the group. 'A while ago we received an accurate account of a lead-lined chest being tipped overboard by German sailors after the battle off Texel. I spoke to Captain Youngson here, and he agreed to search for the container on the sea bed.' He motioned towards the table. 'It appears he was successful.'

There was a chuckle from the men, accompanied by a ripple of applause.

'Would you like to open it?' Hall offered the tools to Churchill, who gesticulated with his cigar.

'No, Captain. The honour is yours.'

Hall removed his jacket and rolled up the sleeves of his shirt. Along both bare arms, two snarling, writhing dragon tattoos snaked all the way up to his shoulders. He approached the desk and eyed the casket, which was about three feet in length, two-foot-wide and two-foot-high and covered in green slime. On the side closest to him, a hasp secured the top to a staple, but there was no padlock through the hoop. Perhaps there had not been sufficient time for the sailors on board to fasten it properly.

He grasped the hasp, pulled it away and tugged hard, but the lid refused to budge. The casket had been in the sea over six weeks, and the metal must have corroded and stuck fast. A smart tap with the hammer and chisel was enough to free the lock. He felt along the sides with his fingertips, sensing the edge where the top met the bottom half and he chased the line with more taps. Finally, he yanked the lid upwards, letting it fall backwards. Bottle-green water sloshed against the interior. Without pausing, he plunged his arms under the surface, gripped the object underneath and dragged it out. Water cascaded onto the floor as he raised a large book to shoulder height.

'Verkehrsbuch,' breathed Admiral Oliver.

Hall noticed a few puzzled expressions among the group. 'The VB is used for diplomatic cables.' He glanced towards Churchill. 'We've been desperate to get an insight into German cables to their embassies abroad. I would be grateful if you allowed my department access to the book?'

He caught a sharp glance from Ewing and turned to face Churchill. After a brief pause, the First Sea Lord nodded agreement.

Ewing spoke up. 'I am sure we all wish to congratulate Captain Hall on the successful retrieval of a codebook used by the enemy.'

Hall gestured to Captain Youngson, 'You should thank him, not me. He did all the hard work.'

'Well we appear to have won one, just as we lost another,' said Ewing.

'Speak plainly, Sir Alfred,' said Churchill. 'What

do you mean?'

'The Kaiserliche Marine changed the entire SKM codebook. We can no longer read any of their messages.'

CHAPTER 28

The rain beat the soaked ground and over the leather top of the suitcase. Constantine switched on the torch, moving it from side to side over the wet grass, shouting her name. The light picked out an overcoat, crumpled and stretched full-length. There was a moment of incomprehension before he realised Evie was underneath.

Her skin was pale. He cradled her head in his arm and touched her neck. She was cold, too cold. He had seen this condition before when even the most able-bodied of sailors were pulled out of the sea. Unless she could be moved to a warm, dry place, she would die.

He placed the torch on the ground, pointing towards her prone body. To protect her from the worst of the downpour, he knelt over her and set about removing her coat. His Navy bushlat was designed for Russian winters and made of heavy material; it would keep her warm, but she was so small, he had problems fastening the double-breasted front. When he had tied the belt about her waist, he pressed her icy face against his. 'Please God,' he whispered. 'Please let her live.'

For several minutes he held her to him and prayed. It seemed as if his voice was being drowned out by the force of the wind and the drumming of the rain, and he cried out. To have come so far, so close, and yet arrive too late to save her. He cursed his decision to follow her and dried her face with the sleeve.

Her eyelids opened, and her mouth moved. He leaned in close to hear her above the torrent of rain. She must have seen him, but there was no sign of recognition.

'Evie, it's me, Constantine.'

He turned the torch on his face, and for a few seconds, he was blinded by the beam. Had she recognised him? He held her close again for several long minutes.

At last he moved above her to watch her face. 'Evie, it's me, Constantine,' he repeated. 'Where were you going with the farmer?'

Her forehead puckered in an exaggerated form of concentration. When she spoke, her words were slurred, as if she was drunk. 'To the hut.'

The news brought a charge of electricity to his body, giving him hope she might yet survive the night. But a hut would be too small to appear on his map, and too difficult to discover in the dark.

'Which way, Evie? Which way did he go?'

Her face relaxed into a rigid mask of the whitest porcelain. When she didn't speak, he thought she had slipped into unconsciousness. After a pause, her left arm unfurled and stretched out, extending along the same general direction he had been following.

For a minute he held her, compressing his coat around her, hoping the warmth would be enough to raise her temperature. When he felt her stir, he brought his flask out of the knapsack, unscrewed the silver top and put it to her lips. She sipped a few drops, then took a longer swallow and coughed.

'Can you get up Evie?'

She lowered her head, and he helped her into a sitting position. When she nodded again, he gently raised her to her feet.

'We have to get out of the rain. Can you walk?'

Another dip of the head. He held her around the waist, and they made the first tentative steps together. After half-a-dozen paces, she turned. He played the light over where she had lain and the beam settled on the suitcase. At the sight, she attempted to go back.

'No Evie. We mustn't; we have to find the hut.'

She appeared reluctant to continue without her case.

'We will have to leave it, Evie. I can't carry you both.'

She straightened and rested a hand on Constantine's shoulder. 'Let's go,' she croaked.

Despite the milder weather, the plane trees in St James' Park had lost their leaves. Bark had peeled away in patches, giving them the air of a group of elderly ladies who had spent too long outdoors. The surrounding paths were thronged with people: many were soldiers on leave or getting ready to go the front; some were naval personnel from the Admiralty hurrying to a meeting in Whitehall or Downing Street. Most though were female, walking with furled umbrellas, pushing prams or escorting young charges.

The rain had stopped, but Captain Hall was too preoccupied to notice. He had found his favourite bench, and let his mind drift, alighting on the occasional passer-by. From a distance, he observed a middle-aged lady approaching. She was dressed in a coat and scarf similar to his wife's, and he rose in anticipation. As she drew closer, he realised it was not Essie, but the sight stirred a memory of their conversation the previous evening.

He had been ranting about the ineptitude of his superior. 'Ewing! No doubt he's excellent in his field. He was a professor at King's College Cambridge, for goodness' sake. But why is a brilliant scientist such an incompetent administrator in running a department?'

Essie, bless her, was sympathetic and supportive. 'He's never been trained to lead men, only to dictate what should be done. How old is he?'

'Late-fifties I would guess. About fifteen years older than myself. You'd think a more senior person would be more mature.'

'There,' Essie said. 'That's likely to be the root of the problem. He sees you, a vigorous, dashing young man, with a vast experience of commanding men at sea. He feels inadequate. Perhaps he thinks he's not up to the job.' She pondered the situation. 'You once told me he was only appointed because he liked puzzles. Decryption was a hobby, not his field of study. Maybe he doesn't understand the science behind it.'

Hall's mouth sagged. Essie's insights into human nature were always astonishing and occasionally profound. He recalled her next comment, delivered with steady, unblinking eyes.

'He is afraid you will show him up and take his post. You know how to use the information from intercepted cables, whereas he does not. That makes him feel inadequate, and his reaction is to pull you down at every opportunity.'

He had considered her remarks long into the night but was too tired to work out a way he might benefit from them.

A young woman held his attention as she walked past his bench. She stepped into the path of an oncoming pedestrian and withdrew a small white feather from her pocket. When she presented it to him, he backed away. But when he caught the disapproving glances of people close by, he reluctantly accepted the unwanted gift.

She sidestepped and continued on her way.

'Excuse me,' said Hall, beckoning the young man over.

The lad coloured, and he moved aside.

'Please, I won't embarrass you any further.' Hall patted the seat beside him. 'Come and sit for a minute.'

He studied the youth as he sat at the opposite end of the bench. His face was lined; the restless eyes and the grimy skin suggested a tramp, used to living on the streets. However, his jacket and trousers were made of decent material, and underneath the waistcoat, the shirt remained white.

'Tell me, what's your name?'

'Arthur, sir.'

'And how old are you, Arthur?'

'Seventeen sir.'

'Do you have a job?'

'Yes sir. I work in the Venesta factory at Crescent Wharf.'

'The munitions place near the Royal docks?'

'Yes sir.'

'Well, Arthur, I want you to know something.' He leaned forward and lowered his voice. 'The lady that presented you with a white feather had no idea what an important job you are doing for the war.'

Arthur's worried frown relaxed into a smile.

'Now, unless you prefer to keep that present, I suggest you give it to me.' He held out a hand. 'I know someone far more deserving of your gift.'

Arthur placed the feather on Hall's upturned palm.

'It must be embarrassing to have to explain what you do. People are ignorant of your contribution to the war effort.'

'It is, Captain.'

'May I give you a tip before you go?'

Arthur nodded agreement.

'Get yourself a peaked cap. One like this, but without the braid.' He touched his hat. 'It'll stop these busybodies from poking their noses into your business.'

'Thank you, sir.' Arthur's smile expanded until it spread from ear to ear.

After Arthur left, he returned his attention to the feather, turning it this way and that in his hand. When he looked up, he spotted Claud Serecold cutting a direct course for his bench. His plan for a quiet spell in the Park was already doomed.

'Hello, Captain. I was told you might be here.'

'I occasionally come here to think; I find it conducive to thought. Not that there is much green space left. And you?'

'Admiral Oliver told me to present his compliments and asked if you could see him this afternoon.'

Hall checked his pocket watch; he had two hours before he would need to return, and the feather had given him an idea. 'Can I request a favour when you get back to the Admiralty? Please find Fleet Paymaster Rotter and ask him to meet me here.'

'Here?' Serecold hesitated.

'Yes, here. Soon as you can.'

Claud disappeared toward Horse Guards.

As Captain Hall sat, he pondered his predicament. If the Admiral was intent on bringing a court-martial, there was nothing more he could do. But there was something he could try, which might lesson the severity of the outcome. It all depended on Charlie Rotter, the person originally responsible for discovering the method the Germans used to encipher their messages. He had sent for him twenty minutes ago.

In the meantime, it was essential to keep abreast on events further afield. News stories were still being published about the huge losses around Ypres, though the battle had ended a week ago. While he was musing at the scale of human carnage, Rotter came to attention before him and saluted.

'No need for that, Charlie. Come and join me. I'm afraid I've finished all the sandwiches.'

'That's perfectly all right, sir. I'm not hungry, anyway.' He sat beside Hall. 'How can I help Captain?'

'I wanted to speak to you about a delicate matter.' He folded the newspaper and put it aside.

'I thought it best if we have our talk well away from the panelled walls of the Admiralty.'

'Understood, Captain.'

'It has been explained to me the German high command know we are in possession of SKM. They have changed the codebook so we can no longer interpret any of their cables.'

'I'm not sure that's correct, sir.'

'Sir Alfred believes it has happened. But you're not certain?'

'No sir.'

'Are we unable to decipher German telegrams?'

'That is true, Captain. Do you remember the method the Germans used to code their messages? First, they take the German text and look up each of the words using the codebook. Then they use a second mechanism called encipherment, which scrambles the code before it's transmitted?'

'I do, indeed.'

'To encipher a message, a key is needed. For SKM this takes the form of a table, called a transposition cypher. We understand from captured sailors that enemy ships carry a main one and an emergency backup. It's possible they changed it, or started working with the emergency one.'

'I didn't know about the second cypher. But if that is the case, why haven't we come by these tables before?'

'Because they are typed out onto one sheet of paper - easier to get rid of if the ship has to be abandoned. They're also kept in a different location to the codebook when not in use.'

'So what you are saying is they could be using a new cypher table, rather than a new codebook?'

'That's correct.'

Hall considered the issue for a minute. It was far too early to be sure, but if the Germans believed their messages had been compromised, they would change the codebook, no matter how much effort was involved. Changing a one-page cypher table would be easy to accomplish.

'How could we prove this, one way or another?'

'If we found the new cypher table, it would confirm they haven't replaced SKM.'

'So how would you go about doing that?'

'The same approach we used to find the original cypher,' said Charlie. 'We identified two messages sent using the same code. I laid out the letters of each message in a line. The first letter of each went under column one, the second under two, and so on. I wrote the two letters of column one onto a card, the next two on another card, etcetera until I had a card for each column. Then comes the hard part - shuffling the cards until both letters on each card and the nearby cards correspond to a keyword from the codebook.'

'Remind me how many codes there are in the book?'

'Over thirty-four thousand.'

Hall's eyebrows arched at the huge number of

combinations. 'I really don't comprehend how you manage. It would be far too complicated for my brain.'

Rotter smiled. 'Actually, it's exasperating. Ninety-nine per cent trial and error, and a hundred per cent boring! When I started doing it, I found getting the initial keyword time consuming and difficult, but afterwards, it became a little easier because I had fewer cards to shuffle to get the next keyword, and so on.'

'And what sort of progress are you making?'

'Progress?' Rotter looked startled.

'Yes. How far have you got with the process?'

'I haven't started. Sir Alfred suspended all attempts when we couldn't decipher the messages. He said there was no point since the Germans knew we had their SKM and they had issued a new codebook.'

He stared at Rotter. 'So it's possible SKM hasn't changed at all?'

'It's feasible.'

'Did you make Sir Alfred aware of that possibility?'

'Of course, Captain. But he wouldn't hear anything about it.'

Hall tucked the feather in the inside pocket of his jacket. 'Right, from this moment, I am transferring you to the Directorate of Navy Intelligence - my department. I want you to return and do your best to understand if a new SKM has been issued, or if it's merely a change to the cypher. Report to me every morning in my office. I will speak to Sir Alfred about this, so don't worry on your account.'

Rotter rose, 'Yes, Captain.'

Evie found Constantine's coat both a blessing and a curse. The bushlat material kept her dry but was so long it dragged on the ground and became caught in brambles. More than once, she stepped on the hem and fell flat on her face. Constantine tucked the excess inside, over her hips, and fastened it in place with the belt.

Constantine was an apt name for her companion, she realised. He was always by her side, helping her over the ditches, through boggy patches and over walls. Every so often, he would stop for a compass bearing, and she would rest before they set off again. How he came to be there was a miracle. When the thought occurred to her, she would reach out to touch his arm, to reassure herself he was real.

The rain had stopped, and a Persian blue tinge began to infuse the pitch-black sky. She could distinguish the shapes of trees and fields, and as they broached the top of the hill, she looked across the valley. A warm orange blush from the as yet unrisen sun silhouetted an undulating vista. She stood to study the horizon, then tugged Constantine's arm and pointed.

He brought up the binoculars. After a moment,

he murmured, 'Smoke.'

The discovery energised them both, and after a fresh compass bearing, they pressed on.

CHAPTER 29

Room 40 was humming with activity. It was second nature to test morale, and Hall stopped to talk with some of the men on his way to Ewing's office. His assessment was Ewing set his staff high-level goals, but gave little scope to them to organise their own work.

He stood opposite the secretary's desk, 'Afternoon Mountstephen, I need to speak to Sir Alfred.' He could tell the secretary was about to refuse his request.

'Immediately.'

Mountstephen rose and knocked softly on Ewing's door and ushered him in.

Sir Alfred's room, once so neat, now resembled a Solicitor's office. Piles of papers were stacked on the floor and windowsill, and his desk was covered in paper.

'First, may I apologise for disturbing you like this - I can see you are busy.'

Ewing gestured. 'Please sit down.'

He dragged the chair out from the table, only to discover several files already occupying the seat.

Ewing looked briefly apologetic, 'Oh, put them on the floor.'

Hall observed the Scotsman. Today he was wearing a green velvet bow tie above a white shirt. His jacket hung on a stand in the corner, making his waistcoat the focal point of the office. Hall's eyes were drawn to the purple and yellow spots of colour, set against a black background.

'Yes, what can I do for you?' Ewing's voice contained a testy note. 'I'm afraid I can't give you more than a few minutes.'

'That's perfectly fine. I wanted you to know I've taken your previous comments on board - about going over your head - and therefore wished to talk to you first.'

'Quite right.'

'I dare say you recall the unveiling of the VB codebook yesterday?'

'I thought you might want to discuss that.'

'Yes, it came as a complete shock when you announced the Germans knew we had SKM.' Hall crossed one leg over the other. 'I wondered what was the justification for that?'

Ewing blinked. 'Isn't it obvious? For the last two days, we haven't been able to decode any of their cables.'

'I gathered that was the problem, but then I began to wonder why? I was told there could be an alternative reason.'

'Ah, I see what you are after.' Ewing steepled his fingers. 'We considered if the Bosch had adopted a different key to encipher messages. I asked two of my best cryptologists to examine them, but they came up with a blank.'

Hall nodded, as though deep in thought. 'Of course, I realise this is only a slim possibility, and I understand why you wouldn't want to waste any effort - or your staff's time working on it.' He indicated the piles of paper. 'I appreciate you and they are very busy.'

'Correct. Was there anything else?'

'Only my opinion that while you are concentrating on other projects, we would lose an immense amount of intelligence on the movement and deployment of the German fleet.'

Ewing folded his arms. 'Yes. I had no other option but to focus our attention on more fruitful areas.'

Hall spoke with gentle firmness. 'If there is even the slightest chance the enemy is using a different transposition cypher, then the War group will look hard at how much time your department has lost by not giving this problem sufficient resources.'

Ewing's ruddy complexion paled, yet he remained silent.

'I have an idea which I would like to broach,' Hall said after several moments had passed. 'Assume for the sake of argument, the cypher key has changed. Assign one of your code-breakers to my department. I would ensure he is given the space and peace to work.'

Ewing's slow shake of the head preceded his remarks. 'I cannot, and will not transfer any of my staff to the Department of Navy Intelligence.'

Hall paused. 'There is a reason I'm making this suggestion to you. If he fails, I will be held responsible, not you. I would be blamed for persuading you to agree the project, and I would also be censured for the failure of the task.' He detected a glint in Ewing's eyes.

'And if you are successful?'

'Then I will make it known the whole plan was yours. I will say you felt your code-breaker would work better in a quieter setting - where he's not constantly harassed by other code-breakers for help when they are working on other things.'

Ewing's eyes narrowed.

'It would also show you in a stronger light,' Hall continued. 'It would demonstrate you can delegate responsibility like the skilled director people believe you to be.'

'And if I disagree?'

'Sir Alfred, I'm a sea captain, not an administrator. I don't plot or scheme in the office.' He caught Ewing's sceptical glance. 'Well, not any longer - we're all on the same side, after all. But the consequences of not following up this possibility - however slim - are so important I would feel obliged to discuss the issue with Admiral Oliver and others.'

'I see.'

Hall leaned forward for emphasis. 'This is something I am loath to do since I know you have not been placed in this position of responsibility by chance - everyone knows of your distinguished academic career. I need to follow this up and eliminate it to save any embarrassment all round.'

In the silence that followed, he caught a subtle curl at the corners of Ewing's mouth. He carried on, 'And if they agree and it is later discovered the German Navy had changed the cypher key and not the codebook, I regret they would be bound to doubt your expertise in this vital area.'

Eventually, Ewing spoke, 'Very well, but there must be stipulations.'

'Name them.'

'You report to me every morning regarding progress.'

'Agreed.'

'The code-breaker returns to my office after a week.'

Hall hesitated. 'I was thinking more like a month. You know how long it took to break the first cypher.'

'A fortnight then. No longer.'

'Agreed.' Hall swallowed, 'Now we haven't discussed which member of staff. I understand Denniston is regarded as one of your best.'

'He is, but he's extremely busy. You can't have

him.' Ewing sounded emphatic.

'If not Denniston, how about Richard Norton?'

Ewing sighed. 'He's up to his eyes on the HVB.'

'I do need someone.' Hall paused, 'What about Rotter? He's helped both of us in the past.'

Ewing pondered the idea. 'Very well. Agreed.'

'Thank you, Sir Alfred, Rotter it is then.'

Constantine had called a halt about half a mile from the hut. The long-dead trunk of a fallen tree afforded a seat for both of them. Even in her exhausted condition, Evie heard a stream trickling over stones a few feet from where they sat. The sun had risen, throwing the shadow of willow trees across the water and birds were calling to one another. In summer the setting would be a rustic idyll, but in the cold grip of dawn, she trembled.

Constantine's arm around her shoulders provided some reassurance. She leant over to support her head on folded arms and felt his body shiver beside her. As she stood up, her limbs ached with the strain. His clothes were still wet, and she removed her coat and gave it to him.

'No, you keep it.'

'Take it.'

He surveyed the scene with binoculars, then handed them to her. She adjusted the focus with help, and a close-up emerged. The cabin was clearly visible, set near a stand of trees on the brow of the hill. Its exterior was made of timber, logs that had been sawn and joined at the corners. She spotted a door, but there were no windows. Smoke rose from a metal chimney.

'Can we stay here a while?'

'No. You need to be in the warm and to rest, and we both have to dry our clothes.'

'I'm afraid.'

Constantine's gaze switched to her. 'Why?'

'Bruno is so... I can't describe how he changed once we left the farm.'

'When I saw you leave with him, I was puzzled.'

'The police are looking for me.' She hesitated, 'I nearly killed a man.'

'Otto Gratz?'

'Yes. How did you know?'

'Through a mutual friend, Captain Hall. He told me you were in danger, and I agreed to come out to search for you.'

'I'm so thankful you did.'

He put his arm around her once more and held her tight. After a minute he asked, 'What makes you so frightened of him? You've been staying with him and his wife these last few weeks.'

'On the way here he stole the money from my suitcase. Then he left me.'

Constantine's jaw muscles twitched. 'He should be made to pay.'

'No.' She shook her head, fiercely. 'Don't provoke him. I think there's something wrong with him.' She pointed to her temple. 'Up here. He scares me.'

'We have no choice,' he said. 'This shelter is the only one for miles.'

She mulled over his words; he was right. 'Will you go first?'

'If you want. Nothing will happen to you while you're with me.'

They approached the hut, and when they were within thirty yards, she hung back and waited as he rapped on the door. A moment later, he entered. Several minutes passed before he reappeared, beckoning her in.

'So that's where you are!' Bruno's voice boomed from inside, and he strode over to clutch her in a bear hug. 'Where did you get to?'

Before she could answer, Bruno interrupted, 'I've been searching all over for you.' He spoke to Constantine. 'I lost her in the rain and the dark. I'm so pleased you found the path.'

Constantine appeared to be taken in by him. She was so startled she didn't know how to respond. She stepped away from his grasp and scanned the small room. Two paraffin lamps threw their shadows against the wall. There was an old wood-burning stove near the door, and a raised wooden section opposite provided a sleeping area. Rumpled blankets bore mute testament Bruno had been asleep before their arrival.

'So kind of you to share your cabin.' Constantine sounded grateful.

'It's not mine,' replied Bruno. 'My father built it

for all the local sheep farmers.' He eyed Constantine. 'I'm really surprised to see you. How did you find us?'

'That's easily explained. I was visiting your farm, hoping to meet Evie, when your wife informed me you had left. I followed, naturally, and eventually caught up with her.' He gave Evie a squeeze.

Bruno didn't reply, and the silence dragged on. Finally, Constantine spoke, 'What a dreadful night to venture out on such a long trek.'

'No surprise the girl became lost then,' said Bruno.

'I wondered why anyone would set off on such a difficult journey, so late in the day?'

'Oh, that.' Bruno flipped his hand as if the reason was unimportant. 'Hildegard decided it would be best to take Evie to the cabin and for her to stay a few days.' He lowered his head and eyed Constantine under dark eyebrows. 'The police are hunting for her, in connection with attempted murder.'

Constantine feigned surprise. 'Incredible.'

'Yes, well we thought so too. Anyway, I intended to return later and take her to the nearest railway station. We were hoping to find a ship in Holland to bring her home.'

'If that's still the plan, I'll need my money.' She extended her hand to Bruno.

He turned away with a muffled, 'Of course.' When he had retrieved the tobacco tin, he handed it to her. 'I only brought it for safe-keeping. Now you have a companion,' he inclined his chin towards Constantine, 'it should be safe.' He paused. 'I have to say your sudden appearance is astonishing. What, may I ask, is your interest?'

Constantine clasped Evie's hand. 'We're to be married.'

She stared at him. Then she remembered she had a part to play and placed her other hand over his.

Bruno's eyebrows rose, but he didn't respond. Instead, he rubbed his hands together. 'Right. You'll be wanting more wood for the fire. In the meantime, you're welcome to use the bed. You must both be exhausted.'

She looked towards Constantine. When he nodded his assent, she folded over the blankets, climbed onto the shelf and squeezed herself against the rough wall. There was barely enough room for him to lie alongside her. She watched him remove his knapsack, and when Bruno wasn't looking, he slipped a leather holder that looked suspiciously like a scabbard underneath.

'I'll try not to wake you when I return,' said Bruno.

She craned her neck to observe him. His back was to her, and she saw him reach down to grip a short-handled axe propped up by the stove. When he left, she forced herself to listen hard for sounds of him moving outside. Weariness overcame determination and her eyelids closed.

Evie's steady breathing indicated she was fast asleep. Constantine swung his legs over the edge and sat upright on the wooden bed. Reaching below the blanket, he grasped the long knife and held it up to the light. The Bebut Kinjal always accompanied him when he was asked to courier documents abroad. A touch of the handle was enough to calm the tension.

Evie was right to warn him about Bruno's state of mind. He seemed unaware they had seen through the false bonhomie as soon as they first arrived. Constantine considered the situation and calculated it was best to keep the man's delusion alive as long as possible. Bruno might allow them to continue on their way. Perhaps he could be persuaded to let him take over and escort Evie out of the country. But dealing with such an unbalanced individual would always be tricky, and he could never trust him.

He unsheathed the knife and examined the blade in the yellow light from the lamps. There were several notches along the cutting edge, a legacy from when his father owned the instrument before passing it on to him. It was too long to be called a knife and too short to be a sword. He recalled the lessons he had learnt, first under his father's tutelage, and later by a professional swordsman. There was nothing Evie needed to fear when he had the Kinjal in his grasp.

He lay down, covered the weapon with the blanket and closed his eyes. Evie's breathing had deepened, and for a while he listened to her, once again offering thanks to God he had found her alive. He had no idea what possessed him to declare they were getting married, but whatever happened, he made a silent promise to the woman sleeping next to him: *I will look after you for as long as I am able.*

Twenty minutes elapsed, and he wondered if Bruno would return. A creak sounded softly as the door opened. Constantine lifted his eyelids a fraction and glimpsed the man's bulky form as he stacked the logs. When Bruno finished, he opened the hatch in the stove and carefully placed one in the fire. Sparks erupted as the still-damp kindling burnt.

For five minutes, there was silence, and Bruno remained standing with his back to the bed. Perhaps he was warming his hands or planning his next move. Through half-closed lids, Constantine watched the shadowy figure advance towards them. He was carrying something in his hand, the implement he used to cut the firewood.

Nearer still and as he raised the axe, its shadow cast an arch against the roof. The arm began its downward strike, and Constantine rolled off the bed straight into the man's legs. Bruno fell backwards and put out both hands to break his fall. The axe flew against the wall, and Constantine brought his own weapon to bear.

CHAPTER 30

Evie woke, jolted from sleep by a loud thud. Still absorbed in her dream, it was several seconds before she comprehended the reality. Constantine was sitting on top of Bruno's prone body, with his knife raised, ready to strike. Bruno had Constantine's wrist in both his hands, and she saw the glow from the lamp reflected in the film of sweat on Constantine's brow. They sounded like animals, grunting with the effort while scrabbling about the floor.

Now the picture was becoming clear. Bruno, the farmer, had enormous strength, more than enough to block his opponent's attack. Constantine was younger and more agile, continually shifting, attempting to find a way through his opponent's defences. Yet Bruno prevented every effort. A sharp spike of fear drilled through her sternum as he gained the upper hand.

She cast about the small room for something to use against him. In the space between them and the door, Bruno's axe lay on the ground. She hopped out of bed, leapt over the bodies and picked it up. By now they were rolling about the floor like two wrestlers, looking for any advantage. While that happened, she could not get an unobstructed shot. She closed on them, lifted the axe in the air and waited for an opportunity.

Again the men shifted, and Bruno became instantly aware of the new threat. He released an arm and punched her in the stomach. The force of the impact sent her flying, hard up against the stove. The hot metal burnt her side, and she rolled away, screaming.

The men carried on fighting. Constantine's knife, now held by both of them, raked the wall, collided with the paraffin lamp and knocked it off the shelf. Both men were weak, having suffered injuries from each other's blows. With a sudden twist, Bruno squatted above Constantine, and the knife flew across the floor. When Evie looked up, she saw Bruno pummel Constantine's unprotected face. She also noticed fuel from the lamp had spilled out and caught fire. Constantine's knife glittered in the blaze. Bruno continued to rain punches, and it was clear Constantine could no longer defend himself. Yet another blow smashed into Constantine's face, and she had to make a move.

Flames raced up the wall of the cabin and she picked up the Bebut Kinjal and staggered over to the men. She lifted the knife high above them, the failure of her mission forgotten, the pain in her side obliterated by hate. She gripped the handle tighter and brought it down with all the power she could muster. At the last instant, Bruno turned to meet the danger, but it was too late. Instead of a non-fatal blow to his back, he unknowingly presented his neck as a target. The blade sliced through flesh. Blood gushed with the pressure of a waterspout, drenching her.

Bruno's body slumped over Constantine as the fire roared along the ceiling.

When Rotter entered Hall's office the following morning, Hall looked twice at the young man.

'Charlie? You look like you've been up all night.'

'Nearly sir. I went home in the early hours.'

Hall blinked rapidly. 'I said this was important, but it's also vital you get proper rest.'

'I know.' Rotter sounded depressed.

'It sounds as if you've not found a solution yet?'

'No.' Rotter used a hand to comb his wavy hair. 'But when you've been working on deciphering cables as long as I have, you develop an instinct. My intuition tells me underneath all the jumble of letters and numbers, they're still using the original codebook.'

'Well, that's great, Charlie. But I can't go to Ewing or Oliver on such little evidence. How long do you think it will take?'

'It's hard to say, Captain. How long have I got?'

'A fortnight. It will be difficult to make a case for any more days.'

'OK Captain, I'll do my best.' He halted by the door. 'Oh, there was something else. I'm aware you've squared things with Sir Alfred, but I'm worried if Admiral Oliver finds out he'll take me off the assignment.'

'Ah, Charlie. There's no need to worry. I briefed him, and he's agreed to everything. In fact, he was positively cheerful to learn that Sir Alfred and I are getting along so well.'

Rotter shot Hall an incredulous glance.

Hall was grinning.

For the following twelve days, Rotter reported every morning. Each day a terse shake of the head or downward cast of the eyes told its own story. On the twelfth day, there was a marked change; Charlie Rotter's face was a mask, but his jaunty step and the gleam in his eye betrayed his excitement.

'Well then Charlie, don't just stand there!'

'Captain.' Rotter executed a sharp salute, and his mouth expanded into a wide grin. He extracted a crumpled sheet of paper, laid it on Hall's desk and smoothed the creases with his hands.

Hall saw a series of rows and columns of letters and numbers. 'What does this mean?'

'It means Captain, that I have found the cypher key. Using this transposition cypher, we can read the Hun's cables again!'

'Have you tried the key on any new messages?'

'Of course, Captain. Works like a charm.'

Hall came round the desk to shake his hand. 'Well done, Charlie. I mean that. You should take the rest of today and tomorrow off.'

'I don't know about that, sir.'

'I do,' replied Hall. 'For the next two days you're still working for me, and I say enjoy a well-earned break.'

'Thank you, sir. But I don't think we've seen the last of these.'

'Oh?'

'They've changed the cypher key once, they'll do it again - just to keep communications secure. Wouldn't surprise me if they change the cyphers regularly, once a month or so.'

'Thanks again, Charlie. That's useful to know.' He watched Rotter leave, then slipped the paper into a plain brown envelope. There was no time to be lost, and he marched along the corridor to Room 40. A brief knock, a short discussion with Sir Alfred's secretary, and a minute later he was in Ewing's office. Taking a cue from Rotter, he kept his head down and his face fixed with a grave air.

'I rather thought you would run into problems, Captain.' Ewing's condescending tone jarred, and his maroon bow tie over a pink striped shirt didn't help either.

'It appears paymaster Rotter has discovered

the Germans are using a new cypher key for the SKM codebook.'

Ewing's reaction was worth the wait; his bushy eyebrows rocketed up, and his jaw sagged. As Hall removed the envelope from his jacket, a small feather escaped from his pocket unseen and fluttered to the floor.

Hall tapped the note. 'Interestingly, he tells me it's not an emergency or backup key, but a special issue. He suspects the Bosch is likely to change the keys more frequently; it's an easy way to increase the security of the codebook. I expect the same goes for the other codebooks such as HVB or the more recent VB.'

'As if we haven't enough to do already,' grumbled Ewing. He rose and walked to the window sill to pick up a file. 'Well, thanks for the information, Captain.' He opened the sash a little and faced Hall. 'At least Rotter can return to the fold.'

A draft of cold air lifted the feather and wafted it across the floor where it came to rest under the desk.

'Not really, Sir Alfred. I've given the poor chap a couple of days off.'

Ewing turned sharply. 'What?'

Hall pointed to the sheet on the desk. 'He's been working on that non-stop, weekends included. The man needs some time off for rest.'

Something in Hall's tone forestalled Ewing's irritated rebuff. 'Oh, very well. If you say so.'

'Will you inform Admiral Oliver about the new

cypher, or should I?'

Ewing wafted his hand in a gesture of dismissal. 'I will be sure to let him know.'

'Thank you, Sir Alfred.' Hall inclined his head. When he left, he made straight for Oliver's office.

There was a brief tap, and Churchill's head poked around the door. 'Ah, so this is where you're hiding!'

Hall looked up from his pile of papers. 'I don't think so; too many people know where my office is. I can hardly get any work done.'

Churchill glimpsed Hall's expanding smile. 'May I take a seat?'

Hall gestured soundlessly towards a chair.

Churchill sat and brought out a cigar, which he lit. He savoured the tobacco and began, 'I came to congratulate you on discovering the cypher key for SKM.'

'Thank you, but paymaster Rotter did the work. I simply gave him the space to achieve the task.'

'I thought you would say something like that,' said Churchill, tapping his cigar on the ashtray. 'But if it hadn't been for you, we would be none the wiser.' He glanced out of the window, and his eyes lost a little focus. 'We might still believe the Germans had discovered our secret.'

'And I might be out of a job.'

Churchill's gaze swung back to him. 'There was

never any chance of that happening.'

'Sir? Admiral Oliver told me in no uncertain terms, I would face a Board of Enquiry.'

Smoke wafted towards him as Churchill waved his arm. 'No. I'll admit he put you under some pressure, but there was no prospect of you leaving the service.' He drew on his cigar. 'Sir Alfred is an outstanding engineer and will usually get to the bottom of matters. Sometimes though, he needs a little encouragement.'

'Which is where I come into the picture?'

'Precisely.'

He paused a moment to absorb the point: Churchill had known about the problems with Ewing all along. But ordering Ewing to continue pursuit of a cypher key would have upset him; the eminent professor would be insulted. If Hall was ordered to lead the task, the distinguished professor would feel undermined, and might still take home his bat and ball.

Churchill had struck a middle course: bring pressure on Hall to find a solution. If Ewing fell out with him, Hall could be blamed. But he must have been confident Hall would discover a way.

'Now what is all this?' Churchill gestured to the mass of documents on the desk.

'It's been a week since the Battle of the Falklands, and I thought we should do an assessment.'

'We have people doing that already.'

'Yes, but *I* wanted to understand what lessons

could be learnt.'

'So what have you got?'

'I've gathered as much information as I can lay my hands on.' Hall pointed to one stack of papers. 'There we have testimonies from the Governor of the Falkland Islands and reports from Admiral Sturdee's Captains and officers of his squadron. Here are the ship's logs and cables between London and Sturdee's squadron. Ship-to-ship signals are here, together with reports from captured German officers and crew. And there is a pile of newspapers covering the period after the engagement.'

Winston blew smoke. 'Very thorough.'

'Sir, about the only thing all the reports agree on was the weather. They say the encounter took place with a clear dawn sky. Unusually, the sea was calm.' He passed over the paper he was reading, dated Tuesday, 15th December 1914. Below the headline "The Atlantic Battle" was a detailed description of the action that ensued when Admiral Sturdee, Commander-in-Chief, South Atlantic and Pacific, met and defeated the East Asia Squadron.

Churchill scanned the first paragraph.

> Sir Doveton Sturdee is a master mariner, and the country is proud of his achieve ment. The King has sent him a personal letter thanking him for his service. We offer our congratulations for his ge nius in tracking and locating Von Spee's

Squadron so quickly and in discharging
his duty.

'But you and I know better, sir.'

'Indeed.'

Sturdee hadn't found von Spee, von Spee had found him. Sturdee had sailed to Port Stanley to take on coal and make repairs. He was expecting to begin his search on the western seaboard of South America and was in no hurry to prepare for what could be a lengthy hunt. But before he was ready, von Spee's advance guard was sighted along the southern coast.

Hall picked up the testimony from the Commander of the *Gneisenau*. 'Captain Maerker survived after scuttling his ship and was rescued by the *Invincible*. He claims that if Von Spee had fired while Sturdee was coaling, he could have inflicted enormous damage. Our ships were so tightly packed together, he would be bound to hit something. And if he had sunk one or two, he could have bottled up the rest of them in the harbour and prevented an escape to sea.'

Sturdee's ships had scrambled to make ready. Hall imagined the initial panic amongst the British squadron, with more than half its warships either taking on coal or waiting for their turn. The *Bristol* was cleaning her boilers and repairing her engines and would take longer than the others to put to sea. But when the *Gneisenau* and *Nürnberg* arrived, *Canopus* was prepared.

Earlier, the *Canopus* had been grounded to give

a stable platform for her guns. She was positioned behind the headland, concealed from the German ships. To make doubly sure she remained hidden, her upper-works were painted in splodges of colour to blend in with the sky and terrain. Her gun turrets covered the outer entrance of Port William, and when the first two German warships appeared, a 12-inch salvo drove them off, giving Sturdee enough time to prepare.

'I believe *Canopus's* guns unnerved the *Gneisenau's* Captain,' said Hall.

'Well, 150-foot waterspouts would send shivers up any commander's spine.' Churchill paused. 'There is a rumour going the rounds that von Spee was led to believe Port Stanley was free from British warships.'

Hall's jaw fell. How much did he know? 'The wireless station on the Falkland Islands is the only communications post we own in the South Atlantic. I considered it would present an attractive target to von Spee.'

Churchill laughed a dry, chesty chuckle. 'Listen, Reginald, I'm not concerned with how you did it, but next time, will you tell our side sooner? When the signal arrived that the enemy was in sight, Admiral Sturdee was having his breakfast. I imagine he choked on his porridge.'

'Yes, I accept your point.'

'Good. What about the performance of our squadron?'

'We had the most powerful force: better ships, faster, longer-range guns, and superiority in numbers. And with the fine weather, the outcome was a foregone conclusion.'

'I agree.' Churchill rose. 'You may be unaware, but von Spee's two sons, Otto and Heinrich, were in his squadron.'

'No, I didn't know, sir.' Hall stood and escorted Churchill to the door. 'I am very sorry for the family. Von Spee, in particular, was a great Admiral.'

'At least the public will see we repaid Germany for Coronel.'

'We won the battle of the Falklands. Surely that's more important in the grand scheme of things?'

Churchill paused in the doorway. 'Unless the country is with you, winning a battle is like a ripple on the sea. With the people on your side, we have a tidal wave that can carry us to victory.' He patted him lightly on the shoulder, once, twice, then left.

CHAPTER 31

Captain Hall returned to his desk. Although Churchill saw the victory in terms of continuing British dominance of the seas, it worried Hall that the battle was overlong and unnecessarily aggressive. Something was not right, and to pin down the problem, he reviewed the action in his mind.

Once Sturdee had signalled 'General Chase' his two battlecruisers overhauled von Spee's two armoured cruisers. When von Spee saw the British catching up, he ordered *Gneisenau* and *Scharnhorst* to turn and face them, allowing his three light cruisers to escape to the southwest.

But Sturdee had anticipated this and sent *Glasgow*, *Kent* and *Cornwall* to chase them while *Invincible* and *Inflexible* remained to take on *Gneisenau* and *Scharnhorst*. The battle between these four capital ships lasted three hours - far longer than Hall expected. As he leafed through the documents, he realised that some of this was down to von Spee's tactics. He had tried every trick to tilt the odds against the enemy. He changed tack, so the wind blew his smoke over the British gun layers. When that didn't work, he drove at the battlecruisers to get within range of his 8.2-inch guns. But like a boxer, Sturdee's superior speed meant he could dance out of reach while continuing to bombard the armoured cruisers with his more powerful 12-inch guns.

But, despite these cunning schemes, the German warships took far too long to die. Hall pressed his thumb and middle finger against his forehead, seeing the destruction in his mind's eye. By 3 pm, the *Scharnhorst* was on fire: her third funnel shot away. Steam hissed from the stricken ship as the sea found the flames. *Carnarvon* moved in to join forces with *Invincible*, and at 4:10 pm *Scharnhorst* turned on her beam ends. At no stage did she attempt to strike her colours and surrender. To Hall's mind, the real reason for her slow, yet fated end was the poor marksmanship of Sturdee's gun layers and spotters.

For a while, he wondered what he would have done in the same circumstances. Von Spee had fought to the end, even though it meant the loss of 840 seamen. What had prompted him to sacrifice himself and everyone else? No doubt Germany had placed a heavy expectation on the man's shoulders, and according to the Commander of the *Gneisenau*, von Spee could be fatalistic on occasion. But for all the honour in death, Hall couldn't agree to the inevitable slaughter of his own crew when there was time to surrender and save them.

He turned to the report on the demise of *Gneisenau*. With three British ships against her, she shouldn't have lasted as long as she did. She received two hours of heavy pounding before hauling down the ensign on her foremast. Confusion reigned as a second ensign remained flying, and she fired one more shot before turning on her side at 6 pm. A total of 186 officers and crew were rescued alive, and 660 men died. Again, Hall put this down to the lack of accuracy by the British crews. Precision had been sacrificed over the rate of fire.

The same story was repeated when *Glasgow* and *Cornwall* went after the *Leipzig*. They eventually caught up, and after a protracted exchange, the *Leipzig* rolled over at 8:12 pm with the death of 270 crew. Eighteen entered the water alive, and of those, only sixteen survived the cold temperatures.

The *Kent* pursued the *Nürnberg*, coming upon her at 5 pm. After a round of desultory salvos on both sides, two of *Nürnberg's* boilers burst, reducing her maximum speed to 19 knots. The two warships closed on each other in a lengthy and continuous broadside. Although *Kent* suffered casualties and a small fire, the greatest destruction was visited on the *Nürnberg*. At 6:25 pm, her engines stopped, and ten minutes later, she ceased firing. As she was still flying her colours, *Kent* continued her attack until her opponent's ensign was lowered. Twelve men were picked up out of the water, and seven survived.

Only the faster *Dresden* escaped.

On his way out of the Admiralty, Captain Hall gathered up some new cables from his desk. He found a bench in Regent's park and began reading as he ate his lunch. The first three messages had been decrypted from the HVB codebook, but the last needed no decoding.

He re-read the cablegram. It was from the port of Dordrecht in Holland.

> *Bene omnia. In via domum nostram.*
>
> *All is well. On our way home.*

ACKNOWLEDGE-MENTS

When I was researching information for another project, I came across a little-known fact on the web site of MI5, the British Secret Service. In the First World War, and unknown to Germany, the Admiralty in London began a systematic interception of German telegrams. By 1917 the process of decryption was well understood and in January of that year the German State Secretary for Foreign Affairs sent a cable, (the *Zimmermann Telegram)* to Mexico. The subject was an inducement to Mexico to make war with the United States, in a calculated strategy to prevent America from entering the war against Germany. When the Admiralty presented the deciphered note to the Wilson administration, America joined the Allies.

And so the concept of this novel was born. Twenty-five years before Bletchley Park, how did the Admiralty assemble, organise, intercept and decrypt Germany's communications during one of the most tumultuous periods of British history? The answer was a fascinating one, and I have attempted to 'realise' the birth of the unit that made such a difference to the outcome of the war.

During the two years to research and write this novel, I consulted a variety of sources for information. There were many variations and interpretations of events, forcing decisions about precisely what happened, when, by whom and why. I concluded I should stick with most of the recorded characters and events. In the novel all the principle individuals existed (except for one leading lady) and all the main events occurred - subject to a dash of artistic licence. For example, I delayed Inspector Woodhall's enlistment into the 1st Scottish Rifles by three months, as he was needed for important detective work in London; and there is no record of Evie and Constantine's mission in Germany.

I would like to acknowledge the following authors and their works.

Count Constantine Benckendorff, *Half a Life*; David Boyle, *Before Enigma*; Paul Gannon, *Inside Room 40*; Admiral Sir Reginald 'Blinker' Hall, *A Clear Case of Genius*; Richard Hough, *The Great War at Sea 1914-1918*; Robert Massie, *Castles of Steel*; Robert Massie, *Dreadnought*; David Ramsay, *'Blinker' Hall Spymaster*; Commander Henry

Spencer-Cooper, *The Battle of the Falkland Islands*; Tom Standage, *The Victorian Internet*; Barbara Tuchman, *The Zimmermann Telegram*; Edwin Woodhall, *Spies of the Great War*; James Wyllie and Michael McKinley, *Codebreakers.*

A copy of the *Signalbuch der Kaiserliche Marine* (SKM) may be viewed at The National Archives at Kew, reference: ADM 137/4156.

The map 'The All Red Line' used at the beginning and again in chapter 18 is in the *Public Domain*, from *The Annals and Aims of the Pacific Cable Project (1903)*

Any factual errors are entirely my own.

I owe a debt of gratitude to those who aided and abetted the book's long gestation. Thank you to my wife, Fran, for the initial copy-edit and her patience during my lengthy disappearances to the upstairs study. Credit to my friends from the Swarthmore creative writing group who helped with the opening and other scenes. A special 'thank you' to Vik who edited the manuscript and saved me from the M4 and to my brother Tony for post-production. And grateful thanks to Leonora, writing tutor, for her guidance and encouragement.

Printed in Great Britain
by Amazon